# A Witch-ish Guide to Protectors & Pendulums

## LILITH AND CO.

### SARAH ZOLTON ARTHUR

IRVING HOUSE PRESS

A Witch-ish Guide to Protectors & Pendulums

USA Today Bestselling Author
Sarah Zolton Arthur



sarahzoltonarthur.com

**Unexpectedly Married**

The Consolation Bride

Marriage (Red, White &) Blues

**Adventures in Love**

Skydiving, Skinny-Dipping & Other Ways to Enjoy Your Fake Boyfriend

Skydiving, Skinny-Dipping & Other Ways to Enjoy Your Fake Boyfriend — **Audible**

Wanted: Willpower Not to Kill A Man

WTF Are You Thinking?

Adventures in Love Complete 3 Book Series

**Holiday Bites (A Lake Shores, MI World)**

Baby, It's Cold Outside (Book One)

Always Be My Baby (Book Two)

**Lilith and Co.**

A Witch-ish Guide to Protectors and Pendulums

**Charleston Copperhead Country**

Angry Puck

Hot Puck

**Standalones**

Summer of the Boy

Summer of the Boy— **Audible**

**Brimstone Lords MC**

Bossman: Undone

Duke: Redeemed

Chaos: Calmed

Scotch: Unraveled

Hero: Claimed

Blood: Revealed

**The Bedlam Horde MC**

Devil's Advocate: Vlad

Devil's Due: Sarge

Devil's Work: Dark

Devil Incarnate: Reaper

Devil to Pay: Cutter

Devil Inside: Green

Devil's Own: Roughneck

I stood in front of the open garage door with my hands on my hips surveying the massive piles of stuff leftover from a love story gone wrong. Some women got happily ever after. I got the castoffs from the life of a man who once existed, who once loved me and I'd loved him, but now? The answer, my friend: dust blowing in the wind.

His parents didn't want the stuff, and I understood. No parent should outlive their child. His did. I didn't want the boxes, either, but when his mother had turned those sad eyes on me and begun to cry—how could I say *no*? I was the loving, grieving fiancée, after all. One hundred percent true. I ate (when I eventually got my appetite back), slept (when the insomnia finally left me), and drank (alcohol didn't help one bit) my grief, day in and day out, over his loss.

That happened two years ago.

Two.

Long.

Years.

Jeffery had that effect on people. To say his death came unexpectedly would be akin to saying the sky was blue or trees had leaves. A big ol' steaming pile of *duh*. What the police could never tell us: Why did it happen? Jeffery had been a healthy, devastatingly handsome twenty-six-year-old financial whiz who'd made a ton of money for his clients.

*He'd made them tons of money.* This meant when the police showed to talk with me that day, to ask if he had any enemies, the answer was a resounding *no*. Who wouldn't like a man who made them rich beyond belief? Then why was he gunned down when he ran into the convenience store to buy me a pint of Chunky Monkey because I'd been having a migraine and wanted to let Ben & Jerry chase my blues away? It wasn't a robbery gone bad. The police were sure of that point. The perp targeted exactly one person with the big *pow-pow* and that one person was Jeffery. He'd driven a fancy car, had a fat wallet in his pocket, and a Rolex on his wrist when the shooter brought him down. The only theft the shooter committed was stealing my fiancé's life.

So here we were. I wiped the tears from my face with the back of my hand. Thinking about the brutal way Jeffery left us always choked me up. No one deserved to die that way.

Standing outside the garage staring at those boxes wasn't going to get them sorted any faster. Sighing, I pushed up my metaphorical sleeves, ready to wade into the mire of memories. The first box contained his clothing—suits, jeans, and button-down shirts for both business and casual wear. Those stayed in the box that I planned to donate. There had to be someone out in the big, wide world who could use a good suit when heading into a job interview. His clothing might change a person's life for the better. So why did it feel like deciding to donate his organs instead of his Armani?

I lost myself in the chore, saving the few mementos special to me like the dancing hula girl bobblehead he kept on his desk. We'd bought it at a truck stop outside Needles, California while on our way home from one of Jeffery's old college roommate's wedding. Then I finished by putting a box together of items making up the sum of Jeffery's early life. Report cards, school pictures, yearbooks, and the like. Things that hurt too much for them to look at now but his family might be happy to have down the road.

Despite working in the shade of the garage, sweat dripped from my brow, and highly attractive pit stains drenched my T-shirt. Of course, the shirt being a medium-dusty blue, the stains showed contrastingly darker. August in Michigan played out more like a rainforest than most people imagined. I pushed my bangs out of my face, tucking a few of the longer strands behind my ear, and chewed on my bottom lip.

*This is taking forever…* No matter. The job needed to get done. I'd grown tired of scraping ice off my windows two winters ago because the garage had been too full of this stuff, but being heavily laden with grief, I didn't have it in me to do anything about it. Fast forward to today, and I felt ready to tackle the emotionally daunting task.

"Hello, Simone," Mrs. Hildebrandt called from her spot on the sidewalk in front of my lawn where she watched me sorting out boxes, as always wearing her signature moo-moo and orthopedic sandals. Today's moo-moo was yellow with large blue flowers. If a smock and a hospital gown had a baby, the baby would be Mrs. Hildebrandt's dress for today. "Finally getting rid of that stuff?"

"Yes, Mrs. Hildebrandt." *Clearly.*

"Why don't you get your sweet fella to help you clean? A gentleman should always help his sweetheart."

Mrs. Hildebrandt currently suffered from early-stage dementia. It wasn't her fault, yet it still hurt to be hit with that same reminder that my "sweet fella" was gone every time she saw me. The neighborhood had loved Jeffery and he would've been out here helping without me ever having to ask. Because of that, everyone in the neighborhood knew of Jeffery's passing. They'd even enacted an emergency phone tree. Those first weeks, I had neighbors helping with everything from cleaning to laundry to mowing the yard. Several of the women even went grocery shopping. Not that I'd needed to shop. The rest of my kind neighbors had filled my fridge and freezer to capacity with any form of noodle dish one could imagine, and even a few that it shocked me they had. Like Mrs. Danbury's Chicken-Pineapple Surprise. The surprise being whatever that mystery meat started life as it sure wasn't chicken.

Picture a dish where ambrosia met chicken alfredo and you'd be just about there. Though she'd thrown in a couple of undetermined spices for good measure, which burned my tongue.

I'd given some to Mr. Pooches, my kitty, and he ended up sick—like take-him-to-the-vet sick. Let's just say that particular gift left me with enough bloating and nightmares to last me a lifetime and call it good.

I shuddered at the memory. Then I called out to Mrs. Hildebrandt, "He can't do it," and I turned back to tackle the task at hand.

Nothing prepared a person for that news. We weren't married and we hadn't lived together yet. The police had no idea to contact me. I called his cell and when someone answered, that someone wasn't my Jeffery. He'd identified himself as Officer Monroe. Asked who I was. Why was I calling? The love of my life had been murdered and did I have his parents' address?

I'd dropped to my knees and wailed. The rest always ended up fuzzy. The huge bubble of grief that suddenly consumed my life blocked out any recollection of when I stopped crying or who found me, if anyone, or how I'd gotten up off the floor. None.

Moving on, I stood, wiped my hands down the front of my dusty jeans, and surveyed the scene. At the end of an arduously emotional and somewhat physical day, I ended up with four boxes to donate.

"Right," I muttered to myself, bending to pick up the first box to load into the back of my jeep. I had it painted bright lilac. Purple was my jam because who could be sad surrounded by purple? So I made it my mission to devote my life to the flowery hue as much as humanly possible. Three more hefty loads stuffed into the trunk and I finally had a space to park in the winter. Once I sorted the 'keep' boxes down to two, I hauled the rest out to the front to be picked up in the morning by waste disposal. Mrs. Hildebrandt remained standing on the sidewalk in front of my lawn watching me work until I got scared she'd end up with heat exhaustion or something.

"It's hot out here, Mrs. Hildebrandt. You should go home and get a drink," I said, which caused her to startle. She blinked several times, murmuring something unintelligible, then walked home. I waited to withdraw completely from my driveway until I saw her enter her house, then I shifted into reverse pulling out.

Sitting at the second stoplight on my way to the big chain secondhand store, this niggling feeling hit my left ear out of nowhere. It felt like a tickle that I couldn't get rid of, not by wiping at my ear with my shoulder, or even scratching at it with my nails. It just kept on, and since it happened to be my left ear, I turned my head to the left when I went at my ear with my shoulder again. It didn't work—*again*—but I spotted a small secondhand store I must've passed by a million times and never realized it was there.

As the light turned green, I clicked on my blinker, merging into the middle turn lane. A small store, it sat between a vacant storefront and a sub shop. After a couple of tries, I backed into a spot in front of the store, stopping to grab the first box before heading inside. The problem being, I had a hard time getting the door open while carrying the large box. Three failed attempts later, I set the box down to open the door and wedged my body between the door and frame to hold the heavy glass open until I was able to pick up the box again.

"We're not cooling off the outside—shut the door," This, someone shouted at me from the area around the checkout.

I looked up, still hefting the box up with my knee and shifting it to my hip. "Excuse me?" I asked.

"The door." The voice came from an irate man. When I

looked up—*bam!* This unbelievable sense of déjà vu hit me from out of the blue. "You're standing in it, neither inside nor outside. I don't care which you choose, but make your choice and close it already."

Seventies porn music played in my head as I watched his mouth move, a mouth putting me under a hypnotic spell until I realized the words coming from that hypnotic moving mouth weren't very flattering. "Are you sick or just dumb?" he shouted at me in a highly aggrieved manner, I might add.

I blinked the brain fog away.

*What?*

My ears felt filled with fluid. I shook my head until the muffled sound cleared and I blinked several times again.

"I asked if you're sick or are you just dumb?" he repeated curtly. "Come in or get out. I don't care which, just stinking do it." Uh, was that a tone? Did I detect *a tone*?

That hardly seemed necessary. I stepped in, letting the glass door slowly ease shut. "Well, you could've helped me and that would've gotten the job done faster." And oh, yeah, did he ever get my mean eyes. The *if looks could kill* eyes that I saved for the worst offenders.

"I could've," he answered. "But it's not in my job description." The jerk, I mean okay, he happened to have been a handsome jerk, but a jerk nonetheless. And he had the audacity to smirk. As if.

Why was it that the best-looking people were always the biggest assholes?

This guy had to be one of the worst because he seriously caused a big-time tingle in my parts. All the parts, not just my girly parts. I was talking rapid-heartbeat, hard-to-catch-a-breath, face-flushing-with-embarrassment-from-being-a-lowly-peon-in-his-presence kind of sexy. His hair appeared so brown that some might've mistaken it for black, and he wore it short but artfully shaggy in that *I know I'm hot* way that ridiculously hot people lived by. And if that weren't enough, he had the audacity to have these black eyes that shimmered and reflected the light in the store like pieces of shiny coal.

Don't get me started on those shoulders—I mean, who gave him the right to have shoulders that broad and muscled while working behind the cash register? Those shoulders belonged on romance book covers. Or now that I was on a roll, how about being that tall? Jeffery was six feet. This guy looked at least a head taller. Who gave him the right to look like that while working in a store where anyone—me, I was anyone—could see him? Everything about him ticked me off on principle.

If that was the way he wanted to play this, *fine*. He didn't know who he was dealing with. I walked that box over to the checkout, dropping it on the floor. "Well," I started in, hand to my hip, leaning into his space with my eyebrow raised—better believe I broke out the eyebrow raise for this one—and I cocked my head, giving it to him straight. "If it's not in your job description to help a girl out when you see her struggling with the door, then you're just going to have to deal with escaping air."

He opened his mouth to spew something highly entertaining, I was sure, but I cut him right off.

"Oh, no... You had your say. It's my turn now," I said. His mouth snapped shut while he bared his teeth at me like a dog. *"Bad puppy,"* I admonished him. *"Heel."* Ever heard that saying *'He had murder in his eyes?'* Whoever made that saying up had clearly been talking about this guy, but I didn't have two cares to give. And for my parting words, I looked him right in the eye and said, "And I have three more boxes in my truck *just like this one."*

Then in the grandest exit I could muster, I spun around on my heels and walked out. If I was being honest, I didn't expect it to work, but he followed me outside. Because he followed me to my jeep pushing in front of me to heft up one of the boxes, I magnanimously ignored his grumbling.

We each carried a box and when we reached the door, he shifted his box into one arm as if holding a tissue box and opened it, holding it for me to pass through first. The last box he fetched on his own.

As he bent his knees to set it down, I pet the top of his head like I would when giving praise to a dog, contemplating whether or not I had enough time to scratch behind his ear before getting the heck out of there. "Good boy," I said and then I ran for my life while laughing my fool head off.

I distinctly heard the sound of a thump against the glass making me pretty sure he threw something against the door. Before hopping back in my jeep, I popped inside the sub shop next door for a veggie sub on parmesan bread, a giant chocolate and raspberry chip cookie, and a diet iced tea to go. Smile still planted firmly on my face.

On the way home, my phone rang. Typically, not a big deal, but today the screen said: *Janet*. Janet? No. I wasn't in the head-space to deal with Janet. It'd been months since I last heard from her. Being Jeffery's mom, and with Jeffery being gone, she'd found it hard to be around me. I must admit, I'd dropped the ball on keeping in touch with my almost mother-in-law as well.

In my contemplation of what she could possibly have to call me about, I almost missed answering the call. And wouldn't that have been a shame? Yes—*sigh*—it would've. I was being mean. "Hello?" I answered.

"Simone, dear… how are you?" She'd sounded sad since Jeffrey's passing, but today she emitted it through the line, filling my car up with her sorrow.

"What's wrong? Is it Charles? Daphne?" Charles, her husband, and Daphne, her daughter—Jeffery's father and sister—were the only other reasons I could think of to cause her this level of misery.

"No…" she whispered. "They're fine. It's… Simone dear, the police phoned. They're finally releasing Jeffery's personal effects." She sniffled loudly. "They told us to collect it by this afternoon." This, she followed by a second, even louder sniffle. "I can't do it, Simone. I can't. *Please…*"

Of all days to ask me to pick up his personal effects, but how did I tell her *no*? She was almost my mother-in-law and this was Jeffery we were talking about. I owed him this much, to see to his parents now that he couldn't.

"Sure," I told her, sighing. "I can head there now."

"Thank you," she said softly. Then we hung up.

And just like that, I merged over three lanes of traffic, horns honking as I cut a few people off in my attempt to make it to the righthand turn lane, taking a hard right at the next light, then flipping around to turn back onto the street I just came from, only heading the opposite direction.

Seven stoplights and two more turns later, I pulled into a metered spot in front of the police station. Right before I opened my door, I remembered I'd been cleaning in a garage all day and sighed. I must've looked ridiculous walking into that second-hand shop, one big, hot mess.

My eyes shot to my jeans. Dirty. Hurriedly, I flipped down the visor mirror, holding back a scream given the horror of my appearance. The soft lavender I'd dyed my hair two months ago to help me move forward now held a sheen of silver from all the dust.

The lavender was part of the *new me* project. The things to do for myself to help me out of the funk I'd been living under since Jeffery's passing.

What normally fell soft and full of body now hung limp and stringy around my shoulders. The best I could do was finger-comb it, which brought back a little life. Well, it'd just have to do. Cobweb chic might not have been my best look, but who did I need to impress?

I really despised this particular favor. My stomach pitched as I grasped the handle and I swallowed back the fear as I opened the door. On a large breath, I climbed out.

*Lord help me.*

**CHAPTER**

*Two*

The suction keeping the door closed because of the temperature differential blew me backward hard enough to land on my butt when I finally yanked it open, with a burst of super-cooled air hitting me as I fell. Clearly, I'd never been a Boy Scout. Wasn't that their motto: Always be prepared, or something like that? Well, I wasn't prepared for the gale-force wind about to hit me, and when my hand slipped from the handle, that was all she wrote. Hoping that nobody saw, I pushed up off the hard cement and brushed off my humiliation along with my bottom, thankful that the door caught on the rubber lip lining the threshold instead of shutting completely.

Because I was busy dusting myself off, I didn't exactly look where I was going—that was until I slammed head, torso, and even legs first into a wall of man. Where I *oomphed*, he grumbled, lifting me by my arms to set me away.

"Maybe you should actually look before you walk," he said, and not nicely.

"I'm sorry," I replied and looked up to smile at the man, hoping to show my sincerity. That idea blew with the wind when I caught his eyes. Dark eyes narrowed angrily on me and not the kind of *you just knocked into me* type of angry, but a deeper-seeded anger where the roots had already taken hold before he ever laid eyes on me.

"What business do you have here?" he asked, posturing menacingly by folding his arms over his immensely broad chest. He seemed overly pissed off given the situation. It was an accident. I wanted to say, "I hope your day gets better," but with another scowl from the man, I rethought that real quick. Was Mercury in retrograde? Why did every man I ran into today have to be an asshole? Okay, so I literally *ran* into this guy, but come on. I apologized. Let the punishment fit the crime, for crying out loud.

"I'm here to pick up my fiancé's belongings. It has to be gone today." Man, I wished I'd stayed in bed. The detective actually seemed to get angrier when I answered the question that *he* asked. His body grew super rigid and the vein in his neck not only pulsed, but looked a second and a half away from bursting through the skin on his neck. This must have been *Pick on Simone Day* and someone forgot to send me the memo.

"Go to the elevator. Basement level. Check in at the desk— they'll help you out."

"Thank you," I said, moving away from him but deciding that maybe he was just upset about the accident, I wanted to try to smooth things over before we parted ways. "And I'm really sorry about running into you."

He gritted his teeth but didn't say another word to me, only watched me until I turned away to get to the elevator. Once the doors slid shut, I pushed the B button and had to grab the wall when the lift jolted. At the bottom when the doors slid open, I had this idea that this floor would be darker with maybe only one or two buzzing, flickering greenish lights illuminating ceilings with water stains and, I didn't know, puddles on the floor. Maybe I watched too many police dramas because this place might not have had natural light coming in from windows but it held a light and airy feel that surprised me. Clean. No water or cobwebs. A bubbly woman sat behind a desk. Blonde hair pulled back in a ponytail and smiling blue eyes that matched the customary blue uniform she wore smartly. Not a scowl in sight. Finally.

"Welcome," she said. "How can I help you today?"

"You guys released Jeffery Myer's personal stuff. I'm here to pick it up."

"Do you have an I.D.?" she asked.

I pulled my wallet from my purse, flipped it open, and slid the license from the plastic sleeve, handing it over. She snapped a picture of it to load into their computer before handing it back.

"Okay, wait here. I'll be back in a minute."

Smiling, I nodded, waiting patiently as she jogged through a door behind her. A few minutes later, the woman appeared holding a smallish brown box. The kind that normally held files, with the lid and everything. I signed the paperwork and took possession of Jeffery's belongings, then got the heck out of there.

On the drive home, I passed the secondhand store again, which made me wonder why that guy was such a jerk. Though I refused to give him too much headspace. I had a cleared-out spot to park in my garage and a box of my dead fiancé's effects. The first I loved thinking about, the second I wanted to avoid, but at the same time, curiosity got the better of me.

While I sat at the table eating my lunch, I flipped off the lid of the box and pulled the first object, Jeffery's phone, out. His phone. I pulled out his wallet and other things they'd collected from the scene, but something kept pulling my attention back to his phone. I walked it into my kitchen to plug it in and waited for it to power up.

Jeffery had shared his lock code with me, the same as I'd done with him. Even after two years, when I clicked on his browser, the last thing he'd looked up appeared as a thumbnail in the corner. I clicked on it and—why would Jeffery have been looking up a strange address? He didn't do house calls. He had an office, a nice office where his clients came to him if they didn't want to video conference.

I turned to the maps app to help me out, and according to the cross streets, it wasn't in the best neighborhood. So I clicked off the browser to look at his call history. Mine was the last call he'd made. But there were several calls from a person named Beetle. The last call only five minutes before he'd called me.

*Beetle?*

Jeffery never talked about a Beetle and we talked, or I *thought* we'd talked, about everything. Well, okay, we talked about everything that had to do with him. Me? Not so much. I held a huge secret, something no one else in the world knew about except maybe my parents, but seeing as they died when I was just a baby, they weren't spilling either.

See, I wasn't exactly human. I wasn't *not* human, either. I considered myself human plus. The plus coming from the magic that flowed through me every full moon. No, not like a werewolf or anything like that. This magic sparked from my fingertips like a witch, but I'd met a few witches and all of them said variations on the same thing: "What are you?"

It'd been my experience that others in the magic community could sniff out their own. Even amongst the odd, it appeared I didn't fit in. At least not until I'd met Jeffery. He went out of his way to make me feel loved. Though, he was also completely human. Kind of like on that old '60s sitcom *Bewitched*, I'd intended to share my secret with him, just not until we were married. That was why we'd kept separate homes. I made sure to have 'cramps' or 'a really bad headache' on every full moon, thus avoiding that potentially uncomfortable talk. Stupid, right? All that time wasted. We could've spent that time in domesticated bliss. It seemed like a perfectly reasonable idea at the time. Like he couldn't have just divorced me after he found out?

Speaking of magic, that familiar pins-and-needles feeling started to spread through my hands, telling me something I didn't need a calendar to remind me of, that tonight was a full moon. I flexed the joints in my fingers. This really was the worst part, the pins and needles caused by the magic uploading onto my temporary… what? Cache, maybe?

The last voicemail recorded on Jeffrey's phone happened the day before he died. Again, from Beetle. "Make the move now," the low, eerily smooth voice ordered. "Or else."

Or else?

Or else *what*?

Or else *he loses a client*?

Or else *he gets written up*?

Or else *he gets a bullet to his brain*?

When I said *eerily smooth*, I meant like when you heard the Godfather talking in that really popular movie. You just knew he was evil, but he never sounded upset. That was Beetle. Could this man be behind Jeffery's murder? And why hadn't the police ever mentioned this to us before? Since no arrests were made, I could only assume that they didn't feel the need to feed us this information. The sandwich sat like a lead brick in my stomach. Wishing that I'd avoided food altogether, I sipped on the iced tea from the sub shop in hopes that my poor tummy would stop hating me as much as it felt like it did.

But… what if the police missed something? My gut told me there was more to this Beetle and the address Jeffery looked up. Crap. Okay. My feet knew what I planned to do before my brain knew probably because my brain started to focus on something else, something more… diabolical.

The word CORRUPTION began flashing in my head over and over in a bright purple neon. Corruption? Was their lack of communication concerning this person purposeful? I'd love to say that my intuition or gut instinct led me to this conclusion too, but I couldn't because as I continued to see the flashing purple neon word behind my eyes, I felt the pulse of magic encircling it. Magic? Surrounding a word? This never happened before. I wasn't sure I liked it now. No. My entire life I knew what to expect from my magic. Taser fingers that sparked with every full moon. Now suddenly the universe decided to change the rules of the game? Why? How? And most importantly, what did it have to do with Jeffery?

While this corruption angle took up major headspace, my feet seized control of the rest of my body. I left the other items on the table, crumpling up the wrappers from my food to throw away then grabbed Jeffery's phone, my purse, and keys and ran out to my garage. Even in the daylight, the power in my veins started to get stronger because of the moon's position. I flexed the fingers on each hand multiple times and shook them out. Then using my maps app, I followed the route from the address provided by Jeffery's phone back to that less-than-stellar neighborhood.

I'd be lying if I didn't say I hoped to see a sign that read: Beetle's place. Did I expect to see it? Of course not. But it would've made this job a whole lot easier. What didn't make it easier was the address belonged to an abandoned building with the bottom windows and doorways boarded up and the second- and third-story windows broken out as if people had thrown rocks through them. It took a great deal of psyching myself up to finally decide to do a walk around. Without full use of my magic, if someone decided to pop a shot off at me, depending on how good a shot they were, it could mean R.I.P. Simone.

If they tried to attack me, maybe take me out with a tackle, enough magic flowed through me to fend them off. A touch from my hand was like being touched by the prongs of a stun gun. But I had to be touching them for that to work.

*This is for Jeffery.* After my mental pep talk, I sighed, shook off my fear, and pushed open the door to my jeep, making sure to bleep the locks after I jumped out.

The entire perimeter was littered with broken beer bottles and fast food wrappers, and around the back, I even found bent spoons and discarded needles, evidence of drug use—totally gross. One of the boards on the window had been loosened and I was able to move it out of the way enough to climb through. The temperature immediately dropped by a good twenty degrees inside and when the board swung shut again, the room plunged into blackness.

It stank of urine with faint hints of excrement. I wrinkled my nose, seriously contemplating turning myself around and getting the hell out of there, but instead, I fished my phone from my purse and clicked on the flashlight, shining it around the open space. Evidence suggested that several of the city's homeless used this building as a camp.

As I walked the room, I heard a clanging like a can falling and spun around with my light, finding the offending can and a giant rat scurrying along the perimeter of the floor closest to the wall. What in the world would have made Jeffery come here?

The hairs on my arms started standing on end, which meant the time had come to move my ass. I ran back over to the window, moving the board and slipping back out into the sun, warming my bones, though not getting rid of that shaky feeling.

The feeling grew steadily stronger as I rounded the building. I prepared to see someone scoping out my jeep or checking out the building. But I could never have prepared to see him. *He* was there. The guy from the secondhand store stood across the street not scoping out my jeep, not checking out the building, but staring straight at *me*.

Arms crossed over his chest, a really attractive chest, even if not quite as broad as the detective's at the police station. It still out-broaded most chests in the chest universe. What was wrong with me, thinking about broad-chested men at a time like this? He glared at me. Those hard eyes struck me harder than any hand ever could. They struck me down to my soul. He had that menacing thing down because I, for one, was intimidated.

Instead of asking him what in tarnation he was doing there, I ran to my truck, bleeping the locks to get in before I reached it. The problem with that strategy one might ask? I'd be happy to tell if I wasn't so scared out of my mind, but one might guess my answer when I reached the door, swung it open, and climbed in, only to be met with him sitting in the passenger seat. How? He was across the street like two seconds ago.

"Drive," he ordered me and the only thing that went through my head at that moment was an episode of a police forensics show where the officer said flat out: *"Never let them get you to a second location."* I didn't want to die.

"No!" I yelled, hoping to take him off guard, and I touched all five fingers on my right hand to his neck. That touch should've knocked him out for like ten minutes at least, but instead of passing out, he grabbed my hand, forcing it back onto the steering wheel again.

"If you don't want to die, I suggest you not try that again and drive."

Well, my next escape strategy involved running us off the road into a busy gas station or grocery store. My baby, beautiful flowery lilac finish, pristine in her condition, would just have to forgive me when I took her into the body shop for repairs because that would mean I was alive to take her there.

As I didn't want to die and for some odd reason, my personal finger tasers neglected to work on my kidnapper, I started the engine and pulled out onto the road.

"Turn left," he ordered. Since turning left took us out of that particular neighborhood, up and over the bridge to an area I was more familiar with, I turned left.

"Why are you doing this? How did you know I'd be there?"

"My boss sent me," he answered.

Uh, his boss? "And why does the owner of a secondhand store care where I spend my free time?"

"Different job. Different boss."

"Who's your boss?"

"Can't tell you that."

"Can you tell me anything?" I asked. "What's your name?"

"Not that it matters, but it's Connor. Feel better?"

"That I know the name of my kidnapper? Yes." I turned a

hard right into a gas station, stepping on the gas. I stopped just short of plowing through the wall.

"Stop!" he shouted, trying to yank the wheel. When I stomped on the brake, I threw her in park, wrenched the keys out of the ignition, grabbed my purse, jumped out, and ran for my life, yelling at the top of my lungs.

*"He's trying to kidnap me! Help! Someone, help!"*

Several men of the big, strong, pissed-that-someone-was-trying-to-hurt-a-woman variety fell in, blocking Connor to allow me to get inside the store. From the door, I watched as those same men surrounded him, closing ranks.

"My girlfriend gets a little dramatic," he said in his lame attempt to cover his own behind. Which I had to admit was weird because it sounded like a radio transmission in my head. With only a glass door to separate us, his words should've sounded muffled, but they came at me clear as a bright sunny day. And I didn't like them one bit. Dramatic? Did he really have the nerve to call *me* dramatic?

Oh, I could show him dramatic. With a great lack of common sense, considering the man kidnapped me and thus I should've kept as many barriers between us as possible, I pushed open the door to yell, "He's not my boyfriend. I met him once today at a secondhand store. I think he might be stalking me."

There might have been some knuckle- and neck-cracking among the men keeping me safe from Connor. The cashier, an older woman who looked at me like this wasn't the first time she'd seen something like this, handed me a phone. "911," she said.

I explained the situation the best I could.

"Are you safe?" the dispatcher asked.

"For now. I'm inside. Men are keeping him from entering."

"Good. Stay inside. Police are on the way."

She kept me on the line, giving her a play-by-play of the standoff outside.

With my stomach all tied up in knots, the cashier kindly

handed me a cup of coffee. I'd swear on a stack of tarot cards that I only turned my head away for a second—a measly, split second—and *bam!* The yelling and painful screams caught my attention. The cup of hot brew slipped from my fingers, spilling a puddle of brown liquid over the floor as both the cashier and I pressed our faces to the door, peering outside, where those big, strong, angry-on-my-behalf men slumped in a heap on the hot cement.

No Connor to be found.

That was when the police showed, sirens blazing. And just my luck, the angry police detective had to be the one to answer my call for help. Great. What could be odder than a failed kidnapping attempt, a dogpile of large protector-type men out cold, and a detective angry I breathed air? Well, that could only be the giant black hound the size of a grizzly running top speed away from the scene. I'd hate to be the animal control officer sent out to trap him.

"What are you staring at?" the detective asked after snapping his fingers in my face to get my attention.

I pointed in the direction of the dog. "Uh… the gigantic *dog.*"

He turned his head the way I pointed, squinting his eyes and covering his hand like a visor to shield his eyes from the sun. "What dog?"

"What do you mean what dog? It's *right there?*" I pointed again. "He's running between the trees and that building."

The man frowned even harder at me, a feat I didn't think possible until I saw it with my own eyes, as he folded his arms over his massive chest taking a "don't test me" stance that I probably should have found more intimidating—but *hello,* gigantic dog on the loose! "Did you hit your head?" he asked and I thought he might've been part dog himself the way he growled that sentence at me.

Hit it? No, but I shook it.

"Listen, just take my statement so I can go home and take a nice bubble bath." Something felt off about the detective. Definitely *something* that I could no longer ascribe to him having a bad day. I wish I could put my finger on the what of his issues, but my head started to throb and I just needed to go home now. Thus, I gave my statement without any further pretense. When he asked me how I'd ended up at that abandoned building, I was honest. "Jeffery's phone was in with his belongings. I charged it and turned it on. I saw his call log and texts. The location puzzled me, so I went to check it out. That's how I ended up at the building."

Then, I kid not, he poked me several times with a beefy finger right in the center of my chest. He did it hard enough that I figured I'd find a bruise in that spot. "I'm telling you now, don't go back there. That's an order." —Uh, *an order*? Last I checked, we didn't live in a fascist state and he had no say in where I chose to go at any given time of day— "You've got no business being in that part of town."

Then he suddenly and completely dismissed me by turning his back on me to take the statements of the big, burly protector-type men who'd kept me safe from my kidnapper and now stood around in a huddle rubbing the backs of their necks and wherever else appeared to pain them. I couldn't read their minds, but I'd say trying to figure out what the hell just happened to them.

Connor. He said his name was Connor. Why would he tell me his name unless he'd planned for me not to make it out of our encounter alive?

And on top of everything, I'd found nothing useful in the abandoned building. Zip. Zilch. I sighed. It was time to call this a day and head home. Vegging until I fell asleep sounded pretty perfect, actually. The magic simmered just below my skin now. It wanted out. It wanted me to let it loose onto an unexpecting world.

"Simmer down," I whispered to my fingers. The magic didn't listen. It never listened.

The problem with the whole *vegging-out* plan was that once I reached my house, ordered takeout from my favorite Chinese place, and plopped down into my favorite chair with a tall glass of icy-pink lemonade, the condensation dripping down the glass —the best way to drink it—my curiosity got the better of me again and I opened Jeffery's phone again. I open the Dropbox app. All boring finance-related files. I couldn't pretend to understand all the jargon, but I understood enough to see that there didn't appear to be any funny business.

File after file, I read for hours. Only stopping to answer the door and pay the delivery driver. Then I hit a file related to a client named "B. el-Zebu." That was an interesting name. I'd seen al-Whatever names before, but never el-Whatever. I clicked on the file. Every word was written in a language that I didn't understand. Not one that I recognized. Yet another dead end, or so I thought. I thought about it until I reached the bottom of the file, only to find a second file. This filename caught my attention because Jeffery had named it "Chocolate Chip Cookie Recipe."

This seemed like a weird spot to put a cookie recipe. I clicked on it. My magic went haywire, burning under my skin, boiling my blood until I feared I'd pass out. "What the—" I whispered, squeezing my eyes shut and shaking out my hands, trying anything I could think of to get rid of the burning.

The words in the file began to rearrange themselves and I blinked several times to rid myself of the hallucination. They rearranged into an address. Similar, eerily similar to the address I'd gone to today, but it was located in a town like four towns over. Could this be why I'd found nothing at the abandoned building? Because it was the wrong location?

Quickly, I shoved the remnants of my dinner into the refrigerator, slipped on my ballet flats, grabbed up my purse, and headed out to my jeep. In so much of a hurry, I even neglected to turn off the TV and lights. Before I backed out onto the road, I plugged this new address, with the new ZIP Code, into my map app.

The closer I drove to this new address, the more my magic

tried to rip itself from my body. It hurt so badly I was forced to pull over two different times to get a grip on the pain. It had never behaved like this before. Once I reached the town of Raven, the town where I needed to be, I took each turn going slowly. Not a star shone in the sky, but the moon burned full and bright.

And then I heard the robotic voice of my map app: *Destination on the right.*

# CHAPTER Three

This couldn't have been right. The only thing on the right was a cemetery. One of those incredibly old ones without modern amenities like streetlights. A wrought-iron gate attached to a rock wall, the kind without mortar, stood proudly stacked with seems tight enough that the thing wasn't ever going to crumble. Too tall to see over. My fingers felt ready to explode wide open.

Part of me immediately got a case of the willies. But another part of me felt compelled to go inside as if returning home. I didn't understand it. I also couldn't resist it. The magic refused to let me. *Refused.* A large padlock kept the townspeople out. I wrapped my hand around the lock to see if I had any chance of unlocking it and the thing popped open. Just like that. As soon as I touched it, the magic escaped my fingers. It pulled me forward, moving my feet for me.

The unbearable pain changed to this weird, out of control tingling sensation that didn't hurt one bit. What. In. The. Hell? Like it or not, I felt that I needed to push on and I sighed, shot a quick prayer into the universe that I came out of this little excursion unscathed and started walking.

Tombstones older than my great-great-great grandmother—I imagined her to be the first of us to immigrate to the US from the old country, as the United States only went back as far as the 1600s—speckled the ground along with looming, dead trees. They had to be dead; otherwise, they'd have been full of leaves and not just twisted, spindly branches. These had none. And forget about asking which *"old country"* my ancestors arrived from because I didn't have a clue. My parents never said because they'd died, leaving me to go into the foster care system with only a small, ancient, handwritten diary as my sole possession of their lives.

As I grew and asked questions, I found out that a woman who identified herself as being from CPS placed me in an emergency foster care home. That my parents had been killed earlier that night. From what I was told, the journal had been strapped to me, under my clothing. Made from leather, the spine cracking from age. I treasured that book. I just wish it had gone into a little more detail. Oh, I'd asked it too many times to count. The book simply ignored me. Seeing as books didn't speak. As a kid, I'd wanted to know in order to give myself roots, a family history I could connect with. But then, when the magic began to manifest, I became desperate to know. Was said old country Transylvania? Or possibly Ireland? What other countries were known for magic?

A path lit up for me. Fiery footsteps led the way. I followed diligently because one didn't simply ignore fiery footprints and my magic made me do it. I followed the trail deeper into the dark. Even my magic started to get a little nervous, twitching along with the tingling, or maybe that was my imagination. Maybe it wasn't as much nervousness as anxious anticipation.

The path led me to a second, smaller wrought-iron gate, this time attached to a wrought-iron fence surrounding a cement building. A mausoleum. I *hated* mausoleums. They freaked me out in a major way. I just knew some disgusting zombie thing waited inside to suck my brains out.

And then the door creaked open. A red light the color of flames lit the space. I struggled to back away. My feet tried to help me run away, back to my car. My magic pulled me forward. The largest dog probably ever in existence lunged from inside the crypt, snarling and gnashing his jaws.

"Good doggy," I said, trying and failing to move out of teeth range. He looked exactly like the dog running away from the gas station earlier this afternoon. The dog blinked. Not kidding. It stopped trying to eat me and blinked as if confused by the situation. *Join the club.*

The twitching and tingling abruptly stopped as my magic stretched out in front of me to run specter-like fingers over his ruff. The moment the magic made contact, a huge, invisible explosion shot out, rippling the air like an atomic bomb, knocking me on my butt, knocking me out. When I came to, Connor, my kidnapper, held me in his arms against his warm body.

I tried to scramble away, but my head still felt dizzy and he held on tightly.

"Settle down," he ordered.

"Let *go!*" I shouted.

Connor looked to the sky. "Is this how it's always going to be?" he asked no one.

"How *what* is going to be?"

He sighed. *Sighed.* Like a hugely affected one.

I rolled my eyes. "Will you please let me go now?"

"No," he said.

No? What did he mean, *no?* "I asked nicely."

"And I turned you down *nicely.* Now that we both know how to be nice—"

"Your idea of nice differs from mine."

"Listen, it goes against my nature to let you go. It's not like I want this connection. What are you, anyway? I've never met a creature like you before. And I've met every level of creature, or so I thought."

"Rude much? What are you?"

"I'm a hound."

"So you're a dog."

"A *hound*."

"Is there really a difference?" I asked. This close, his eyes gleamed like shiny, black coal rocks, even in the dark. His skin looked soft. He had these plump lips that I wanted to—*no. Bad Simone.* We did not want that thing you were just thinking. A thing so wrong, I couldn't even say it in my own head.

He laughed salaciously. "Trust me, sweetheart, there's a difference."

Connor let his guard down enough for me to push up into a seated position. "Oh, this is one of those 'I have a bigger penis' things, right? Hounds are hung?"

"As a matter of fact, we are."

"Well, good for you." Unsure of what else to do, I lightly patted his shoulder. "Now if you don't mind, I need to know what's in there—" I pointed to the open door to the mausoleum.

He narrowed his eyes on me. "What do you mean, *what's in there*?"

"You seem to understand English, *so…* I'm not sure how to answer that."

"You really don't know?" he asked, to which I shook my head in answer.

"Hence me asking."

"Hades," he said.

I pressed the back of my hand to his forehead to check if he was feverish. "Are you feeling okay?"

He narrowed his eyes. "You really *don't know.*" This was said as a statement. "So your parents never…" He let the thought trail off.

"I'm afraid not. They died when I was a baby. I didn't know anything about this stuff until I hit puberty and got more than my period." I laughed uncomfortably. "Why couldn't the detective see you?"

"Only supers can see me in hound form. And ghosts and spirits."

"Supers?"

"Supernaturals. Magic holders. Since you're not having a nervous breakdown, I assume you know about magic holders."

I nodded. "Yes. When I was twelve, I ran into my first witch. She told fortunes at a festival."

"They do work the circuit," he answered dryly.

"Of course, I thought it was all a bunch of hooey until she revealed she knew about *my* magic. That got my attention and it marked the first time someone asked, 'What are you?'"

"And you have no idea?"

"None. I'm clearly not a witch. I only get my magic at the full moon."

He cocked his head. "Seriously?"

"Seriously."

"Not even Lycans are constrained by the full moon."

"They're not?" I asked now very curious about the evolution of their legend. *Remember to look up Lycan legends when I get home.*

"Nah, that's a rumor. They're just strongest at the full moon."

"Why are you hanging out in a cemetery?"

The beautiful man looked on me somewhat indulgently for the first time in our acquaintance. And let me just say, indulgent was a good look, not that I thought he had a bad one. Not even when he was being an ass or scaring the crap out of me today. "Sweetheart, what's your name?"

"Simone."

"Well, Simone, I'm a death hound. In some cultures, we're known as 'hellhounds.' I guard the entrance to the underworld."

"Does that come with a good benefits package?" I joked. He didn't so much as crack a smile. "You aren't laughing."

"That's because I'm not kidding."

"Why did my magic bring me here? And why did you kidnap me this afternoon?"

Connor pulled me in closer to his body heat, keeping his

hands resting on my hips. He didn't even look aware of the action. "After you showed up to the store this morning, I got a call from my boss. He said, 'Something's started.' And told me I needed to keep an eye on you."

"What's started? And who is your boss?"

"I have no idea what's started. But I guard the entrance to the underworld. Who do you *think* my boss is?"

Yikes. Fire and brimstone and all that. "Well, can I go down there and talk to him?"

Connor looked at me like I'd been touched in the head. "No, you can't talk to him. Go home. I'll stop by when I get off shift."

I stood, brushing off my backside. "I'm not going home. Who do you think you are, ordering me around?"

He stood, too. And the poor, suffering man pinched the bridge of his nose, letting out a long breath. "Listen, I'm working right now. I don't have time to get into it. I said I'll be at your place when I get off shift."

"Okay. We're going to pretend for the time being that you're actually listening to me rather than blathering out your pie hole. But here we go. One: I don't want you coming over to my house. Two: I'm not going home because three: I'm following the leads from Jeffery's phone."

Even in the dark, I saw Connor narrowing his eyes on me. "Who's Jeffery?"

"My fiancé."

*That* got his attention. His back went rigid and he barked, "Your *what*?"

"My fiancé," I answered a bit more timidly. Now, I was hardly a timid person, but the force of his reaction took me aback.

And how I missed that somewhat indulgent look from just a few minutes ago when he narrowed his glisteningly angry eyes on me and if I looked hard enough, I saw plumes of superheated breath leave his nose and mouth in a highly aggressive manner. "From this point on, you no longer have a fiancé."

"Not that it's any of your business, but I haven't technically had a fiancé for two years. Not since he was murdered. Still, he *was* my fiancé, so that's how I address him when I talk about him."

The plumes of breath and angry eyes subsided as he glanced up at the sky.

"The universe hates me," he mumbled under his breath. "It's the only explanation."

Okay, well none of this made a lick of sense since the moment I stepped foot inside this miserable place. I needed answers. Tomorrow being Sunday meant I had the day off, but after that, my snooping would have to wait until next weekend. Some of us had to work and thus staying up late while digging into my dead fiancé's murder didn't help with the whole being a responsible adult thing. Given that, Connor, who did the universe really hate?

The door to the mausoleum creaked open further and I watched in awe as a black shadow ascended the stairs, cast against the red light. Probably the most beautiful man I'd seen in my life walked through the door.

"So this is her," the man said in a masculine yet melodic voice. Connor replied by jumping in front of me and growling, his back to my front.

"Come any closer and I'll end you." Connor sounded serious. "It won't last forever, but you'll be gone for a good long time… and it'll hurt."

"Down, boy," the beautiful man said and I snickered. Come on, I couldn't help it. A man after my own heart. Both Connor and the beautiful man shot me looks. Connor's was irritated, whereas the beautiful man's was amused. Then the latter cast his startlingly sky-blue eyes on me and he smiled. His bright-white teeth glinted off the moonlight. He flipped his wavy, blond bangs back. "I'm Luc," he said.

"Simone," I said back, ten kinds of breathy.

Connor growled at me this time.

"You're being rude," I admonished him.

He turned his whole body around in order to glare at me. "*I'm* being rude? You sound like you're seconds away from ripping your clothes off for the guy and you're doing it right in front of me. How would you *expect* me to react?"

"Stop," Luc ordered. "You know she can't help it. The ladies all love me. And you know even I can't go against the universe on this one."

"I'm standing right here. You'd think she could control it a little better," Connor replied. Then Luc did the best thing: He moved his eyes between himself and Connor, the look in them saying, "*Brother, please.*" As if the idea of anyone finding Connor more attractive than Luc was ridiculous. And sorry Connor, but Luc wasn't wrong. He had this… this… magnetism that pulled my gaze to him and wouldn't let go. Not that Connor was anything to sneeze at. The man was *foine* with a capital F, at least when he wasn't speaking. The whole *opening of his mouth and letting words out* thing diminished the aesthetic. Connor definitely had the dark, broody thing working in his favor, though.

"Okay, what is he talking about? And what does the universe have to do with anything?" I asked.

Rather than answer, Connor reached his massive man paw out to draw me in close to him. "Honey, go home. I said I'll be there when I get off work." Then, I kid you not, he bent in and *kissed me*. Like he kissed me, kissed me. With tongues and everything. I began to soften. As my heart rate sped up, I leaned into his body, wrapping my arms around his shoulders and neck, and I *kissed him back*. This was my first kiss since Jeffery and it felt good. No, it felt phenomenal. I opened my mouth wider for him, drinking in everything he had to offer until I came to my senses and kneed him in the boys.

He tore his mouth away and bent over, cupping his junk in one swift move. "What… was… that… for?" he sputtered out.

I felt bad because I probably went in a little harder than

necessary. And Luc, Luc stood off to the side laughing his fool head off.

"Go home before I kill you," Connor growled.

Yeah, that time I took his warning seriously.

# CHAPTER Four

Leaving Connor in pain last night didn't sit so well with me. I had a terrible time sleeping. Tossing and turning something fierce. I probably had bags the size of sleeping bags under my eyes. Still, I needed to apologize. He'd caught me off guard by kissing me, but that didn't give me the right to be violent, especially since I'd liked the kiss. It felt good. It felt right. Like of anybody in the world, somehow, I was supposed to be kissing Connor.

Once I got up, I made the bed then showered. For some reason, I decided to go with a pretty white sundress with bright-pink hibiscus flowers and vibrant, green leaves, which tied at the shoulders instead of relying on straps, and my cute wedge strappy sandals. I messy-braided my hair and applied light makeup. He might not be so mad at me if he saw that I made an effort before showing up to apologize. The last thing I did was clean out the litter box and leave my precious baby some food, *then* I headed to the secondhand shop to see if Connor was working. If he wasn't, I'd have to do some major groveling to get his address from whoever worked there today.

I happened to be a freaking fantastic baker, but as I'd gotten dressed before coming up with the idea to bring Connor a peace offering, I opted to stop at Egor's Bakery. That man had a way with baklava that was so good, it should have been illegal. Of course, I had no way of knowing if Connor actually liked baklava, but if he didn't before, he would once he tried Egor's. It was *that* good. And like always, I left with way more than any one person could eat in a week. The man certainly knew how to upsell.

The secondhand store looked closed. I pulled into the left-hand turn lane and turned into the parking lot. Then, slinging my purse around my shoulders, I picked up the pink box tied closed with red-and-white-striped twine, said a brief prayer that Connor would actually happen to be inside and that he wouldn't try to kill me, and pulled on the door handle. It opened.

Gorgeous Connor stood behind the register. His face heated when he looked up from his paperwork at the sound of the bell over the door jingling.

"Burning the candle at both ends?" I asked as my icebreaker.

The heat stayed in his eyes, though he sounded bored. "The other job, I *have* to do. This one, I *want* to do. It's my store."

"And a nice store it is. But if I might suggest some customer service training. You weren't very nice yesterday." Okay, I came here to say I'm sorry yet here I was insulting him again. Why did that happen whenever I was in his presence?

He let out a long, slow breath. "What are you doing here, Simone?"

I held up the pink box. "Peace offering?"

He *almost* cracked a smile. "You're unsure if it's a peace offering?"

"No. It is. I'm just unsure if you want it," I replied, still standing close to the door should I need a hasty escape.

"I want a lot of things." He looked at me pointedly and yeah, I felt that in my girly parts.

"Will you hurt me if I bring the box to you? It's *baklava*."

Connor sort of snicker-sneered. "I'm not the one with a lethal knee, now, am I?"

Okay. But what did he expect me to do? "You kissed me."

"Yeah," he answered. Just "yeah."

As I walked the box over to him, I asked, "What did you expect me to do?"

"Kiss me back. Exactly what you did—at first. That's how these things work."

These... *things*? What things?

Once I reached the counter, he pulled me around behind it with him, taking the box to set down next to the register. He lifted me up, setting my bottom on the edge of the counter, pushing my legs apart to step between them.

*Shit.* This close, he smelled really good. Like really, really good. This musky, manly scent that I wanted to bathe in. My heartbeat started racing again. Why did he affect me like this? My nostrils flared. My lips parted. I licked them, wanting nothing more than to have his mouth on me.

He placed his hand on my thigh, skin-to-skin contact, pushing my dress up as he leaned in. "You can't keep doing this to me," he whispered before pressing his lips to mine.

"*Connor*," I whispered back, but with the feel of him, of his mouth working its magic, I forgot what else I wanted to say.

He only stopped the lip-lock when the bell jingled again. We both turned to see a short woman in a T-shirt and jeans that had been cut off into long shorts that reached her knees. The outfit was a bit of a mess, but she paired it with gray converse so she had some cool in her. She snickered when she saw us, then she glanced away from us, walking over to a display in front. I took that as my cue to hop down from the counter and tried to escape. He held me prisoner with his light touch to my arm and his blazing stare.

"You going to let me into those panties of yours?" he asked, whispering into my ear before dragging his lips down to bite the lobe.

"Whoa! Slow your roll, there, Clifford." I softly slapped his nose. "Bad dog."

"Woman, seriously—enough with the dog jokes. I'm a hound. I told you that."

"Crying all the time," I muttered.

"*Simone.*"

"What? You haven't even asked me out on a date yet and think I'm just letting you into my panties."

Again, he sighed. Connor did that a lot around me. "Our kind doesn't date," he said.

"Maybe your kind doesn't, but my kind does."

"Sweetheart." He tugged on the bottom of my braid gently. "You *are* my kind."

"Uh… no, I'm not. Last I checked, I get a magic power-up on the full moon. I don't go all Scooby-Doo."

"No—that's not—" he started to answer until he noticed the woman walking up to the register with a bunch of baby clothes. She dropped them in a heap.

"I'll let you get back to it." Then, because it felt wrong not to, I bent in to peck his lips. "Seriously, try the baklava. Egor makes the best."

Connor shot me a confused sort of look. "Yeah," he said. "He does. Where are you going now?"

I thumbed through a box of old costume jewelry, picking up a brooch that caught my eye. A gem so dark red, it almost appeared black. A gold snake slithered around it. "This is beautiful," I said, holding it up to show him.

"Keep it. Now, where are you going?"

"I'm off to find Jeffery's killer," I answered offhandedly.

He roared, *"What?"* so loudly that when I spun around, I actually knocked the box I was looking in on the ground, spilling the contents all over the floor.

"For darkness's sake. You're a disaster area and you're not going after your ex's killer." He stormed from around the counter stomping over to where I'd bent down to pick up the things that spilled onto the floor.

"His name was Jeffery and *I am.*" I took out my anger on the poor tchotchkes, slamming them back into the box. What gave him the right to order me around? I was an independent woman. I was going to marry Jeffery. Someone took that future from us. I saw it as my duty to figure out why. My last gift to him and his family.

"Honey," the woman with the baby clothes said. "Your boyfriend is right. You shouldn't be going after a killer. That's dangerous."

Boyfriend? She thought Connor was my boyfriend?

Of course, she did. What else would she think when she walked in on us mid-lip lock? I snickered to myself thinking of my answer. *"No, ma'am, he's not my boyfriend. He kidnapped me yesterday and I made out with him before kneeing him in the boys and running away."*

What was more, why wasn't Connor correcting her?

"Connor, I have to. The family needs closure."

"Leave it to the police," he replied to me. "Let me ring you up," he said to her as he started scanning tags and placing the baby clothes into a plastic store bag. "That'll be ten dollars and eighty-two cents."

The woman fished in her purse and pulled out a wallet where she tapped her credit card against the card reader to complete the transaction. Connor handed her the bag.

"Have a great rest of your day," he said to her, then turned back to me expecting her to leave, as if waiting for me to argue. He acted like he'd known me forever and just knew that was how I'd react. That frustrated me to no end. Still, I decided not to give in to the aggression he so readily brought out in me, deciding to answer calmly rather than knee him in the boys for a second time in less than twenty-four hours.

"It's a cold case," I said tightly. "They've given up. And truthfully, I don't trust them. There's this detective who leaves a bad taste in my mouth."

"He shouldn't be leaving *any* taste in your mouth," Connor grumbled.

"Oh—would you stop? It's a saying. You're the only man I've kissed since Jeffery died two years ago."

He smiled then, looking incredibly cocky. "Don't do anything until I get off work."

I huffed. "Why?"

"Because I have a vested interest in you staying alive."

He gave way too many mixed signals for my sanity. First, he cut me down, and now he acted as if he actually liked me. What? And as for me? I actually liked that he seemed to like me now. I returned the sentiment, even though he drove me nuts most of the time we'd been in each other's company.

"What's going on here, Connor?"

"If you don't feel it, I'm not telling you."

"The truth is, I don't know what I'm feeling. Last night I felt —it's embarrassing the thought that went through my head. I won't bore you with the details. That's why I stopped you. I had to. But this morning, no magic—I… I still feel something. It's just not that clear."

Connor looked over to the woman, who still stood by the counter watching us intently. "Store's closed for lunch."

The woman startled, but she slung her bag over her shoulder and walked out. He walked from around the register to follow her, locking the door behind her. He stomped back over to me, bent down to grab hold of my hand, pulling me behind him through the rest of the store to a door at the back. Most of the back room consisted of a large receiving center, but off to the left, he dragged me toward a hallway.

One door on the left in the hall. Three on the right. He stopped us in front of the door on the left, opening it and dragging me through.

An apartment. He brought me to an apartment. "You live here?" I asked stupidly because clearly, he did.

"I own the building, so it made the most sense. Now, you're going to tell me about what you were feeling."

"Connor—*heel*," I ordered him. The smile he flashed me

turned positively wicked. The next thing I knew, he had me up over his shoulder marching us toward another location. We entered what turned out to be his bedroom, and then I went flying, landing on a huge bed. He followed me down—using his arms to brace himself, looming above me.

"Now… tell me what you were feeling."

"Connor," I protested. "You seriously don't want to hear that. No man wants to hear that from a woman he just met."

"Spill," he grumbled.

"Fine." I flitted my hands in the air to mimic my *"fine."* "Last night, as you were kissing me, it felt like we'd known each other forever. It felt like… like… This is humiliating."

He dropped his mouth to mine. The corded muscles rippled underneath the skin of his strong arms. "What did it feel like?" he growled low, like a sexy, sultry whisper.

Defeated, I gave in. "Like we were meant to be together."

"Finally," he said. "Was that so difficult?"

"Excruciating," I replied. "When our lips aren't attached, we're biting each other's heads off."

"You can put your mouth on my—"

"Okay, Rin-Tin-Tin, I get the idea."

"Rin-Tin-Tin? Really?"

"What?" I asked innocently. "Besides, that was yesterday. Today, with no magic—"

"You sure you don't have magic?"

"Nope. It leaves me once the moon wanes. It has to be full."

"Then what's that?" He pointed to the magic reaching out to him from my fingers—it wasn't as bright and strong as yesterday, but the fact that it even existed at all was huge.

"How is this happening?" I whispered.

"Because we're connected. I didn't know it was you—but I've been waiting for you." Oh, lordy, he had on his bedroom eyes. The nerves in my belly fluttered like I'd never been kissed before, let alone been intimate with a man.

Jeffery and I had an active sex life, and he hadn't been my

first. Yet it took everything in me to not giggle like a schoolgirl. I looked around frantically to avoid making eye contact with Connor. He was too much. Too intense. Took up too much of the air in the room.

"Simone," he growled my name—a good growl, the best growl. I ignored him. "Look at me," he demanded.

Strategically keeping my eyes averted, I shook my head.

"Look at me, Simone."

I shook my head again. That was when I noticed a picture of a pretty woman sitting on his bedside table. She had all the dark features of Connor but looked to be in her early twenties.

"Who's that?" I asked before thinking better of it. The mood in the room turned icy.

"My sister," he said. "That's Madigan."

"You're tense now. Did something happen to her?" The moment was ruined anyway. What could it hurt to find out more about him, about his life?

"She disappeared. Two years ago. She came to me one day, told me she'd stumbled on something huge."

"What was it?" I asked.

"Don't know. She didn't want to elaborate. She called me the next day. She was scared. Begged me to meet her. I told her not to move, that I'd be there as soon as possible. She was gone when I got to her location. I never saw her again."

I gasped.

He nodded once then pressed his forehead to mine. "Thing is, she's a hound just like me. Not much in the world scares us."

On its own accord, my hand moved up his body, gliding over his silken skin in order to rest two fingers on his face below his eye. With my thumb, I gently stroked his afternoon stubble.

Connor closed his eyes, breathing in a sharp breath through his nose, sinking into my touch.

"She was petrified," he whispered after a few long seconds.

"Have you been searching for her?"

He shook his head *yes*.

"I'll help you find her."

That got his attention. His whole body stiffened above me. His nostrils flared. His eyes stared down at me, angry and intense. "No," he bit out.

Confused, I waited for him to continue. If you gave people enough silence, they felt compelled to fill it.

Predictably, he filled it.

"Did you not hear me? My sister went missing. Think I'm risking you? Your life is tied to mine. For whatever reason, the universe wants us to be together."

For whatever reason?

How romantic.

I shut down, turning my head away to not have to look at him. "Get off me," I said.

"What?"

"I said, *get off me.*" I pushed at him, my hand making contact with his rock-hard chest. It lit me up on the inside, exactly what I didn't want to happen.

Why would the universe want us together? We didn't even like each other. I mean, I was starting to like him, but then he had to go and open his mouth. If the universe wanted us together, they should've made him mute. Mute would've worked. Or maybe made him a French speaker. I didn't understand French. Therefore, he'd have been able to say all the rude things in the world and I'd never have known.

Thoughts shifted behind his eyes. The frustration. He looked about a second and a half away from throttling me or kissing me.

Neither worked for me.

With his lack of concentration, I managed to roll out from under him.

"What are you doing?" he barked.

"None of your concern." I ran my fingers through my hair, just knowing that I needed to fix my braid, and I straightened my dress. "You probably need to get back to the shop," I said, and then I ran, heading through the store and out to my jeep.

Okay, so it wasn't my proudest moment, and yes, I'd made a fool of myself, but honestly, something inside me withered, turning brown and ugly when he'd said "for whatever reason."

He didn't actually like me. He was simply drawn to me by some stupid cosmic misunderstanding. Once I reached my driveway, I hit the garage door opener and then proceeded to drive into my clean garage. I shut off the engine while the door closed.

I loved my little abode, decorated in midcentury modern. All blond woods, and instead of the traditional pink, I, of course, used lilac and the traditional teal from the time period, along with chrome accents. It made me happy. But it also felt lonely. It didn't used to feel lonely, but Jeffery used to come around all the time. Now, as I glanced around the empty space, I thought that maybe I needed to get another pet. One that liked my attention. Possibly a dog—no. *Not* a dog. A gerbil? Fish?

Something. My one requirement was that it actually had to like me. My precious kitty took care of me, but he kept himself aloof most of the time. What I craved was unconditional affection without having to bother with people, as it was clear the universe had cursed me when it came to interpersonal relationships with humans or human/death-hound hybrids, as it were.

I walked to the bathroom to fix my braid and then it hit me. I had to ask Jeffery's mom again if she knew of any enemies Jeffrey might have had. Maybe now with the shock having worn off, she could think of someone that escaped her memory before. He never talked to me about work. He'd always said I was his safe space, where he didn't have to think about all the crap in the world. So, could he have told his parents about someone that he chose not to tell me about? Had she ever heard of Beetle?

She answered on the second ring. "Simone," she started. "Is everything okay?"

"No, actually. It's not."

"Is there something I can do?"

My opening. "Yes," I said. "Here's the thing. I picked up the box of personal effects like you asked and I plugged his phone in to charge, connecting it to my Wi-Fi."

Even her breathing sounded sad. I shook it off. That was exactly why I needed her to answer my questions.

"The last several calls were from a person named Beetle. Did he ever mention a Beetle?"

"No," she said quickly. "Never."

"Did the police ever ask you about a person named Beetle?"

"No. We never got any kind of updates from Detectives Morgan or Shift, you know that." —*Uh, no I sure as hell didn't*— "They said they couldn't find any leads. What kind of name is Beetle, anyway?"

Detective Shift. I never met a Detective Shift. Suddenly a horrible thought hit. The detective. The one who gave off all those bad vibes. What was his name? And here, I didn't think the situation could get any worse. Jeffery had been killed. But somehow it kept spiraling down, down, down.

I sighed. "I don't know. That's what I'm trying to find out. What about B. el-Zebu?"

"No."

"Janet, please. I need you to think. Did he have any enemies?"

"Everyone loved him. If Jeffery had enemies, they certainly weren't known to me."

"Right." I sighed a second time because it was that or cry. "Thanks for your time."

Before I got the chance to disconnect, she called, "Simone?"

"Yeah?"

"Please don't do something stupid like call that number."

Call the number? Why hadn't I thought of that? I stayed silent until she whispered, "Be careful," before hanging up because we both knew in that moment, I was about to do something stupid.

I typed the number for Beetle from Jeffrey's phone into mine. My magic twitched beneath my skin, exactly as it would have if we were close to the full moon.

How? It never happened before, not in the twelve and a half years that my magic had been manifesting. It should've gone back to zero. A reset. At this point in the lunar month, the magic hibernated.

A deep voice answered. "I've been waiting for you to call."

"This isn't Jeffery," I said.

"I know," he replied, causing me to suck in a sharp breath. "You want to meet."

"Yes," I whispered.

"Meet me at Monnie's in fifteen minutes. It's a pool hall off of Porter Street."

I ask you, what other choice did I have? "Okay. I'll be there."

He only gave me fifteen minutes, but my outfit didn't feel safe enough for a pool hall. Too easy access to my girly parts. Quickly, I slid on a pair of jeans and pulled on a white T-shirt. A man's shirt. Haines. V-neck. I'd always found them comfortable and made of a lighter-weight cotton, which helped keep me cooler in the summer. Then, I tied on my Converse.

I could run, jump, lunge, or any necessary movements to help me get away should the need arise. After shoving Jeffery's phone in one pocket and mine in the other, I grabbed my purse and keys and took off for Monnie's.

Finding Monnie's Pool Hall on my map app, I backed out of my driveway and drove like my life depended on it. I actually arrived only a minute late. *Go me!* Though it would've been preferable to have someone at my back, seeing as I'd never want to pull any of my friends in on this mess, I went in alone.

A dark air surrounded Monnie's. It felt thick, tense. Goosebumps prickled my skin. It gave me the heebie-jeebies. When I walked inside the smoky, dimly lit place, heads turned to take me in. The way the room was situated, the bar sat to the front and right. To the left and back, there were several pool tables. The rubber on the soles of my Converse stuck to the wood flooring covered in years' worth of old, dried alcohol and—*crap,* I hoped it was only alcohol. A green hue covered my skin from the trapezoid-shaped green-glass light fixtures hanging from the ceiling.

Oh, and I knew *immediately* when I locked eyes with Beetle. A large man. Swarthy with a thick scar that cut across his cheek from his nose to his ear. His eyes looked at me with curiosity and disgust, black like Connor's, but dead. So *not* like Connor's.

He looked like a beetle.

Before I lost my nerve, I walked across the bar to stand in front of the man himself.

*Show no fear.*

"Something to drink?" he asked me. Voice even gruffer than over the phone.

"I'll get it." I didn't trust this guy as far as I could throw him and I knew from the size of him that I couldn't even pick him up. I didn't need him slipping something into my drink.

I ordered a cola because impairment of any kind equaled death or defilement.

"Do you play?" Beetle asked, gesturing to an empty pool table.

"I do."

I'd learned to play when I was a young teen. Jeffery and I actually met in a bar. He saw me playing with a couple of girlfriends and walked up to call next game. We were together from that day on.

I found the cue stick I wanted and chalked up.

"You first," he said.

I bent over the table, aimed at the cue ball for the break, drew back my stick, and made my shot. The satisfying crack of the ball always made me smile as the triangle of balls spread out, hitting and bouncing off the sides of the green-felt covered table, sinking the seven ball. Solids. In pool, I had game. In interrogation, no game. Being completely out of my league and accepting it, I decided the best course of action was to simply go for it and ask. I mean, he'd been *expecting* my call. What did I have to lose?

"What business did you have with Jeffery?"

"Oh, Simone..." He tut-tutted me, shaking his head. "Are you sure you want to go down this road?"

Okay. Score one for Beetle. I took my next shot, sinking both the five and the one balls.

He raised his eyebrow in my direction. Clearly, he'd figured revealing he knew my name would mess me up.

I'd bite. "How do you know my name?"

"I make it a habit to know everyone close to the people who work for me. How do you think I got him to work for me in the first place?"

"Fair enough." My ball narrowly missed the corner pocket. "Your shot."

Beetle nodded, surveying the table. He lined up his shot, drawing his stick back, but before he took his turn, he said, "Tell you what, I miss this shot, I let you walk away scot-free. Neither me nor any of my people will bother you again. I make it, you belong to me."

I laughed, managing to make it sound incredulous rather than the freaked out that I was. "You're not the Devil. This ain't Georgia and unlike Johnny, I'm not willing to make a deal," I answered, referencing The Charlie Daniels Band's biggest hit, "The Devil Went Down to Georgia."

"Sweet, innocent Simone…" He paused for what appeared to be dramatic effect. "You have no idea who I am." Yep. Dramatic effect worked perfectly. Anyone who said that didn't ooze threatening would've been lying.

"Where is she?" someone barked loudly in a voice that sounded remarkably like Connor's.

I whipped my head up to look at Beetle, who glared at the door, and I turned my head in the same direction, locking eyes with the man himself. Then, twisting back to say something, I didn't know what, to the man I suspected was responsible for Jeffery's death, I found him gone. *Poof!*

"What do you think you're doing here?" Connor yelled my way, so I had to presume he was yelling at me.

The room went quiet.

His eyes raged with molten heat as he stomped over to me, then, wrapping his hand around my upper arm, he started pulling me, dragging me when I stumbled over my feet, out of the bar.

"Stop," I demanded.

Connor didn't stop.

"Stop!" I yelled louder, wrenching my arm out of his hold.

Rather than argue with me any further, he flipped me over his shoulder again, storming out to my jeep. I pounded on his back.

"Put me down," I demanded.

But the jerk didn't put me down, he fished my keys from my pocket, bleeping the lock then dropped me into the passenger seat. He rounded the hood to climb into the driver's seat, started the engine, then sped out from the parking lot.

"What in the hell do you think you're doing?" I railed against his caveman-like treatment of me and the situation and whatever else I could rail against at the moment. Oh how I wanted to hurt him.

"Have to work tonight," he grumbled. "But I had to come after you…"

"Whoa," I said. "I never asked you to come after me."

"Yeah, I know you didn't, which is why you snuck off without telling me where you were going." He was yelling by the end of his tirade.

"Calm down, Cujo."

"Cujo? *Cujo?* You haven't *seen* my level of crazy yet."

I rubbed out the knot of tension at the base of my neck between my shoulder blades. "Take me home."

"Right. So you can do something else ridiculously stupid again?"

"It wasn't stupid. I needed to meet with him to see what he knows about Jeffery's death." Hearing Jeffery's name seemed to set him off. What? Like it or not I was going to marry the man and he died because I needed ice cream. I *owed* Jeffery this. He lost his life essentially because of me. I wouldn't ever forgive myself for that. But note to self: With the way Connor gripped my steering wheel hard enough that I was pretty sure he could rip it right off the mount, never bring up Jeffery without a leash and muzzle handy.

"Jeffery's dead," he barked, like I wasn't totally aware of that by now. "He's dead and you're alive—at least for now. Those guys are bad news and you just waltzed your fine ass in there like other people don't have a stake in whether or not you survive."

He thought my ass was fine? That made me feel good—*wait, no. Focus, Simone.*

"What are you talking about?" I asked.

"You would've never married Jeffery."

"What? Why would you say that?"

"Because you weren't supposed to be with him. You're supposed to be with me."

"*Connor.*" I sucked in a deep, lengthy breath, then let it out gently, gradually, trying to calm the vibe inside the vehicle. "We didn't know each other then. And you don't even like me."

He slowly turned his head to glare at me, almost like he was possessed—yeah, like one of those possessed ventriloquist dummies—and I would have sworn on a stack of tarot cards, I lost my breath completely.

Connor drove us to his store, continuing around the back, where he pulled into a spot and cut the engine, then predictably, a little bit roughly, and totally aggrievedly, dragged me inside. "There's food in the fridge. You know where the bedroom is. Watch TV or whatever."

"Where are you going?"

"Work. At the cemetery."

"Then why am I here?"

"Because I need to know you aren't going to do anything else stupid when I'm not around to bail you out."

I had the overwhelming urge to punch him right in his handsome face. "I had it under control. You didn't need to show up."

Connor rolled his eyes.

"I'll just leave as soon as you do," I threatened.

"If you think you've got it in you."

"I don't need my car. I can call an Uber."

"You could. But you couldn't get outside to catch it."

Excuse me? "What do you mean?"

He threw his hand out. "Try it."

Challenge accepted. I walked confidently over to the door, twisted the knob, and pulled. Nothing happened. I twisted the deadbolt to make sure it was unlocked and tried again.

And nothing. Again.

"What did you do to the door?" I demanded to know.

He shrugged. "Wards."

Oh, I narrowed my eyes on him, all right. "*Wards*? What in all of Hades is a ward?"

"Depending on what you need it for, they either keep supers in or out of a place. These wards keep *you* in."

"But not you?"

"Not me."

"Where did you get wards that keep me in but not you?"

"My boss, Luc. We're tight. He felt bad for me and wanted to make sure I wasn't late, seeing as I can't exactly call in sick."

"You don't get personal leave days?" I asked, affronted for him until I remembered to be upset with him, then I started to pace. I didn't like being trapped. As an adult with all my capacities intact, I couldn't figure out how I'd ended up in this mess. "Why in the world do you even care what happens to me? I still don't get it."

"Because you're mine," he roared so loudly that I actually took a step back, hitting the door from the back of my head to my bottom, and I blanched.

"What do you mean, I'm yours? We kissed a couple of times, so what?"

"Are you being serious right now?"

"Yes," I snapped back.

He pressed his palms to his eyes then dragged his hands up to rake through his thick, messy hair. "Simone, you said it yourself. It felt like we were meant to be together."

"I was just… *turned on,*" I admitted. He couldn't really believe that he and I were… well—that was just ridiculous!

"No. You were just admitting the truth. You felt it because it's true."

"There's no such thing as fate."

I swore the guy looked to heaven for help. "You have so much to learn. Unlike humans, most supers have an '*other half.*' A life mate they're meant to be with."

"And you think that's me?"

"Unfortunately."

"Well, don't let me cramp your style."

"Simone—you aren't getting it. We've met. Connected. There's no going back. I couldn't go out with someone else if I wanted to." He gestured to me. "And from the death glare you're shooting me, you can't stand the idea of that, either."

I lifted my hands up to my face, feeling the scowl I thought I'd been hiding so well.

"Yeah," he said, stepping close to me, reaching his hand out to snag my T-shirt to tug me against him.

"That means you're staying here. I'm going to work. Then we'll figure out what to do about you now being on a bunch of bad guys' radar when I get home."

"How do you know I'm on any bad guy radar?"

"Because you're hot and you were playing pool in Monnie's. No good guys hang out there."

I geared up to argue my point again, I really did, but he bent in to press his lips to mine. I hated that it felt good. I didn't want it to feel that good.

Connor drove me insane.

He didn't even like me. The more I thought about that, the angrier I got. The angrier I got, the more frantic the kisses became. I pressed harder. My hands roamed. And unfortunately, I moaned into his mouth.

"No," the infuriating man grumbled, tearing his mouth from mine, pushing himself back from me.

We were both breathing heavily. *Sexy times could be had at any moment* level of heavy.

"I don't have time," he said, staring at me through eyes declaring they were ready to devour me. "I need to get to work."

Without so much as a goodbye, he walked out the same door I couldn't pull open, slamming it behind him. Great. Just freaking great. I found myself trapped in someone else's home with no way to get out. And as far as I knew, I was stuck for the entire night.

Why did my parents have to die before having a chance to explain about my magic and supers, for that matter? I hated not knowing. One thing was certain: Connor might have locked me up in here, but he clearly forgot about Jeffery's phone.

My life's ambition was never to be Nancy Drew, but a man dying took precedence over any other life choices. Especially when that man meant something to me. When I turned on the phone this time, an image appeared in my mind. It took me so off guard that I dropped the phone onto the rug. The image of a woman with long, dark hair, dark eyes and mediterranean skin filled my inner vision. She opened her mouth and I'd swear in a court of law that I heard her say, *"Simone."*

My legs buckled underneath me, sending me down to the carpet along with the phone while I tried to slow my racing heartbeat. What in all magic was going on here? I'd never had a vision before. *Never.* I had taser fingers once a month. The month should've reset. Not fair for the universe to change things up on me now. We had a system. I (mostly) held back from touching people one day a month then went on with my life all the other days. But visions?

*Visions?*

A person really needed to be mentally prepared to deal with this revelation and clearly, I was *not*.

Since Connor really happened to be the only one who knew about the mess my life had become, I wanted—like, *really* wanted—to talk to him. The problem being, he'd neglected to leave his number and he never told me his last name for me to look it up. Even if I tried google searching every Connor with a phone in the Tri-County area, I'd be here till next Thursday making phone calls.

I walked to the kitchen, rummaging through cabinets. This was a coffee moment. Coffee: the delicious elixir to ease the cruelty of life. Where did he keep the stuff? I needed it *stat*. He had a refrigerator filled with fresh fruit and vegetables. In his pantry: oatmeal? Protein shakes? What exactly did he expect me to eat? Where were the snack cakes or processed food? I thought Connor might've been trying to torture me. How about bread? Or mayo? Some cheese and olive loaf... Was that too much to ask for?

Heathen—the man was a complete heathen.

Now I wanted to eat more than ever because he didn't have any real good food. I paced the floor of the kitchen like a caged animal, getting more and more irritated. Too restrictive. I needed more room to roam. I needed freedom. I needed—

Finally, I found myself in front of the door again, more frustrated than I'd been in forever and I screamed out that frustration, kicking at the door. I grabbed the handle again, jiggling it, and screamed once more, "Open already!"

Then the craziest thing happened. It popped open. He supposedly had wards keeping me locked inside like a freaking prisoner. I tried the door. It'd refused to open for me. I was far from crazy. It would *not* open. Now, just like that, it opened?

Whoa. I walked outside into the fresh, clean air. It felt like I'd been locked up for fifteen years. Okay, *maybe* I exaggerated a bit. Still, it felt good to be out. My beautiful jeep sat parked where he'd left it, but my hopes for escape were dashed when I realized that he never gave me back my keys.

"Universe," I said to the sky, "How do you expect me to drive without my keys?" Again, with the angry reflex actions, I threw my hand out, bringing it down on the hood, yelling at my jeep. "Why can't you just start?" I cried out, only to have the engine turn over.

It did.

At first, I thought I might be cracking up. To test it, I climbed inside, then pressed the brake to shift into drive. I expected it to stall when I pressed the brake, like when I pressed the brake on my old car after engaging the remote start, but I'd forgotten to put the key in the ignition. It didn't stall. Good jeep. Another hurtle down. So I drove.

To Raven.

To Connor.

He'd be pissed to see me, of course. But what could I do? This was huge. Huger than huge.

When I parked in front of the cemetery, I sighed, relieved that the jeep never stalled on my way. "Thanks for getting me here safe," I said to my car. "You can shut off now." The magic twitched under my skin in more than just my hands and the jeep shut off. "Wait here," I told the car like an idiot.

The padlock unhooked before I reached it tonight. The path lit up for me, even though I remembered the way. The burning footprints led me back to the mausoleum, where the darkness seemed both darker and not nearly as dark simultaneously.

Once I reached the wrought-iron fence, I told the air, "Don't let him know I'm here just yet." Nothing happened when I reached the door except that the footprints disappeared and —*poof!* The door popped open. I waited, set off to the side of the mausoleum in the darkness, for Connor to come charging at me. The only light in the cemetery came from the stars and a slightly less-full moon. I gave it a few minutes to make sure he wasn't going to get the jump on me. When the coast seemed clear, I entered the stairwell, glowing red, with no shadows this time. It actually felt like I'd been invited inside. It would've been rude not to go. I *wasn't* rude—I mean, unless I landed in the unfortunate circumstance of dealing with Connor. At least when he talked.

If we were really meant to be together, the universe messed up. I did a quick check to make sure I was alone and then slipped down the stone staircase. The red light shone up from the bottom of the ancient building. The wall had metal plates with images of demons and other magical creatures all along the spiraling stones.

It looked like I'd walked into a real-life version of Dante's *Inferno* meets *The Goblin Market*. And it was warm, but not overly hot. Considering the red light, I figured it would be boiling. My feet should have made noise against the stone steps, but every step remained silent. And I finally saw where the red light came from: a wall of fire. As soon as I reached the bottom, I became surrounded by those walls of fire on three sides.

The space opened up wide—no place to hide. I watched silently while scantily-clad women hung all over each other and the men in the room. It appeared I'd entered a waiting room. There was a hallway off the waiting room where the bottom half of the walls were made of fire, but the tops had windows showing the inside of offices, where people milled about working. I thought I might've stumbled into a supernatural office building.

And no one noticed me. No one. I moved through the waiting room to the hallway, completely carefree. This was amazing. The door at the very end of the hall opened and I stopped short—sucking in a sharp breath because Connor emerged from the office with Luc's hand pressed in a friendly manner to his back. They were both laughing. Connor laughing was a thing of beauty.

Luc suddenly looked over to where I stood and we locked eyes—or I thought we locked eyes until he twisted his head left and right like he was looking for something, but he didn't call me out. He leaned in to say something to Connor, who stuck his nose up and sniffed the air.

I mean, come on, it wasn't my fault. He stuck his nose in the air and sniffed like a bloodhound. How could I not laugh? But I kept it down to a low snicker. Well, I kept it to a low snicker until he picked up the trail heading straight for me. He stopped abruptly only inches from my face, reaching his hand out too. I managed to dodge it, stepping to the side.

"It's not possible," he grumbled to Luc, who followed him.

"You sure it's her?"

Connor directed a *"Please"* glare at the man.

"Right." Luc laughed. "I'm not sure if you're the luckiest or unluckiest SOB in the world."

"Pity me," Connor said.

Luc folded his arms over his rather large chest. "She's hot. How bad can it be?"

"Yeah, she's gorgeous," he said and I stood a little taller. "But then she speaks," he finished and I deflated, accidentally letting out a small *harrumph* of annoyance.

Both men whipped their heads in my direction. Connor looked to the ceiling for apparent deliverance. "Please tell me *no*," he said to no one. Then when I thought he was going to grab for me, he fooled me by stepping on my foot. We all watched his boot hover above the ground. Or well, that was what it had to look like to them. I saw my shoe trapped under his massive boot. Connor had seriously large feet, although completely proportional to his size. I should've kept vigilant. But his foot was trapping my foot... and then, out of nowhere, he grabbed my arms.

"Show yourself," he barked.

"Didn't you use the wards?" Luc asked.

"Of course I did. She couldn't get the door open."

As there was nowhere for me to run, I whispered, "Let them see me now." But then because I was me, I tacked on, "But give it some flair." And just like that, I shimmered into view. Yes, a full-on shimmer. It was so cool if I did say so myself. Every eye landed on me. Not just Connor's. Not just Luc's. There were unloquacious gasps and shouts of, "What the—"

A couple of the men gave long, slow whistles. I stood straighter and smiled in the direction of the whistlers.

"Do that again, and I'll rip your throat out, Egyn," Connor threatened.

There were snickers from the others before Luc asked bizarrely, "How'd you do it?" At first, I thought he was asking Connor how he did it, as in *put up with me,* and I waited for Connor to give a snarky answer. Then I realized he'd actually been talking to me.

I shrugged. "Don't know."

"I gave him witch wards," Luc said.

"I'm not a witch," I replied.

"Clearly," he chuckled.

"This isn't funny," Connor bit out.

"Oh, no—it is," Luc answered. "But I also gave him demon wards, too."

"You thought I was a demon?" I asked, aghast.

"Truthfully, I don't know what you are. It's been ambiguous from the first time Connor here"—Luc patted Connor on the back—"got a good look at you."

"Leave it to the universe to stick me with an unrecognizable thing," Connor said.

Thing? *Thing?*

Instead of screeching in his ear and kneeing him in the gonads, I turned to Luc. "Is there a vet nearby? I want to get him debarked."

Connor, predictably, growled at me, baring his teeth.

"Oh, no!" I gasped. "Old Yeller's got the hydrophoby."

Luc threw his head back, laughing. It was a sexy, melodic laugh. I liked it. I bet it got him a *lot* of booty. "If you don't want her," he said to my other half and I was wholly unsure if Connor would agree that Luc should have taken me, or if Luc was taking his life in his hands.

Connor spun, stepping in front of me just like last night. "Back off," he said, and then he turned back to me, "What are you doing here?"

Hmm... I supposed Luc *was* taking his life in his hands after all. I really couldn't call it.

"I needed to talk to you, but I don't have your number."

"Connor." Luc admonished the man-dog that I was becoming very fond of. "You didn't give your woman your phone number?"

It was Connor's turn to shrug. "I forgot."

"You're a terrible boyfriend," he said.

"Don't I know it," I replied.

Luc turned that killer smile on me again. Then my *boyfriend* sighed, shifting to reach up to cup my cheeks. He looked deeply into my eyes. And oh, lordy... I could get used to that look. This Connor. "What do you need?" he asked.

"I got a vision."

"A vision?" Apparently, he didn't expect those words to come out of my mouth. What? He expected me to say I was lonely or something? His brows drew together in confusion, though. That was fun. "Of what?" he asked.

"A woman. I've never seen her before but she knew my name. It weirded me out—like really weirded me out, and for some reason you were the first person I thought to talk to about this. Now that I hear myself say it out loud, it sounds incredibly stupid."

"Simone, of course you wanted to talk with me. Mated remember? So what happened next?"

"Well, I said I needed to tell you—I kicked the door and it opened, then my jeep started without keys. And when I got here, I casually said I didn't want you to see me, and you didn't. The door to the mausoleum opened and here I am."

"I take it these aren't normal occurrences for you?" Luc asked, leaning in close to our little huddle.

"Nope." I shook my head. "Not at all."

"If we can narrow down your origins, then we can figure out what you are. We figure that out, we can figure out why this is happening."

"You don't think it's—" Connor pointed up.

Luc shook his head.

"No. I still play cards once a week with Mike. When he starts winning, he gets chatty. So whenever I need a heads-up on what they're doing, I let him start winning."

"What is he talking about?" I asked.

"I'll fill you in when we get home."

"Why are these powers coming now?"

"I wish I knew," Connor said. He rested his forehead against mine. The magic twitched under my skin. When he kissed me, it felt like we lit up the whole room. "Maybe it has to do with whatever you are. Like Luc said."

"Does magic usually change?"

"I've never heard of it doing so. Powers develop, get stronger. But what I know about it, you get your powers at puberty. That's when I started shifting."

"But my taser didn't work on you." I tried it out yesterday when he kidnapped me. The first time.

"Maybe because I'm your mate," Connor said. "Try it on Luc."

"*Hey,*" Luc argued. "I thought we were friends."

"We are, but Simone needs to see if she's still got it. And you know, she's my mate. I have to side with her."

"You just want to touch her fun bags," Luc said.

"I mean, you're not wrong," Connor answered. "But it's more than that. Hos before bros. Sorry, dude."

Luc huffed. "Fine. But you owe me."

I stepped around Connor, my belly all aflutter. I wanted it to work, but at the same time, I liked Luc. "Okay," I told the man.

"I'll go easy on you."

"I'd appreciate it."

Sucking in a breath, I called up my taser fingers, pressing them to Luc's shoulder. He screamed, dropping to his knees and breaking contact. He rubbed at his arm. "I thought you said you'd go easy." Was it bad that I kind of felt powerful knowing my taser fingers brought Lucifer himself—the morning star— down to his knees? *Yes, bad Simone. You like Luc.*

"I *did*."

"I don't want to consider what full force might feel like." The fine man continued rubbing at his arm. Watching him, those feelings of power fled leaving me simply feeling bad, well, until he spoke again. "But warning, Simone," he said in a tone that had gone a little hard. "I don't care that you're our boy Connor's mate. Try that again, I won't be responsible for what I do."

"That sounds ominous," I said, swallowing hard, at the same time Connor barked, "*Luc*."

"What?" Luc asked innocently. "I was kidding..." And now my fingers itched to show him full force. "Simone, help me out here. Try it on Connor."

If one thing could help me forget about zapping Luc, it was the idea of zapping Connor. "My pleasure."

"Seriously?" Connor asked with a tone dripping incredulity. It really *was* the little things that brought the most happiness.

Cracking my knuckles, I called up the power again. Still not snapping as much as on the full moon, it fizzed and popped from my fingertips more than when I touched Luc. A big smile spread across my face. "Ready?" I whispered.

"You don't have to look so excited."

"It's like *Christmas*," I gushed.

He laughed, shaking his head like he couldn't believe that I'd just said that and I struck, pressing my whole hand to his shoulder in a sneak attack.

Nothing.

"Wait—let me try again," I pleaded as I moved my fingers to his neck.

Nothing.

My face dropped. Excitement gone.

"Aw, Simone—you look like someone kicked your puppy," he said, obviously getting enjoyment from this.

"Not yet," I answered, then I surprised him by kicking his shin. Not enough to hurt, of course. I wasn't sadistic. I mean, the man was still my mate. "There. Now I do."

"Woman," he sighed, pulling me in for a hug. "What am I going to do with you?"

"I've got some ideas," Luc cut in.

Connor growled, pressing his fingers to his eyes, trying to rein in his temper. So, what did I do? Why, teased him, of course. "Luc *is* pretty hot. I think I might want to hear his ideas."

"*Simone*," Connor snapped. "Luc, I warned you."

I rolled my eyes at the man. "Settle down, hothead. You know I only have eyes for you," I said then once he had himself under control, I pinched his cheek, speaking to him indulgently. "Now, be a good puppy and give mama some sugar."

Connor would either end up loving me or killing me. The jury was still out in my opinion, but I'd certainly have my fun along the way.

He looked to Luc. "When does this shift end?"

"Not for several more hours."

Okay, wait… when did Connor get to sleep? He went from guard duty to the store. That really didn't sit right with me. "When do you sleep?" I asked softly so he knew I wasn't kidding.

He tilted his head to look at me, and when he did, I mean, he *looked* at me. He saw through all the bullshit and he brought his finger up, swiping it under my eye. "I don't sleep much."

"*Connor*," I said, feeling that word to my core.

He cleared his throat then whipped his head in Luc's direction. "Can I clock out early?" Connor's sweet turned to heat behind his every word. Sexy heat. Dripping with it.

"Sorry, man. I'm all for young love, but I can't bend the rules," Luc answered.

"Why not?" I asked.

"You know how it goes… if I do it for one, then I've got all my employees whining to go home early. Things would never get done. It'd be a mess."

Something about his answer didn't quite fit. I knew he wasn't telling me the truth… or the *whole* truth. I hated not knowing things.

"Do you want me to go home?" I asked both the men, really. I mean, I didn't actually want to because—though I'd never tell them this—I enjoyed our banter. I'd never had this even with Jeffery. We were always that gaggy-sweet couple. The type people made fun of behind their backs.

This somehow felt more… *me*.

"No," Connor said, giving me another nugget of sweetness from him. He held me from behind, nuzzling my neck with his nose. "Something's happening with your magic. We need to figure out what or more to the point, why."

"You can't talk to me in that voice and expect me not to, like, strip myself naked and tackle you right here."

"*Keep up the voice, mate*," one of the other men in the room shouted.

"Better join me in my office." Luc placed his hand on my shoulder. "We can try our hand at research because as much as I'd like to see you strip naked and mount my boy here, I don't want him ripping out the throat of anyone who might get a look at you, including mine."

Connor's arms squeezed harder around me as he pulled me in tighter against his body. His very strong, solid… *whoa!* "You really need to let me go," I whispered to him. "I'm so turned on with you this close that I could probably orgasm without you doing much more than this."

"Simone," he whispered, pressing another kiss to the skin right below my ear.

"What? I haven't had sex in two years and you're hot. You smell so good, it's making me light-headed." I closed my eyes, pressing my butt against his groin, and I maybe sort of began to grind against him. I couldn't help it. Like it was literally beyond my control.

He growled in my ear. "Simone, baby, you've got to stop that."

"Not gonna lie, Con," Luc said, cutting in. "This is really hot."

"That's it," Connor returned. "She's staying with me." No matter how forcefully he wanted me to stop, he refused to let me go, keeping my body exactly where I was, pressed against him.

"Obviously she can't," said Luc. "She's coming with me into my office."

"I'm really not comfortable with that," Connor snapped.

Luc turned his impatient eyes to me. "Will you put us all out of our misery and bed him already? This overly protective bit won't end until you play a couple rounds of slap and tickle."

"Are you trying to pimp me out, Luc?"

"It's not me. The universe pimped you before you were even born."

"Would you two stop talking about pimping my mate?" Connor got that sexy, low growl to his voice and I officially hated the universe. Who did the universe think it was, giving me a mate with a low, sexy growl and a job he couldn't leave for several more hours?

I snickered as a deliciously wicked thought popped in my head. "Is there a coat closet around?"

"Say, that's not a bad idea," Luc agreed.

"The first time I sleep with my mate is *not* going to be in a coat closet at work."

"Connor, Connor, Connor, no one said anything about sleep..." I said. "Then I'm sure Luc will let us use his office."

"Only if I can watch," Luc countered.

"No—you *will not* watch," Connor yelled.

Too easy. Way too easy.

"Listen." I twisted in his arms to put my hand on Connor's chest. "I promise to pick a fight with you when you get off shift so we can have incredibly hot make-up sex in a bed. Deal?"

He smirked, and wow—that shot him up from ridiculously attractive to *phenomenally* attractive. "Why do I get the feeling any sex with you will blow both our minds?"

"Have you seen me?" I teased. "The universe must really love you, seriously. As hot as I am, I'm a hundred times that as a lover."

But instead of giving in to my compromise, Connor flipped me the rest of the way to face him, still keeping his arms tight around me, my body pressed to his. His mouth descended, pressing against mine, covering it, and I lost myself. He filled me with his warmth soul deep. My heart rate sped up, my breathing intensified, and I *moaned*. Like that deep, guttural, *well on my way to the big O* kind of moan. I had to give the man credit. He could kiss. Next-level lip-locking technique.

"Connor," I whispered against his lips. He sifted his fingers through my hair. Keeping his eyes closed, he pressed his forehead to mine, breathing heavily himself.

"I can't take this anymore. Simone, you're in my bed tonight."

"No," I replied, too caught up in all that was Connor to register his reaction.

"Why?"

Why? Too easy. "You have no food at your place."

"My fridge and pantry are full, baby." He snickered.

"With oatmeal and protein bars. I didn't see one bag of potato chips." I pushed up to kiss him again. "Or one pint of ice cream. I need sustenance, Connor. Feed me and I will rock your world."

"We're stopping at the store." Then he set me back from him. "But not until I'm off the clock." He sighed, gritting his teeth, and we both dipped our heads to take in the tent he sported in his jeans.

"Sure you don't want a closet?" I asked.

"Fuck it—I want the closet," he said and he started for Luc's office, grabbing my hand, dragging me along with him. "You're not watching," he warned Luc. "I *will* rip your throat out."

And I realized just how real things had gotten once we were in Luc's office and Connor had locked the door. He pushed me up against it, taking my lips in a hard, punishing kiss. It lit me up inside and I returned it just as hard, just as punishing, letting my hands roam.

He growled.

# CHAPTER
## *Seven*

Connor dropped his hands from my back to grab a hold of my butt, hefting me up until I was able to wrap my legs around his waist, locking my ankles to keep myself from slipping—not that the man would've let me. Hard to ravage my lips without access to them. It appeared that death hounds liked it rough. I had no idea that I liked it rough until this moment, when he moved me from the door, tossing me on the black leather sofa that Luc had in the corner of his office. I bounced only once because he threw himself on top of me.

One thing could be said for the man: He moved with precise quickness when the situation called for it. Say, like when you were about to bed your mate for the first time and *really* wanted to get her naked to commence that bedding.

And not to say that I had a world of experience in the bedroom—again, I hadn't been a virgin when I met Jeffery, but I'd hardly been open all night for business. Still, judging by the handful of lovers I'd taken to my bed once upon a time, I could say with authority that Connor told the truth about his assets. No exaggerating here—so not exaggerating. *Thank you universe!*

A little bout of panic hit me as I wondered how he was going to make it fit. The fear quickly abated, however, when he dropped his lips *there*. The magic spot. And the best part was you didn't need to be a super to take advantage of that little nub of sorcery. Just a willing partner with a willingness to learn. I was partial to the swish and flick—but that was just me.

I widened my legs to show that I welcomed him having his wicked way with me in *all* the wicked ways he planned to be wicked.

Maybe because of this whole being Connor's other half thing, I didn't know, but… I'd had great sex, phenomenal sex with Jeffery, the kind that would've kept me happy for the rest of my life. Yet the moment Connor slid inside me, I knew no other man would ever satisfy me again—there could never be another man. Other men no longer existed in my world.

Though that was as much as I thought about it because *rough*. Gloriously so.

I wouldn't have been surprised if they heard us on the international space station.

Connor's intensity—*whoa!* I warred between never wanting it to end and needing it to because I couldn't take a minute more.

Thankfully, our tsunami wave crested, wiping out the entire coastline of my body in the process, and I floated on the calm sea that was Connor holding me, nuzzling my neck with the tip of his nose while pressing tiny kisses to my jaw.

*Sated* didn't begin to cover it, and who knew Connor could be sweet?

Really sweet.

"What's your last name?" I asked, thinking on the situation and how funny it was that I let this man into my body in all the ways, yet I didn't really know him.

He smiled, a kind that looked depleted of energy but highly satisfied.

"Baghest. I can't believe I never told you."

"Honey—" I patted his chest. "You haven't even told me your phone number."

"When I can move again, I'm going to have to rectify that,

too. Though, I'd be lying to say I didn't enjoy you showing up here tonight."

"Good boy," I said and I scratched behind his ear. "I'll point out that you weren't singing that tune earlier tonight."

"Different song drifted down." He smiled, rolling in to kiss me for real. I tingled all over. "What's yours? Your last name?"

"You mean you haven't looked me up?"

"Been sort of busy working two jobs and trying to keep you safe from bad guys."

I couldn't believe that I'd never given him mine, either. We'd certainly dropped the ball on the whole "getting to know you" portion of mating.

"Lamia." I pushed my lips up to kiss him again. "That's the only thing I know about who I am. It was in a book left with me when I was abandoned as an infant."

Connor's face hardened when I talked about being abandoned as an infant.

"What?" I asked. "You knew that."

"Doesn't mean I'm happy about it. Any thought of you being alone and vulnerable kicks in a protectiveness that I've never experienced before. It's annoying as fuck."

Well, that just pissed me off. Here we'd shared this amazing, wild—did I say amazing?—experience and he was going to complain that he felt protective? Screw him and screw this. I didn't need it. I pushed him off me and stood from the sofa gathering my clothing that until minutes ago I was happy he'd torn from my body.

Why did men have to open their mouths and… and… *men*?

Was it the best situation? Not remotely. Especially not for a girl with supernatural powers being raised around regular old humans, but I was over it. Some things just were. My childhood wasn't so different from a whole lot of other kids'—well, aside from the whole zappy-zap fingertips on the full moon. And I didn't need his protective bit when he neither meant it nor wanted it, but was stuck with it because of some cosmic blunder tying us together.

Upon opening my mouth to tell him just that, I got cut off by an annoying knock on the door and Luc calling through. "Sorry, lovebirds. I tried to give you as much time as possible, but there's some stuff going on in the cemetery. We've got alarms going off down here. Need you to check it out."

*Ha!* Love birds? As if, but curiosity got the better of me and I wanted—no, *needed*—to know what set off the alarms. "Want me to come with you?" I asked, rather hopeful that he'd say yes.

"Are you *nuts*?" he snapped. *Snapped*. Whatever. It wasn't like I didn't have a few specialties. Or one. One that would work bringing a baddie down. In light of that, his response hardly felt like the correct response after getting to know each other in all the ways. The man should've had faith in his mate, in the universe giving him an other half who could keep up with a death hound.

I tried to look badass as I pulled up my panties. It wasn't easy to look badass while gliding up panties, so I did it with a scowl on my face.

"Simone." He used his lightning-Connor-quickness to pull my still-almost-completely-naked body back against his still-very-naked one, which created quite the conundrum because I didn't like being snapped at. He had an inside voice—everyone did—and he needed to learn how to use it.

But at the same time, my body reacted to his nearness. To his *naked* nearness. It was a lost cause. I hated myself for melting beneath him.

"You're aware of what just happened between us?"

"Uh, yeah," I replied. "Since I gave you my consent to rock my world."

"Right. So why in the hell do you think that I'd want you anywhere near trouble?"

"Because I have powers. I can help. Besides, do you think I want anyone else to get all the fun of kicking your ass?"

Uh, yeah… that answer went over about as well as I expected it to. As in, it didn't. At all. He growled at me. How did a man who'd just been spectacularly laid—in my opinion—find enough annoyance in him to growl?

"Get dressed," he ordered.

"Say *please.*"

What did you know… Rather than growl again, or even sigh, he smiled as he bent in to press a kiss to the hinge of my jaw. "Please, Simone, baby… get dressed so I don't have to kill my best friend."

"For clarification—" I did sigh, leaning into him. His breath dancing over my skin. His delectable scent filling my nose. I couldn't help it. "Your best friend is…"

"Luc."

"Gotcha."

Given the state of our relationship now that we'd bumped uglies, he wasn't kidding. He'd end Luc for seeing me *au naturel.* Something he found annoying. But in this instance, I chose to be the bigger person and take pity on both men by hurriedly pulling back on my clothing.

Once I had my last button buttoned, Connor called, "You can come in."

Luc stepped inside the room with a knowing smirk on his face. He did a cursory glance around the room and that smile fled when his eyes landed on me.

"You were hoping to see me naked, weren't you?" I put a hand on my hip.

He shrugged. Shrugged—of the sheepish, *why bother to deny it* variety.

"*Luc,*" Connor yelled.

"What?" He threw out his hand toward me. "We both know she's hot."

"Yeah, she is. And she's *my mate.*"

"At least tell me, did she rock your world? I need to live vicariously through you, brother."

Connor narrowed his eyes. "Watch her—*don't* touch her," he warned, but as he passed by Luc, he dropped his voice, smiled slightly, and whispered, "You don't even know." And I watched the high-five eye-volley between them.

Part of me couldn't help but get really happy that he felt that way. *Focus, Simone.* I needed to figure out how to get outside to help Connor. I'd already lost one man and that just about broke me. Jeffery, he'd meant the world to me. I had the feeling that I'd never come back from losing Connor.

He grabbed a handful of my shirt to tug me into his arms and crashed his mouth down onto mine in a hard kiss. "Behave," he warned and I decided to forgive his earlier comment because Connor kisses magically healed all wrongs in my world, even if those wrongs came from him. Then the coolest thing happened: He dropped to the ground, and where the all-man Connor just stood, now stood a giant, black, death hound with glowing, red eyes. His clothing lay in a shredded heap on the floor. He chuffed then turned to run out the door that Luc left open for him when he'd entered.

"So, Simone," Luc said. "What should we do until Connor gets back?"

"Are you flirting with me?" I asked and he smiled another sexy smirk, then winked. "Oh, I can't wait to tell Connor."

Luc's face immediately dropped. "Let's not do anything hasty."

"Connor's going to kill you," I singsonged, liking the way I got this big, strong fallen angel to squirm.

For an office in Hades, Luc's was surprisingly cozy. The crazy-soft sofa I got to break in. Framed western prints on the walls painted a deep maroon. His huge desk looked like mahogany. Two leather club chairs sat opposite the desk, and he even had a large, stone fireplace taking up the entire wall across from the sofa. I couldn't deny that the man had good taste.

"I think you ought to get some work done while you're still

alive to do it," I said. "I'd hate for you to leave this place in a state. It'll be hard to get someone to fill your shoes."

"What are you going to do?" he asked.

"Probably take a nap on your incredible sofa. It's so soft."

It's not as if I wanted to nap, but I needed Luc to forget about me long enough for me to get the chance to escape. No matter what Connor said, I knew he could use my help.

As providence or whatever worked in Hell came to play, one of Luc's employees… I guessed a demon? A demon made the most sense. He knocked once on the door then entered before being told to.

"Sorry to bother you, Luc," the swarthy man said in a distinctly cockney accent. "But there's an incident in quadrant three." I felt bad for him. Not that he was necessarily unattractive, but given he worked around Connor and Luc every day, I figured that'd give anyone a complex.

"Incident?"

"It appears as if one of Lev's people left a cage unlocked and at least one kraken escaped."

*Lev? Who's Lev?* Luc apparently sensed my confusion as he turned his head toward me to say, "Leviathan," before turning back to the demon. "You've got to be kidding me." He pressed his fingertips to his forehead, taking in a long, cleansing breath, or it could've been a suffering sigh, given the situation. The two sounded so similar, it was kind of hard to tell. But Luc looked at me again. "Stay here. I'll be back as soon as I can."

I shooed him off. "Not to worry. Tell Lev I said 'hi.'"

Both men looked at me like I had just gone round the bend and I got the distinct feeling that Lev wasn't nearly as personable as Luc.

"Or not," I mumbled, but neither of them heard me, as they'd both already left the office. Still, it couldn't have worked out better for me. I gave Luc plenty of time to forget I existed, which equaled about another five minutes, before I said, "I don't want them to see me." Just as before, my body faded from view. I watched myself starting with my feet become invisible, but it was like I could still see myself at the same time. Magic rocked, but it was also screwy.

No one saw me as I walked out of Luc's office. No one saw me as I took the spiral stone staircase up to the cemetery. Then, after I whispered, "Don't let anyone in the cemetery see the door open," no one saw me leave the mausoleum and join the group facing off in the dark. Eerily dark. The unnatural kind—or what I considered unnatural.

It seemed smart to hang back and get a feel for the situation before I joined in the rumble. Connor had his back to me. He growled one of those deep, rumbling, *shook the ground beneath us* kind of growls.

Badass.

Well, except for the acid drool that singed the ground as it soaked in. That was pretty gross. My other half was a drooler. The singular Connor stood between the mausoleum and six brawny, angry, gritty-looking men. Beetle's men. Not only did I know it because I simply felt it, but I recognized most of them from Monnie's.

The hulking figure who stepped forward, cloaked all in black, narrowed his beady eyes on Connor. "Give us what we want," he said.

Connor didn't speak as he was in death hound form, but he growled again, and I got the feeling that Beetle's man understood exactly what he said.

"You'll regret that," the man warned, then the six of them lunged. At my Connor. Uh… forget that. Only *I* got to manhandle Connor. Well, that wasn't exactly true. I'd never actually manhandled him aside from that time I'd kneed him in the boys, but—*focus, Simone.*

"The war starts now," another man shrouded in a dark cloak shouted, lunging toward Connor with some kind of black, glowing knife while Connor was occupied defending himself against the other five. I didn't even think, jumping into action, pressing my taser fingers to the dark figure's exposed skin on his neck. He literally never saw me coming.

The air in the cemetery went wired when he screamed and dropped to his knees. I kept right on pressing until he passed right out. Beetle's men looked frantically around trying to figure out what they'd just witnessed. Connor took the opportunity to lunge at another. I went after another man, too.

We'd taken out all the men save one. We left him standing. His hood had fallen off during the fight and really, with his dark beady eyes and that thick scar running down the length of the right side of his face, he looked like every stereotype a girl could come up with to describe a *henchman* for a *bad guy* named *Beetle*. Then a very naked Connor shifted back from his death hound form. I bit my lip to keep from giving myself away, but the man just did it for me. I couldn't help it. He stared down the last man in quite the menacing fashion. "You tell your boss that he'll get her over my dead body, and I'm damn hard to kill." When the man just stood there, Connor barked, "*Go!*"

That lit a fire under his feet. As the man ran like a coward, Connor then shifted back to his hound form, but not before yelling, "Simone, back inside. *Now.*"

Clearly, I'd given myself away with my sizzle fingers. As I headed back down, a group of demons passed me and instinctively, I knew they were the cleanup crew. Well, Connor could be angry all he wanted, but I did the right thing going out to help him.

He found me back on Luc's sofa waiting patiently. Okay, so Connor didn't need to slam the door. I sensed when he walked in the room now. That was complete overkill. But I looked up and smiled. "Hey, how'd it go?" I asked, hoping to both head him off and make him think I'd been in here the whole time.

"How'd it go? *How'd* it go?" If he wasn't careful, his head might explode.

"Yeah. You're here, so I take it you took care of things." I blinked big eyes to appear innocent.

One second, he stood by the door running his fingers through his hair and the next, he stood right in front of me, lifted me up with a firm grip around my arms, flipped us around so he could take my spot, and deposited me on his lap. "What in all of Hades were you thinking?"

"First of all, can you put some clothes on before you yell at me, especially while I'm in your lap? I find your nakedness distracting. Secondly, what do you mean?"

"Simone." He shook his head. I smiled as I bent in to peck his nose. "You're going to be the death of me, I just know it."

"No. It'd hardly do me any good for you to die."

He sighed. "Where's Luc?"

"Kraken escaped in quadrant three."

"Please tell me you aren't serious."

I shrugged. "Lev's people aren't very reliable."

"What do you know about Lev? Did he come here? Did he see you?"

"No. One of Luc's guys popped in to give him the good news."

"Woman," he grumbled, shaking his head as he wrapped me snuggly in his arms.

"You're not going soft on me, are you?"

"Baby, you're going to beg for me to go soft on you when I get you home."

Yes, please.

This whole work thing put a crimp in my ability to keep looking into Jeffery's death and how Beetle was related. But at the same time, I loved my house and my jeep and didn't want to lose them because I lacked the funds to continue payments. Payments only got made when I worked.

I owned a shop specializing in crystals and other valuable rocks, plus special plants: herbs, bark, roots and flowers for making teas, tinctures or potions. I employed a reiki specialist and a past life regressionist. Some people didn't believe in such practices, but some people didn't believe in supers, either, and I was living proof they existed.

Most people were surprised to find out that someone my age owned their own business. To my good fortune, as it turned out, supers liked to help other supers succeed in this world. We'd come a long way since the "Grab your torches and pitchforks" days, but that was only because we'd found ways to assimilate into the normal human world. Such as open businesses. And once humans began to open themselves up to the idea of alternative medicines and new age lifestyles, we got to come out from the dirty underground market completely. They might not have believed in supers, but they believed in the power of crystals.

Two counter girls worked the weekends for me. They got Monday and Tuesday off and I had to remind myself that my shop was worth getting up for as I reached over to shut off the alarm.

At the same time, Connor rolled over in his sleep, draping his arm across my belly. Now that we'd consummated the mating, he refused to leave my side or my bed. Well, his bed would've been preferred—by him. But I loved my home and my bed. Not that his was bad by any means. I simply liked mine better.

If I didn't like the feel of him next to me so well, we'd have to have a serious talk about boundaries. Although I'd planned to cohabitate with Jeffery, I'd never actually lived with anyone since the days when I had a legal guardian, and I'd tried my hardest not to people in those homes. That tended to be my safest option when fireworks sparked from my fingertips every full moon.

What did he, Connor, expect from me? From this situation? Did he think we were just going to live together? *Were* we going to live together?

Okay, being this close to Connor muddled my mind. It might've been a good thing that I had work to occupy my time. Gently, so as not to wake him, I lifted his arm, moving it back onto his side of the bed.

His side.

He already had a side?

We'd so naturally shuffled into our spots without even talking about it.

*Whoa!* I crawled out of bed and since I'd lost every stitch of clothing last night before we'd ever tumbled into that bed, I didn't have anything to take off once I reached the shower.

He slept the whole time I showered, dressed, and walked out to the kitchen to toast myself a couple of Pop Tarts. I put a full pot of coffee on so that Connor could have a cup or two before leaving for work.

Then I headed for my shop.

I loved my shop. Located at the end of a strip mall, it appeared very unassuming from the outside. The inside smelled of sandalwood and lavender for a very calming vibe.

Regular old humans expected calming vibes. Supers *needed* it. People had no idea how draining it was to keep our powers hidden throughout the day because powers had minds of their own and wanted to be seen, to be acknowledged.

I felt very at home here and owning a shop allowed me to keep up with the latest super-related gossip from the ones who came in for my crystals or tea blends that they loved to use in casting spells or rituals.

At about 9:00 A.M., Connor strode through the door looking his normal Connor irate. "You left without telling me."

"I'm an adult. I'm allowed. But I left you a pot of coffee, so really, you should be in here thanking me. Plus, how do you keep finding me? I don't remember telling you about my shop."

"The bond. Your scent."

"Uh, I showered this morning, buddy. I don't have a *scent*."

"Simone, this isn't funny."

"*Connor*, I wasn't trying to be."

"I told you to stay put unless I'm with you."

"You should get used to disappointment."

He ran his hand through his hair and growled. Connor and his growling.

"Go to work, Connor."

"Are you dismissing me?"

"How astute of you."

"I'd prefer you come to work for me at the store." Rather than try to strongarm me, he leaned against the counter, putting weight on his arm to lean in close to me. Man, Connor this close did stuff to me. All the stuff. All the good stuff and that was bad because it made it hard to do what needed to be done. Then, with his voice dripping with sensuality, he said, "That way, I can keep an eye on you."

So caught up in his hotness bubble, it took a second for me to realize what he'd said. I blinked a couple of times before the bubble popped and it hit me. I straightened right up. "*I'd* prefer you never say that to me again. Guess which one of us is getting what she wants?"

He actually thought weaponizing his hotness would work? I kicked him out, though not before giving him a proper sendoff. What? No one was in the shop and we locked the door. And let me just say, up against the wall, storeroom sex made for a fantastic start to my workday.

Fan-freaking-tastic.

The problem with giving him his proper sendoff was that he'd worn me right out, and once he left, I had a parade of customers, mostly witches, in and out all day long.

By the time I locked the door at the end of the day, I was ready for—I'd decided earlier that day on Mexican takeout, my comfies, and a movie.

Before leaving, I called ahead and since I couldn't decide on what I wanted, I bought several dishes. A Mexican smorgasbord.

In my softest, gray jersey shorts and a pink razorback tank, I had the bounty of food spread out over the coffee table with my plate in hand, a tall glass of iced tea sitting on the lamp table next to my elbow, *Practical Magic* cued up when the door opened. I turned to watch Connor stride in.

"Connor. My door was locked. How did you get in?"

"I took your extra key this morning before I left. Which, seriously, baby, you should've left it set out for me. I had to take extra time hunting it down in those wasteland of junk drawers you have."

*Shoot.* I never even thought about leaving him a key.

What did that say about me?

"Smells like Mexican."

"Yeah." Thank all the tarot cards in the world that I'd been particularly indecisive today and bought extra. Man, I was rusty at this girlfriend gig. I needed to get with the program here. Solo

Simone had a partner in crime again. "Get a plate. I didn't know when you'd be um… home."

He smiled. *Phew! And the Oscar goes to…*

"Let me change out of my work clothes first."

I stared at him. "Do you have clothes to change into?"

He shrugged. "You didn't want to sleep at my place last night. So I stopped off there before going to your store this morning."

"Oh… okay." This… this… *situation* with Connor suddenly started to feel a bit too *domestic* for my liking. Aside from the whole *him being my mate* thing, our relationship was moving at lightspeed. The last time I'd gotten loved up, well, it ended up sucking big time. Did I have it in me to go through that again? Knowing what could happen?

Because the feelings starting to develop for Connor weren't all negative. In fact, I'd venture to say the opposite.

Before I had the chance to get out of my own head, Connor walked out of my room in a pair of low-hanging shorts and nothing else. We were so getting naked again. *No. Bad Simone. You are eating dinner and watching a movie.*

My mouth salivated at his nearness, and my heart skittered a wonky rhythm when he reached up into the cupboard to grab a plate. His muscles bunched under his skin. I cleared my throat. "The, um, forks are—"

"I know where the forks are, baby."

He knew where to find my forks?

I watched him pour himself a tall glass of iced tea and continued to hold his gaze as he dropped down onto the sofa next to me.

"What are we watching?" he asked.

I blinked. "Sex."

He broke into a wide smile. "We're watching sex?"

"What? No. It's *Practical Magic*."

Connor snickered as he bent to pile food on his plate. While moving back into a comfortable position, he stopped to press a kiss to my lips. "Since Sandra Bullock doesn't star in porn, I'm going to guess that's not what you meant. If you want sex, Simone, just say the word."

I opened my mouth and somehow got "food first" to fall out.

*Whoa.* I totally needed to figure out how to turn the dial down on this connection. It seemed a bit too unhealthy for my liking because being with him simply felt better than anything else in my life. I wasn't ready for that level of intensity. We'd only just met. Okay, well, we didn't exactly *just* meet. I'd known him long enough to get the business at least ten times in three different locations. Still my point held validity—even if only to me.

Today was a good, easy day. Connor joined me in bed and we slept. Like actual sleep. He held me throughout the night.

When my alarm went off the next morning I tried to be quiet for him again, but as it turned out, he woke up right along with me.

"I can't have sex right now, Connor. I need to get ready for work."

"I wasn't actually thinking about sex, but good job. Now I am." He rolled over to pin me down and he kissed me. "As it turns out, I don't have time this morning, either."

"Did Luc give you the night off? I just realized that you slept here."

He eyed me like I'd gone around the bend again. "You *just* realized that?"

"No. I knew you slept here, I meant that it just hit me you were here all night."

Connor shrugged. "Luc got called away on business. Usually I join him unless he's working with upper management."

I furrowed my brows. "You mean Lucifer is *middle* management?"

My mate smiled indulgently, pointing up. "No. *Upper* management." Ah… okay. I got it now. That seemed reasonable.

"What are your plans?" I asked.

"Calling a realtor."

"What are you selling?"

He chuckled. "This is a nice pad. You should get a good price for it."

"I know it's nice. That's why I bought it. I have no intention of selling. Why would you say that?"

"Because you're moving in with me," he said with as much nonchalance as one might say the bed had pillows.

"What a silly boy you are." I reached up to scratch behind his ear. "*I'm* not moving. But feel free to stay here anytime you like. When you aren't moving your mouth, I actually enjoy your company."

"Stay anytime I like? Simone, we're mates. The universe wants you in my bed every night and waking up next to me every morning for like… *ever*."

"So you want to move in together, like, *officially*?"

"Don't blame me. Blame the universe."

"I mean, it's fast… It's not as if I haven't clued in from the universe, but that's a big step."

He pulled out one of his *what in the hell is wrong with you?* faces from his repertoire of faces that I knew he kept just for me. "Bigger than mating?" he asked on the verge of shouting. "We've mated. It's the supernatural equivalent of getting married with the universe officiating. It's a done deal, baby. We started down the path the moment we locked eyes. But when you let me take you on Luc's sofa, you said '*I do.*' No going back now."

"That's a lot to take in."

"We have forever, Simone."

"Okay… but I'm still not selling my home."

"Did your dead guy live here?"

That was quite the brusque, uncalled-for way to ask if Jeffery and I lived together. "His name was Jeffery. And not that it's your business, but *no*. We never lived together because he didn't know about my condition. I planned to tell him after we'd married."

"Condition? You're a super, not arthritic. And it *is* my business because I'm not living in his house."

I got it. He didn't like that I'd been engaged before him. Tough turkey. He needed to get over it and stop being so hurtful. I loved Jeffery. Even if I was meant to be with Connor, I loved Jeffery. A tear fell from my eye, and I turned my head away to keep him from seeing it. "Well, it's never been his house. It's *my* house."

"Good, baby," he whispered softly. Good? *Good*? I prepared to let him have it, but Connor rolled into me, nuzzling my cheek with his nose and I lost all my aggression. "I'm sorry, Simone. I know you cared for him but it goes against every instinct I have in me to think about you being with another man. You're mine."

His nuzzling along with his sweet apology, something that I instinctually knew Connor never gave out before now, caught me so off guard that I freaking sighed.

Since when did I, Simone Lamia, sigh like some girly girl because a hot guy nuzzled my cheek? I mean, okay, I'd sighed a time or two with Jeffery, but that was years ago. His death forced a new Simone to emerge. A stronger, badass Simone. Strong, badass Simones didn't sigh all girly-like.

"Then I'll move in here. Not sleeping in a bed that you're not in."

"You're not?" I whispered because he pressed his lips to my throat and I got lost in the feel of him.

"No." He dragged his mouth up to my jaw.

And I was officially screwed.

"Now I've got plenty of time for sex," he said through his kisses.

Then I was literally screwed.

The more time I spent with Connor, the harder I found it to be away from Connor. Maybe we needed to take a honeymoon.

While I sold crystals, Connor officially moved into my place.

Or I guessed it was now *our* place. He wasn't messing around. He closed his store while he lugged things over from his apartment, and texted me pics throughout the day of where he'd put his things. Secretly, it excited me to get those texts, to see him moving his things in with me as my mind and heart began to sync with this whole idea of being his mate. He said it. I'd never be alone again. The thought thrilled me now. Funny how fast that happened. When I arrived home, Mrs. Hildebrandt stood outside on my front lawn as if she'd been waiting for me to get here.

"Hey, Mrs. Hildebrandt, what are you doing out here?"

"There's a man in your house. He moved boxes inside. Are you moving?"

"No, Mrs. Hildebrandt, that's Connor. He's living here now, too."

"What about your fine young man, Jeffery? Is he okay with another man moving in?"

"Mrs. Hildebrandt, Jeffery is—"

"Don't tell me you broke up. He was such a nice young man. And handsome, too."

She wasn't wrong. Jeffery had been nice and incredibly handsome. But *hello!* Mrs. Hildebrandt needed to open her eyes because Connor—he beat out the sun for hotness. It radiated off him in waves.

"It's going to get dark soon, Mrs. Hildebrandt. Why don't you head home? I don't want you hurting yourself."

She looked around as if just noticing where she was and turned to walk home. I waited to go inside until I saw Mrs. Hildebrandt step through her front door. Then I got to step through mine... right into a wall of wondrous smells.

"Connor?" I called out.

"In the kitchen," he answered. I followed my nose to where I found him pulling a roasting pan out of the oven.

"You cooked?"

"Been single a long time, baby. I like to eat."

"No, you don't."

He stared at me, head cocked. "I don't?"

"Oatmeal and protein bars? Kale? Speaking of—" I tried to peek at the roasting pan to figure out what he'd cooked. "You aren't trying to feed me anything... *healthy*, are you?"

Connor snickered. "I wouldn't dream of it."

"Good. Then you get a kiss." I did exactly as promised, walking the few steps over to the man, dropping a kiss to his lips. "Thank you for doing this," I added and when he smiled —*whoosh!* Air evacuated my lungs.

"Why don't you get comfortable? I'll get this to the table," he said. I nodded, walking to the bedroom, where I changed into comfy shorts and a T-shirt. Then, after washing my hands, I joined him at the table.

"Eating at the table today? Who's fancy?"

"It seemed like an *eat at the table* kind of day, the first meal with us officially moved in together."

I sat down.

After my first bite of succulent roast, two things about Connor became fact. First, he was the best bed partner a woman could ask for. Second, the man could cook. *Really* cook.

That night, after a full belly and a highly pleasant evening doing nothing in particular with Connor, I went to bed and that was where the weirdness started. I lay down next to my what amounted to a universal common law husband, snuggling against him with my head on his chest and my arm draped over his stomach. I seriously couldn't think of a more comfortable spot.

"No Luc tonight?" I yawned.

"He'll be back tomorrow. I'll have the graveyard shift again."

I laughed lightly at his little quip. Graveyard shift, indeed.

Sleep came easier with Connor here, too. I could only assume that it had something to do with the connection we shared as mates. But the easy ended there. From the moment I felt myself fall into a sleep state—and yes, I *felt* it—the dark-haired woman showed up again. All I got from her before was *"Simone."* Tonight, however, I got a total *Chatty Cathy*.

"Simone," she started off the conversation again, and I waited for her to continue. "You've connected with your mate?"

"Yes."

"Oh, thank the darkness," she replied.

I narrowed my eyes at her. "Why?"

"He is your key—you must use him."

"My key? Use him?"

She wasn't making any sense.

"The brooch presented itself to you?"

"Brooch?"

"A symbol. A snake."

"Yes. It was at Connor's secondhand store. He let me have it."

"Use it, Simone… let it guide you."

"Guide me?"

She whipped her head around left and right as if she'd heard someone enter the room with her, or wherever she was at, but it was a dream, so I didn't see how it could be possible.

"I have to go. Stick with your mate… He is your key…"

"Where are you?"

"Be safe." She disappeared.

Connor is my key? Use him? Let the brooch guide me? It seemed too real to just let go, but at the same time, dreams for regular, old humans had to do with their subconscious thoughts and feelings. What did talking to a person in a dream mean for a super?

To tell Connor or not to tell Connor, that was definitely the question. In the end, I moved away from him so as not to wake him up and accidentally did just that. The moment he felt me leave my spot, his eyes popped open.

"You okay, baby?" His hand sifted through my hair, then ran down my arm to relax me.

"I was actually trying not to wake you up."

"Simone, I feel it whenever you aren't next to me."

"Well, that's bordering on supernatural creepy stalker."

He laughed and it tickled as he continued to run his hand up and down the skin of my arm.

"What woke you? Bad dream?"

"Not *bad*, per se—more odd. I saw that woman again."

"Woman?"

I nodded. "Do you remember the day I came to find you at the cemetery because I heard a woman call my name in my sleep?"

"*Yeah…*" He suddenly became very tentative about how casual to react to my news.

"She talked to me this time."

In a flash, he sat up straight, silky, groggy sleep-voice gone. "What did she say?"

"She asked if I'd connected with my mate yet. And when I told her *yes*, she visibly relaxed. She told me that you're my key."

"Key to what, untold carnal pleasures?" The idiot laughed.

"Um… she wouldn't be wrong."

My mate smiled a super-cocky smile, but I couldn't lie. He rocked my world. Rocked my universe. Rocked my dimension. "But," I went on, "I got the feeling that wasn't what she meant. She said you're my key. I'm supposed to use you."

"Any way you want, baby."

"Mind out of the gutter, stud. She asked me about the brooch—the one you let me take from the shop the other day."

The way he squished his face, it appeared he was trying to recall the brooch in question and simply couldn't. I crawled from the bed over to my dresser where I kept my jewelry box. Flipping the box open, I picked up the fine piece of jewelry. It felt like its power tried to burrow under my skin, to meld with me. The next thing I knew, Connor was at my side.

"What's wrong?"

"This is the brooch." I held it up. He took it from my hand, looking it over.

"I never checked it in. I'd recognize this. It has magic."

"That's curious because I picked it up from a box that held jewelry odds and ends sitting on one of your shelves. When I picked it up just now, it felt like it tried to meld with me."

"Meld?"

I shook my head.

"Maybe you should get rid of it."

"I can't. The woman made it seem like I was supposed to find it. She said it 'presented itself to me.' Then she said I'm supposed to let it guide me."

"To where?"

"Your guess is as good as mine."

"Don't you do business with witches?"

I felt the need to hug him. "I do."

With his arms wrapped protectively around me, I felt better. He kissed the top of my head. "Maybe we can talk to a witch to help us figure out what this thing is." He flipped the bauble in the air then caught it. "Maybe you can get your cards read. They might be able to point us in the right direction to figure out who this woman is and why she's contacting you."

"So you don't think it's just my subconscious?"

"No. I have a bad feeling she's trying to warn you about something that's on the horizon. As protection is sort of my gig, it's rare that I'm wrong."

"One witch, Agatha, comes in every Wednesday. She feels powerful. Maybe she might be willing to help me."

"I'm coming with you to the store."

"What about your store?"

"I like my store. My store is in no way as important as my mate, Simone. I'm coming with you."

"You said '*in you*' wrong."

He laughed. "If that's what you need… it'll be a sacrifice, but for you, I'll make it."

CHAPTER

*Nine*

onnor led me back to bed this morning, but we didn't fall back asleep for a while. He'd definitely changed "with me" to "in me" a couple of times before we passed out.

When we reached my shop, he became all business. Not that he didn't hold me or drop kisses to my head, but those appeared more about his protection instinct kicking in than anything lovey-dovey.

At around 10:30, the bell over the door jingled as Agatha walked in. She'd reached what I liked to call her "Stevie Nicks" stage of life, wearing her hair down long and flowing. Long flowing skirt and a black shawl. Just because she didn't admit to being a witch didn't mean she didn't dress like one. I smiled, feeling her power. If she would be willing to help me, she'd definitely have the power to do it.

"Simone, merry meet."

"Good morning, Agatha. What can I help you with today?"

"I need black cohosh, evening primrose, and red clover."

I walked over to my jars filled with herbs. "How much of each?"

"How about two ounces of each? That way, I'll have extra. I have a feeling that I'll be getting more orders."

"Of anybody, you'd know." We both chuckled. While I weighed out the red clover, I casually threw over my shoulder, "I was wondering if I could pick your brain for a moment."

"Sure, what do you need?"

"Give me a minute." I walked back behind the counter and waited for the non-super customer in the place to find what she wanted. After I checked her out, I looked back to Agatha. "Can you read my cards? I'd be happy to pay, but this is important. I need someone powerful and I feel your power radiate off you from the moment you step inside the store."

"What's going on?"

"Connor," I called out to him. He smiled his panty-dropping smile at the both of us. "Can you lock the door and put the lunch sign up?"

"Oh, my," Agatha murmured, noticing Connor standing off in the corner of the store on the opposite wall, but in reality, he'd just slipped in from the back room.

"This is my mate, Connor Baghest."

He waved as he locked up the shop for me.

She eyed him up and down, eyes narrowed, assessing. "You're a protector."

The tension between them ratcheted up at least ten notches. "I am. How did—"

Agatha put her hand up to stop him. "Not just a shifter, but a *protector*. You're Simone's protector. That's why you've mated. Why would Simone require a protector?"

Then she pivoted to look me in the eye. "What are you, Simone?"

"We've talked about this before. Your guess is as good as mine. I take it most supers don't have protectors?"

"Not in the form of shifters. Familiars more so, but shifters are saved for..." She trailed off.

"For?"

"Sorry—for important people."

"I'm *not* important, I can assure you."

"Your mate tells me different. Do you have a table? My cards are in my purse."

I walked Connor and Agatha into the back room, where I had a table set up for when we ate lunch or dinner, depending on the work schedule. She set her purse down on the table, unzipped it, and fished through it until she pulled the deck out. She dumped them out of the box into her hand.

"Please, sit," she said and both Connor and I pulled out chairs, dropping into them across from her. "Tell me what you needed from me this morning. Why did you seek me out? I need to know everything."

"I've been gaining new powers."

"New powers? At your age?"

I nodded. "Yeah. They've been growing since I connected with Connor. Aside from my taser fingers, I've been able to manifest my desires and now, I've started seeing this woman in my head. The first time, she said my name, but I couldn't get more than that."

"Was this before or after you connected with your mate?"

My cheeks flushed. "Um… we'd connected but hadn't *connected* yet, if you get my meaning."

"So that was the first time. I take it there's been a second?"

"Last night," Connor answered for me.

I elaborated. "When she came to me—it was while I was sleeping—anyway, she seemed relieved that I'd connected with Connor."

"Relieved?" Agatha repeated questioningly.

"Yeah. She told me to use him. That he was my key."

"Your key? She said that specifically?"

Again, I nodded. "Yes." When Agatha dipped her chin, I went on. "She asked if 'the brooch' had presented itself to me." I pulled the brooch out of my pocket to hand it to her. She reached her hand out but pulled it back right away with a hiss when she saw it.

"How are you able to handle that?" she asked.

What was she talking about? "I just picked it up. Connor can too. Why?"

"That's an athame."

What? I looked at her confusedly. "It's a brooch."

"No. That was once inset in the handle of a dagger."

"A dagger—this?"

She eyed the piece and then me. "The dagger disappeared millennia ago."

"Then how do you know that this is from that?"

"I feel the power and it's been passed down in grimoires, detailed drawings. Witches can't touch it. No supers can touch it."

"Why is that?"

"That belonged to the dagger of Lilith."

Connor barked out a laugh. "You had me going for a minute there. Simone, she's not being serious. There's no way you've been carrying around a token from the dagger of Lilith in your pocket."

"Why?" I asked.

"Mostly because it's impossible. It's been gone for millennia as she said, and you and I have held it without any ill effects."

"What kind of ill effects?"

"Excruciating pain. Draining power. Endless suffering after death. You name it, it's responsible."

"And how do you know so much about the dagger of Lilith?" I asked him.

"Luc has a book in his office. Sometimes on my down time, I'll peruse his shelves."

"Was there a picture?"

He shook his head. "No. It just talked about it."

"What did it say?" Agatha asked. We both looked to her curiously. "I only know what was passed down in my grimoire. I'm very curious to know if there's anything more."

Connor shrugged. "Basically, it said that she and Adam weren't a well matched couple because he thought a lot of himself, wasn't real nice, and tried to act all superior. Lilith didn't go for any of it. They had a couple of kids. The kids dug their mom way more than their dad because of above reasons. They divorced. She got the kids. He got Eve and used his new platform to continuously run down his ex."

I bristled.

"What he didn't understand," Connor continued, "is that a true badass doesn't need someone around to massage their ego."

"Aw… honey, is that why you like me to massage yours?"

Agatha laughed while Connor hauled me over onto his lap, pressing a kiss to my temple.

"I like when you massage things, but my ego isn't one of them." Woo. The way he said that shot a thrill right through me.

"So it didn't say anything about the dagger, then?" Agatha asked.

"Just that her daughter got into a heated argument with Adam and he ended up striking her. Lilith flew into a rage, attacking Adam with the dagger. She didn't kill him."

"She could have," Agatha put in. "Lilith was the first witch. She cast a spell using the blood of Adam to protect her daughter and all of her daughter's descendants from any men. Then she gave the dagger to her daughter."

"So then how did it disappear?" I asked, totally enthralled by this story.

"Lilith's daughter was betrayed… by a *woman*. A woman who'd been coerced or forced into hurting her. No one knows what happened after that."

"Okay, but how does anyone know that this brooch belonged to that dagger?" I pushed.

"Because Lilith wrote it down in her personal grimoire. She

showed it to those she trusted so they would know when they saw it, it would provide protection."

"But I thought it was only protecting her daughter and daughter's descendants."

"Her daughter had children."

Yeah, I got that. "How many?" I asked.

"That, we don't know."

"Do you know, Connor?"

He shook his head. "Lilith has been out of commission since well before I made my appearance into the world."

"Would Luc know?" I asked.

"I'll talk to him tonight."

"So back to the matter at hand," Agatha said, "you've somehow ended up with part of the dagger of Lilith. We don't know why and we don't know how you can touch it."

Understatement of the century.

"We know you're an orphan. You've told me as such," she continued. "I think you need to tap into your past, to access memories that you don't realize you have."

"Can you do that?" I asked.

"I can, but not here. You'll have to come to my home, where I have the things I'll need." She pulled a piece of paper and a pen from her pocket, writing down her address. "This isn't my home where I sleep, but where I practice away from prying eyes."

"Thank you."

"Meet me there at midnight. The magic is strongest then."

I leaned in to hug her. "Blessed be, Agatha. We'll be there at midnight."

As Agatha turned to leave, I told her not to forget the herbs on the counter. They were on me.

"Can you believe that?" Connor asked.

"No. But I knew if anyone could help us, it would be her. She's strong."

"I'm not leaving you alone today. Something about the day is giving me an off feeling—don't argue."

Snickering, I smiled through it. "I'm not arguing, believe it or not. I feel something on the horizon, too, and I don't like it."

We tried our best to get back to business as usual, opening the store back up. He actually behaved himself and stayed out of the way, pulling back his protective instincts with me, especially when men approached me for help. I put him to work as a salesman. When Connor Baghest wanted to be charming, he nailed it. Women and even a couple of men swooned when he turned it on.

Now, when a few of those women got a little too friendly with *him*, I may or may not have walked up to him, planted a huge kiss, and let him know explicitly what I planned to do to him when we got home tonight. He totally forgot about anyone else standing near us.

So maybe I had protective instincts, too.

At the end of the day, he helped me close up shop, we stopped off for BBQ takeout tonight, and headed home. Despite keeping up the low-key, nothing to see here vibe throughout the day, I thought both of us were a fair mixture of excited and apprehensive about tonight's festivities.

"Had your sister met her mate?" I asked totally out of the blue—well, out of the blue to Connor. I'd been thinking about it since we'd talked to Agatha this morning.

He snapped his head back looking at me. "What?"

"Your sister. Your sister is a death hound, like you. You're a protector and we mated, which—correct me if I'm wrong, but it felt like Agatha insinuated that you are supposed to be *my* protector. That's why we mated."

"I haven't thought about it since this morning with everything else going on, but no, you're not wrong. That's how she made it seem." He ran his hands over his hair. "And to answer your question, not that she'd told me."

Well, shoot. "I was hoping that if we knew who she'd mated with, who she'd been tasked with protecting, that might help out in this situation."

"Situation?"

"Well, it seems odd that all this is happening now. Your sister went missing around the same time Jeffery died. This Beetle guy is after me. You're not just my mate but my *protector*. I'm no Nancy Drew, but even I can connect dots."

"Simone, I'm liking this less and less."

"Already beat you to it. But the events have been put in motion."

"Because you went to Monnie's."

Uh… no. "I'd be careful going down that road of accusation if I were you. The day we met, you told me Luc told you 'something's up' or something close to it, and he'd sent you to that abandon building. I hadn't contacted Beetle yet. Whatever this is, it's bigger than you and me."

"It can't be bigger than you and me with us at the center of it."

I spun my finger in the air. "Semantics. The point still stands."

"Get your shoes on. We'll grab ice cream before we head out to Agatha's place."

"Connor Baghest, I'm going to say this once and if you bring it up again, I'll deny it until my death, but you are amazing."

He laughed, pulling me in for a hug and kissing the top of my head. "I'll never bring it up."

"Bull," I countered.

"Okay. You're right. Be prepared to deny it until your death."

That was fine. I'd suck it up for ice cream. We pulled our shoes on, grabbed my keys, and headed out to the jeep. Connor had a truck. A nice truck, but he must have sensed that I needed my jeep. The purple. He didn't have to fully get it to get it.

He drove us through the drive thru at Dairy Queen and we both got Blizzards. Mine, strawberry cheesecake with chocolate chips. His was an amalgam of M&Ms, Reece's Pieces, Reece's Peanut Butter Cups, and chocolate chip cookie dough.

We reached the address Agatha had given us about a quarter

to midnight. She stood in the open door, anticipating us. Her witchy powers were so cool. As we stepped inside, I noticed Connor's nose wrinkle as the air hung thick with incense, a highly flowery scent. It might not have been my jam, either, but clearly, Agatha needed it to get this party started, so to speak.

As it appeared that she grew several plants and dried them here, I wondered if she came to the shop more to connect with other witches than for my actual products.

"You've got quite the green thumb," I pointed out.

She dipped her head sheepishly. "Okay, I'll admit, I went to your store the first time because I was drawn to it, not because I actually needed anything."

"Why didn't you tell me?"

"Because I haven't been able to figure out what drew me. So I kept coming back, figuring that the reason would present itself. Today, when you stopped me in the store, it presented itself. I'm supposed to help you."

"Well, I hope after tonight, you'll still come visit me, even if you don't buy anything. I look forward to our Wednesday chats."

"You do stock bark and leaves from trees we can't grow here."

I'd like to think that was her way of saying she enjoyed our Wednesday chats, too.

She ushered me over to a recliner. The soft, brown leather looked well-loved. "Please sit," she said, then she looked to Connor. "You can take any of the other seats."

We waited for Connor to get comfortable before Agatha walked over to the hearth, where she had an overly large, scuffed and dented tea kettle that I'd bet money had been passed down in her family for years. She used the hem of the apron she wore to lift it from the handle that it hung from over an open flame, bringing it over to the white mug sitting on a table made from a tree stump. She poured the bubbling liquid into the mug, set the kettle down to drizzle honey into the cup before dropping a tea ball into the drink, then brought the mug over to me.

I watched the brown from the tea swirl through the water in a very unnatural fashion. Once it stopped swirling, Agatha pushed the mug up to my lips. "Drink. Drink it all."

Steam rose up from the surface of the tea. I blew on it so as not to burn my mouth and sipped carefully. It tasted of warm spice, something bitter, and the honey.

"What is this?"

"Shh… drink. I can't start until you finish."

I tried to drink fast, but the stuff still steamed. No matter. I chugged and gulped until I'd finished every drop.

"Good, good… close your eyes," she directed. I closed my eyes. "Now take slow, even breaths in and out." Right. In and out. I breathed, feeling a calm wash over me as soft words in some distant, foreign language reached my ears, knowing that Agatha spoke those words. "I need you to dial back the years as if flipping back a calendar."

In my mind, I pictured a calendar, flipping back in time.

"I need you to go back to when you were born."

The calendar flipped back through the years until I reached the time of my birth, or, I thought it was my birth. It looked well past my twenty-five years in a time period I failed to identify. A woman with raven hair, brown eyes, and a smile full of love held me in her arms. She spoke in a language I didn't speak, yet I understood her.

"My Simone," she said. Okay, well, she definitely used my name. A man stood next to the woman, one arm wrapped lovingly around her, the other brushing gently over my head looking down on me with his warm brown eyes. His hair he wore long. The brown strands tied back with a strap. He and the woman and I all shared the same tan skin tone. They made such a handsome couple. All I felt was love until suddenly, the man and woman whipped their heads up, fear on their faces.

The woman I'd spoken to in my dream stepped into the

movie frame playing in my mind. "They're coming. Get her out."

Then a different man's voice filled the room. "Give the babe over."

The man I knew to be my father charged, the woman I'd spoken to in my dream grabbed me from my mother, and then we were surrounded by darkness, as if we'd traveled through a dark tunnel.

An explosion ripped through the room. My eyes opened in time for me to see splinters of wooden door shrapnel flying at Agatha and me. Connor dropped his man form, charging the intruder, whom I couldn't see because I was trying to keep the wood from getting in my eyes.

Agatha's eyes glowed warm orange, the color of flames, but she didn't wield fire. The tea made me too sluggish to move with enough effectiveness to help them out. Still, I managed to think that Connor, Agatha, and I needed to get out of there.

The next thing I knew, the three of us landed by the base of a tree just inside the woods at the back of Agatha's property. I saw the house in the distance.

"How did we get here?" Agatha asked.

"I told you I can manifest," I said. "I thought that we needed to get out of there."

She looked at me in amazement. "I've never seen anything like it. No spells. No chants. No teas or tinctures? You certainly have witch power, but you are no witch."

"Well, we already knew that."

"Did you see anything?" she asked.

"I saw my mother and father. But it felt like a time way in the past. So it couldn't have been me or my parents. The woman I talked to in my dream showed up. Someone attacked and she grabbed me from my mother, then we were surrounded by blackness. That's the last thing I saw."

"Does it trouble anybody else that at the moment Simone is attacked in her memory, we were attacked here?" Connor asked.

Yes. That troubled me. It also troubled me that Agatha was seeing my mate naked. *Connor needs clothing,* I thought and it took everything I had to try to make that happen but I couldn't. Agatha's tea packed a punch.

"Someone is following you, Simone," she added. "You and Connor. You can't go home."

"Where are we supposed to go?" I asked.

"Whoever they are, they know I tried to help you now. It's not safe for us to keep going."

"Then we're back to square one," I said, sighing.

"No. You need to go talk to my ancestor."

"Your ancestors? How would I go about that?"

"Get to Ireland. I'll tell you whom you need to seek out. She's a relative and she'll help you reach the ancestors. Do you have your phone?"

I fished into my pocket to pull out my phone, unlocking it for her, then handing it over. She opened the note app and typed out a name, then handed it back to me.

"Now, go."

I looked down at the name and tried to manifest us out of that treeline.

Nothing.

"What's wrong?" Connor asked.

"Well, aside from you being naked right now, that tea she gave me is still in my system. Manifesting us out of there used up my strength. I need to rest, to recuperate before we can move."

Connor looked down at himself.

Agatha laughed uncomfortably. "I was trying not to bring attention to that. Though, you should be very proud of your... um... physique."

I used what strength I had to step in front of him. "She's not wrong," I said. "Very, *very* proud."

"Woman." He laughed.

"We have two choices here: You can either change back into a hound as we move out or I can give you my jeans."

Connor stared at me incredulously.

"What? My shirt will cover my undies and the pants are stretchy."

"Not that stretchy."

"Then be a good boy and change for mama."

I looked to Agatha. "I'm sorry to drag you into all this."

"You didn't. This is the universe's plan for all of us."

"Where will you go?" I asked.

"Don't worry about me. I have places to lay low without you around to track."

"Safe travels, Agatha," I said.

"Safe travels, Simone."

Connor gave Agatha a silent thank you, dropping his head right before he changed into his hound form. "Get on my back," he said inside my head. I climbed on his back and with a wave to Agatha, we took off.

"Where are we going to go?" I asked him.

"Only one place I can think to go where you'll be safe."

In an instant, I knew it.

Hades.

# CHAPTER Ten

Connor ran through the night. A blur of animal running faster than any human eyes had the ability to focus on until we finally reached Raven, the cemetery, and finally, the mausoleum.

"What are we going to do for clothes?" I asked once he stopped. "You can't go down there naked."

"Since I don't usually have the time to strip before I change, Luc keeps a special closet that's always stocked for me."

"Okay, but you won't change back until you have something to dress in?"

He laughed in my head. It came out sounding like a gruff grumble in real life. "Doesn't take much, does it?"

"No. And it's annoying." This whole *protective mate* bit. But then again, I wouldn't have been too pleased with Jeffery going completely buff in front of other people. Not that he couldn't have done it if he'd wanted to. His body, his choice, and all that. I just wouldn't have liked it much and I *really* didn't like the idea of Connor baring it all to the masses.

"How are you feeling?" he asked.

"Still a bit tired. I should've asked what she'd given me."

"From now on, we ask before you drink."

The door to the mausoleum opened. Connor started down the stone spiral steps. The door closed again behind us.

Luc stood at the mouth of the hallway with his arms folded over his chest, glaring at my mate and me. "Took you long enough. Do you realize how late you are?"

Connor gestured to Luc's office with a tip of his head and continued past the fallen angel without stopping. Once the three of us got to the room and the door was shut, Connor walked over to the closet that I hadn't noticed the last time I'd been in here. He changed to a man, only giving me a glimpse of his tight behind as he ducked inside.

A few moments later, he stepped out in jeans and a T-shirt. Blue jeans. Red T-shirt. He had socks and a pair of red-and-white-checked Vans in his hand. He walked over to the infamous sofa, the one we'd first—*ahem*–on. Yeah, that one. And he dropped down to slide on the socks and shoes.

I stood mesmerized, watching him. "*Damn…*" I accidentally let slip. Both Connor and Luc looked at me. "What?" I asked. "I'm a lucky woman. I get to hit that." Connor chuckled as I pointed at him.

"So why are you late?" Luc asked. "You should've started hours ago."

"*Shit*. Forgot to call. Simone was visited by a woman in her dream. She had some important things to say to Simone, but we didn't understand it all. We met with a witch to see if Simone could remember when she was born and we were attacked."

"Attacked?"

Connor nodded.

"By who?"

"That's the ten-million-dollar question," Connor added. "His face was blurred."

Luc cocked his head. "Blurred?"

"As if a spell had been put on him to purposely obscure his features. He was large and wore head-to-toe black."

"That could have been anybody," Luc unhelpfully answered.

"Luc," I said to get his attention. When I had it, I asked, "What do you know?"

His chin jerked back as if I'd hit him. "Excuse me?"

"I don't mean you were involved with my attack, but when Connor and I first met, you told him to get to me, that 'something started' or something along those lines. My gut tells me that everything going on is a whole lot bigger than me. I think there's a reason Jeffery died, and that Connor's sister disappeared. And I think they're both related to why I was attacked."

Luc walked over to sit at his desk. "We all have quadrants down here." He pulled open a drawer to grab an ancient-looking —but in remarkably good condition—map, unrolling it. "Obviously, this area falls under my jurisdiction." Luc's quadrant encompassed all of North America, Central America, and South America, along with all the islands in close proximity. "Lev gets the oceans because none of the rest of us wanted to take that on." Luc then went on to point to different quadrants on the map with different names in each quadrant. "As you can see, some of us have larger quadrants than others—Mo was so ticked that he didn't get South America. He's always thought of himself as a Latin Lover."

"Mo?" I asked and both he and Connor narrowed their pretty eyes on me like I was the dim kid in class.

"AsMOdeus," Luc replied. "Demon of Lust. You might have heard of him." I crossed my arms over my chest and shot him my meanest *'say one more word and I'll end you'* eyes. "Anyway," he went on, looking back down at the map while snickering. "It has the potential to equal out because some smaller quadrants have vastly larger numbers of people to corrupt."

"Right." I checked my temper. "That makes sense. But what does any of this have to do with Connor and me?"

"That, I don't know. Think of it like the mob. Bosses want more territory."

I nodded my understanding.

"We all keep track of the goings-on in the other quadrants.

When Connor first met you, even though he wasn't sure it was you… Actually, I have a theory about that. I think your powers were bound as a baby. Whatever you are, you're too strong to keep them bound forever. But that's why our boy here didn't exactly know it was you." *Wow!* That made total sense. "Anyway, when you two first crossed paths, the other quadrants lit up. I'd had a feeling that something was coming; I'd had that feeling a long time. When the quadrants lit up, I knew whatever is coming started that day and it started with you and Connor meeting."

"And you neglected to tell me this why?" Connor practically growled at his friend who I felt, even as a fallen angel, was taking his life in his hands.

"I told you what I could. You knew I had that bad feeling. You also knew when I felt it start. But I can't tell you everything. It would take away the fun of watching you swing."

"Even if it involves me and *my mate*?"

"Even then. I hate that it's that way, but it *is* that way. I don't make the rules. You get an audience with the big guy upstairs, feel free to ask him why. Until then, my hands are tied sometimes."

Connor chuffed a couple of times. "Can we go back to Simone's powers?" Given the chuffing and the tone of his voice, it was clear he vacillated between sulking and wanting to tear Luc's office apart in a fit of anger. "Tell me more about your theory."

He turned thoughtful eyes on me. "It's just something that I've been thinking about."

"Why did my powers only show on the full moon?" I asked.

"Because it's the most powerful time of the month. With your strength and the power of the full moon, the binding couldn't hold. And you both know you two are more powerful together. That's the purpose of mates."

"But we're not regular mates," Connor said, stepping closer to me. He wrapped his arm around my waist, tugging me taut against his chest. Luc waited, hands folded over the map, for Connor to finish. "Agatha—that's the witch we sought out to help us—she told us that I'm her protector."

Luc raised his eyebrow. "You're Agatha's protector?"

"No, come on, man." He *tsked*. "I'm Simone's protector. That's why we're mates."

"But protectors are saved for—"

"Important people," I finished for him. "Yeah, we heard. Who else besides fallen angels get protectors?"

"You don't have to be fallen. Anyone important to the world, you know, that whole good-versus-evil dynamic, gets a protector. But when you're mated to your protector…" He trailed off as if forming another thought. "That's huge," he finally finished.

Huge. Of course. Why would it have been anything different?

"Who is this Agatha?" Luc asked next.

"She's a very powerful witch," I said. "Old family. Goes back centuries."

"Did this Agatha tell you anything else?"

"Only that we need to get to Ireland. Her relative should be able to help me access my memories again. We need to find out who my parents were so I can find out what I am. Agatha, Connor, and I believe that whatever I am, it's relevant to what's going on."

Luc pondered this a moment. "At the end of your shift, you can take her through the catacombs. It'll be the fastest way for you to get her to Ireland without being seen."

"Catacombs?" I asked.

He nodded. "They connect the quadrants. A lot of us don't go topside often. It tends to lead to trouble. But that doesn't mean we don't take meetings."

I looked to Connor. He dipped his chin once. Although we were still new to this silent communication thing, I thought he got me. We didn't have time to wait until his end of shift. Even as much as I hated to leave Luc in the lurch, he had to understand why Connor would do that.

People attacked us tonight.

To kill us.

Kill.

Us.

I let that thought sink in. I hated that thought.

"I'm showing Simone around the place," Connor said. "Call me if you need me." Then he held his hand out to me. The moment I grabbed it, Connor started pulling me out of the office, and with his long stride, I struggled to keep up with him.

"Take it down a notch there, Beethoven. There's plenty of time to show me around."

"Beethoven? Now you're really reaching."

"*Huh*—I thought it was a cleverly used example of a lesser-talked-about dog movie."

Connor rolled his eyes at me while shaking his head in what I thought looked a lot like humorous exasperation. But I'd like to note that although he found me exasperating, he slowed down, too. We moved down a hallway that I'd never been in before, obviously, since I'd only ever been down the hallway that led to Luc's office.

The farther away from Luc's office we walked, the grumpier the faces of the people or demons around us grew. It both said good things about Luc and bad things about the others who ran Hades.

Eventually, we hit a set of stairs that appeared to head down into a basement. "Do I want to know what's in the basement of hell?" I asked.

"In this case, you do." He tugged me to get moving along with him down the steps. The stone walls on either side gave off a rotten egg smell. I fanned my hand in front of my nose. "Ugh… no more chicken for you. Bad dog."

He glared. I snickered. Quietly, of course.

"Connor, where are you taking me?"

He didn't answer until we reached the bottom step, which opened into a kind of narrow hallway made of stone that seeped water from the water table and left puddles on the ground. "Catacombs."

I stared at him, approvingly. "Are you breaking the rules?" I asked giddy that he not only totally got me in Luc's office, but he went off script for me. "I mean, didn't Luc say you couldn't use these until the end of your shift?" So I really didn't think my look back in Luc's office would work on Connor as much as annoy him. Score one for Simone.

"Luc doesn't have a mate who was attacked tonight."

"Aw, Connor Baghest, does this mean you like me?"

"Not by choice," he deadpanned and I threw my head back laughing but quickly covered my mouth to keep others from hearing us. He pulled me in for a quick kiss before leading us into the hallway.

"Wow, you really do like my booty, to go all rogue guardian." I bumped his hip with mine.

"I've had worse."

"And by worse, you mean everyone who wasn't me?"

"If you absolutely need that confirmation to massage your ego."

"Massage me harder, baby."

"Not joking, babe. Stay close to me and stay alert. We're heading into Sat's quadrant. He's a nasty piece of work."

"Sat?" I asked. Connor stared at me, lips pursed, waiting for it to click. Then it clicked. "Sat? Do you mean Satan?"

"There you go."

"Give me a break. We aren't all on a nickname basis with underlords."

"Man acts like a tyrannical Goodfella."

"Um… yikes!"

"Ever wonder why that part of the world has historically seen so many wars?"

I wrinkled my nose.

"Exactly."

"I thought Satan and Lucifer were one and the same," I said while it hit me that we were actually heading into *Satan's* quadrant.

He shook his head. "Nope. That's something the mortals got wrong. Although, some theologians got it right. There're a few lists floating around." Then he put a finger to his lips.

I nodded and kept in step right beside him as he led me through the maze of dank tunnels. Finally, we hit a stairwell.

"I need you to make it so they can't see us," Connor said, stopping me before ascending the steps. "Probably better if they can't sense us, either. Think you can do that?"

"I'll do my best." Then I began to think the words: *"Don't let them see us. Don't let them sense us."* I chanted those over and over in my head.

"I can still see you and myself," he said, sounding defeated.

"That's because I didn't manifest for *you* not to see us. Is that what you want?"

"No. Not if you're sure this'll work."

"I think it will. It has in the past, but there's a reason I don't offer a money-back guarantee."

He pressed his forehead to mine. "You got this," he whispered. I smiled. For Connor, for Connor and I to have a chance at a future together, I believed I had this.

Nodding, I took the first step up the stairs with my mate at my side. To be on the safe side, I continued to chant my chant in my head until we reached the top of the stairs, entering into a beige, governmental office straight out of the 1970s, sucking all fun and happiness out of the air. If working in a place like this didn't make one vengeful, I didn't know what would.

"This is horrible," I whispered. "Maybe if we painted his office lilac, he'd give up the wrath."

"Sweetheart, he chose the color scheme to make his employees hate their lives. Wrath is in his blood."

*Oh, right.* With that little ditty of information floating around in my head, it was now or never. We walked holding hands down the ugly hallway, unforgiving incandescent lighting and all, passing cubicle after cubicle without anyone turning a head. We weren't out of the woods yet. Those employees could've been conditioned to keep their heads down, nose-to-the-grindstone, and all that.

A man in an ill-fitting business shirt and beige slacks with pleats walked out of one of the offices along with a woman in a very unflattering gray dress and her hair pulled back in a tight bun. They moved right past us without a second glance, and I melted against Connor. As he led us to the stairwell that opened to Ireland, another office door opened. In the doorway stood a man. He scared the crap out of me. Black hair slicked back. Dark suit with a white button-down, the top two buttons undone at the collar. He wore thick, gold chains and all his fingers sported thick, gold rings. A scar ran down the left side of his face.

That had to be him.

*Satan.*

Connor tugged me to keep moving. For just a moment, I swore he glanced in our direction, but it passed quickly and we ran up those steps. My calves and thighs burned by the time we reached the top, but the door opened and we stepped outside, finding ourselves next to a mausoleum that might have been even older than the one in Raven. The cemetery definitely was way older.

"Don't take the juju off us yet," Connor whispered.

I didn't plan on it.

We walked to the edge of the cemetery, out the old gate, onto Irish soil.

Now we had to find Agatha's relation.

That should be easy.

Not.

# CHAPTER Eleven

"We need to head to County Cork. That's where Agatha's relation is located," I said, in awe of the fact that I actually stood in Ireland. Both feet on the ground. Here. "Do we know where we are now?"

Connor pulled my phone out of my pocket to check our location. "It looks like we're in County Kerry. Cork is the next county over to the southeast."

"But Cork is a big county."

"We'll make it work. We don't have a choice."

No truer words. We had to make it work. Period.

As I still felt sluggish, I had Connor remove his clothing and drop down into his hound form in order to carry me. I ended up compromising with myself, manifesting the directions we needed to go to get us to Agatha's relation rather than just trying to manifest us there because I just didn't have it in me. It took extra juju to cloak myself from the non-supers we passed because explaining how I zipped across a field faster than most humans could run, and doing it not touching the ground because only supers could see Connor in his hound form, might've gotten a little tricky.

Turn by turn, directions sped through my mind, but they

gave me enough time to relay them to my mate before leaving. I was my own personal GPS. How cool was that?

Connor, for his part, didn't act at all winded. But if anyone got a look at his physique, they wouldn't question why. The man had it going on in all the ways.

The directions headed us toward an old town called Youghal, which upon our arrival, we found to be a quaint seaside town. But we weren't done. We needed to find a section of town called Moll Goggin's Corner.

How did I not know this place existed? Clearly, my worldly education lacked, if not in all the ways, then definitely in this one. What wasn't lacking? The power that radiated off of one little stone home in particular. The front of the home had been decorated with a plethora of plants, unlike all the other homes surrounding it. And as I made money from plants, I knew that these had special powers. To keep away evil. Disease. Unwanted guests. Rue, oregano, rosemary, and thyme, just to name a few. A cook wouldn't hang their herbs outside the front door, so far from the kitchen.

"This is it," I said to Connor. He stopped, allowing me to climb off his back. It seemed too big a risk to uncloak myself in broad daylight. Hoping I wasn't making a big mistake, I walked up to the front door and knocked. The plan was to slip inside and uncloak then. Though as a super, she'd see Connor. I hoped he didn't scare her out of opening the door enough for that to happen. From what I understood, it wasn't usual for a death hound to show up on your front stoop.

The door opened to reveal a wrinkled, old woman, possibly arthritic, as she hunched over, her hands mangled. She had a wild, dried bird's nest of hair and a mole bigger than her nose under her left eye. She stood in the doorway, her eyes traveling from where I stood still cloaked, as if she saw me, then behind me to Connor.

In an accent almost too thick to understand, she ushered us inside. "Best come in before any sense you out."

We stepped inside and I turned to shut the door. When I turned back, the woman who'd been withered seconds ago now appeared as young as Agatha. I stepped back, shocked. Her deep-auburn hair shimmered like strands of copper flowing down her back. She looked at us through eyes of buckwheat honey.

"The protector can go in there"—she pointed to a small half-bath—"to change." She knew I stood there? How?

I handed off Connor's clothing to him, well, I laid them on his back, and he walked into the half-bath. I pulled the door shut.

"You may reveal yourself now," she said. Mind totally blown. No one, not even Luc or Satan, had been able to truly sense me the way she did.

Part of me wondered if I needed to be cautious, but the more dominant part knew that she was the one I needed to see and so I manifested myself to be seen again.

"I'm Ainsling," she said. "You are?"

"My name is Simone."

"And your protector?"

"Connor," I answered for him because he was still in the bathroom dressing. "We were sent to you by Agatha—"

"I know of Agatha." She cut me off. "She's a powerful witch, indeed. I knew to expect a visitor, though the winds didn't tell me who."

At that point, Connor walked out of the half-bath. He draped his arm around my waist to pull me in close to his body. Ainsling watched us.

"Your protector is *very* protective, I see."

"Yeah, he's kind of a lug, but he's growing on me." I laughed as Connor kissed the top of my head.

"We don't get mated protectors around here often."

"But you do get them?" Connor asked.

She nodded. "The last one was a couple of years back. She and her mate needed my help."

"With what? If you don't mind me asking," I asked.

"Well, he had great powers, like the ones I sense in you. And like you, his felt bound."

"His? The person like me was a man?"

"Please, come sit. You need refreshment before we continue."

Connor looked a second and a half away from going all hound smash on her, but I reached up to scratch behind his ear and he shook his head at me instead. At least for now, these antics worked on him. Though I couldn't say for how long.

We followed her into a sitting room with air thick with incense just like Agatha's place. What was it with witches and flowery incense? She already had tea and cakes waiting for us, as she'd known we were coming.

I accepted the tea and a buttery cake and I scowled at Connor, who tried to refuse. The cake made the trip worth it. It was *that* good.

"What can you tell me about this other who had bound power?" I asked after swallowing the bite.

"He was strong, but yours is stronger. The bindings bound tighter. Someone really needed you not to have access to them."

"Agatha had me go back in time to my birth, but it felt like lifetimes ago. Can you help me figure this out?"

"His name was Simeon. I could never forget him. He reminded me very much of you Simone. And his mate, a beautiful woman. Different name. A surname here."

"Madigan?" Connor asked and he looked ready to puke doing it. His sister. Wow. His sister had a protected mate, too. Just like Connor. I knew this whole thing was connected somehow.

A feeling of dread swooped in fast almost overwhelming me. What were we about to get ourselves into next?

Whatever we were about to face, Ainsling sensed it as she nodded once solemnly. Immediately, I set my tea and cake down in order to move to Connor's lap to best give him comfort. He held me close.

"Where did you send them?" I asked.

"Before I tell you, you must know, that like the protector mates Simeon and Madigan, you have an air of destiny about you. His, as yours, comes from a far-off place. One I cannot put a lock on. But I can give you a tea to talk with my most powerful ancestor long departed. She can guide you in a way I cannot."

"No," Connor said at the same time I said, "Yes, please."

Another tea. I already wasn't at my full strength yet. But if this was my only option, then I had to take it.

"Connor, baby—I have to. You know I do."

"You haven't recovered from Agatha's tea yet."

"I get that, but it's the only way. I'm agreeing with Ainsling and you have to let her do her magic."

He kissed me, pressing his forehead to mine, and hugged me tight. "I can't lose you," he whispered. "I can't let you be hurt."

"I won't be hurt. Just drained."

"You don't know that."

It was on the tip of my tongue to make a dog joke, but I held back. The situation simply didn't abide any levity.

Finally, he gave in, sighing. "Yeah, okay."

He gave his permission even though we'd both known I wasn't asking for it. I simply wanted him to be okay with the decision I'd come to. Ainsling stood up and hightailed it to her kitchen, my guess in case he changed his mind. But I wasn't planning on changing *my* mind.

While she was gone, Connor took my hand, squeezing it gently while placing our linked fingers on my knee. Dare I say, lovingly? *"Please.* I don't want you drinking that tea. I can't protect you while you're under."

I pressed my head to his neck to snuggle in further. "Think about it, babe. Really think about it. We have people trying to kill us. Your sister and her mate, a mate I'll add she never even told you about, showed up here then went missing?"

"I know." He huffed out a breath. "But I can't lose you. We're tied together, Simone. It hurts, but I can live without my sister. I can't live without you. As fucked-up as this is, I wouldn't want to."

"Wow, Connor Baghest, I think you *do* like me."

He kissed me. One of those power-packed, *giving you everything he was feeling without saying a word* kind of kisses.

Way too soon, we heard a throat clear and he pulled out of the kiss. I was simultaneously ready to meet this ancient ancestor and ready to punch Ainsling for interrupting such a monumental moment.

"Can I ask you to sit over in this chair?" Ainsling pointed to a ratty, old, well-worn, well-loved brown leather chair similar to Agatha's but not a recliner. This had an equally ratty, old, well-worn, well-loved ottoman moved in front of it for me to prop my feet up on.

Giving Connor's hand one more squeeze, I moved from his lap to the chair. The soft cushions enveloped me as I sank down into them and I set about getting comfortable by propping my feet up on the ottoman while I waited for Ainsling to pour the hot brew.

"You must drink it all down," she said while handing me off the cup.

I nodded, blowing on it to cool down the surface, and whispered, "Bottoms up," before gulping it down. Two gulps and I'd emptied the cup. My mouth tasted heavily of licorice, which I was sure she'd added to aid the flavor, which otherwise tasted heavily of rosemary, mugwort, and passionflower. There were other herbs in the brew; those just came out the strongest.

It only took a second for me to begin feeling the power coursing through me. I closed my eyes, though I didn't have to because the tea lulled them closed to allow me to travel. I left my body, flipping back through history until reaching the correct moment in time. A beautiful woman of maybe forty waved me in exactly like those men with the orange vests and flares on an airport tarmac did for the jets.

And when I landed, she smiled, speaking to me in a tongue I didn't know yet fully understood again. Magic was trippy.

"I've been waiting for you, Simone Lamia. I am Sirona."

"That's a beautiful name."

She graciously dipped her head in a thank you. "You seek the other."

"Yes."

"Then he did not succeed in finding you."

I snapped my head back. "Me?"

"Yes. The other came to me looking to seek you out."

"What? How? Did he say how he knew about me?"

"The other, his powers were bound as are yours. Your protector is key. He will help break the binds."

"That's why I've started getting more powerful since we met? He's supposed to help me break the bindings?"

She nodded. "There is evil in the works, Simone. Pure evil prepared to destroy the beauty of the world for greed. They sought you out years ago. Should you fall, the world has no chance."

"Then why did they go after Simeon? We never met. I grew up in foster care."

"You are him. He is you."

"That makes no sense. What does any of this have to do with the amulet from the dagger of Lilith?"

"Reunite the amulet with the hilt. The blade will appear. Only those gifted the powers from the mother of witches may wield the dagger."

"The mother of witches? Lilith?"

She nodded again.

"What is my connection to Lilith?"

"The answer you seek has been blocked from me. I fear the evil follows you to keep you ignorant. Knowledge is power. Seek out the knowledge."

"Where?"

"There are witches' archives located far out on Orkney. You

must head for the Knap of Howar. The Knap of Howar. This is important. Speak the words: *Cuir isteach mar chara*. A stone staircase will open for you. Only you and your protector will be able to enter because he is connected to you. Follow the steps down. If you are safe, the archives will present themselves to you."

"Okay. God, I hope I can remember those words."

"We are not finished. To close the archives, you must speak the words: *Fág mar aon ní amháin*. It is vital that you close the archives, Simone. Do you understand?"

I nodded. "Yes."

"Devastation and death will come to all witches should you fail to close the archives. The balance of power will shift to the darkness. Those who seek the light will perish, for once the witches fall, one by one, all supers will fall." She shuddered.

"But I thought you said only Connor and I could enter because of our connection."

"Evil has attached itself to you. I feel it even now. Your power keeps it in check. It cannot act, only watch, but if you forget to close the archives, evil may leave a piece of itself behind without your magic to fend it off."

As if life wasn't complicated enough before. I let out a slow breath. "Okay. Knap of Howar, Orkney. *Cuir isteach mar chara* to open the archives. *Fág mar aon ní amháin* to close them. And make extra sure no matter what to close them. Yeah?"

"Yes. You must return to your time now. I sense the protector growing agitated even through the loop."

"Connor's a little overprotective."

"You will be glad of it in the coming weeks. Blessed be, Simone. Until we meet again."

"Will we meet again?"

"Blessed be," she repeated, then she swiped her hands in the air as if shooing me off and disappeared from view.

My eyes popped open to find the beautiful Connor squatting down next to the chair, holding my hand. "Hey, babe," I said groggily through a half-smile.

He audibly relaxed. His taut shoulders melted back into a position of calm.

"You were gone an hour, Simone. I thought… I thought…"

I brought my hand up to hold his cheek. "I'm back. I'm fine. Sirona had a lot to say."

"Well?" he asked.

"We're headed for Orkney." *And our impending doom,* but I thought better of relaying that bit of information for now.

I had a connection to Simeon. I am him. He is me. Whatever the hell that meant. We both had a connection to Lilith.

Dread filled me.

I literally carried the fate of the world.

But Connor, Connor carried me.

We could do this.

We had to.

"Eat more of the cake before you leave," Ainsling said. "It will help to recharge you."

Once Connor heard that he immediately spun to grab my only partially eaten butter cake, dropping that and the regular, old lemon ginger tea onto the table next to my chair.

"Eat," he ordered.

I picked up the cake, taking a huge, overly exaggerated bite to make him feel better, but also to get him to see he was being a bit pushy. Yes, I needed a power-up. But I wasn't dying.

"You must eat, too," Ainsling ordered Connor. "The road ahead is fraught with danger. To protect yourself and your mate, you must fuel your body."

He looked about ready to argue, but I raised my eyebrow in challenge. He dropped back down into his seat and proceeded to cram the whole slice of cake into his mouth. I laughed when he started to cough.

"Serves you right for being an idiot," I said, taking another daintier bite than him.

Once we'd finished with our tea and cakes, I used the bathroom and then I dropped a cloak over myself again. Ainsling gave me a backpack to carry Connor's clothing in. Although the cakes started to help, we moved faster with Connor in hound form. She opened the door for us. I called up Orkney in my mind and the directions began to flash for me again.

Nobody told me they were located in the Atlantic Ocean off of Scotland. Seriously? The scenery flew by in a blur. Despite how fast Connor ran, it took us way longer to reach the ocean off of Scotland than it had for us to reach Cork from Kerry.

Once we made it to the shore, and after we made sure no one was around to see us, I dropped the cloak and Connor shifted back to man. He dressed quickly because neither of us wanted to waste time with me keeping him out of jail on exposure charges.

"How're you feeling?" he asked.

"A little tired."

"Can you get us to the island or do we need to find other transportation?"

"I think I can get us onto the island."

"You *think*, Simone? I'll find us a boat."

"No." I threw out my hand to stop him. "I can. I can get us there. Trust me, babe. I can do this."

He pinched the bridge of his nose, squeezing his eyes shut. "You're going to be the death of me." Like I hadn't heard that before. We could consider it Connor's mantra by this point in our not-so-long relationship. The universe had a sense of humor, that was for sure.

"Nah. I have too many plans for you later on. But I need you to hold on to me—as tightly as you can."

As asked, he stepped behind me, pressing our bodies together as he wrapped his arms around my waist. He moved my hair off my shoulder with his chin and rested it there.

"Ready, baby," he whispered. I closed my eyes, chanting the words over and over in my head. Knap of Howar, Orkney. With Connor holding on tight, we moved from the pebbly beach on Scottish soil to standing in tall, lush green grass surrounding two stone dwellings without roofs. They looked thousands of years old. Neolithic.

The wind picked up when we stepped inside, a sudden rain event pelting us, and I had to wonder if the site felt our power and was trying to keep us out.

"Now what?" Connor asked.

Because I didn't know where to speak the words, I stood in the center of the room of the larger dwelling and spoke the words Sirona told me to speak. *"Cuir isteach mar chara."*

God, I hoped I pronounced that correctly. Did magic give points for trying? I guessed not since nothing appeared to happen, other than Connor and I getting pummeled by the wind and rain. I took in a big breath and tried again. *"Cuir isteach mar chara."*

"What's supposed to happen?" he asked.

"A staircase is supposed to open up for us, leading down into the archives."

"Would it open out here where any mortal could see it?"

That got me thinking. Probably not. I tugged Connor along behind me over to the—the best I gathered, it had once served as a connection like a small hallway between the two dwellings. No mortal would see inside unless standing right by the opening.

I spoke the words one more time. *"Cuir isteach mar chara."* Then I watched in awe as crumbling rocks dissolved into thin air, revealing an archway with stairs leading down. "Come on. Hold me and stay close," I ordered my mate. The moment he cleared the archway stepping down onto the first stone step, the entrance closed behind him.

Flames illuminated the steps for each one to come, extinguishing on their own once we'd passed it. Almost a hundred steps down, we entered into a large, stone room that should've been wet and dank but felt dry and warm from the purple flame burning in the hearth, which burned smokeless and I assumed fumeless because I smelled nothing.

The room was set up like a library. Shelves and shelves of books. Beyond the books, we found shelves and shelves of scrolls from the time before books.

"Where do we start?" Connor asked.

"I don't know. Is there a card catalog?" I laughed at my own stupid joke. "If you find one, we need writings on Lilith."

Apparently, the room heard me because several books moved forward on their shelves to be plucked up by me or Connor. And in the very back of the section of scrolls, three moved from their spots. I walked back to get those while he grabbed the books for me and we walked them over to the table that rested in front of the hearth.

While the books clearly held some importance, I opted to go for the scrolls, opening what I thought to be the oldest first. I didn't know how I discerned this; the idea just popped into my head, drawing me to it. Carefully, I unrolled the scroll to reveal a form of writing I was sure had been lost to the world for millennia.

The words began to flame blue, lifting from the pages to arrange themselves in midair, dropping back to the page as I read each one. I knew a dead language. Mind blown. But that wasn't even the best part. As I continued to read, pictures surrounded Connor and me. The exact pictures the words described.

*"Adam is a lie, claiming superiority over me and my children. He brings no power to this land. The fertile garden imbued me with all the magic. Magic I have passed on to my children. With his every attempt to lord over us, I find myself more disdainful of the man and my life with him."*

Wow.

That said so much.

I kept on reading. *"My children find comfort with me. None with the man. If he does not leave them be, he will pay for his crimes."*

Connor pulled on my sleeve, pointing to one of the pictures of Adam raising his fist to a boy and the woman from my dream —she pushed in between the boy and Adam, taking the blow to herself instead, but as she slowly stood, recovering, the woman punched Adam back. Clearly, he hadn't seen it coming, taking a couple of steps back to keep from going down, but she moved in, swiping his legs out from underneath him. I watched in horrified fascination as he hit the ground and his head bounced off the hard, packed dirt. She dropped down, pinning him to the spot with her knee to his neck.

*"Hear this, Adam," she says. "Should you raise another fist to my children, it will be the last thing I ever allow you to do."*

"Connor—that's her," I whisper-shrieked.

"Who?"

"The woman from my dream. The one who talked to me. That's her."

"It couldn't be her. That's Lilith."

"Duh. I get that. And I also know I talked with her."

Believe me or not, I didn't care. I had to see what happened next. We moved further down the scroll, but it seemed to be about how hostilities had grown between Lilith and Adam, yet he never made another attempt to hurt the children physically. That didn't mean he wasn't a verbally abusive asshole. The pictures showed more than I wanted to see. It physically hurt *me* to witness those poor children wounded by someone who should have loved them and protected them.

I opened the next scroll.

*"He proved himself too much of a coward to raise a hand to the children again. Rather, he berated and belittled them. Innocent children. This was no haven for them, living with this monster. Having had enough, I stole away with them, leaving him to wither alone without my magic to keep the bounty of the gardens flowering lushly.*

*"As the children grow, they flourish. I met another, a man who calls himself Zohor. He is light. He is love. He teaches the children. Gives them guidance. We walk side by side, hand in hand. I consider him my equal as he considers me his. I gift him my love. We create more beautiful children together. I choose this life with Zohor over any time spent in my garden."*

"Wait." Connor turned to me confused. "I thought Lilith had an affair with Satan."

"It doesn't appear so. She sounds happy."

"This is playing out like a soap opera."

*"My garden is no more,"* she wrote. *"Adam, he ruined it, blaming it on the poor one who replaced me. He remains bitter and hateful. I have learned he has besmirched my name, telling lies by shifting the blame onto me as well. This poor woman, I know with whom she lives. But I cannot decide if I should help her escape as clearly, she holds none of the power bestowed upon me in the magic garden."*

Connor leaned into me, pressing a kiss to my temple. "What was that for?" I asked.

"I was just thinking it's no wonder so many human men are dicks if everyone can be linked back to him."

"Where do supers originate from then?"

"Well, clearly, other people lived close by if she found a new man. Just not in her garden."

"Oh, it sounds like he lived quite a bit of life in her garden," I quipped back.

He laughed, kissing me again, this time on my lips.

"Do you think he was given life from the mud the same as Adam and Lilith?" I asked.

"I don't know. It wasn't mud from the garden if he was. I mean, aside from being good and kind, he seems completely human."

It was my turn to laugh, punching him in the shoulder. "I can't believe you said that."

"What? You know it's the truth. Supers are far more accepting than humans."

Okay, I had to give him that.

We moved on to read more.

*"My children have continued to grow strong in heart and strong in magic. But as we remain isolated and my two oldest children have come of age, Zohor agreed to stay behind with the younger ones while the three of us travel to seek out acceptable mates for them.*

*We have been in the city two nights when we come face to face with a woman, eye blackened. I hug her, this stranger, then press my palm to the injury to remove it. She begins to cry in my arms. As I am holding her, I am met with a voice I never wished to hear again. 'She belongs to me. Take your hands from her.'*

*My children move to stand next to me as I turn.*

*'She does not belong to you.'*

*His mouth drops open in shock.*

*'Hello, Adam.'*

*'Is that the girl?' he asks. 'She'll fetch a good price.'*

*'She is none of your concern. Come near and die.'*

*The woman with us whimpers. He orders her back over to him. I offer my protection, but knowing not of me, she thinks me simply a woman the same as she, unable to protect her or myself from his fist. He flies into a rage upon her approach, striking her repeatedly. I raise my hand, using the wind to pummel him until my son stops me as a crowd begins to gather.*

*We find men and women whom we believe would suit, bringing them back to our land. There, we put Adam out of our minds while the men court my daughter and my son courts the women to find which one would suit the best. They are welcome to stay, should they not be chosen. I have younger children who will soon come of age and they are free to court one another as well.*

*As the days move by, I teach all the uses of magic. My children hold more magic than those not of my blood. My oldest two hold the most magic of all my offspring as they came into the world in my garden. But as Zohor holds a form of magic of his own, a magic not bestowed unto Adam, not as powerful as mine, but magic nonetheless, all my children have gifts above others.*

*I have started a grimoire with which they are to study.*

*My son has made his match. She is lovely."*

I stand to stretch. "This is getting intense."

"Is it bad that I want to bang you against this table right now?"

"Connor!"

"What? All this talk of magic is turning me on."

"Sorry, bud. Not the time for slap and tickle."

"Simone, baby, it's almost always the time for slap and tickle."

"I could use something to eat, though. I'm starved. How long have we been here?"

He pulled out my phone from the backpack. "Uh... *hours.*" Then he stood to stretch as well.

"I don't suppose we could get a meatball hoagie around here?"

"Baby," he sighed. "We get home, I'll buy you a hundred meatball hoagies."

"One footlong will suffice."

As we stood there talking about food, the strangest thing happened. A pot appeared bubbling away over the fire in the hearth. Freshly baked bread, bowls, spoons, and tumblers of wine materialized at the edge of the table away from where we had the scrolls and books piled.

"You do this?" he asked.

I shook my head. "But it's good to know witches."

# CHAPTER Thirteen

While we filled ourselves on the bounty given to us by witches—the stew needed a bit more salt, but otherwise was delicious—we read on. These scrolls grew darker in tone. And I had a feeling we were going to find out what we were after.

The blue, flaming words lifted from the paper again. *"My daughter has chosen a mate. Baruch is a good man. His powers grow as he learns the ways of magic. My daughter is truly happy."*

"Okay," I said, taking another drink of my wine. "So it looks like these early men and women, the ones Lilith chose to bring back to her land, held some magic like Zohor. Where do we think that came from?"

Connor shrugged. "I think humans have always had some sort of magic in them. Look at psychics. They aren't supers. They just have the ability to tap into a magic that most people no longer have access to. For whatever reason, mortal people decided to suppress their magic to the point that it's not there any longer."

*"My beautiful daughter grows heavy with child,"* Lilith wrote. *"Baruch dotes on her, keeping her comfortable. He is more of a partner*

*and caregiver than Adam ever was to me when I carried my children, and he is every bit like my Zohor. She has chosen well."*

Her daughter was beautiful, looking very much like her mother. The pictures showed Baruch, his dark hair and tanned skin very much in keeping with that area of the world. But his eyes. They looked on his wife with so much love, I felt like crying, and it took a lot to get me to cry.

*"Adam has shown today. Out of nowhere, he has invaded our land with his cruel heart looking for my dearest Shoshana, my eldest child, my flower who grew in my garden amongst his cruelty.*

*'Where is she?' he demands.*

*'She is with her mate. Do you not have another woman to subjugate now? Your concerns are with her. Leave this land now.'*

*'You took my due.'*

*'I took nothing but what was mine. I grew those children in my womb. I brought them into this world without help or kindness from you. I nurtured them. They are* mine. *They have* always *been mine.'*

*'Eve is useless. She holds no magic. I want my magic back. You will give me my due. Shoshana will marry my son. She will give us back our magic, which you stole.'*

*'Shoshana has a mate. The magic was never yours. It was gifted to me. She will not marry your son. Children born to her will bring good upon the world, not the evil in your heart. This is your last chance, Adam. Go now and never return or I will end you—'*

*'Mother Lilith,' Baruch calls to me, running from the home he shares with my daughter. 'She needs you. Is time.'*

*'Go now, Adam—your last warning.'*

*Zohar and my son, Peter—fathered by Adam—race down over the hillside with their hands raised, prepared to defend me and their homes. They need not a spear or sword, or to take up any such arms against the intruder, for their magic is enough to defeat him.*

*'Mother Lilith,' Baruch calls to me again. 'Please.'*

*'Go,' Zohor says. 'Help our daughter.' Then he turns to Adam. 'Leave or die.'*

*'Peter?' Adam asks. 'You will come with me now.'*

*'My home is here, with my family,' Peter answers. I need to get to my daughter, but I worry for my dearest partner and my eldest son.*

*'I am your father!' Adam shouts.*

*Peter laughs humorlessly. 'You were never anything but cruel. Zohor is my father.' Then he shoots out his hand. A gust of strong wind blows Adam off his feet. 'Never come back,' Peter orders.*

*As Adam scrambles to his feet and runs away like the coward I always knew him to be, he calls over his shoulder, 'You will be sorry you went against me.'*

*Once he is far enough away, I run up the grassy knoll to my daughter who needs me."*

It appeared that Agatha's family grimoire was wrong. Lilith wouldn't ever have left her son swinging. She loved him. That meant she cast her protection to her daughters *and sons*. Her daughters simply held more magic. *Women* held more magic. And that had to be why men spent so much effort trying to keep women down. All thanks to Adam.

"Wow," I said, wiping my face. "Adam was a real piece of work."

"So much makes sense now," Connor teased. "So much. Good thing our kids won't have a dick for a dad."

That got me. We'd never discussed kids. Not that there had really been time since we'd hooked up. But still… "Our kids?"

"Yeah, I figured we'd have a couple eventually. Don't you want kids?"

"Is it possible for me and you to have them, given you're a death hound and I'm whatever I am?"

"It's very possible, baby. The universe wouldn't have paired us if it weren't. And besides, it might be a good idea to bring a couple more protectors of the world into the world."

He had me there. "Can we discuss this topic when we no longer have men trying to kill us? I'm a little jaded at the moment."

"Simone, I won't let them hurt you. You're mine to protect and I will do that until my last breath."

"Which I'm hoping won't be for seventy or eighty more years."

"Seventy or eighty?"

"Well, I'm guessing I'll be tired of your old, wrinkled Shar Pei butt by then."

"*Woman.*" He shook his head before pulling me onto his lap. "What am I going to do with you?"

I nestled against his chest. "Thank you for not being Adam, well, at least not now. You were kind of an Adam when we first met."

"I was never an Adam, baby. I was confused, which made me a bit surly. But once I figured out who you were to me, I was surly because you liked to put yourself in dangerous situations."

"This will be the only time you'll get this, so mark it in your calendar, but I'll give you that point."

He threw his hand to the part of his chest not blocked by my body and whipped his head around. "The world must be ending. We need to find shelter."

"You're an idiot."

"Ah, but I'm *your* idiot." Then he pecked a quick kiss to the top of my head. "Shall we get back to it?"

I nodded, stretching out my legs and back again, doing a couple of bends and squats. Research took a lot out of a woman. When I felt ready, I took my seat again and went back to the scroll. Connor dropped down next to me and we both watched with rapt attention to what came next.

*"'My beautiful Shoshana, you are doing well, my love.' Baruch pushes her sweat-soaked hair back from her face.*

*'One more push,' I urge her, waiting to help bring my second grandchild into the world. She carried two. Two. Shoshana's sister, Libi, my oldest daughter with Zohor, holds our beautiful girl while Shoshana pushes with all her might.*

*'I cannot,' Shoshana shouts.*

*'You can, my love,' Baruch urges her on while I take a different approach.*

*'You will. Now Shoshana. You will do this now.'*

*My sweet daughter bears down one last time and I am able to help ease the babe out.*

*'A son,' I cry with a full heart. 'You have given our family a daughter and son.' I help to detach the boy and finished up the delivery while Baruch holds his son.*

*'My beautiful Shoshana, you have done well. He is strong and perfect, just as our daughter is. No man has more blessings on this night than do I.'"*

"Connor, did you see that?"

"Uh yeah, I'm scarred. You going to want me in the delivery room?"

I slapped him. "Not that part—and yes. If we have kids, your butt will be in there with me because I didn't get *myself* pregnant. But let's focus. I'm talking about the part where Shoshana had twins. A boy and girl."

"Yeah, that's crazy and highly sus."

It was more than sus and I needed to read more to confirm what I thought deep down I already knew, though, I'd admit, I had no idea how it was possible.

*"I take the baby girl from Libi, placing her on Shoshana's lap. Baruch approaches, placing the boy down next to the girl. He holds his family lovingly."*

"Connor—this is the part from my vision at Agatha's, only I never saw the boy. Just me."

"Keep reading," he ordered.

I looked back to the scroll. *"'My Simeon.' Shoshana softly breathes his name. 'My Simone.' We all whip our heads up in the direction of the commotion outside the dwelling.*

*'They are coming. Get her out.'" Lilith says to Baruch. We should have ended Adam when he'd shown up before. It is him. I know it is him coming for my Shoshana.*

*"'Give me the babe,' Adam says. My lovely Shoshana, so tired, holds almost no strength.*

*'No," she says. 'Libi.' My Libi bends down to grab Simeon.*

*'Get him to Peter,' I order, using my magic to protect her as she uses her own to escape. The sound of fighting rings through the land and I know my Zohor and my dearest sons and daughters are defending our home and our family.*

*Adam lunges for the innocent babe, Simone. Baruch throws himself onto the man as I lift the tiny girl into my arms. 'I will be back. I will fight.'*

*'Simone,' Shoshana cries and that is the last we hear. I move her to where Adam will never lay hands on her. 'My beautiful Simone,' I say with tears in my eyes. 'You are loved, my Simone. You are loved. Adam wanted your power. I fear that others worse than Adam will seek it for themselves as well.' I place my grimoire inside her swaddle. 'The universe will send you a protector when you need it. Until then, I must bind you—I am so sorry. You must know, dear child, that I do this to help you. I pray you understand.'*

*I bend down to kiss her head, then I step away from the building, using my magic to compel someone inside to find her. 'I must protect your brother now.'"*

"Holy—" Connor started.

"That's what I was afraid of."

"Baby, do you still have that book you had since you were born?"

"It's back at home. Connor, did you hear that? Simeon is my twin brother. He's... We're..."

"The grandchildren of Lilith and Adam. Yeah, I got that. I'm just not sure how to process it."

"*You* don't know how? Imagine being me."

"So now we know what you are—*wow*. I can't wrap my head around it. I've been sleeping with a direct descendant of Lilith."

"She spoke of you. The universe would send me a protector when I needed it. And here you are. Your family must be special for the universe to send you to me and your sister to my brother."

"What happened to Shoshana and Baruch?" he asked. "And to Zohor and the children he had with Lilith?"

"I don't know. But maybe they've had family lore passed down that might help us with whoever is trying to kill us now.

"And maybe they've been in contact with Simeon."

"But, Connor, we have to get the grimoire. With that, Simeon and I can join the amulet to the hilt of the dagger and the blade will appear."

"Did she say that?"

"No. But Agatha's ancestor told me and I feel it. I feel the action, the joining, coursing through my veins as if it's already happened. It *wants* to be joined again. I don't know how else to explain it."

"It's not safe to go home now. We know you were being followed."

"I think we were both being followed," I countered. None of whatever this was started happening without Connor. Beetle, the man I was sure was behind all this saw Connor the day he showed up to Monnie's Bar to protect me. Or more like retrieve me, but semantics. Connor was on bad guy radar, too. Period.

"Any ideas for what to do next? I'm practically useless because my whole body has gone into protection mode. Rather than coming up with plans, I'm on edge, waiting to eliminate any threat against you. It's annoying as hell, to tell you the truth —and before you get all bent, it's annoying because I want to help more. Not because I don't want to protect you."

"Is it bad that I want to bang *you* right now? That was… that was…"

"Baby, focus."

"Focus. Right. I think we need to find out if Lilith has any living descendants aside from me and Simeon."

"Then we've got more work ahead of us. We've got a few more scrolls and plenty of books to look through. One of them has to give us an idea of where to seek out more of Lilith's descendants."

We read for several more hours. In Lilith's own hand, we read that she'd gotten back to Shoshana and Baruch too late to save them. Shoshana had been too weakened from the long birth to fight and although Baruch had tried to protect her, Adam had used a hidden knife to end them both.

My parents. Adam murdered my parents. No wonder Lilith never came back for me. It was so unfair. I never got to know them. They never got to know me. I hated Adam. He robbed me of my family. He forced me to grow up scared and alone.

"I know what you're thinking," Connor said. "You shouldn't play poker."

"He took my family."

"He did. And I'm sorry about that, but if he hadn't, then I wouldn't have met you. That would've robbed me of *my* family—the one I have with you. And maybe it makes me a dick, but I can't be sorry that I've got you in my life."

I moved to straddle his lap. "Maybe there's time for a little rub and stroke?" I asked through my tears.

He kissed me, but my clothes stayed in place. "You were right before. We'll wait until we're in a bed where I can get creative and not have to think about witchy spells watching us."

The last book that we read had nothing to do with Lilith. Or at least not at first glance. It talked about a lab in England collecting DNA, like a 23andMe for supers. The book had been written just last year. The lab was in Birmingham.

"We need to go there, right?" Connor asked. "It wouldn't have presented itself for nothing."

"They might be able to put me in contact with other members of my extended family."

He shook his head. "Then I guess we're going to Birmingham."

We wrote down the information that we needed and when I stood and said, "It's time to go," the stairwell opened up. Connor grabbed my hand to lead me up the steps. He tried to keep walking, but I tugged my hand away to stop him.

"*Fág mar aon ní amháin,*" I said, hoping that, again, the witchy spell on the archives appreciated my attempt at pronunciation.

When Connor gave me a weird look I shrugged. "What? Bad things could happen if I don't close the archives. It has to be done."

"Anything else? Put your left hand in? Pull your left hand out?"

"I'm not doing the hokey pokey."

"Do you have the strength to manifest us to Birmingham or are we running?"

"I ate. We've been sitting for hours. I can't be sure, but I felt something tingly when I drank my wine. I think it had some healing properties like the witches knew I needed it."

"I love being a death hound, but witches are damn cool."

"Yeah, they are. So hold on tight and I'll manifest us to Birmingham."

Getting Connor to do anything that involved getting close and personal with me clearly wasn't a hardship for the man. Pretty much the moment the words left my mouth, he had himself pressed to my back, his arms around my shoulders. I sucked in a breath, closed my eyes, and pushed the thought of *Weik Laboratories, Birmingham,* out into the world. At full strength, the manifesting came easily to me.

It literally took us the time from me closing my eyes and pushing the thought to opening my eyes again to find that we'd landed in an alley between two brick buildings. Huge buildings. Several stories up. I couldn't know how wide until we headed out of the alley and I got to take in the full scope. Each building took up the length of the alley on their respective sides. Where I lived in my little corner of Michigan, we didn't have these massive modern monoliths—ooh... all M's. I liked how that sounded. Massive modern monoliths—*No. focus Simone.* It almost felt like the more my magic downloaded into my system, the more all over the place my thoughts traveled and I had a strong suspicion that little side effect would either become my best friend or get me into a world of trouble one day. I voted for best friend, but so far I didn't feel like my vote counted for much in the universal elections. If there even was such a thing.

"Which building do you think it is?" Connor asked, snapping me out of my head. I startled then smiled at him. His eyes dropped to my mouth. "What's that for?"

"What?"

"The smile. You take my breath away when you turn that smile on me. I can't think straight."

"I'm just glad you're with me now."

"Dammit, woman—" He snaked me into his arms again, pressing his cheek to the top of my head. "You can't say shit like that when we don't have time for me to act on it."

"I'm sorry."

"Don't be sorry. Just save that thought for when I can get you alone. Now, before I say screw the world, which building?"

I shrugged. "Don't know. It could be either one of these or it could be across the street. Magic lands us where it's safest, where we're least likely to be seen by someone who wants to burn us on a stake."

"So you don't have a feel yet?"

"It's harder to pinpoint because there's a lot of magic users here. That, I feel one hundred percent. And for the record, I'd rather you screw the Simone. I don't want to share with the world."

"Right," Connor grumbled, wiping a hand down his face. "We need to start looking." He reached for my hand and started to walk, leading us out of the alley onto the bright, sunny street.

"It's that one." I pointed to the building across the street from us.

"You sure? How do you know?"

Laughing, I dropped Connor's hand to move his head in the direction I wanted him to look. Namely, at the sign on the front of the building that read: *Weik Laboratories*.

"I'll be snookered," he mumbled. "They just put it out there?"

"Sometimes the best defense is to hide in plain sight. No one is going to go there unless they're seeking out their services."

Because Weik Laboratories was located on a busy street, we jogged up to the closest crosswalk and crossed with the others, mostly non-supers, needing to get wherever they were going, too.

Connor pulled the glass and metal door open for me to pass through first.

Magical energy filled every nook and cranny of the building.

"Oh, my…" The pretty, blonde receptionist with her plump, rosy cheeks said as we approached her desk. Her eyes grew wide. I couldn't discern whether she was 'oh, my'ing my mate or if it had to do with me.

When she tilted her head and asked, "What are you?" I sighed, knowing it was me. Well, until she turned to Connor and whispered, "Oh my," with a completely different meaning.

I snapped my fingers to get her attention back to me. "He's taken."

Her face pinked. "Um, yes. So sorry. How can I help you today?" But before I had a chance to answer, especially since I had no idea how to answer her or how much information to give, her eyes grew wide once more as she looked between Connor and me and she put her finger up to tell us 'one minute' and picked up a phone receiver.

"Ms. Rivers," she said into the phone. "You should come down here."

After she hung up, Connor, always on the defensive when it came to me, pushed me behind him. "Is there a problem?"

"No. There's no problem. It's just—" She was cut off by another voice.

"I'm Victoria Rivers." A woman who looked to be in her mid-thirties with short, curly, brown hair and a navy suit jacket and pencil skirt clicked her heels over the marble flooring toward us. "We've been waiting for you to show."

She stuck her hand out. I reached around Connor to shake it.

"You've been waiting for us?" Connor asked suspiciously.

"The protector," she said, still smiling. "Would you like to join me in my office? It'll be easier to show you than try to explain."

"We're not going anywhere with you."

To move this little party along, I stepped out from around Connor. "Honey," I whispered in his ear, "we'll be okay. I feel it. She's not going to hurt us."

"You're lucky to have such a fierce protector."

I leaned in closer to her conspiratorially. "Don't tell him this, but I agree." Then I turned and winked at Connor. "I'm Simone, by the way. And this guy is Connor."

"I can't tell you how thrilled I am to finally learn your names, but I'm also a little nervous as to what it means that you both are here."

Well, that sounded ominous. I knew we had bad men trying to kill us and all that, but did she know something that we didn't?

Victoria Rivers led us to the bank of elevators. She pressed the *up* arrow, the one that took us all the way to the top. So it appeared that Ms. Victoria Rivers was an important person in the Weik Labritories world.

Her office was huge. Huge. And full of windows. Bright sunlight shone in. Luc would have been jealous. The heat in his office didn't come from the sun.

"Please, have a seat." She gestured to two leather club chairs situated in front of a large, oak desk. We sat and watched her walk over to a room that wasn't a room when she opened the door because inside that door was another, a safe door. The expensive, airtight, fireproof, waterproof, bombproof variety. That part was the human magic. It'd also been imbued with witch or some sort of super magic. Given the location, I was going with witch.

She punched in a code and waited for the lock to deactivate. Victoria opened the safe and walked in. I lost sight of her for a minute and then she returned wearing white, cotton gloves that she used to protect very fragile, yellowed paper, walking it over to her desk.

"We've had this in our possession for more generations than I can count. It was given to an ancestor of mine. She was told to read it and to keep it safe. Above all else, she was to pass it down to someone who would follow the instructions."

Victoria carefully pulled the paper from the envelope, laying it open on her desk. I craned my neck to see what was written. "What are the instructions?" I asked.

Turning the letter for Connor and me to get a better look, she began to explain. "When the mated pair seek you out, you must help in any way possible. The dark protector and the one you will not be able to discern. They are the key. The world will be unraveling, unable to recognize itself. I cannot say when they will present themselves, but they will present themselves. To save all that is love and beauty, you must hear them. You must aid them. Without the mated protectors, all will be lost."

"That's ominous." I swallowed hard.

Connor turned his head to look at me. *"Babe."*

"What? We've got bad dudes after us who want us dead. But that whole 'all will be lost' thing is creepy."

"Really? After everything we've seen, everything we've survived, *that*'s what gets you?"

"Yeah. Literally carrying the fate of every living thing on the planet, all the people and animals and even the plants on my shoulders, is a little daunting. I'm not going to lie, it fills me with a tad bit of anxiety. How doesn't it for you?"

"Because I'm selfish," he said, completely straight-faced. "I only care about keeping you safe. That's my job. I lose you, I lose everything. You stay safe, the world stays safe, but to me, that's neither here nor there. It's you, Simone. For me, it all comes down to you."

I bit my bottom lip to keep from attacking him with kisses

and to keep from breaking down in tears. Man, we'd come a long way.

"So what can I do for you?" Victoria asked.

"This might sound odd," Connor started, "but no other mated protectors have visited you, right?"

"*Are* there other mated protectors?" she asked.

"Okay, so that's a no. I just had to ask."

"I need you to test my DNA," I said, just putting it out there because a.) she asked and b.) the time for niceties passed us when she read us that note. "I need to see if I have any living relatives. This is so important."

"Of course," she said. "Is that it?"

"How fast can we get the results? It's kind of a matter of world-ending importance."

"With the use of magic, we have technologies that the non-supers can only dream of. Let's go down to the lab. They'll take some blood and we'll get this process going. A few hours at most."

For the first time in a while, I felt a sense of hope.

Fingers crossed it wasn't premature.

"Can she have the letter?" Connor asked as we stood from the chairs.

"I'm sorry?" Victoria asked in return.

"The letter. Can Simone have it? We're here, so you've fulfilled your contract. I'd like my mate to have the letter. We believe it was written by her… *ancestor.*"

"Oh, well…" I read the shock on her face. "It's, um…" The thought of parting with that letter never crossed her mind. The woman was an open book. And Connor said *I* should never play poker.

"It's okay, Connor," I said. "Thanks for thinking of me."

"I'll always think of you. And it's not okay. That was written by your grandmother."

Victoria whipped her head up to look—no, she didn't simply look. Her gaze felt heavy. She *glared* at me.

Before she could ask, I held my hand up to stop her. "Get me the test and I get the information I'm looking for, I will tell you. We'll *need* allies in this. All of us. We live together or we die apart. There is no in-between."

She handed me the letter. "Here," she said. "It's been in my family for so long, but it belongs to you."

"Thank you."

"Right," she said. "If you two will follow me, we'll get that testing done."

I slid the letter inside the backpack and then replaced it on my back as I stood to follow her, Connor at my side. She led us back to the bank of elevators, this time taking us down to the lowest level.

Now, when the doors opened at the bottom, we were met with the exact image of a laboratory I had in my head. The exact. Bright, overhead white lights illuminated the entire floor. Floor-to-ceiling glass windows rather than walls. Glass doors that slid open. People in lab coats wearing latex gloves and goggles. Computers and machines. I had no idea what they did or how they were used.

She led us to the closest room and the doors automatically opened for her. We followed her inside, where we were met by a woman who introduced herself as Margaret who wore a pleasant enough smile but was otherwise covered by a white jumpsuit and goggles. "What can I help you with today?"

"These are very important clients, Margaret," Victoria said. "She needs a blood draw and her results need to take precedence over all others waiting in the queue."

"Really?" Margaret eyed me up and down. "That's an unusual request for DNA testing."

"I'm sure it is," I replied. "But it's important. So…"

"That's not a problem. Have a seat." She pointed to a rolling stool and I sat in it. It rolled backward until it hit a bank of pull drawers behind me. Connor walked over to stand next to me, placing his hand on my shoulder.

I wasn't particularly eager to get stuck by a needle. On the list of my favorite things to do, that wasn't close to the top. Still, necessary for saving the world and all that.

"Name?" Margaret asked.

"Simone. Lamia," I replied.

Margaret typed my name on the computer along with other

things I didn't pay attention to before walking back over to me with a syringe that she'd printed a label for while we waited. It said: Simone Lamia. *Priority*

"Please put your arm on the counter," she said. I did so, watching as she ripped open an alcohol pad. She swabbed my skin, let it dry for a second, and then I got the stick. The vial filled with dark, oxygenated blood. Margaret pulled out the glass tube, stuck the label on it, and laid it down while she pulled the needle from my arm, and stuck a cotton ball and tape over the puncture.

"There. That's it. We'll get this processed and let you know the results as soon as possible."

"Thank you, Margaret," Victoria said.

"Yes, thank you," I said, too. Connor gave a head nod.

"Do you have other business in Birmingham or would you like to wait in our cafeteria?" Victoria asked.

I looked at Connor. Even though we couldn't do anything for a couple of hours, there was no way he'd let us go sightseeing and risk us becoming one of the sights being seen.

"Cafeteria," Connor answered for the both of us. "Thank you."

We took the elevator to the third floor. The whole floor encompassed the "cafeteria." They could only call it that because they served food, but they had it laid out like an all-you-can-eat buffet in a major hotel resort on the Vegas strip. Jeffery and I had vacationed in Vegas once. I remembered eating cheese and mushroom ravioli while he snacked on sushi rolls in the same visit. I smiled at the memory. Finally. With Connor as my mate, I was finally able to remember Jeffery without all the grief attached. I liked that for both Jeffery and I.

"High class," Connor muttered. Understatement. In every respect. "I'm going to have to tell Luc about this place," he said to me. "There's no way witches should eat better than we do."

"What? Luc buys the wrong brand of kibble?"

Rather than grumble, he pulled me against his side to kiss the top of my head. Although I wasn't super hungry, they had a dessert bar. Uh… yes, please! "Meet you at a table, sexy." I winked then sauntered over to grab up a plate.

And when I sat down holding a plate filled to capacity with every chocolate or cream-filled treat imaginable, I realized that Connor and I couldn't go any further together until I confronted this travesty of justice. "I think we need a break, Connor."

"What?" he laughed as he asked.

"I thought I could do this, ignore what was glaringly evident. But I don't think I can."

"Do what, Simone? What's glaringly evident?"

"I thought I could accept it, but…" I pointed to his plate. "Fruit, Connor? In a room full of eclairs, tarts, puddings, sundaes, cream puffs, cakes, and pies, you chose fruit?"

He bit back a laugh. "Baby—what am I going to do with you?"

"Nothing, seeing as I'm leaving you."

He dropped some blueberries on top of a tart that he snatched from my plate, picked it up, and took a bite. "No, you're not. Can't get rid of me, Simone. We're connected. That's forever."

His voice got all drippy with sex and I'd never cursed a huge buffet more in my life. A huge buffet or the fact that I had demons or whatever they were trying to kill me.

"Promise me that when this is done, you'll do that one thing —the twist—that I loved so well. I need a few rounds of the twist."

He raised his eyebrow at me. "I thought you were leaving me?"

"You put blueberries on a tart. Eat a cream puff and I'll do that thing where I drop down and—"

Connor shoved his hand over my mouth. "Woman," he grumbled. We both looked down at his rapidly tenting jeans. "I'll give you so many rounds of the twist, you won't know what day it is when I finally let you up for a breath." Then he dropped his hand to pop a few blueberries into his mouth, sans tart, so I raised an eyebrow and he took another bite, shaking his head at me and snickering. I loved his body, but I made my point.

"Thank you, you know, for being here with me."

"Wouldn't be anywhere else."

"I know. This was all set up by the universe; it's not that you particularly like me—but thank you."

"Hey—" He twisted my chin to get me to look at him. "It might've been set up by the universe, but I like everything about you, sweetheart. The universe gave me you because it knew you were the exact woman I needed in my life. The woman I'd have the most fun with. The one I'd care for the most. The universe was just our matchmaker."

"If you don't kiss me now…" I whispered until he pressed his lips to mine.

"Damn," said a woman's voice somewhere behind us.

"Where can I get me one of him?" another asked.

"Sorry, ladies," I called out over my shoulder. "He's one of a kind."

The women laughed as they went about their business.

And, in my humble opinion, to get me to believe that he really cared about me, he ate—gasp, horror!—*cake*. The kind with coconut frosting. Tender and moist. He piled berries on top, but he ate it.

If they'd given us a private room, Connor and I would've had time to play several rounds of slap and tickle before Victoria finally showed up to retrieve us. But thank the good universe, she did.

"Come on up to my office again," she said. "I can go over your results with you."

*Phew!* We hopped up from our seats to follow her out of the cafeteria. The elevator ride felt like it lasted forever. When we walked into her office, Connor and I dropped into the same seats from before while Victoria rounded her desk.

She turned her computer screen for us to see. "This," she

said, "is your genetic profile." Victoria pointed to one column. "These"—she pointed to another section on the screen—"are your closest relatives." We looked closely at the names. "But this is curious." She clicked on one of the names. "See?" Victoria pointed out a string of horizontal lines in a column that I figured had to be a section of my genetic profile.

"What am I looking at?" I asked, squinting my eyes because everyone knew that if you squinted your eyes, you understood things better.

"You and she share a common ancestor. But you're here." She again pointed to my column of horizontal lines. "She's here." Victoria pointed to a different column of horizontal lines. And that was when it clicked. "It appears as if you're cousins. But she has all this as part of her genetic profile, but you—yours stops. I don't know what to make of it."

Well, I promised I'd fill her in on everything even with Connor literally breathing down my neck in full-on mated protector mode. Clearly, he'd changed his mind. But Victoria deserved to know.

Why was keeping this secret so much easier than spilling it? The truth shall set you free and all that. I was pretty sure the people who said that didn't have demons or whatever out to kill them, though.

"This might sound crazy," she said, sounding a little sheepish. "But to me, it looks like she's your first cousin hundreds of generations removed. I know it doesn't make any sense, but the DNA doesn't lie."

My heart seized up knowing what I was about to do next. Understanding clicked in for Connor through our bond. I not only felt his emotions, but he gave my shoulder a squeeze and when I looked at him, he raised his eyebrow while nodding his agreement.

I sensed goodness in Victoria. I sensed her family lineage. An old family. Powerful. Of course not as old or powerful as mine, but considering my grandmother was *the first* witch, we sort of had to count me as an outlier.

"What I'm about to tell you is *definitely* going to sound crazy."

"*Okay…*" she answered, drawing out the 'kay' to like five syllables worth of unsure expression.

"The reason I'm here is because a powerful witch had me connect with an even more powerful ancestor—"

"You spoke with an ancestor?"

"A couple of them," Connor said, giving my waist a reassuring squeeze.

Her mouth dropped open, as it would have. Communicating with the ancestors wasn't something your average witch could pull off. And even though neither said, I got the feeling that those who could manage it only talked to relations. But again, considering where I'd come from, it seemed that I belonged to *every* witch's family.

"They sent me to the witches' archives in the Orkneys," I continued.

She jerked her head back. "You went to the archives?"

"Yes. Connor and I spent hours inside."

"The archives let you *inside*?" she almost shouted.

"You get she's important." My mate jumped in, clearly losing patience. Victoria looked at him and slowly nodded. "Right. So if you know that, what are the chances that the archives wouldn't?"

"They're the reason I'm here in the first place," I said. "And I can tell you that she"—I pointed to the computer screen again—"registers as my first cousin hundreds of generations removed…" I let out a heavy sigh. "Well, it's because she is."

"I'm afraid I don't understand," Victoria answered.

"Yeah… I'm pretty sure you do. Not wanting to accept an answer is way different from not understanding it."

"But you can't… You can't…" She repeated herself without bringing anything more to the table.

"I am the granddaughter of Lilith."

Victoria gasped and stumbled back from me far enough to hit the window behind her.

"Adam, my biological grandfather, was a nasty piece of work. That was why Lilith left him. She and Adam had Peter and my mother, Shoshana. So if we're first cousins, then she has to come from Peter's lineage."

"Peter and Shoshana were the children of Adam and Lilith?" she asked while she slowly moved back to her chair behind her desk and sat down. "Peter and Shoshana?" she repeated.

"Yes. The magic of the garden wasn't gifted to Adam. It was gifted to Lilith alone. When she left with the children, she took the magic with her. There was no serpent or forbidden fruit. Lilith was a strong woman who took her kids and left an abusive marriage. But Adam wanted the magic back. Eve hadn't been gifted it. So he searched out Lilith and Shoshana, who by then were both married to strong, confident, loving men. The man my mother and Peter considered their father, Zohar, and my father, Baruch."

"Zohar and Baruch…" Victoria mumbled.

"Both men held magic, although not as strong as Lilith, my mother, or even Peter. That gift of powerful magic was gifted to women. My grandmother helped them to grow as witches."

"So what happened?" she asked, leaning way in conspiratorially.

"Adam launched a surprise attack on the day my brother and I were born. My grandmother used her magic to help me escape."

"But why attack? Killing the magic users wouldn't give him magic back."

"He wanted my mother to marry his son with Eve to gain control over my mother's magic and, well, mine."

She sucked in a long breath. "I have to say, what you're telling me sounds unbelievable. If this is true, then why haven't we sensed you before this? Every super in the world would've ended up at your door, drawn in by that kind of power."

"Lilith bound her," Connor said. "She bound her magic until she was old enough to meet her protector."

"And that's you?"

"That's me," he agreed. "But you knew that."

She nodded. "I did. I feel like something bad is about to hit. Like imminently." She sighed. "I can't shake it."

"That's because it is," I said, wishing I could give the woman better news. "When I found my mated protector would be when the shit was starting to hit the fan, so to speak. The bindings could only hold me for so long and they were slipping, which is how Connor and I were finally able to come together. With our meeting, the bindings are slipping more every day and at an expedited rate."

"Who's coming after you?"

"We don't know. But whoever it is aims to control my power by controlling me—and they're *bad* news."

"That doesn't fill me with joy," Victoria responded.

"Nor I," I said back. "But the time is coming when everyone will have to choose. Do you side with good or do you side with evil? No one can escape this."

"So you're talking Armageddon-level bad?" she asked.

"Unfortunately… Yeah," Connor said.

"What can I do?"

"You're choosing us, then?" I asked.

Victoria jerked her head back as if I'd smacked her. "What kind of witch would I be to go against Lilith? Of course, I'm with you."

I relaxed a bit. I felt her goodness, but that didn't mean she'd jump right to helping me. We all had free will. "I need the name and location of my first cousin if you have it. Then I need you to start finding supers and at this point, mortals who understand the stakes and want a future for their children and grandchildren. A fight is coming, whether we want it or not. We need to prepare."

# CHAPTER

## *Fifteen*

Lily Joy. My cousin. What a pretty name. Victoria kindly gave us her address. Before we left, both Connor and I made sure she understood how important it was for her to keep my info on the down low, but also to prepare. Get as many people she trusted on our side as possible. I hated being the prophet of doom and gloom. I mean, for the rest of my life, however long that might be, Victoria would remember me as the woman who'd brought on the end of days.

I'd much rather be remembered as the spunky woman with the cute hair and sassy sense of style always ready with an intelligent quip and a mostly kind word. Was that too much to ask for?

"Well, if you'll excuse us," I said as I reached for Connor's hand. It made things easier for us to be touching when I moved us with magic. Plus—and I would never tell him this in fear of giving him an even bigger head—I craved his touch right now. It settled me. Heading into the unknown and all that, Connor kept me anchored to a reality that I hoped we'd get to live rather than the one that currently faced us. Then I closed my eyes and focused my mind on Lily Joy's address somewhere in the middle of the English countryside. Some little town I'd never heard of. I knew it was the middle of the countryside because the moment I concentrated on the address, I saw the home in my mind.

When I opened my eyes again, Connor and I stood in front of a thatched-roof cottage trimmed in natural, aged wood. The window glass reminded me of the window glass used in a colonial village I'd toured once. Natural wood and utilitarian shutters framed the outside of each window. A stone path welcomed us to the front door. Plants and flowers lined the path.

I found so much comfort around witch-owned cottages. Even though I wasn't a witch, I still kind of was. Lavender, rosemary, and sage—I got that *kid at Disneyland* feeling all over again.

"You love this," Connor said reflectively.

"I do."

"You're glowing."

"That's nice of you to—"

"No, Simone, you're actually glowing. Look."

What in the ever-loving—no way could this be possible? My skin glowed a golden, shimmery light. Uh… this was definitely new.

Connor reached his hand over to brush it along the skin on my arm. "It's warm," he whispered in what I considered awe. "So a new achievement unlocked."

"It appears so." I smiled sheepishly, but then Connor pulled me into his arms and my glow engulfed the both of us.

"I feel it inside me," he went on. "I feel you and the glow. Like you're separate entities but joined at the same time. I've never felt anything like it. It's not just your emotions, Simone— it's literally you. What do you think it means?"

"I have no clue," I answered him dreamily, sighing. Then I shook my head, realizing it was a spell. Not the glowing, that was all me. But the dreamy quality I felt, it was an enchantment that Lily Joy must have placed on her home.

"What?" Connor asked, drawing his eyebrows down in evident confusion.

"Part of this is a spell. I'll explain later."

Let me just say, I struggled to free myself from the feeling that engulfed me. Of everything in the world that I had to do, being held close by Connor was something I *wanted* to do. Still holding his hand, I walked us up to the door and knocked.

After a minute or so, the door cracked open. The woman's eyes went big when she took us in. I expected her to ask, *"What are you?"* I mean, I always got the "What are you?" question. But she surprised me with a, "How did you break through?"

"Really?" Connor asked. "That's your first question for us?"

Her exasperated sigh sounded so similar to mine. I laughed.

"Oh yeah," Connor went on. "She's definitely related to you, sweetheart."

"We're related?" Lily Joy asked.

"My name is Simone."

Lily Joy gasped. "Lamia?"

Shocked, I nodded, blinking like an idiot.

She looked from side to side then held the door open. "Please, come in."

We walked inside the home filled with comfortable furniture. Big. Old. Lived in. A fire roared in the stone fireplace, filling the room with peaceful warmth. "I *love* your home," I said and she smiled.

"Thank you. It's taken me a while to get it how I wanted it." Then I watched as she shut the door behind us and swiped a flat hand through the air above it. The cracks between the door and doorjamb glowed an orangey hue before dissipating. "Please have a seat."

Now that I got a good look at her, and this might've sounded crazy to most people, considering the distance between us in the family tree, but she looked like me. Same dark eyes. Same natural hair color. Although a bit thinner than me, she had those same soft features, cheeks, chin, and nose. She even dressed similarly, I mean, not to what I wore today, but an all-around style. She wore an oversized, pale pink sweater and black, skinny jeans. If I scanned my wardrobe in my mind, I was sure I'd land on that exact same sweater.

"Can I get you something to drink?" she asked.

"Water?" I responded and I half-expected her to wave her hand and have the glass appear in my hand. That wasn't what happened. She walked to the kitchen and came back expertly carrying three tall glasses of water, handing one each off to both me and Connor before taking a seat across from us.

"Thank you," Connor said.

"Does it just kill you to be pleasant?" I asked him teasingly.

He winked. "Only with you." Then he took a sip of his water before setting the glass down on the table in front of us.

I noticed Lily Joy's eyes moving between Connor and me as we bantered. "Your words make it sound like you don't like each other, but the feeling I get from you is far different."

"He grew on me," I answered. Then tacked on, "Kind of like a fungus."

She pointed between the two of us. "So he's your protector…" Connor and I both nodded. "But he's also your mate?"

"Guilty," he replied.

"I've never met a mated protector before."

"Well, I've never met a relative before," I said and she turned her head to look at me in apparent disbelief.

"You were orphaned, too?" she asked.

Uh… why did her *too* hit me as ominous?

"Yes, I was orphaned. How did you know my last name?"

"My parents died when I was a baby. I don't know how. But life was very difficult. I have power like a witch, but I'm not a witch. Not really. Every year, I'd get a little more power—like the universe was doling it out in increments. Then a couple of weeks ago—*bam*! It was like the magic smacked me between the eyes."

I looked to Connor. A couple of weeks ago? Like when Connor and I had met? What did I do with this information?

"Anyway," she continued, shaking her head as if to clear it, "I jolted awake in the middle of the night. A woman's voice said, '*Simone Lamia. Remember Simone Lamia.*' Then she was gone. I couldn't go back to sleep to save my life."

"You don't sound like you've grown up in England," Connor said.

"Oh, that's because I didn't. I'm American. I was drawn here a couple of years ago by the will of some long-lost relative who left me this land."

"No way that's a coincidence." Connor voiced exactly what I was thinking.

"Here's the thing," I said, then I let out a long breath and went for it. "You're not a witch. I mean, you are, but you aren't. Just like you said. The same as me. I... well... Our family history is a bit hard to hear."

Lily Joy gripped her glass in one hand, resting it on the other as she leaned forward, listening.

"I think the woman you heard—the voice that woke you up —was Lilith," I said bluntly.

And cue the disbelieving eyes in five... four... three... two... There they were. "Excuse me?" she asked.

"It's kind of a funny story. See, Lilith is my grandmother. She took me on the day I was born because Grandad Adam led a surprise attack and killed my parents, Shoshana and Baruch. You're my cousin through my uncle Peter, Shoshana's brother, and one of the two children of Lilith and Adam."

"Lilith and Adam? Like Garden of Eden Lilith and Adam?"

"That would be them," I answered.

"And you call that a funny story?" she asked taken aback.

"*Funny curious,* not *funny ha ha,*" Connor answered for me.

"How are you here, now?"

"Lilith could time jump. She left me here as an infant."

"So... we're *Lilium?*"

"'Lilium'?" I asked.

She nodded. "The children of Lilith. My parents left me with a book. More like a diary, I guess, because it was handwritten. One of the passages said Lilium are the children of Lilith. Stronger than any witch. Stronger than any super. Most would kill for what we're apparently capable of. I just never put it together. They're rare—or, *we're* rare. I'm embarrassed to say that I thought it was super superstition."

"*Surprise!*" I joked.

"You'll have to excuse me here, but I'm still having a hard time wrapping my head around this. *I'm* a direct descendant of Lilith. *The* Lilith. The woman so powerful that men demonized her in the Old Testament."

"It's a lot to take in," I agreed.

"Why do you seem so calm about this?" she asked.

"Connor, plug your ears," I ordered.

"I'm not plugging my ears."

"Connor," I repeated more forcefully. "*Plug your ears.*"

"Fine," he grumbled, but he grumbled while plugging his ears.

"He's not supposed to hear this?" Lily Joy asked.

I shrugged. "I don't want him to. He gets a big head."

"About?" she hedged.

"He grounds me. Connor is why I'm so calm. Without him, I'd be a mess."

"Finally, you admit it," he said, drawing a laugh from me.

"You're supposed to have your ears plugged."

"Have you learned nothing, Simone?" he asked, and yeah—his coal-black eyes smiled with heat and love just for me. I was putty in his highly capable hands.

"So you need my help," Lily Joy said. "That's why you're here."

"Pretty much," I agreed. "Hey—what was that spell outside? It was…" I felt my cheeks heat thinking about the way Connor had held me. The tenderness of his touch. A trill of goosebumps ran up my arms.

"It didn't work," she replied and I cocked my head, looking at her curiously.

"What do you mean, it didn't work?"

"It's a spell to keep supers away. You two should've started fighting, completely forgetting why you'd shown up at my door. If the spell had worked, you'd have fought as you left me alone."

"Damn right, achievement unlocked," Connor mumbled.

"What?" Lily Joy asked him.

"Simone changed it. She changed the spell. Her skin started to glow and then I felt her inside me. She made me remember the tenderness I felt toward her. The bond from being mated."

"Can you teach me how you did that?" Lily Joy asked excitedly.

"If I knew how," I said. "My powers were bound. They've been coming back more and more since I connected with Connor. I had no idea I *could* do that before it happened. And I knew it was a spell that you put up. But…"

"So your parents were killed by Adam. Now you show up at my door. As much as I like this 'hey, cuz' get-to-know-you type of visit, I think Lilith led you here."

"I mean, I wish it was just a 'hey, cuz' visit. I like you," I said. "But I think Lilith led me here, too. I sort of have men—possibly demons—trying to kill me."

Lily Joy's mouth dropped open. "Demons?" she asked. "You couldn't have said shifters? I have tons of shifter repellent. Easy-peasy." She ended with a flip of her hand.

"Have you ever heard of a person, man—witch or demon— named Beetle?" I asked.

"Beetle?" she asked. "No. Never. But the name doesn't fill me with warm fuzzies."

"Me either," I replied. "He killed my fiancé. Connor's sure Jeffery and I never would have married—"

"You wouldn't have," he cut me off.

"Testy," Lily Joy teased.

"It's a trigger subject for him. But the gist of it is, Beetle got to Jeffery to get to me. I met Beetle once in a bar. He's a bad dude."

"Tell the truth," Connor said. "You met him because you *went* to meet him. Get this," he said to Lily Joy. "She thought it was smart to hunt down her *ex*-fiancé's *killer*."

"He wasn't an ex when he was alive."

"Can we *stop* talking about him?"

"You're jealous?" Lily Joy asked Connor.

"It fucking guts me whenever she brings him up. Physically guts me. I can't handle thinking about her being with another man."

"I think the universe put a little too much punch in the destined mate mojo," I replied as I stood from the chair that I occupied to drop down on Connor's lap, surprising him. Then I grabbed a hold of his cheeks, turned his head, and planted a big, ol' kiss to his lips. "I'm sorry," I said low. "When we're alone again, I'll do that other thing you like, you know—" I ran my nose along the side of his face. "To make it up to you."

"Do yourself a favor, Lily Joy. *Don't* find your mate," he said this right before kissing me hard again.

"I think that means he forgives me," I said after he tore his lips away.

"Nope," he said. "Though I think I'm ready to try…"

Lily Joy huffed, clapping her hands together once. "Right. Let's get you two a room. We need to work on finding all your powers. Or at the very least, getting you to understand the ones you've already harnessed so you can recreate them."

She stood and stretched. Lily Joy held a great deal of power. The house felt protected. Coming here had been the right choice. If we were going to be safe anywhere, it was here. I made a mental note to ask her more about the wards and charms she put around the property tomorrow. The day had finally caught up with me and I felt exhausted. "If you'll follow me," she said, leading us upstairs to a hallway. She pointed. "That's my room." Across the hall, she pointed out another room. "That'll be yours.

The bathroom is at the end of the hall." She finished by pointing out the last room. "It's getting late, so I'm heading for bed. We can start first thing in the morning."

Connor pulled me into the room and shut the door. "I believe you promised me that *other* thing I like."

A shiver ran down my back. *I believe I did, Connor Baghest... I believe I did.*

**CHAPTER**

*Sixteen*

s I lay naked and blissfully asleep in Connor's arms, I became aware of the fact because I saw my body. My disheveled hair. Sated smile spread across my lips. My mate holding me protectively. I looked down on us. Connor rolled into me, pressing a kiss to my neck without opening his eyes. I reached up to touch the spot and I couldn't touch it because I had no arm to manipulate. No body to make contact with.

My body was in the bed. *What's going on?* I silently asked the universe and a door opened up out of nowhere. Not a physical door on the ground, but ethereal, in the air, like me. The pull to move through proved too strong to resist. I glanced down at Connor one more time and gave in to the urgency. As soon as I passed through the door, it clicked shut but stayed floating, as if waiting for me when I was ready to return.

*Jiminy Crickets!* My heart slammed inside my chest, or it would have if I had a heart or a chest because I was in a dank, dark cave. Cold—so cold, I saw my breath, which again made no sense because one needed lungs to expel breath. I looked down and saw a man huddled against a woman. Their clothes were torn. He held a great deal of power, I definitely felt that, so then why wasn't he using it? This made no sense.

Without a second thought, I drifted down to get a closer look at the couple, and seriously, *nothing* could've prepared me for this. I gasped. The man looked exactly like me, only in a man's body. I knew without a doubt that this was Simeon, which meant, the woman he held was... She was...

"Simone?"

I whipped around to see energy shaped like the man sleeping on the ground.

"Simeon?" I asked hesitantly.

He let out a breath as he smiled. "I have to admit, I wasn't sure if any of this was real."

I outright laughed. "I'm *still* not sure any of this is real. What's going on here?"

His energy shrugged. "My guess, astral projection? It's all new to me."

"Tell me about it. Is that—" I pointed to the woman with him. "Madigan Baghest?"

Simeon's energy radiated warmth and love. "My *mate*."

"Her brother is just through that door." I gestured to the door still hanging midair.

"Her brother is your mated protector?"

"Crazy, right? Thanksgiving at our place this year?"

He shook his head. "If we live that long."

That brought a damper on this little family reunion. "Why are you sleeping in a cave?"

"It all happened so fast. I was driving past a café and got the strangest urge to go inside. Madigan looked up the moment I stepped through the door and everything in the world made sense. She said, 'Are you going to sit down?' and that's how it started."

"Not exactly the first meeting for me and Connor. I kind of insulted him and kneed him in the balls."

My brother laughed loudly, the sound resonating off the

walls of the cave, though it didn't wake the sleeping couple down below. "I take it there's a story there."

"You have no idea."

Then he sobered. "I grew up alone. I knew I was a super, but I wasn't a witch. It was Madigan who figured out that I'd been bound. A woman showed in my dream. She told me to find my sister, Simone. Clearly, I was taken aback. I mean, I had a sister? After being alone my whole life, I suddenly had a mate and a sister?"

"But you couldn't find me?"

"I didn't have the chance. Madi and I were confronted by some men who claimed to work for a man named—"

"Beetle?" I asked.

Shock spread across his energy's face. "We barely got away with our lives. More powers show up all the time, but I'm not in control of them. They track us everywhere I use magic, so we've had to resort to traveling without it. But our money ran out. We went to an ATM to get more and were ambushed. I have no idea how they'd tracked us. Madi was injured. I had to get us somewhere safe for her to heal."

"Where are you?"

"Faroe Islands."

"Can you get to Guilford, in Surrey—um, England?"

"I don't know."

"Our cousin lives in the country, outside Guilford. Lily Joy. She'll help. She has power."

"I think I'm too weak to carry her there. She's too injured to shift or walk."

*Great. Think, Simone. Think.* I closed my eyes and concentrated on my brother's body sleeping down below. A slight shimmer moved over his pocket. *Please, universe, let this have worked.*

My energy started to fade. Not now. I wasn't done. I wanted to stay with him. It felt wrong, too soon, to leave him behind. The floating door opened, drawing me to it again. "I have to go. Check your pocket. If it worked, I'll see you soon." Before the door shut on us completely, I shouted, "Remember, Guilford. Lily Joy."

The door snapped shut and I felt myself being shaken violently. "Simone? Baby—*goddammit*, wake up."

What? It felt as if every bit of energy had drained from my body. I ached. It was hard to open my eyes, but I managed. Connor leaned over me, fear coating his expression, emanating out of every pore.

His eyes glistened and when they landed on mine, he crushed me in a hug that made it hard to catch a breath. "What the fuck happened, Simone?" he sort of barked against my neck.

I lifted my hand weakly to brush loose hair from his forehead. "I'm here," I whispered. "I'm here, Connor."

He peppered my face with kisses. "Dammit… Don't you ever do that to me again…" More kisses.

Lily Joy stood next to the bed wringing her hands and I sort of felt embarrassed, what with the way my mate wouldn't let up on the PDA *and* I realized I was still as naked as a wee baby. "How do you feel?" she asked me.

"Tired. Weak."

Thankfully, Connor had the presence of mind to pull the covers up over my exposed skin, and the way he positioned himself, shield me from Lily Joy's view.

"I'll bring you some tea."

I didn't see her leave, but I heard the door click shut.

"Where'd you go?" Connor asked. I shivered, even though I wasn't cold. Connor's body heat saw to that. Still, I couldn't stop.

Connor held me like he never planned to let me go. About ten minutes later, Lily Joy showed back up with an American *mug* full of tea—not a dainty English teacup. Connor helped me hold it because I lacked the strength. The tea smelled of peppermint along with other fragrant herbs.

As the tea started to take effect, I was able to talk without my teeth chattering. "What happened?" I asked Connor.

"I was sleeping. Then I sat up in bed, ripped from my dream by this horrible pain. It felt like half of me died. Then I turn to you and you're hardly breathing. You won't wake up. With all the things that have happened to us, I have *never* felt that level of fear. You were just gone, Simone. I couldn't feel the connection."

"The door," I mumbled. "It had to have been…"

"What are you talking about?"

"Well, it looks like I've unlocked a new power. Astral projection."

"Astral what?" Connor snapped.

"Could you reach for your T-shirt? I'm feeling a little exposed here."

He sighed the kind of suffering sigh that could only come from a man unlucky enough to have been mated to me. But he still reached his long arm down to the floor to where I'd thrown his shirt after ripping it from his body in the heat of passion. The taut muscles straining along his ribs turned me on—no. *Bad Simone. It's not time to get turned on by your mate.* In my defense, the universe did this to me. Jeffery and I had a wonderful sex life, but I'd never felt the need to ravish him anytime he got close to me, so it wasn't like I was some crazed nympho who couldn't keep her sexual urges in check.

The universe made me do it.

Once my little talk with myself ended and the T-shirt covered me, I went on to explain. "I was dreaming, or I thought I was dreaming. I saw us sleeping in bed. You're such a cuddler," I threw in for good measure.

"Simone," he admonished.

"Okay. Keep your—" I pulled up on the blanket to check if he wore any drawers and nope. I smiled. "We'll change that to hold your horses." The poor man rubbed his hand along the back of his neck while he looked to the heavens. "Right," I went on. "A door appeared, just floating in the air. It opened and pulled me through it. I didn't really have control. When I got to the other side, it snapped shut."

"So you were no longer here with me."

"You won't believe where I was, Connor. I saw…" How did one go about telling their mate that they saw their missing sister? I guess the way I did everything. Right to the point. "I ended up in a cave. Babe, I saw your sister."

His whole body went rigid. "You *what*?"

I shook my head. "And I met my brother. He looks just like me, but you know, manly… and without my awesome lavender locks."

"You talked to him?" he asked.

"Yes. He didn't know that we were mated."

"Where are they?"

"Hiding out on the Faroe Islands. He said they were attacked by Beetle's men and went on the run. He's too tired and injured to use magic. Your sister was injured." I placed my hand on his chest to calm his rapidly beating heart. "She was sleeping. My brother is taking care of her." Then I turned to Lily Joy. "Lily Joy, if a manly version of me and a girly version of Connor show up, it's Simeon and Madigan. I told them to come here."

"You don't think they will?" she asked.

"Well, he couldn't use magic so they were using cash, but they ran out and tried to get to an ATM but were ambushed. Somehow, they ended up in a cave on the Faroe Islands. I started to fade, getting drawn back through the door. But I tried a spell. If it worked, then he'll have money to get them here."

"I pulled you back through the door when I shook you," Connor said.

"Seems like it. Please don't look sad. This is good. My brother and I have met. Your sister is in good hands."

"It's not that I'm sad…" He ran a hand over his face, presumably organizing his thoughts. "I'm glad my sister is in good hands. This sounds low in my head, so I know it'll make me sound like a dick when I say it out loud, but she's no longer my main concern. She has a mate for that. You, though, Simone, you traveled out of your body thousands of miles away without me there to protect you."

"I didn't do it on purpose."

"I know that, baby. But you can't know how I feel. You feel our mated bond—but every part of who I used to be is overwritten by the bond *and* my need to protect you."

"That sounds highly unpleasant," I said softly. While I'd said it to lighten the moment, I also meant it. Poor Connor. Tears actually rimmed my eyes.

Connor lifted me onto his lap, wrapping his arms around me, and he bent in to kiss the side of my head. "It's not so bad."

"Maybe—do we think there's a way to bring Connor with you during your astral projections?" Lily Joy asked and in truth, I'd forgotten she was in the room with us.

"I don't know. This was the first time it happened."

"We could practice while you're here."

"That's a great idea, Lily Joy," Connor agreed and I smiled. He really had the sweetness down when he wanted to use it.

"Since I'm up," she said, "I'm going to dress and get breakfast going. We've got a lot to do and it appears, not much time in which to do it."

I felt the invisible noose tightening around my neck. I only hoped we were prepared for the fall.

After a hearty breakfast of fruit, oatmeal with pecans, and a plant-based sausage, along with copious amounts of coffee, the three of us put our heads together trying to figure out any new powers and getting a good handle on the ones I already had.

That was the plan. Where to start, though?

"What can you do?" Lily Joy asked to get us going.

"I have taser fingers. When I want to shock someone, I press my fingers on them, and an electric current moves through them."

"Are you kidding?"

"Trust me, she's not kidding," Connor said. "I've seen her in action. It's amazing."

"Thank you," I said, smiling stupidly back at the man.

"You caught me on a good day," he replied, winking. "She can manifest her desires. That's so convenient."

"'Convenient'?" I asked sarcastically. "You wanted to pull your hair out the first time we figured out that ability."

"Right. Because I was trying to keep you safe. But then you took me into Luc's office to have your wicked way with me. After that, I loved it."

I rolled my eyes at him, snickering. "You're a pig."

He shrugged. "*Oink.*"

"Oh, yeah—I'm definitely ready to meet my mate," Lily Joy said, almost to herself.

"It has its perks," I replied, startling her.

She sort of jumped as if a thought had just come to her and asked, "Is that all?"

"Well, you know I can talk to ancestors. So I can do witch magic."

"That's a very good start." She pulled out her pendulum from her sweater pocket, making me feel like a very inadequate witch. She kept her pendulum right on her at all times? I didn't even own one. "I think we should ask your spirit guides. They should be able to tell us a little more." She excused herself to the kitchen and came back out a few minutes later with a small, clear, glass bowl with water in it and I saw some pink granules that hadn't disintegrated yet.

"Moonwater?" I asked.

She nodded. "And Himalayan pink salt. To cleanse my energy from the pendulum. It'll help you connect with your spirit guides better."

Lily Joy dropped the simple gold-plated object into the water and we gave it about five minutes.

"Now you pick it up and hold it between your hands to imbue it with your energy," she directed and I reached into the bowl of water to retrieve the thing by the chain. I held it between my hands and waited. "Don't forget your protections."

"What kind of protections?" Connor asked as Lily Joy sprayed a rosemary spray around the room.

"Witch wards," she answered, and I nodded. I knew a thing or two about witch wards.

So I cleared my throat and said, "Only spirit energy with my greatest good is allowed in this safe space. All others must go."

"That takes care of demons and any other manner of supers who might want to find their way in here?" asked Connor.

"Only if demons try to jump in from Hades," Lily Joy replied. "If they come in human form, it doesn't work. You need a different set of wards that involves a blood sacrifice. It's not pleasant—oh, remember yes or no questions."

"Got it," I said. "Is my spirit guide here with me?" The pendulum swung in the 'yes' position. "Can you whisper your name in my ear?" Again, it swung in the 'yes' position, and I heard the name *Lilith* whispered in my ear.

"Grandma?" The pendulum swung in a huge *yes* arc. "You're my spirit guide."

"'Grandma'?" Connor asked. "You mean Lilith—*the* Lilith is your spirit guide?"

"It appears so. Have you met your great-granddaughter, Lily Joy?"

Then I heard, "Tell her I'm proud of her," whispered in my ear. "I check in on her whenever I can."

"Uh… Lily Joy, Lilith says she's proud of you and that she checks in on you whenever she has the chance," I told my cousin. Lily Joy's face lit up with pure happiness. "If I can hear you, is it possible for me to see you, too?"

"Make it happen," Lilith said and that shocked me. I could make it happen all by myself?

"What did she say?" Connor asked.

"That I can make it happen." Then I began to manifest my desire for all of us to see and hear Lilith. After repeating and repeating it in my head, a beautiful woman with long, flowing, raven-black hair stood in the middle of us. This was her. Lilith. I'd recognize her anywhere. Both Connor and Lily Joy gasped.

"You look so much alike," Connor said. "It's uncanny. My mate is the spitting image of Lilith."

Lilith turned her smile onto my mate. "My granddaughter's mate. You come from a long lineage of protectors," she said. "Your ancestor rushed in to help my family when Adam launched his attack."

"Seriously?" He pulled me into his arms almost reflexively. "That's amazing."

"The universe had granted him a small amount of magic and he lived with my family and me, learning more. We had no idea transfiguration was one of his powers. But he saved the life of my second-oldest daughter by changing into a large, snarling beast dog while I was getting my Simone and Simeon to safety. When I returned, he had taken out several of Adam's men. He married my daughter, joining our family."

Lily Joy looked between Lilith, Connor, and me. "That's unbelievable."

"It's beautiful," Lilith added. "Adam turned men against us, convincing them to harm any magic holders. Once again, if he couldn't have it, then no one else could. Adam was the biggest mistake the universe ever made. The only good that ever came from that man was my Peter and Shoshana. My beloved Shoshana didn't survive the attack. But my Peter did. And you, my dear, Lily Joy, are the product of his union. I'm blessed to know you."

A tear slid down Lily Joy's cheek.

"When magic holders were forced into hiding, that was how the Baghests entered into service. The universe tasked them with protecting magic holders in their hiding spot, which the mortals deemed Hell, to scare any off from seeking magic holders out."

"So it's a PR game," I said and my grandmother smiled at me, nodding. "Do you know who Beetle is?" I asked then, bringing this fun conversation back into the serious realm.

She shook her head. "Their magic is cloaked. I cannot sense who is behind it."

"Cloaking magic? Is that something I can do?"

"We don't yet know the full extent of your powers, my Simone. Whoever this Beetle is, they've somehow harnessed powerful magic. No magic holder should have the power to block me. I *am* the embodiment of magic in humans. When I left the garden, the universe saw fit to give small amounts of magic to those deserving of it, a sort of checks and balances."

"Checks and balances?" Connor asked.

"Can you believe that the universe feared that *I'd* be the one to go off on a power trip?"

"The universe didn't plan that one too well," I replied.

"So what should we do about her powers?" Lily Joy asked.

"If an idea comes to you, then try," Lilith said back. "The universe is whispering its secrets to you. But I'm not privy to those particular ones. I am sorry."

"Are… Are my parents around?" I asked. "Can I speak with them?"

Lilith smiled and nodded. Two people, a man and a woman, appeared together and my eyes immediately filled with tears. "Oh my god," I whispered. Connor's arm squeezed tighter.

"My beautiful Simone," my mother said. "Isn't she beautiful, Baruch?"

"She's a vision. Hello, my daughter."

"Dad?" I threw my hand over my mouth to stifle an ugly sob.

"I'm sorry we were not there for you as you grew. We would have never left if we could have helped it."

"You died trying to protect Mom. This is all on Adam. Not going to lie, I hate that I have any of that man's blood running through me."

"Magic was an experiment for humanity," Lilith said. "The universe tracked my ability to yield it. The garden was created to make sure that no one was hurt should it go wrong. If Adam had been a good man, then I may not have wanted to leave. But the universe knew there were people ready to receive it. Thus, I had to *want* to leave."

"But he took everything from me," I protested. "You, my parents, my brother. I grew up completely alone when I could've had a family if it hadn't been for him."

"Oh, my dear girl," my mother said. "You have a family." She looked to Connor behind me, then to Lily Joy. "Your family is now. It is in your future. The children whom you will one day hold in your arms."

"Only if we can defeat Beetle, which I'm not so convinced—"

"*No*," Lilith said sharply. "Do not manifest negative thoughts. You will defeat him. You must."

I sighed. "*Will* and *must* are very different, Lilith."

"This is a lot for her." Connor defended me, and yeah, despite our rocky start, I felt his love in every word. I wouldn't tell him this, but the universe picked well. It still made me salty that Adam had taken away my birth family. That I spent my youth scared and alone. But if I'd lived out my life with Baruch and Shoshana, I wouldn't have been alive to meet Connor. Life had its tradeoffs.

"I've been watching you with my daughter," my father, Baruch, said.

I blanched. "Not at *all* times, right?" I asked, feeling a bit green.

He smiled in knowing indulgence, appearing to hold back a laugh. "No, Simone. There are some things a father does not need to know about his daughter."

"Thank god," I mumbled.

"Given that you're here, sweetheart, I'm pretty sure he's aware of how things work between mates." Connor kissed my temple, then, and I scowled.

"I *know* that. But what if he popped in at the wrong time? Say, Luc's office? Ring any bells?"

He nipped my earlobe. "I'll never forget it."

"Standing right here, son," my father clipped and I threw my head back laughing.

"Call us whenever you wish to talk," my mother said. "But our energy is waning. We need to recharge."

"I'm not ready to let you go," I admitted.

"You're not letting us go," Lilith said. "We're always with you."

Before our eyes, my parents and grandmother shimmered and faded out of view.

Lily Joy sighed. "I wish I had that power."

"Do you *know* you don't?"

"I guess not."

"Well, we should try. But if you can't, I can do it for you. Say, if you wanted to meet your parents."

Her eyes shimmered momentarily as if she were holding back tears. "I'm so glad you came into my life," she answered and I took that as a 'thank you.'

"I have a feeling you'll come to eat those words," I answered, deciding that we needed a little levity in the room again. Knowing everything we were about to charge head-first into, I needed to surround myself with as much happy as possible to take with me when things got decidedly *not* happy. How were we supposed to defeat an enemy if we didn't even know where to find him or what exactly he was after?

"Not possible," Lily Joy countered, thankfully cutting into my dwindling levity. "Whatever is coming, at least I have you and Connor. After spending my life alone..." She didn't need to say more. I totally got where she was coming from. But again, we couldn't go back there. We had each other now. Moving forward, neither of us would be alone ever again. Not unless we wanted to be.

I clapped my hands together making Lily Joy jump, and I even noticed Connor give a little start. Maybe I might have gotten a bit of enjoyment from that, but I'd admit to nothing. "Right," I said abruptly. "So, I can speak to spirits."

"And make them visible for the non-Simone around you to see and hear," Connor amended. "That has to be a rare ability. I've known supers all my life and never heard of that ability."

"Neither have I," Lily Joy agreed.

"So what do we think it means?" I asked.

"It means we need to make sure you're really familiar with your powers," Connor said. "Because if we've never heard of them happening to other supers, then chances are good we can take Beetle and his men off guard."

"Ooh... true," Lily Joy said, nodding her head. A smile spread across her face. "This is going to be fun."

Fun? Debateable. I think Lily Joy and I had differing ideas of fun at the moment. Connor was right, though, I had to get familiar with my powers.

We spent the day working on the abilities that I knew I had, paying special attention to witch magic. I figured some good spellwork might come in handy in the coming days. Beetle was cloaking himself from even Lilith seeing him. How did one go about cloaking their identity from the likes of the first witch?

Beetle had to be super powerful to accomplish that.

The three of us worked until my head ached too badly to go on. When I looked at the time, it was well past lunch, edging toward rounding the far side of the dinner hour. My belly took that time to grumble loudly.

"We need to stop," Connor said.

"Do we have time?" I snapped.

"If you make yourself ill, then you won't do any of us any good," he argued back.

"Normally, I'd cook, but I'll order us something," Lily Joy offered, probably to get us to stop bickering.

"No need." I waved my hand in the air. The next thing I knew, we heard pans clanking in the kitchen. The three of us walked in there, already smelling the mouthwatering aroma of meatloaf.

Lily Joy walked over to the stovetop. "There are mashed potatoes." Then she pulled open the oven door. "And there's the meatloaf along with dinner rolls. If there is a salad in the fridge, I'm never letting you go."

"Why not manifest the food on the table?" My mate asked.

Oh, really? I rolled my eyes. "Because I can't keep carrying you, Baghest. Now, be a good boy and set the table." That could've gone one of two ways. He could have found me cute and endearing or I'd taken my life in my hands.

Thankfully, Connor walked over to the refrigerator, yanking the door open. "Oh, Lily Joy, FYI, you're never letting her go," he teased. Good. I really didn't have the energy to fight with him right now. Okay, that probably meant I shouldn't have started anything with him then, but exhausted or not, I still had to be me and few things gave me more enjoyment than giving Connor a hard time. "Thank you, babe," he said. "You thought of me with the salad."

"What does he mean?" Lily Joy asked.

I wrinkled my nose at the memory. "He only eats—*healthy*—food when I'm not around. Can you believe he left me stranded at his apartment with only fruit and protein bars? It was torture."

Both Connor and Lily Joy laughed. I tried to laugh, but I still felt like crap.

"No more magic today," Connor ordered. "The food smells amazing, but you're as pale as a ghost. You need to rest."

Yeah, I wouldn't openly agree with him—no sense giving the man a bigger head than he already had—but he was right. I ate my body weight in meatloaf, mashed potatoes, salad, and dinner rolls. Lily Joy whipped us up some super yummy coffee drinks, the ones that tasted like dessert. And by whipped them up, I meant the traditional way. As in, she used her hands, corporeal ingredients, and a blender.

I offered to help clean up, but she and Connor refused. "You cooked, babe," he said as he chuckled. Oh, he thought he was so cute.

"Then I'm going to go lie down."

No one objected. I went upstairs, changed into a T-shirt that I manifested, causing my stomach to go queasy for a moment, and then fell face-first into bed. Although it took a lot out of me at the moment, I couldn't help but smile at how easily the manifestation came to me now. Part of me couldn't wait to find out every one of my powers, while the other part knew that these powers showing meant I'd need to use them at some point to save us, to save everyone.

We had so much practice ahead of us if I was going to feel ready enough to take on Beetle and stand a chance of winning.

Universe, please help us.

# CHAPTER
## Eighteen

T he next morning, we took things outside. The weather was gorgeous. Bright sunshine and not too hot or too cold. I took off my shoes to let my toes squish in the grass, simply because I could. Poor Connor kept checking his texts distractedly.

"Do you need to leave?" I asked, knowing that Luc—or should I say *an incredibly pissed-off Luc*—was the one blowing up Connor's phone. He'd been sort of forbidden to go on this little adventure with me. And although he wouldn't tell me what Luc had said back at the witches' archives, I knew it couldn't have been pleasant.

"Fallen angels don't have mates," he said rather than answering my question.

"Oh-*kay*." I patted his shoulder. "Good of you to inform me of that."

"No, Simone, I mean, he's angry with me, but my mate comes before his hissy fit."

"Your mate should *come* before everything. It's only the nice thing to do." I pinched his cheek teasingly, causing him to swat my hand away.

"*Woman*." He sort of warned me with that one word.

"Okay, okay..." I held my hands out in front of me with my feet shoulder-width apart, ready to fake fight off an attacker with witch powers. "It's good to know my mate won't slink back to work with his tail between his legs," I mumbled, laughing as he stormed at me. He'd moved away when I'd gone all fighting stance. Connor flipped me up over his shoulder as he carried me behind Lily Joy's house and I shrieked with laughter, kicking my feet and slapping his back until he dropped me to the ground, pressed me up against the plaster siding on the cottage, and proceeded to kiss me stupid.

"What's between my legs?" he whispered, all sultry and turning me on like no one's business, well, until we heard Lily Joy scream. The scared kind. We took off running to get to my cousin. That was when I stopped short, briefly taken aback by the three large, dark figures charging Lily Joy.

"What are they?" I shouted at Connor.

"Demons."

Demons? What in the ever-loving Hades? How did demons find us? We were so careful. Demons should *not* have found us here. "Luc?" I asked.

"No. I know all Luc's minions." That was the last he said in human form. He stripped down faster than I'd ever seen anyone disrobe, and dropped, his gigantic death-hound form stood in his place. Eyes glowing red. Baring razor-sharp teeth as he squatted forward, ready to attack.

Lily Joy retreated back next to me and moved into her fighting stance. I hated that my sweet, beautiful cousin needed to utilize a fighting stance to begin with. When the largest one got a bit too close for comfort, Connor lunged.

I threw out my hand, meaning to create a strong enough wind to push the other demons back, but instead, a small hill formed on the grass, tripping one and sending him toppling to the earth. Yeah, I needed to practice that one more. The last demon kept charging. Lily Joy threw out a spell, but he managed to sidestep it at the last minute. With nothing else coming to me from my vast repertoire of spells—yeah... *I know*—I cloaked myself and threw my body against his beefy one in a move he literally didn't see coming. Thank goodness I got this one down. Connor had the biggest demon down for the count. This left the last one for Lily Joy. She used a badass spell to lift him off the ground and throw him. Unfortunately, she couldn't see me and he landed hard right on top of me. I screamed as I scratched and clawed to scramble out from under him, but I still had the presence of mind to manifest a demon-proof cage, trapping the invaders.

My cloak faded. Connor popped back into his human form and I couldn't even enjoy all that olive skin on display as he quickly dressed because something hurt really bad. He dropped down at my side. "Talk to me. What's wrong?"

"I think my shoulder is out of joint," I told him. But when he tried to pick me up, we found out it wasn't just my shoulder. One of the demon's long, blue-black, razor-sharp talon fingernails jutted from my side in a bloody mess.

"Damnit," I whined. "I liked this top." It was so cute. Peasant style with embroidered flowers around the collar and arm holes. And now stained red with blood.

"Get her inside," Lily Joy ordered. "I think she's good and trapped them for now."

Oh, yeah, I choked hardcore in that particular fight, but I'd gotten that cage right. Connor tried to be so gentle, but each move he made jostled me and I bit my lip trying not to scream as that razor-sharp talon ripped at my flesh with every one of his movements. I whimpered and winced.

"Let's deal with the shoulder first," Lily Joy said. "That will go quicker."

She meant it. Lily Joy cast a glorious spell where we all watched as the end of the bone shifted, then popped back into place. My arm felt sore, but it no longer had me wanting to pass out. The demon claw, now that was another story.

"We have to get it out now," Connor snapped at Lily Joy,

staring down at the torturous blade jutting out from my side. "The longer it's in, the sicker she'll get."

"I need to brew a—"

"No time. This is a demon claw. Do you know how toxic they are?"

Uh, toxic? And yeah, I felt sick with some lightheadedness, and a little bit of nausea thrown in for good measure, but I thought that was from the blood loss.

"Sorry, Simone," she whispered right before separating the wound with her fingers and easing the blade back so as not to rupture any more tissue. I screamed bloody murder and promptly passed out.

When I awoke, I felt like shit, like if the worst flu of my life and a third-degree burn had a baby and the parents used me as a host for their demon spawn. My wound screamed red and angry at me; the skin burned to the touch. I had a fever, and my entire body ached. Was I dying? Was this what dying felt like?

"Simone?" Connor dropped down to my side, smoothing my hair back from my face.

"I… hurt…" I managed to say.

He pressed his face to the side of mine as he breathed in sharply. "Lily Joy is in the kitchen trying to brew something. As pissed as he is at me, Luc even showed up to try to help."

"Luc… was here?"

"He's outside interrogating those demons. There are rules, even in Hades. I work for him; therefore, no demons should attack me unless he puts the hit out."

I tried to laugh. I really did. "I'm burning up… but I'm so cold, Connor."

My mate lifted me, sliding behind me to set me on his lap. There, he held me. "You're going to be okay, you hear me?"

"I don't know… that I am…"

"Don't you say that." He kissed the top of my head. "*Lily Joy!*" he shouted.

"Here." She returned with a mug of what smelled like rotting vegetation and a small bowl of salve that looked like it. She rubbed the salve on my wound where it bubbled and hissed when it made contact with my flesh. The god-awful smell burned the inside of my nostrils. It stung despite starting to cool the skin there. Then she lifted the mug to my mouth. I felt too weak to hold it myself. Connor helped me drink.

"How long before it starts taking effect?" he asked.

"I don't really know. I've never brewed a fallen angel blood tea before."

I coughed, choking on the drink. "Fallen angel… *blood*?"

"He says it's one of the only things to help counteract the poison, baby."

And right on cue, the man himself appeared in the room. "You gave her the tea," he said.

"How'd you know?" Connor asked.

"I'm moving inside your mate as we speak."

Connor growled. "I will end you if you say that shit again."

"Too soon?" Luc asked all innocently and when no one gave a response, he mumbled, "Right, right…" under his breath. "Make sure she drinks it all. If it works, she should be back to her normally charming self in an hour."

"What if it doesn't work?" Lily Joy asked and Luc's face fell. That didn't bode well for me.

"She'll need a blood transfusion from someone with her blood type—and I don't mean A, B, O, or any of those. I mean Lilium, like her."

"I'm Lilium," Lily Joy said. Her face lit up with hope.

"We could try it, but I think your blood is too diluted." He looked at Connor. "Yours, too." Connor's head jutted back. "And you know how strong demon toxins are. I'm so sorry."

Lilith had said that yesterday, that Connor's magic came from the man who'd married her oldest daughter with Zohor. That only made us kind of related, right? Like our family tree branched enough for our future children to be fine? Connor, it seemed, paid no attention to my internal struggle, putting his own thoughts together. No, I wasn't a mind reader—I mean, yes, I could talk to Connor in his head when he was in death hound form, but I didn't need to connect with him like that and couldn't right now even if I wanted to.

I knew Connor was putting his own thoughts together because he muttered, "*Simeon*."

"What?" Luc asked.

"Simone's brother. Simeon. If the tea doesn't work, then we need to get him here."

"We don't even know exactly where he is," Lily Joy reminded him.

"Let's just hope the tea works," Luc said.

I finished the entire mug and even choked down a second for good measure, but after an hour of me progressively deteriorating, getting weaker and weaker, it became apparent that we needed more than Luc's blood. I needed my brother's.

My entire body shook violently. Connor did everything he could to keep me comfortable, but some things were just out of our control. "We… had a… good… run," I said.

"It's not over yet, Simone. Don't you dare give in. I need you."

It took so much effort, but I managed to lift my hand to his cheek. "I… love you… Connor."

He pressed a kiss to the meaty part of my palm. Dying sucked, both physically and emotionally. As I started to phase out, Connor screamed, "*Lily Joy!*" The fear… Even in spirit form, I doubted I'd ever forget the fear in his voice. Lilith shimmered into the room before my eyes.

"Are you… bringing me… home?" I asked her.

"Who are you talking to, sweetheart?" Connor asked.

"*Lilith*," I answered.

His arms grew tighter around me. "No… no, no, no. You can't have her, Lilith. Not now. She's mine." Connor's words sounded as thick as they did angry and I felt one of his tears hit my skin.

"Hold on, my sweet granddaughter," she cooed softly. "Help is coming."

I felt myself transitioning out of this world. Lilith's features began to sharpen. The room lit up with swirls of energy. Universal energy that mortals couldn't see.

Then we heard a woman's voice. "*Connor?*"

"Where's my sister?" Simeon pushed past his mate and Lily Joy to drop down at my bedside. He lifted one of my hands into his. "What's wrong?" he asked.

"Stabbed with a demon claw," Connor answered. "We were attacked and while I fought off one, she was injured by another."

"What can I do?" he asked.

Luc stepped back inside the room. "The only thing to save her now is a blood transfusion."

Both Simeon and Madigan stood mesmerized by the fallen angel's glowing beauty. "Luc?" Madigan breathed out. "I've never seen you outside the office."

"I don't get topside much."

"It's a good look," she answered.

"Can we stop?" Simeon asked, snapping out of his fog. "*She's my mate and my sister is dying.*"

"Luc's an old friend, Sim," Madigan said. They both looked tired, and I meant that in a physical and mental way. Her injuries had healed for the time, but that didn't mean they hadn't taken a toll on her.

"Sim?" Luc asked.

"Simeon," he grunted.

It didn't bother Luc one bit. "Well, Simeon. We need your blood. She needs a transfusion to live."

"Does anyone know how to do one of those?" he asked.

"I know a guy," Luc said. "But I don't know if he'll do it. We didn't part on the best terms."

"Are you talking about Raph?" Connor asked, highly surprised.

"If anyone can do it, it's Raph."

"But do you think he will?"

"I guess we'll find out." Then Luc looked at me. "Simone, don't die. I'll be back." He popped out of the room right as my consciousness began to wane again.

"Simone?" Connor's voice sounded like he was shouting at me from the end of a very long tunnel.

Sorry, humanity. I think I just screwed over the world.

## CHAPTER
## *Nineteen*

"Lilith's granddaughter?" someone shouted as the blackness lifted. "Only you, Luc. Only you would get involved with Lilith's granddaughter."

"He's not *involved* with her," Connor spat.

"Does your mongrel know who I am?"

"You know he does, and he's not a mongrel. But she *is* his mate. Can you help or not?"

I opened my eyes to see a handsome, dark-haired man with a copper glow surrounding him. He had deep-brown eyes and a strong jaw. One could call him conventionally handsome, but not drop-dead gorgeous like Luc or even blow-my-ever-loving-mind like Connor. He wore a copper breastplate, which seemed a bit over the top for the situation.

"She's pretty, I'll give you that," the man said. "And she's coming to. It's best I knock her out again so she doesn't feel this part." He ran his hand over my body and the blackness settled in again. When I started to regain consciousness, I was… well, I was in an operating room. Bright blue-white lighting. The dark-haired man stood over me in a copper surgery gown and mask. His head was covered in one of those ugly paper head coverings that surgeons wore. I saw an IV and my brother on a bed next to mine. "Not yet," the man said to me.

When I woke up next, the room had shifted to a type of recovery room. "How are you feeling?" the man asked.

"Tired," I answered.

"I thought we lost you a couple of times. Rest now. I'll check on you in a bit." Who was I to argue? I closed my eyes again.

After drifting off to sleep a couple more times and waking up in the same recovery room, the last time I woke up, I was beyond glad to have Connor sitting by my bed holding my hand.

"Hey," I said in a voice so scratchy, it sounded as if I'd dragged it over sandpaper. His head lifted, showing me those coal-black eyes I couldn't get enough of.

"Don't you ever do that to me again," he ordered while pressing his forehead to mine and he breathed in slowly.

"It's just a scratch," I tried to tease, but I ended up in a coughing jag from too much speaking so soon after almost dying. It hurt, too. Like, really bad.

"The one time I *want* you to talk," Connor muttered. I opened my mouth to try to relieve some of his worry, but he stopped me with a kiss of the *heart-melting, this man truly loved me* variety. I sighed instead.

"How's our girl?" Luc's soft, sexy-melodic voice interrupted our moment.

"Alive," I replied.

"Listen, I have some bad news. Can you handle it?"

"No—" Connor said.

At the same time, I answered, "Why not?"

"Sorry, man. This is important, so I'm going with her answer. The demons wouldn't talk for a ridiculous amount of time, no matter what I did to coax it out of them. Finally, I got one to break. They were sent by Beetle. Something about Simone controlling all the world's magic."

"I don't—" I started. "That's not right."

He shrugged. "I'm only telling you what he said. It's like a super highway with you as the hub. He's either going to control you or kill you."

"Why?" Connor asked as he gave my hand a squeeze.

"Supers keep the world in check."

"Easier to take over," my mate mumbled. "*Shit.*"

"Shit, indeed," Luc replied.

"Let me get this straight… This Beetle person wants to take over the world, and he either needs me on his side or dead to do it?"

Luc nodded several times in short succession. "Seems like it."

"How unoriginal. Why do the bad guys always have to be so trite?" I asked, causing both men to laugh at me, which, with the way Connor scowled so deeply that it caused the skin to wrinkle around his mouth, was a feat. If he didn't let up on the death grip on my hand, my new nickname would be 'Stumpy.' "Connor," I whined and he snapped his head to look at me then down at my hand beginning to turn purple.

"Sorry." He let go and that pins-and-needles feeling spread through my hand and up my arm. "I want to talk to them," he said to Luc.

"No can do, buddy."

"You're really going to try to stop me?"

"I wouldn't dream of it," Luc answered what I felt was earnest. "But one of them managed to get his hand down his boot, where he apparently kept two sort of tiny death grenades because he tossed one at the other demon and the dude disintegrated right before my eyes. And while I was distracted, he smashed the other one against his own chest and the same thing happened. I've never seen that kind of magic before. You have to behead a demon to kill it."

"I don't like the sound of that," I said.

"I fucking hate it," Connor countered. "Do Simeon, my sister, and Lily Joy know?"

"Lily Joy was with me. She witnessed the whole thing. Madigan looked after Simeon while he recovered."

And speak of the devil, or should I say Lilium. "Knock, knock," Lily Joy said from the doorway. She carried a tray of tea. "This is either an illegal party or strategy session. Neither of which my cousin is strong enough for yet." She walked the tray over to me, set it down on the bedside table, and began to pour me a cup. "Move," she ordered Connor, who simply growled at her and scooted his chair back slightly. I'll note, he did *not* move.

Next, I heard, "This must be the cool kids' room."

"You too?" Connor barked at his sister.

"Sim wanted to check on his sister and I'd like to meet my sister-in-law. Since they're one and the same, here we are. Deal with it, big brother." She held my brother's hand as they walked in together. He appeared tired, but not much worse for wear. He made it to the bed, dropping down on the opposite side of Connor.

"Hey," he said, smiling at me.

"Hey," I said back.

"It's good to see you finally awake. You were kind of a mess when we got here."

"It was just a graze," I said, watching as Connor dropped his head and then turned it up to the sky. Possibly for deliverance?

"Of all the mates in the world..." Connor bemoaned his plight.

"I feel you," my brother replied in commiseration. "Madi's like a trouble-seeking missile."

"Then we keep them apart," my mate grumbled. "Who knows what kind of trouble they'll get into together."

"All the best kinds," I replied. "Hi, sister-in-law. It's good to finally meet you in person while not actively dying."

Madigan approached the bed, sitting down next to my brother. "It's good to meet you, too. Thank you for helping us."

"It's what families do," I replied, loving the fact that I'd gone from being totally alone in the world to having this crazy, eclectic family of both the born and made variety. "Now, that you're all here, we were talking about Beetle and his boring plan to take over the world."

"Bad guys always want to take over the world," Madigan said, waving her hand in a very blasé attitude. "Why can't they ever come up with something new?"

"*Madi,*" my brother admonished in a distinctly disgruntled tone that I recognized from my own mate.

"Not now, dear. The women are speaking," she replied, shutting him down and I seriously had to bite my lip to keep from giggling out loud. Normally, I wouldn't have cared, but the man *did* just save my life by giving me his blood. Simeon rolled his eyes to the heavens. Something else he and Connor had in common.

I drank from the cup forced into my hands by Lily Joy. The tea tasted mostly of lemon and ginger, but I knew it packed a recovery punch. Lily Joy had a knack for that. I'd drink a gallon of this stuff rather than ever have to imbibe on fallen angel tea ever again. Even remembering the taste made me want to vomit, but I magnanimously held it back, giving my friends the boon they didn't know they almost didn't receive.

"Did the demon say anything else before he disintegrated?" I asked Luc.

"Only that time is ticking or something along those lines," he replied.

"How long do we think until they come back for me?"

"I guess it depends. Were the demons able to communicate that there were three of us here?" Connor asked. "Beetle would have to prepare. He's already planning something. I mean, if I sent henchmen to do my dirty work and they stopped checking in, I'd figure the plan had gone wrong. One thing we know about Beetle, he's not stupid. He knows something went wrong."

Yeah, I thought of that, too.

"But he couldn't know about us, right?" Simeon asked. "He couldn't know that Madi and I made it here. The last he knew, we were injured, on the run, with no idea that Simone even existed."

"*Shit*," Luc said, startling me and I jumped. "I just remembered, I hung back before starting my interrogation, listening for anything useful before they clammed up. I heard one say, 'What about the book?'"

"Book?" Connor asked, and it hit me. Bam! Right between the eyes. The book Lilith left me with. The family's grimoire.

"I have to get home," I said.

"Talk to me," Connor said.

"The book. I need to get it."

"Shit, I forgot about that. It's at home?"

I nodded.

"Someone want to fill me in?" Luc asked. Madigan and Simeon stared at me, clearly confused.

"Sim," I asked. "do you still have the hilt of a dagger?" He narrowed his eyes at me. "Connor, can you grab my bag?" He nodded once, standing to walk over to the corner of the room where my bag sat on the floor. He walked it back over to me. I dug inside, pulling out the jewel, holding it up for Simeon to get a good look at.

"What is that?" my brother asked.

"It's part of Lilith's dagger," I said. Mouths dropped open. "You found a—"

"Solid gold hilt," he said, cutting me off. "I recognize the shape."

"We didn't bring it," Madigan said. "We didn't know we needed to. It was just a pretty piece of gold."

"How could you have known?" I asked. "A witch told me. Did you consult any powerful witches?"

"We never had the chance," Simeon said. "Madi and I tracked down a powerful one named Agnetha, but we were attacked before we got to her. Then we were on the run, trying not to die."

"What about the book?" Luc asked.

"It's the family grimoire," I admitted and I swore you could hear a pin drop in the room from the dead silence. Yeah, that was quite the bombshell.

"The family grimoire?" Lily Joy asked. "As in *our* family?"

"As in Lilith's grimoire," I replied. "She left it with me with it. The gem found me."

"The gold knife hilt found me," Simeon said. "I was metal detecting in a farmer's field about three years ago. I got a hit and dug that out of the dirt. Since it was clearly worth something, I kept it."

"Did Lilith leave you with anything as a baby?" Connor asked my brother. And now more than ever, I needed to know the answer too. She had to have, right? If she left me the grimoire, she had to have left Simeon something important, too.

"A book. A handwritten book with leaves or flowers pressed between the pages. A description of each of the plants on the page."

"Do you still have it?" Connor asked then.

"It's at home, with the hilt."

"You don't think she left you—" I started to say.

"Plants from the Garden of Eden," Lily Joy finished for me. Yeah, she was smart.

"So let me get this straight," Luc said, pausing for effect. "Lilith left you"—he pointed at me—"her grimoire and you"—he pointed at my brother—"plants from the freaking garden of Eden? And you left them unguarded?"

"We didn't know their significance," Simeon said in our defense.

"How could we have?" I defended us, too.

"Not helping," Connor snapped at his best friend.

"So here's the plan," I said because someone had to take charge. "We need Luc to do some snooping and try to identify Beetle for us. Lily Joy, you start researching what kinds of magic those demons got a hold of. How did they find us? How did they off themselves without a beheading?"

"I'll get right on that," she agreed.

"Sim, Madi—you need to get back to your home to get the botanical book and the hilt. Connor and I will go after the grimoire."

"All right, I'm out," Luc said. "Check in at least once a day, okay? I need to know you all aren't dead." Then he kissed Lily Joy's cheek and she blushed. Then he kissed Madigan's cheek, and my brother gave him a death glare. When he bent in to kiss my cheek, Connor growled, baring his teeth. "Down, boy," Luc teased and my mate narrowed his eyes at the fallen angel who was totally taking his life in his hands once again. "You're right, Simone, this *is* fun. But seriously, I could no more bump uglies with you than I could Connor here. You're like a sister now… Unless—are you and my boy here solid?"

"Hades, Luc!" Connor snapped. "Quit hitting on my mate. Today is *not* the day, man."

"You're right. My apologies. I'll try again tomorrow." Luc dodged my bag that Connor threw at his head and jogged out of the room calling, "Later," over his shoulder. I tried to use magic to keep my bag from falling and spilling out the contents all over the floor, but I lacked the strength to do more than slow the descent so it hit with a small *poof*. The flap opened, but only a couple of trinkets rolled out.

"We're not going anywhere today, sweetheart," Connor said, his eyes moving between my bag and me. "Please don't argue. You're not ready and I can't—" He cut himself off, shaking his head.

I felt what he felt. He'd almost lost me. It gutted me to even imagine what he'd gone through while waiting for me to get through the transfusion and time in recovery.

"I won't argue," I said and he stood from the chair so fast that it tipped backward, hitting the floor as he dropped into a fighting stance.

"Who are you and what have you done with Simone?" he barked, and at first, I thought he was serious until he winked at me. "What?" he asked cheekily. "My Simone takes every opportunity to argue with me. I figured you had to be a demon in disguise."

"You truly are an idiot."

"But you love me."

"Unfortunately," I replied, rolling my eyes.

"You seriously aren't going to argue with me on this?"

I shook my head. "If I had been in your place…" Tears actually pricked my eyes.

Connor scooted me over on the bed so he could sit down next to me. He caught the one tear that fell with his finger. "You don't have to worry about that, babe," he replied low, but with lots of feeling.

"It's not that I like you," I countered through my sniffles. "It's just you do that thing with the twist and I'd miss that."

"And this is where I nope out of this conversation," Madigan said, patting my arm. "I don't need to hear those details about my brother."

"But I mean, it's life-changing," I said to her, laughing. "If we compare notes, you might—"

"La, la, la, la, la," Madigan singsonged.

"You shouldn't go today, either," Lily Joy told them. "Simeon still looks tired. Rest today. Leave in the morning."

It felt wrong to waste another day, but we needed to be healthy for this to work. The world depended on us, and most of humanity didn't even know it.

I heard them all downstairs talking at the dinner table and it pissed me off to miss it. Somehow, Lily Joy got it in her head that I needed to stay in bed to rest. I understood she was trying to get me strong enough to use my magic, but alienating me from the rest of the group totally hurt my morale. In a big way. I needed people around me. I needed stimulating conversation mixed with the adoration of my mate. Okay, so I laughed at myself for even thinking that last part. But I missed the big lug's face and his scent, and the way he held me. I missed how gently he stroked the skin on my arm totally unaware that he was doing it. I *did* say I needed people around me.

The four walls closed in on me to the point that if I didn't get out, I'd go mad. Could some call me overdramatic? Yes. Did I remotely care at this point? Hell no. Even though I stood slowly, my head spun, causing me to put a hand to the bed for balance. Then once I felt ready, I pulled the quilt from the end of the bed and made my way downstairs. The food smelled good. Connor laughed at something Madigan said. I felt completely alone as I slipped out the front door. Slowly, I made my way over to a two-person swing that Lily Joy built around the side of the house to watch the setting sun.

The big, orange ball burned beautifully in the sky. I wondered how Mrs. Hildibrant was faring. I needed to check on my cat. At least he knew how to get into his food and her water fountain lasted for weeks.

So much had changed within such a short span of time. I missed my Jeep and my store, and the days when there weren't demons and a man named Beetle trying to kill me. Lilith had been selfish to bring me here, to lay all this on my shoulders. A good man died because of her decision. Jeffery didn't deserve that. If I'd stayed in my time, then he might have met a nice, mortal woman and they would've lived in a nice house with a couple of beautiful kids. He could've led a blissful life.

But then there was Connor. Surely, the universe would've picked a woman better suited to be his mate. Maybe another death hound. Lilith set all this in motion, now leaving me to clean up the mess caused because of it.

Even thinking of my mate with another woman hurt, though. What I needed to do was try to manifest myself away from this place right now so that nobody I loved got hurt fighting this foe who had it out for me in particular in a big, fricking way. But I wasn't so naive to believe that Connor wouldn't get himself killed trying to find me. He'd set the world on fire to get to me.

I pressed the palms of my hands to my eyes, frustrated by the whole situation. What did I do? What was the right course of action here? How much clearer could the universe make it? I wasn't strong enough to take on an enemy like Beetle. The state of my injuries proved that.

If I only had the power to go back in time and take out Adam before he had the chance to attack. Or at the very least keep this Beetle from discovering my secret.

My thoughts kept me occupied for a while longer. I supposed that was how Connor dropped down next to me and I hadn't seen him coming. I sensed him, but I always sensed him. Our bond made sure of that.

"What are you doing out here all alone?" he asked as he

wrapped his arm around my shoulders and pulled me in close to his body.

"I felt a little left out. You all were having such a good time at dinner and I needed to clear my head."

"You weren't thinking of doing something stupid, were you?"

"Technically, stupid is relative to the person or situation in conjunction with performing an action. But to put your mind at ease, no. I was just out here lamenting our situation."

"What exactly are you lamenting?"

"That I'm not strong enough to protect you. That I'm not strong enough to defeat Beetle when that inevitable battle comes."

"Simone," he said softly. "I'm not exactly helpless and you won't be alone."

"It's not fair. Lilith shouldn't have ever put this on our shoulders. I have a target on my back and you're forced to wear one too—you weren't given a choice."

"Neither were you. I have to believe she had her reasons. This might've been in the works with a much worse outcome because you weren't here and we didn't find each other."

"I just..." I sniffled. "I got Jeffery killed and he was a good man. He shouldn't have ever been involved in this. What if I get you killed? I couldn't live with myself, Connor."

"That's where this is coming from," he muttered under his breath. Then in a slick yet loving move, Connor lifted me from the swing to deposit me on his lap. He wrapped the both of us in the quilt, tucking it down around our thighs, and he held me, rocking gently. "Baby, you have to listen to me. I'm sorry Jeffery got caught up in all this, but it's not *your* fault. You had no idea about any of this. And no matter how long or brief my life is, I will *never* resent meeting you."

"You say that now—"

"I say that because I mean it. But just to say, I'm not going anywhere. My life is tied to yours, so I have to survive for you and for the kids we'll someday have. So see… I have a family to create with my mate. It'll be a hardship, but I promise to practice until we get it right."

"I'm scared," I said honestly, showing him the vulnerability that I tried not to ever show to anyone. "And if you repeat that, I'll deny it to *your* dying breath."

He chuckled. "Your secret is safe with me."

Then, rather than use his words, he used his mouth to tell me everything he felt in that moment. A kiss of epic proportions. Dammit, I loved this man. Things would be so much easier if I didn't.

As our kiss reached the inevitable conclusion, Lily Joy came running out of the house shouting for us.

"Here," Connor hollered back.

She rounded the corner with fear written all over her face. "A witch coven was hit outside of Boston. The news is calling them a preservation organization, but the Sisters of Salem—"

"Is one of the largest covens in North America," I finished for her. "How?"

"Bomb. It was a gathering night."

"Shit," Connor mumbled. Gathering nights were nights of celebration to bring new witches into the congregation. From what I understood, it was the night when they each declared a field of study, whether it be spellwork, herbology—like making teas and tinctures—crystal work, divination, or any other field of study.

"It's started," I said.

"It's started," Lily Joy agreed. And as if on cue from a stage director, Madigan and Sim ran out of the house shouting for us.

"Bamburg was hit," Sim rushed out as they reached us, breathing hard. Bamburg? The German coven? No, no, no… This couldn't be happening.

"Where are the other large covens?" I asked.

"Navarre and Edinburgh," Lily Joy answered.

"Don't forget Western Australia," Madi said.

"There won't be a continent unaffected. I see it now," I said and I meant it. Like, as I spoke, this clear image of witch strongholds being attacked filled my vision. I felt lightheaded and sick like I had to puke.

"Simone?" Connor grabbed me before I passed out. "Talk to me."

"Visions," I managed to get out at the very same time my brother bent over in pain.

"I… feel… it…" he cried.

Madigan grabbed a hold of him to keep him standing. Then everything sort of happened at once. A large portal opened up from Hell, and thousands of demons started spilling out into this world. Once again, they'd breached all of Lily Joy's spells and wards. They shouldn't have been able to breach the wards.

A man appeared in the far-off distance right as Connor and Madigan dropped into their death-hound forms. The man in the distance disappeared as a death hound took his place, all this happening in the blink of an eye. He ran full speed toward us, tearing up grass and dirt in his charge. Lily Joy turned to look at the hound barreling down the hill and missed a demon aiming a nasty shot of something at her. I pushed her out of the way right before it hit her and Connor managed to knock me down before I got hit, but that put Connor in the line of fire until the unknown death hound launched himself at another demon, knocking him into the path. The demon dropped and vanished.

Who was this hound? Where did he come from? Despite the field around Lily Joy's house having filled with demons, this new hound jumped right in fighting alongside us.

"Lilith," I screamed, summoning her. Although I couldn't see her, a ripple of energy radiated out from the field. I just managed to grab a hold of Connor's ruff when the ripple hit, knocking us off our feet. I had the presence of mind to manifest our safety. I meant it to protect all of us, but when we landed in the hot, hard-packed sand, only Connor and I made it.

The sun blazed down on us. We had nothing for protection. My backpack was still up in our room at Lily Joy's cottage—and that had the gem to Lilith's dagger in it.

Connor had to stay in his hound form because whatever happened drained me and I didn't have the power to manifest clothing for him.

"*Where are we?*" he asked in my head.

"I don't know. I don't know what happened."

"*It'll be okay.*"

"What about Madigan, Lily Joy, and Sim? And who was that hound?"

My mate shook his head.

"If they planned to just attack us, then why hit the covens?"

"*Something else is going on,*" he said. "*I don't think they meant to kill us. I think it was a distraction.*"

"We need to find shade," I said, holding my hand over my eyes like a visor. A person could go blind out here. "And we need to find water."

After several hours of walking, we found an oasis. Connor dug down fairly deep to find us water, but he found it and we greedily drank our fill. It might've been gritty, sandy water, but it was safe to drink.

The sun began to set at our oasis, meaning England was hours ahead. Connor lay down, leaving a space open for me to settle in a way that he would be able to keep me safe and warm throughout the night. I managed to drift off until I didn't-know-how-long later. Connor startled me awake when he stood abruptly, his head low, baring teeth at something in the distance.

"*Stay back,*" he ordered me as several giant dogs moved into view. *Great. Just freaking great.*

"Who are they?" I asked him in my head.

"*I don't know.*"

The pack leader stared at us, nodded, and then turned to run back the way they'd come from. Connor started off after them but then stopped so I could climb on top of him, then he took off at full speed. He followed the giant dogs back to a camp, where each transformed back into a man when they had clothing to cover themselves with.

One of the men threw Connor a pair of blue, cotton pants in rough shape and a faded, red T-shirt. We must've been in South America, given the look of the men, and I was pretty sure they spoke Spanish. The men eyed me like a raw steak. One asked in very broken English if Connor would be willing to trade me for goods he might need.

"No women near," the man managed to say and so not my problem. The man had very tanned skin from living in the desert, black hair, dark eyes, and a strong physique that I was sure other women found attractive. *But sorry there, fella—my mate has everything over you.* Connor rose up to his full height, which let's be honest, towered over these men.

"Touch her and die," he said in a fierce growl, and with the way their eyes grew wide, each and every man here clearly believed it.

One of the men began whining, *"El infierno,"* over and over again. *"El infierno."*

"That means 'Hell,'" Connor said to me.

"So they know what you are?"

"Seems that way."

"But they aren't death hounds?"

"No. Just your garden variety shifters."

Then it hit me. "Do you think, since they know what you are, that they've seen other death hounds? Are we close to a portal?"

"I'm not fluent by any means, so I hope I'm saying this right."

"Saying what?" I asked, but he ignored me.

"Sorry if I get this wrong," he said, then he followed with, *"¿Estamos cerca de un portal?"*

"*¡Sí, sí!*" the men shouted.

"*Necesitamos comida y agua primero,*" Connor said. They nodded and ushered us over to their little nomadic settlement. "I taught myself some Spanish through Google Translate when I was younger. I have no idea if it's grammatically correct, but it's close enough for them to understand me."

"You taught yourself through Google Translate?" I laughed in spite of the situation, picturing a young Connor on Google Translate while other boys his age were playing video games.

He shrugged. "When I'm not trying to keep my mate alive or save the world, it gets slow at work sometimes."

Well, I couldn't argue with that. But, um… just how long had he been in service to Luc? Did he go to public school at all? Was he homeschooled or could it have been like with Richard, a Jewish boy I'd gone to school with? He went to public school during the day and then had to go to Hebrew school afterward. Once we had the time for more 'get to know you' conversation, I'd have to ask about that. I refused to put my future kids into service for Luc, fallen angel or not. They were going to have a regular childhood just like any other children. Even death hounds deserved a childhood.

We sat on raggedy rug mats that the men laid out around a fire. One man shoved a cup in my hand. I smelled it first. Just water, which out here made sense. Then they shared roasted meat with us. Once they'd realized that Connor could end them all pretty much at the same time, they stopped assessing me for mating purposes.

After I ate my fill, I curled up against Connor, using him as a body pillow, and he let me drift off for a while. Eventually, he shook me awake. Aside from the stars in the nighttime sky, blackness surrounded us.

The men held little torches. I stood and stretched before Connor took my hand to lead me behind the men through the desert. One of the men put up a hand to stop us before we reached a rocky outcropping, but he stayed eerily silent, as did the rest of the men. They doused their torches. We waited maybe fifteen minutes before a door opened out of thin air and someone stepped out.

I looked at Connor, but he shook his head once in warning because what emerged from the portal wasn't a death hound. It was a demon. A curvy woman with short, bleached blonde hair —a pixy cut—and red glowing eyes. She scanned the area. Connor pulled on my hand as he dropped down to the rocky, sandy soil. I dropped next to him.

Our nomadic friends slunk off back into the dark, leaving me and my mate alone. The demon sniffed the air and kept walking in a direction away from us. Thankfully, we were downwind from the portal.

"Isn't this still Luc's area?" I asked in a very soft whisper.

Connor nodded. "But I don't know that demon."

"Do you know all demons who reside in Luc's territory?"

"I work directly under Luc. It's my job to know everyone in his territory."

My mind was officially blown. His job seemed so much more complex than I'd originally thought. My respect for him grew exponentially.

He pushed up from the ground, grabbing my hand again, and began walking softly toward the space where the portal opened for us. As a death hound, it would. We started down the stone steps and the heavy portal door shut behind us.

"Baby, can you cloak us?" he asked.

"I can try."

Taking in a strong breath, I closed my eyes and tried to use manifestation to cloak us, but I still felt too weak. I'd shot us into the desert before I was ready.

"I'm sorry… I can't cloak us both," I said, feeling ready to cry.

"Then cloak yourself."

"No, Connor. We do this together."

He kissed me good and thorough. "I don't know what we're going to face down there. Please, I need you to do this for me."

My protector as well as my mate. I kissed him one more time. "Love you, Connor Baghest."

"Love you, Simone Lamia—even though you're a huge pain in my ass."

I covered my mouth to keep from giggling. "I promise you can be a huge pain in mine if we make it home alive." And I gave my eyebrows a good waggle so he understood exactly what I was talking about.

He sighed, pressing his forehead to mine right before I cloaked myself and we continued the rest of the way down the slick staircase. Rather than walking into a lit office space like we would have back in Raven, we emerged into a dark, dank tunnel that smelled strongly of rotten eggs. More catacombs? We managed to access a portal that bypassed Hades to lead us to the catacombs underneath Hades? Given the stern look on my mate's face, he didn't know this kind of portal existed either.

Why couldn't we have found our way to a sloth sanctuary or a beach resort? Fear and exhaustion sapped my energy as fear and exhaustion were wont to do. Why did bad things happen when you were the least prepared to deal with them? I gripped Connor tighter, getting a sick feeling in the pit of my stomach. Nothing good ever came from dark, dank tunnels. And this was the last thing I needed to deal with given that I still had no idea if Lily Joy was okay. Did my brother and Madigan get away? Beetle wanted my family's grimoire, why? We needed to get a look at the book Lilith left with Simeon. I felt that down to my little Lilium soul.

And lastly, who was that death hound who jumped into the fray? I didn't know him. Connor didn't know him, either. All those questions deserved answers, yet here we were moving through the darkness in a tunnel filling me with dread. *Dread*. I *hated* dread. Especially when it came with no answers in sight.

Connor stepped into a puddle, making a soft splash. From

nowhere, a cage dropped down out of the blackness. I managed to dive against the stone floor and roll before it captured me. My mate wasn't so lucky.

A disembodied voice came at us from the darkness. "Connor Baghest, how nice of you to join us."

*Oh. Crap.*

**CHAPTER**

*Twenty-One*

A hugely tall, strong, and dare I say, beautiful man stepped out from the shadows. He wore an updated commando uniform—all black. Boots. T-shirt. Cargos. Beret. I bet back in the day, he flaunted his strength as a Roman gladiator. The man just looked the part.

"*Kimaris*," Connor said, nodding and looking terribly unimpressed. Given the situation and how well I knew my mate, he was feigning his nonchalance at this dubious situation. "Long way from home, aren't you?"

Kimaris? Who the hell was Kimaris? I never lamented not growing up in the super community as much as when we encountered bad guys. Bad guys made me feel so inferior. My legitimate grandmother gave rise to all witch culture. Given she'd brought the magic from the Garden of Eden into the world, I felt a little disgruntled at my lack of knowledge. My mate needed me and all I could discern was that a big demon guy had trapped him.

"What are you doing so far from your master, puppy?" Kimaris asked in this condescending tone that made me want to slap him across his dark-skinned, chiseled face.

"My *master*?" Connor scoffed. "I work for a living. You're the only one here with a master—marquis. Given Luc pretty much created this whole realm, I'm not sure where your bloated sense of self-confidence comes from."

*Go, Connor.* Bloated sense of self-confidence. God, his smart use of vocabulary made me so stupidly happy, especially in the face of this nasty situation. Though the nasty situation was probably why I honed in on smart vocabulary. It kept me from panicking. Panicking always helped, said no one ever.

As big and intimidating as Kimaris appeared, he snickered like a weasel. "He might've been the first, but Lucifer is far from the smartest or the strongest."

"Hmm… If you think that, I pity you," Connor replied. It hit me then, of all the demons of hell, Luc had angel power. Fallen, yes, but still freaking angel power.

"*Enough,*" Kimaris snapped. "Where is your mate? You've been traveling together."

"That's cute that you think I'd tell you even if I knew. We got separated."

"Bullshit. What kind of imbecile do you take me for?"

"Well, given the cage here, knowing who I am and who I work for—I'd say the biggest kind. And black salt. Bravo. Someone did his homework."

Black salt? Homework?

Kimaris snickered that weaselly snicker again. "Black salt. Weakens and can even kill hellhounds. It's pretty brilliant."

"How'd you know I'd end up here?"

"I just got lucky. Too many of your kind have started siding against us. Why? You pledge your lives to protect supers who don't care about you. We're offering power and instead of accepting the offer, you double down on your unrequited loyalty."

"Unrequited?" Connor asked and I heard the eye roll in his voice.

"Do you think Lucifer cares what happens to you? He'll replace you faster than you can bark."

The byplay fascinated me. Clearly, Kimaris had no idea about friendship. Luc would no sooner turn his back on Connor than I would. And the cage was made from black salt? It weakened and could even kill a hellhound? I needed to get my mate out of there—*stat*. Who thought making hellhounds vulnerable to something like salt was a good idea? And who had the power to implement it?

"Listen, you made a mistake with the cage," Connor said. "You weren't even on my radar. Now, I'm going to have to kill you." He sounded confident, but I heard the softest wince at the end of his statement. This black salt cage hurt him. My mate.

"Oh, Connor…" He tutted. "Do you honestly think that can happen before you die?"

"Well, I'll give it the old college try."

"Dare to dream, mutt."

Okay, no. That was one snarky cutdown too many! Nobody got to make dog jokes with Connor but *me*. It was our thing. Insults were our love language. I had a problem, though—I needed witch tea or time to get my strength back. I didn't have witch tea, but I *really* didn't have time.

"As much as I love getting together," Connor said, forcing an easy smile. "I have things to do. Let me go and I'll deal with you later. You can go about your business for now."

"I can go about my business? Connor Baghest, I thought you were smarter than that." The demon held two fingers out in front of him and raised his hand upward. The cage and Connor raised off the floor. As the cage lifted, a black salt bottom formed under my mate, giving him no means of escape. Then the demon pushed his hand out and the cage started to move.

Of course, we were moving. Why wouldn't we? It took everything in me to keep myself cloaked. I *did not* sign up for this. But then again, Connor would burn down the world to save me. He deserved no less.

He pushed the hovering cage deeper down into the bowels of the catacombs. Keeping myself masked became more and more difficult as we entered a dark tunnel with water dripping through the porous stone and puddling on the floor. I timed my steps the best I could with Kimaris's steps to hit the puddles at the same time. If he heard the splashes from my footsteps, I'd be toast—demons, fire. I carried no illusions that he wouldn't burn me first and find out my identity later.

Connor's face had grown pale by this point. I wouldn't have been able to see his face if not for the red glow signifying Kimaris as a demon engulfing his entire body—Kimaris's body, not Connor's. But the glow lit the way enough for us until we halted in front of a stone staircase.

The demon lifted his hand to raise the cage and ascended the stairs that led us into well... It looked like a third-world prison. Or like one out of the sixteenth century.

So far, my presence remained unnoticed. At least there was that. We stopped in front of a cell. A woman with dark, almost black hair, and deeply tanned skin—she appeared of Middle Eastern descent, maybe?—approached Kimaris with a set of wrought-iron skeleton keys on a large keyring. She wore the same commando garb as Kimaris.

"Connor Baghest?" she asked. "How'd you bag him?" An air of awe resonated in her words.

The man shrugged. "I got lucky."

"Do we kill him now?" she asked next.

He shook his head. "And lose this bargaining chip?"

"I thought... he had no... loyalty to me," Connor said, straining to speak now.

"Just because he's not loyal doesn't mean you aren't useful to him. We'll see what B—" He stopped himself before finishing and then redirected his thought. "We'll see what the big man in charge wants to do with him."

The woman unlocked the closest cell and Kimaris pushed the cage inside. The door snapped shut and the cage dropped, disintegrating into a pile of black dust on the floor. The bars on the cell door were made of that same black salt. Connor slowly stood, wobbling as if about to lose his balance, and stepped gingerly over the pile of salt. He pressed his back against the wall and slid down until his butt hit the floor. Even though the walls and floor were made of stone, the salt had clearly weakened him too much to fight back. It killed me to see my mate so vulnerable. Connor Baghest was *never* vulnerable.

As weak as I felt, I still used what magic I could to push a thought into his head. *"We need to get you out."*

My head filled with static and a crackling noise before I heard, *"You aren't strong enough. Find a witch to heal you."*

*"I won't leave you."*

*"Please, Simone… I need you to do this."* His eyes closed and his breathing went shallow. My stomach plummeted as fear filled me.

*"Connor!"* I shouted in my head.

His eyes blinked open. *"Sorry."*

*"Don't you die on me."* Tears rolled down my invisible cheeks. *"I'll kill you if you die on me."*

*"I won't die… I have too much to live for."* Because that didn't make me cry harder. *"Follow the hallway… away from the chamber,"* he continued. *"You should find another set of stairs… Take them up."*

*"I love you,"* I whispered to him. When he said nothing back, I ran as fast as I could out of the chamber and down the dank hallway. I found the stairs he'd talked about and rushed up, stopping abruptly when a demon stepped around the bend going down. These staircases hardly allowed for more than a person's body width to begin with. I flattened my back against the wall and sucked in, holding my breath, fingers crossed, that they wouldn't skim me as they passed.

Apparently, they were all part of the commando club. All-black, the required uniform. As this one passed me, she sort of sniffed the air but kept on walking. Once she'd cleared the stairs, I bolted up the rest of the way. Where the portal opened up to wasn't much better than what I'd left behind. I emerged into a bombed-out sandstone building. Heat more stifling than the temperature-controlled Hades assaulted me. I smelled sand. From this, I gathered I'd made topside in the Middle East or Northern Africa. But I could literally be anywhere—at least anywhere with a desert. Just peachy. Northern African and Middle Eastern countries didn't exactly have the witch-friendly stamp of approval. I didn't mean to imply *every person* held a prejudice against our kind, just the *regions as a whole.*

*Now* I faced a different problem. Keeping myself cloaked in my weakened state for such a prolonged period of time wore my butt out. I had to rest and that just pissed me off because Connor needed me. But I felt so weak, I could hardly keep my eyes open. Literally. Some savior of the world I turned out to be. I found a dark corner of the room and dropped down. There, I passed out.

A dream filled my head as I slept. Dreams didn't usually penetrate this level of consciousness for me, but here we were. Mr. Pooches, my gorgeous black kitty, hopped up on my lap and sat, looking right at me.

"Mr. Pooches?" I scratched behind his ear. "Are you okay?" He pressed his head into my hand to really get his scratch on. "You should have enough food and water."

"I've had my fill," he responded, winding his tail around my wrist, and I jerked back in surprise. Mr. Pooches never talked to me. Of course, I didn't remember ever dreaming about Mr. Pooches, either.

"You talk?"

"I talk—but only to you."

"Why only to me?"

He cocked his head and shot me a *'really?'* look. I wasn't trying for obtuse. Mr. Pooches had never talked to me before. Sue me.

"Okay," he went on. "We don't have time for all the explanations the situation requires. I'm here to tell you there's a witch nearby. She's somewhere in your vicinity. Open your mind to sense her. She'll help if you explain the situation."

"'A witch nearby'?" I asked stupidly.

Mr. Pooches got very impatient with me. "Listen—" He turned away as if distracted. "There's been trouble at the house and I think they're back. Go find the witch. I'll join you as soon as I can." Then he popped out of my dream, leaving me all alone.

That was the last I was aware until my eyes blinked open. I remembered every part of that dream. It was just a dream, right? At this point, I couldn't tell if I was coming or going. One thing became clear, when I heard men talking in a foreign tongue I knew I needed to get the hell out of here. They walked right past my dark corner. Lilith knows how they didn't see me or smell me because my cloaking ran out. Once they'd passed me, I gave it a few more seconds to ensure they wouldn't see me before leaving the building and I moved through the darkened streets, pressing myself against walls when necessary and running at other times. The whole time keeping my senses open to sniff out any witch in the area.

I turned down street after street until coming to the end of a road. A dead end. Yeah, if I survived this, I'd lobby to change that term. No one needed that kind of trauma reminder. The only structure left looked like one good wind would blow the thing right over. Still, my Scooby-sense told me that the witch was here somewhere. I walked up to the building and tried to open the door, but it was locked. A locked door, here? Right. Despite being scared out of my mind, I lifted my fist to knock.

No one answered. So I knocked again. No one answered again. I knocked a third time and the door finally creaked open. Very frightened eyes peered out at me. Then once they'd taken me in, they grew huge. The door swung open. Someone grabbed my arm and dragged me inside, slamming the door behind me.

She spoke, but I didn't understand her.

"English?" I asked, hoping beyond hope that she had a better education than I did. She nodded once. Her eyes assessed me skeptically. I know… trust me, I know. What was a purple-haired, English-speaking American doing knocking on her door, especially in the dark? She was in for a whopper of a tale… if she helped me.

"Who are you?" she asked in almost-perfect English. Just with an accent of the region attached.

"My name is Simone Lamia. I need help."

"What are you?" she asked next and yes, I rolled my eyes, even in this precarious situation. I always got that question. Why would it be any different here, while my life was on the line?

"That's a long story," I replied.

"Your name is Simone Lamia, and you need help?" she asked, and okay, we were going to play the repeating game now.

"Yes. I need *your* help."

"*My* help? Why me?"

"You're a witch. I require a witch."

"How did you find me? All the witches have gone into hiding. I have wards around the building."

"I sort of have witch powers," I replied.

"'Sort of'? So you're a witch? I don't get 'witch' from you."

"Well, I have witch-*ish* powers."

"Witch-ish powers? I don't understand."

"Can I sit down? I'm exhausted and feeling a little vulnerable here. More than that, I'm running out of time. Are you willing to help me or not?"

"You will explain?"

"I'll explain everything."

She nodded once and turned, walking inside.

I followed.

*Please let Dream Mr. Pooches be right.*

**CHAPTER**

*Twenty-Two*

The woman led me into a very homey room with a flowered sofa and a fire flickering in the fireplace. Despite the fact that we were in a desert, the temperature dipped when the sun went down, giving the night air a nip. A muted-puce wingback chair sat across from the sofa. The furniture looked old and worn but comfortable.

"Please, sit," the witch offered. She didn't have to offer twice. I dropped into that ugly puce chair and sank down. Oh, yeah—old and worn but comfortable, indeed. "Can I get you something to drink?" she asked and there was my in.

"That's what I'm here for," I replied and she stared at me, head tilted, blank look in her eyes and a slacked expression on her lips. I sighed. "I'm in pretty desperate need of a healing tea."

"That's why you needed a witch," she mumbled. "Oh—I'm Shafira. Welcome to my home, Simone Lamia."

I laughed at the way she'd just remembered to introduce herself. But given the way I'd barged in on her at night, this one was on me.

"First, let me say 'thank you,' Shafira, for helping me," I told her. She nodded as she filled a kettle with water. "Second, Shafira is a beautiful name."

"I was named by my great-grandmother, who transitioned the day I was born. My name was the last gift she'd given to our family."

"That's quite a legacy," I responded, knowing the time had come to spill my guts. She needed to know who she was helping. But I got distracted for a moment while watching her measure herbs into a mortar and then crush them with the pestle. I shook my head to clear it. The fragranced air could lull the most energized person to sleep, so I fought the smell tooth and nail to stay awake. "This is going to sound odd at best and fabricated at worst, but I promise you it's the truth."

"'Fabricated'?" she asked, and I nodded, though her back was to me.

I cleared my throat. "Yes. There's a reason you don't sense me as a witch. Because I'm not *exactly* a witch."

She turned to face me. "'Not exactly a witch'?"

If she kept repeating me, this would take all night. As we didn't have all night, I rushed on, hoping I could get it all out before another interruption. "I'm more than a witch. Have you ever heard of Lilium?"

She startled, dropping the spoon in her hand. The aluminum clanked against the stone floor. "*Lilium*?"

"I'm not just *a* Lilium… I'm sort of *the first* Lilium, or second if you count my mother." When she squinted her eyes at me, I shook my head. I needed to carry a laminated explanation card in my pocket for moments like these. If I survived saving the world, I'd get on that.

She laughed as if she thought I was teasing until she caught my eyes and saw anything but. "Are you serious?" she asked and I nodded. "How is that possible?"

"Okay, here's the CliffsNotes version. Adam was an abusive bastard. Lilith took her two children, a son and daughter, and fled the Garden of Eden. The magic of the garden was with Lilith and Adam wanted it back. Lilith got remarried and raised my mom, my uncle, and the children she had with her new husband. They were happy. Adam hunted them down wanting to get the magic back by getting my mother to marry his son Cain. Are you following?"

She nodded.

"Great. Okay, where was I?"

"Adam hunted them down."

"Right. My mother was already married to my father. She was pregnant with me and my twin brother, Simeon. Adam and his disciples attacked on the day we were born. My parents died that day. To keep us out of Adam's hands, my grandmother, Lilith, escaped through time, depositing my brother and me in different locations. We never knew each other existed until a week ago or so."

She blinked several times before saying, "This is a lot to take in."

"I know, and I'm sorry. But here's the thing. My mate is Connor Baghest. He's a—"

"Hellhound," she replied. "The Baghests are a very old protector family. He's your mate, too?"

"Yup." I popped the 'p.' "Anyway, long story longer, we found my brother and his mate, who is Connor's sister, Madigan—"

Her eyebrows shot up to her hairline. "So your brother's mate is a Baghest protector, too? This is incredible."

"Well, we found them, and Connor and I hunted down one of my cousins, a Lilium named Lily Joy. We were at her place in the English countryside when we were attacked by a horde of demons. I'd already been recuperating from the last time we'd been attacked and I had to get us out, so I manifested and Connor and I ended up in a desert in South America. I hardly had any energy left, but Connor made me use what I had to cloak myself. I couldn't cloak him. He was captured by a demon named Kimaris—"

She gasped. "As in one of the marquises of Hell?"

"Yeah. " I sighed. "That would be the one. It seems he has a team of commando demons working for him. I have to rescue Connor, but I don't have the energy. That's why I need the tea. I need to heal so I can rescue my mate."

"You can't rescue him alone."

I sighed again. This one longer and weightier. What choice did I have? Given our team consisted of me, Connor, Simeon, Madigan, and Lily Joy, and that I currently didn't know the whereabouts or health status of any of them, save for Connor, kind of... "I have to. Did you know there are catacombs under Hades, the corporation?"

"Hades, the *corporation*?"

"Hell is the place you want to avoid. The part of Hades I've visited was nice. And under Hades, there's a sixteenth-century prison? They trapped him in black salt. He's so sick and worn down. I'm worried he won't survive there much longer. I don't know where my brother and Madigan or Lily Joy are. I have no choice." My stupid eyes teared up again. Yes, I turned into a softy where Connor was concerned.

Shafira spooned two spoonfuls of the mashed herbs into a mug, then she drizzled it with honey. She lifted the whistling teapot from the fire and poured the steaming liquid into the herbs. Then she handed it off to me. I closed my eyes, breathing in the healing smell before taking my first tentative sip. What? It was hot. As I sipped my tea, she walked off into a different room. She came back with a plate of... well, it looked like baklava. She handed it to me. It smelled like baklava.

"Eat," she said. "This will help you to heal faster." Didn't have to tell me twice. Eating was better than crying over this crappy situation. "We have to make a plan."

"We?" I asked around a mouthful of food. "Me, not *we*."

"Someone needs to have your back while you rescue your mate—or you need to have *my* back while I rescue your mate. Given your family, I assume you have more powers than me."

"Did you not hear me?"

"Yes. I heard you. But you can't take on Kamaris and his minions alone."

"This is so dangerous. I can't ask you to go up against a marquis of hell. I need you to locate other witches and recruit them into the cause. Witches will win this war."

"Witches *will* win this war. That's why they've sent us into hiding, why the covens have been attacked. They are scared of us. But look around. Where I live *is* dangerous. I face it every single day."

"But—"

"How did you find me?"

Okay, this question got me a bit confused. "I opened my senses to finding you."

"But with all the witches gone into hiding, how did you know I'd be here?"

Oh, I got it. "My cat visited me in a dream and told me to search for you." Yeah, it sounded stupid to me too.

"Your… *cat*? Do you not think that the universe led you to me?"

"I never thought about it."

"We all have a destiny. Your cat sending you to find me is far from coincidental. We are tied. To refuse my help is to deny me my destiny."

"You could die. You get you could die, right?"

"If that is my destiny—if my death brings safety to my nieces who are in hiding with my sister, then I will accept this. I have no children of my own, but my nieces mean as much to me as any ever could. I will do anything to protect those girls."

"I still don't like this…"

"Neither of us like this. But what choice do we have? Evil is sending the witches into hiding—a greater evil than that of mankind. If you were sent a protector as your mate, then we need to save him. He is a part of this. You must fight with him at your side if you have any hope of emerging triumphant."

No truer words.

"You will sleep now," she went on. "The herbs in the tea will help you to rest your mind and body in order to heal." Then Shafira walked out of the room. She came back with a pillow and a throw, placing them down on the sofa. "Please"—she gestured to the makeshift bed— "lie down. We will go once you have your strength back."

Sleeping seemed like the last thing I needed to be doing, but the woman had a point. We needed my power back to full strength if I stood any shot at rescuing Connor. I stood from the ugly chair, stretching, and then walked the few steps over to the sofa, where I lay down.

The sleep took me just about as soon as my head hit the pillow. Fatigue eased from my body and I felt that sense of floating again. This time, I knew the drill. A door opened up and my consciousness floated through. I found Simeon and Madigan on a bed, sleeping. It had to be an old motel. It looked abandoned but still had the old furniture. In Michigan, where I lived, there was this State Highway, M-13. It led up north and was the road hunters especially had used before the construction of I-75. All along the highway, you'd find these little motels tourists and hunters stayed in for the night or longer. Once the interstate went in, most of those little motels had gone belly up. But the buildings remained, as did the furniture inside.

This reminded me of one of those.

"Sim?" I whispered, not wanting to wake up Madigan—and then I laughed at myself. She wouldn't see me; she wouldn't hear me. Simeon's eyes blinked open and his consciousness rose above his body.

"Simone—oh, god, we've been so worried about you."

"I'm okay. How are you?"

"Unhurt. Whatever you did—there was this flash of bright light and I grabbed on to Madi just in time. We were flung into a different place."

"Lily Joy?" I asked, worried and hopeful at the same time.

He shook his head. "I don't know. We got separated."

My heart sank. "Where are you now?"

"I don't really know yet. We found this place and thought it best to hide out until nightfall."

"Best to keep out of sight. I agree."

"Where are you?" he asked, and oh, boy, wasn't that a long story.

"I'm either in the Middle East or Northern Africa. Connor was captured by a demon named Kimaris."

"Kimaris? Why do I know that name?"

"I guess he's sort of a bigwig in Hell. They've got Connor trapped in a black salt cell—did you know black salt can hurt, even kill a hellhound?"

His face dropped as he raked his hand through his ethereal hair. "I had no idea. Shit, it's a good thing—"

A huge explosion ripped through the air and a hand grabbed my arm. I couldn't tell if I was asleep or awake until Shafira's wild eyes met mine. "*Run,*" she whisper-shouted. Definitely awake. Bricks from the wall, ceiling, and roof partially blocked the gaping hole in the side of her home. Shafira yanked hard on my hand to help me up after I stumbled when rubble shifted and slid under my feet. We paused only long enough to get a bearing, then she and I ran, dodging behind buildings and at one point under a truck so as not to be seen.

Demon attack? Mortal attack? At this point, neither of us knew. Men could kill us just as easily as demons. Bullets worked just as well as magic. I opened my senses to find us a portal to escape through.

A giant dust cloud plumed into the nighttime sky above where her home had been. Her home? Dammit.

"I think we'd be safer in Hades," Shafira teased with sadness, but she wasn't wrong, and that got me thinking.

"The portal I came in through is lost to us now. I don't remember exactly which building I left and it's too dangerous to go back into the city to look."

"I'll keep an eye out. You find us a portal if you think one is close by."

"Oh, I have no doubt."

I opened up my senses, feeling the power radiate away from my body like fingers reaching for the empty space in front of us as we walked. It was nighttime and we were in a desert, but a niggling feeling kept telling me we were heading east.

Just as the sun started to peek above the horizon line, we stumbled into a ghost town, one of those places that years ago held a population, but they'd all left now. The moment we stepped into town, I felt the portal draw me to it.

"Over there." I pointed to a partially crumbling building on the perimeter of the town. "It's inside. I feel it."

"Lead the way," Shafira offered, and I did. We ran along the perimeter of the town to the building in question. The pull of the portal grew stronger with every step. "I feel it too," she said.

Shafira had to have power running through her because as I'd learned during my first encounter with one, most witches didn't feel a portal. She wasn't a Lilium, though. She reminded me of Agatha.

Once we reached the building, I felt around the ground finding a stone, I picked it up throwing it inside. We listened as it skittered along the floor, and then we waited a bit longer to make sure no one came to check on the noise. When no one did, we walked inside. The portal opened right up for us. We never even had to search for it. Shafira gripped the back of my shirt as we descended the stone stairs. She gasped at the red, glowing walls. Having recuperated well enough, I cloaked us near the bottom step. When we emerged, it was business as usual.

"Keep hold," I whispered to her, and I felt her give my shirt a tug in the affirmative. The demons working around us looked terribly unhappy. The offices looked exactly like what one expected offices in Hades to look like. I felt like I'd been through this office before. And then it hit me. Connor had navigated us through here once. This office belonged to Satan. It had to.

Where had Luc said Satan ruled? Well, I wouldn't dare speak until we cleared this place.

My current partner in crime picked up on my cues and stayed completely silent. But hey—plus side, I remembered how to maneuver us through this nasty quadrant. If I turned us left at this hallway… *Holynowway!* I did it! I got us to the stairwell that led down into the catacombs.

And the air grew damper, smelling stronger of sulfuric, rotten eggs with each step down, but I confess, I jumped up and down once we reached the bottom.

"We're here," I whisper-shouted. "This is the catacombs."

"This place is horrible. It smells."

"I know. But at least we found it. So where did you live? Hades has quadrants. If I remember correctly, Satan's quadrant is Africa—and that office building we passed through belonged to Satan."

"I don't live in Africa. Couldn't you tell by the surroundings?" she asked and I sort of shrugged in embarrassment.

"I'm not really familiar with this area of the world. When I first saw you, I thought you were Egyptian."

"I am *not* Egyptian. I'm Iraqi."

*Crap!* Could I have been more insensitive? Not to say there was anything wrong with being Egyptian. But they'd originated from completely different peoples. Now that I knew where we were, something about this bothered me. Iraq was located in the Middle East—the Middle East was located in Western Asia. What demon ruled Asia? I thought about it, and then I thought some more.

This made no sense. At least not when I remembered who ruled Asia. Beelzebub. He ruled Asia. Gluttony. Gluttony in this quadrant? Nope. I was getting nothing. It didn't fit Iraq, or many of these Middle Eastern countries. So much fighting. Baghdad had once been one of the most beautiful cities in the world. So… it hit me. Luc once told me that several of the big seven continuously fought for control over quadrants. What if Satan had taken over that section of the quadrant? Wrath. How much more wrath could you get?

"Okay, I think whatever is going on, Satan is behind it."

"Satan?" she asked, sucking in a sharp breath.

"I'm not happy about it, either. He's a nasty piece of work."

"So what are we going to do?"

"Well, we have to try to find Connor again. The problem is, I have no idea how to navigate these catacombs. They all look the same."

"Can't you—how did you put it? Manifest, yes. Can't you just manifest us to him?"

I shook my head, wanting to kick myself for not having that ability. "Not yet. The catacombs won't let me yet. My powers have been coming to me in spurts. So maybe I'll be able to do it, but for now…" I closed my eyes and really tried to concentrate on manifesting us to Connor. Nothing happened. Not even a shimmer of magic. To make sure my magic still worked, I cloaked us again. Then I zapped a crumbling piece of wall. It disintegrated the rock to dust. I wanted to scream, cry, and shout obscenities as loudly as a toddler throwing a temper tantrum. Alas, I sucked it up, shaking my head again. "No."

"I guess we pick a direction and start walking." Shafira was right. What else could we do?

I shrugged. "We're off to see the wizard…" I teased while picking a direction and we set off on this new leg of our adventure.

"Wizard?" Shafira asked. "Now we are finding wizards?"

"It's a movie—*never mind*. If we survive this, I'll show it to you."

We picked a direction and went for it. The dampness made my clothing stick to my body. I hated wearing damp clothing. We walked for what seemed like hours until we came to another set of stairs.

"Should we?" I asked.

She shrugged. "Why not? I doubt any stairs are going to land us in a beach resort with beautiful cabana boys bringing us drinks."

"What do you know about cabana boys?"

Shafira laughed. "My country might have its issues, but I'm still a part of the world."

Fair enough. "To be clear, I'd direct the cabana boys to you because Connor would blow a gasket if he found out I was getting drinks from scantily clad men in speedos—or whatever they wear at beach resorts."

"And to be clear, I'd welcome that."

We both snickered, but it was time to put on our game faces. We didn't know what we were about to walk up into. I used my power to cloak us. The bubble enveloped the both of us, but I made sure Shafira saw me.

"This is so weird," she said.

"You get used to it."

I took the lead, starting up the stone steps. The air grew dryer and warmer the higher we climbed. We emerged into an empty hallway, continuing on until we found the office space for this quadrant, whatever quadrant we were in.

No one appeared to be as happy working here as they did back in Luc's office, but Luc was a fun guy. I couldn't blame them. Still, they didn't look as hopeless as those back in Satan's office. I had no idea whose office we found ourselves in.

None of the demons noticed our presence. My cloak held just as I commanded it to. We walked until we stumbled upon the stairs leading up and out of Hades.

"This is it," I whispered. She nodded, following me up. I pushed open the heavy, wooden door, bracing for where we were about to find ourselves.

Hardpacked dirt.

Brown, dying grasslands.

We emerged by a dead tree, or it *looked* dead. There weren't any leaves. They had probably been swallowed up by the giant trunk. I wasn't kidding. The trunk had to be as big around as a compact car. I'd never seen anything like it before.

"Where are we?" she asked.

"Your guess is as good as mine at this point."

I scanned the area to suss if we had any company and I didn't pick up on anyone, so I dropped the cloak.

The air felt hot and dry against my skin, in my throat, and with each breath dehydrating my lungs—not to be melodramatic, but okay, melodrama seemed apropos in the situation.

I turned left, lifting my hand to shield my eyes like a visor, and then I turned to the right, doing the exact same thing. Nope. No clue where we were. I had no clue which way to start walking. I basically had no clue about anything. I hated feeling clueless. But Connor needed me and Shafira relied on me to get us moving, so I did a quick eeny, meeny, miny, moe and started walking with Shafira next to me.

When a weird creature crossed our path, a very marsupial-esque creature, I sort of started thinking I knew where we'd landed.

"I think we're in Australia," I said, breaking the everlasting silence we'd found for ourselves, given we didn't have water and at least for me, my mouth had gone dry several miles ago.

"Australia is… *interesting*," she replied.

"To say the least."

I heard it, but I never said it. Who'd said it? I whipped my head around and out of nowhere, Mr. Pooches pranced over to sit in front of Shafira and me, blocking our path forward.

"Please tell me you're seeing this," I said to Shafira.

"The black cat blocking our way—yes. I see it, but I'm having a hard time believing it."

"It took me time to find you," said Mr. Pooches, causing me to blanch.

"Please tell me you heard that, too," I begged.

"Oh, I heard it. Do you know this cat?"

"Yeah, this is Mr. Pooches. I told you about him visiting in my dream."

"So, wait—you have a familiar? You never said you had a familiar. This is incredible. Not many witches are gifted companions."

"Uh… he's my pretty kitty. I found him wandering around outside my house looking for food. He's *not* a familiar."

"I'm a talking cat who showed up to help you. You've officially lost this argument," Mr. Pooches said.

And he was right. I'd officially lost this argument. But I'd always thought of them as myths. I bent down to give him scratches under his chin. "Why didn't you tell me?" I asked him and he glared at me the way he always did. "You know I wasn't raised in the life. How would I have known? How did you find me? Who sent you to me?"

"Your grandmother time-jumped with me not long after she escaped with you and your brother, but your foster family called animal control when I kept coming around. I had to lie low until it was safe to join you. Then it took me a hot minute to locate you."

"My grandmother sent you to me?"

Mr. Pooches nodded. I still felt like I was being pranked, but I went with it because what other choice did I have?

My new friend introduced herself. "I am Shafira."

He smiled, eying her up and down, and *ew*—not cool.

"Do *not* mack on my friend," I demanded.

"I'm a cat. It's not like I can act on anything. But she's beautiful."

Shafira's cheeks pinked. "Thank you."

I clapped my hands to get their attention. "Okay, people. Eyes on me. We need to find help because Connor needs us. There's no saving the world without him."

"Every party has a pooper," he whined.

*Really?*

"Once I honed in on your location, I went scouting. We aren't far from the Western Australian coven." Mr. Pooches for the win!

I felt the first twinges of confidence I'd felt since we'd left Iraq behind for the catacombs. The Western Australia coven was known world over as a large and powerful coven. And it appeared they hadn't been hit yet.

Okay, after several more hours—or that was how it felt in the sweltering heat, anyway—of walking, I began to doubt Mr. Pooches's ability to judge distance. Not far? I guess if you meant relative to reaching the moon. Otherwise, way far.

"There," he said, tipping his nose up in a direction kitty-corner from the path ahead of us.

"There what?" I asked.

"The coven."

"There's nothing there." Shafira looked as dried out as I felt. We needed rest and we needed water.

"Oh, they're there. It's a village about a hundred feet that way."

"Simone, I think your cat is broken."

"They've put up wards. You just have to trust me."

"If they're using wards, why can you see them still?"

"I'm not a witch. Familiars are—"

"Demons," I answered helpfully, and when he glared at me, I smiled.

"If you want to get technical," he said. "Yes, we'd be closer to demons than anything. But we're our own subspecies and have our own union."

Shafira popped out a laugh. "Familiars have unionized?"

"Okay, okay… Let's focus here, people. Mr. Pooches, will you lead us into the town?"

"I'd be glad to."

He turned his little black body in the direction he wanted us to go, prancing smugly with his tail in the air. Oh, how I wanted to give him a little zappy-zap from my Taser fingers to wipe out that smugness, but I decided to be the bigger person and let it go.

"We're just about there," he said. I reached over to grab Shafira's hand. If the witches had put up wards, I didn't know how they'd affect her walking through them, so I manifested us walking into the town square without any issues.

A blue light shimmered around us and I knew we'd passed through the invisible barrier. Once inside, a medieval village sprouted to life around us. Buildings and houses all with thatched roofs. Cobblestone streets. Window boxes blooming with brightly colored flowers. Several doors had these wrought-iron symbols hanging on them. I didn't know what any of the symbols meant, but they gave off positive energies.

Okay. I liked this town.

That was when I noticed several eyes peeking out at us from behind window curtains. I waved at one set and they ducked out of sight. "Hello?" I called out. "My name is Simone Lamia. I need your help."

CHAPTER

*Twenty-Three*

We waited for what felt like forever for someone, anyone, to greet us. Finally, a beautiful man with flawless makeup and eyebrows to die for stepped into the street from one of the homes. He wore a multi-colored, butterfly caftan and a long string of pearls knotted at his chest. He had on a gorgeous 1920s-esque headdress with a peacock feather. My mouth dropped open. I mean, I hardly considered myself Quasimodo, but this man upstaged us all.

"Hey," I called out and he smiled. A smile. Thank you, Lilith. I needed someone to smile. Shafira and I still had so much to get done and a nonexistent amount of time to do it.

"Hey, girl," he called back. "What's up?" The man did *not* sound Australian. Like at all. He sounded American. West Coast/SoCal, maybe?

I sighed. "We need help."

"Help? Ooh… spill the tea." He watched me intently with his arms folded over his chest, waiting me out. He'd never even introduced himself, but okay.

"I'm Simone Lamia. This is"—I pointed to Shafira—"my friend Shafira. Shafira is a witch, but I'm—okay, this is always the hard part—I'm a Lilium."

His mouth dropped open.

I mean, he had to wonder how we'd made it through the wards. So the idea of me being Lilium couldn't have been that crazy.

"She is not just any Lilium," Shafira helpfully put in. "She is *the* Lilium. CliffsNotes version." She looked at me. "Is that what you said?" When I nodded, she smiled and went on. "She is Lilith's granddaughter. She has to save the world, but we need to rescue her protector mate first."

His eyes bugged. "You cannot CliffsNotes, long story short that, girl. Long story long. Now."

We didn't have time for long story long. His tanned skin glistened in the sun as he stared us down.

"Sorry, but we seriously don't have time for more. I can fill you in while receiving the help, but this is pretty time sensitive."

He waved his finger around in the air, suggesting he was about to refer to the rest of the coven. "It's bad out there. Time sensitive or not, they won't help until they trust you. Trust *me*. I know."

I shoved my sticky, sweat-soaked hair away from my face in frustration. "They *have* to help. That whole 'bad out there' thing is exactly why I'm here. Do they want to die?" I ended on kind of a shout and his eyes bugged again. He used his hands to suggest I quiet down. "Oh," I said. "I didn't mean that *I* would do anything. I meant the bad guys out there." I pointed behind me with my thumb.

"Listen," he said placatingly as he moved to wrap an arm around my waist. He ushered us forward to the little thatch-covered bungalow that he'd stepped out from. "Why don't you tell Uncle Karro all about it?"

"Who's Uncle Karro?" I asked.

"I am."

"Your name is Karro? I love that."

"The one good thing I got from my father, aside from this flawless skin tone."

"What did you get from your mother?" I asked as he opened the door to usher Shafira and me inside where it looked like a pink glitter bomb had deployed only moments ago. I'd never seen so much pink, glitter, and pink glitter in my life.

"Beautiful, isn't it?" he asked, but I could tell he meant it rhetorically.

"It is. I'm more of a lavender girl"—I pointed to my hair—"but this is amazing."

"What did you get from your mother?" Shafira asked my question again.

He smirked wickedly. "Witchcraft. And my love of big, strong men. Though I didn't know it, about the witchcraft. An imposing specimine of man always snagged my attention. Most of my life, stupid little things would happen, but I chalked it up to coincidence or told myself I was seeing things. I grew up in foster care—"

"So did I," I cut in.

He rolled his eyes. "Girl… then you know. It was a struggle just to survive. One of my foster dads liked to get a little rough, if you know what I mean. The other kids called him 'Dad.' I called him 'Daddy.'"

"'Daddy'?" Shafira asked. I shot her the 'come on, put it together' eyes and she blushed. "Oh…"

Karro held his arm out for us to sit and I flopped down onto the softest, fluffiest pink chair imaginable. I sunk into the cushion. The man could pick furniture, that was for sure.

"You were saying," I said, "about foster care?"

"I went to this Renn Faire—this was after I aged out—and I saw these card readers. They said they were witches. And I was all, 'Real witches? Yeah, okay.' But then all three of them were like, 'What are you?' 'What am *I*?' How rude, right? But they didn't mean it how I thought they meant it."

I understood. I'd felt it coming off of him from our first meeting outside. Those witches hadn't known what he was, just like witches never knew what I was. Because Karro had Lilium blood. *Welcome to the family, Karro.*

"They asked me," he continued, "'What is your magic?' But magic? I didn't have any magic —well, not until it clicked. All those things I'd convinced myself were figments of my imagination or had been mere coincidence. Magic. But it was only a small amount and I didn't know where it had come from or what to do with it."

"How'd you end up here?" Shafira asked.

"You sound American, like me," I stated helpfully.

"I'm from SoCal." So I was right. Point to Simone.

"It's a fun little story. This happened about a year ago. I was with the mayor's son and we were in the middle of—you know —doing it. And as I was being ram-rodded, I shouted, 'Plow me with your jackhammer!' and well, I don't have good control over my magic—or I didn't until about a week ago. Then it sort of started settling. Anyway, I felt his member shift into the shape of a jackhammer, still covered in flesh. Hard and soft—greatest orgasm of my life. But when he pulled out, he had a jackhammer for a member, so I couldn't let him leave until I figured out how to change it back. He was considered missing for a little over a week.

"Then he kind of cracked up and the mayor accused me of slipping him something. The town grabbed its torches and pitch-forks, which is how I ended up here. Witch covens started getting hit, just the little ones back then. Once I'd let my magic in, I locked into the world witch web." The world witch web? Why didn't I get the world witch web? Any lingering bindings needed to be gone yesterday. Given I was the one who was supposed to save the world, I should've been the one with the most powers. "Anyway, I remembered my mom saying my dad was from here. So I pawned everything I could get my hands on to buy a ticket and *poof!* That's how Uncle Karro ended up in his ancestral home."

"Can I let you in on a little secret?" I asked. Karro leaned way in from his seat kitty-corner from me on the sofa.

"I love secrets. The saucier, the better."

"I don't know that it's saucy, but it will explain a lot about your life," I replied. He stared at me puzzlingly. "You're not a witch."

"I know. I told you that."

"You're a Lilium. We're cousins. I'm cousins with all Lilium."

"I'm sorry?" Karro pressed the back of his hand against my forehead. "Are you feverish?"

I shoved his hand away. "I'm not feverish and I didn't hit my head. Lilith—*the* Lilith, first witch, first wife of Adam, Garden of Eden Lilith is my grandmother. She time-jumped with me and my twin brother on the day we were born because Adam attacked. He killed my parents. I didn't know any of this until I connected with my mate. He's a hellhound."

Karro's eyes flared. "A hellhound? Are you trying to make me jealous? I've heard stories. A hellhound even slightly in the mood would make Jackhammer Boy feel like he was working with a floppy, dead fish."

"I wouldn't know. I've never been with Connor while only *slightly* in the mood. He tends to go all in all the time."

Karro clutched the pearls knotted at his chest, fanning himself with his other hand. "You don't think he'd mind if we shared?"

My heart pounded in my chest. My nostrils flared. I cracked my knuckles.

Karro registered my response and I knew this by the way all the color drained from his face. "You know, just once."

"You did hear her say they were mated, correct?" Shafira asked indignantly. "Do you want to die?"

"Sorry… Sorry… I spoke without thinking."

*Calm yourself, Simone. He was kidding. Probably.* I willed my heart rate to slow by taking in long, slow breaths through my nose until I felt calm enough to continue speaking without ripping him to shreds like... like... didn't Tasmanian Devils do that or was that just in *Looney Tunes*?

"My apologies," I said. "Connor isn't just my mate. He's my protector mate. Our bond is... *strong*. I can't help my reaction. What do I need to do to get them to help me?"

He shot me an incredulous look. "Can you prove you're Lilith's granddaughter? That'd help."

"Can you gather them into the town square? I can summon her and—"

"'Summon her'? As in Lilith?" Shafira asked.

"Yes. She's my grandmother and my guide. I can manifest for the whole coven to see and hear her. Will that work?"

"Yeah, I think that would do it," Karro replied. His voice squeaked on the 'yeah.'

I chuckled, pushing up from the softness of the chair, and clapped my hands together. "Then let's get to work. There's not much time."

We walked outside his cozy home to the town center where we stood when we'd first cleared the wards. As I looked around, I realized that Mr. Pooches had left us again. He'd led us into the town and that was the last I remember seeing him. The cat had to know I'd worry about him. Great. One more thing to add to the list.

Karro cupped his hands around his mouth. "Ladies. *Atención*. Simone here needs our help. We really need to help her."

Slowly, I scanned the homes, watching eyes appearing in window after window. He'd gotten their attention, at least. The door of a bungalow at the far side of the town square opened and an older woman with flowing gray, black, and silver hair entered the square with us. The waves of her hair rippled. Her gown, similar to something the movies portrayed the Bride of Frankenstein wearing, rippled around her feet. There wasn't any wind. She made the ripples, trying to look intimidating. It probably worked on most people. But *hello*—granddaughter of Lilith. Not much in the way of witches scared me now.

"Calm your tits, Adi," Karro said, smirking. "Simone here is good people."

The now-known Adi tore her glare from me, throwing daggers at Karro. He continued to smile that 'I know a juicy secret' smile.

"I am Adalaide," she boomed in an echoing voice with a thick Australian accent, which, to be honest, took away from the intimidating factor because that Australian accent always sounded so friendly to me. "Leader of the Western Coven."

"I'm Simone Lamia and this is my friend Shafira. Thank you for meeting us."

"Despite his eccentricities, Karro has good instincts. If he says you need our help, I'll give you five minutes to explain your situation."

Whelp, it was now or never. I thought it best to let Grandma explain for me. "Lilith, I need you," I said into the void between us. Lilith shimmered into her celestial form. Not human but not spirit. "I'd like for everyone here to see and hear you."

"It is done," she replied, smiling that loving grandmotherly smile that sometimes a person just needed to see. I heard the collective gasp from not just Adalaide, Karro, and Shafira. But others had joined while my eyes had been closed. Every member of the coven stood surrounding us.

"I am Lilith, first witch," she started. "Simone is my granddaughter." Lilith, always ready to give a good show, paused for effect. All eyes shot to me, then I nodded and she started to speak again. "Witches will save the world. We are the most powerful. We were granted the power of the Garden. Eden flows through all of your veins. Eden, the universal mother, is within all of you. Harness your collective power and take back what should have always been yours."

"She's good," Karro whispered. "I've got chills listening to her."

He was not prepared for what happened next. "Step forward, Karro." His eyes went huge and his back stiffened. I gave him a little shove of reassurance to get him to step forward. He took these tiny steps and from our meeting today, I knew this man didn't do anything tiny.

"Simone has explained that you are my many-times great-grandson. You are my family. Your destiny brought you here."

"My destiny?" he asked timidly.

"I am proud of you, Karro. Your life has not been easy. None of my family has lived easy lives. I am sorry for this. You will see in the coming weeks how necessary, though heartbreaking for me, that it was. Simone will explain what she needs from you. She will explain what she needs from you all. It is a dangerous endeavor you face. Not all will live to see this end. But if you care for the world, for humanity, for your families, evil must not win."

"I have theories," I told my grandmother.

"I know. I am always with you, my dearest Simone. I hear everything. All you have to do is talk to me and I will answer."

Lilith shimmered out of sight for everyone, but I felt a tingle on my cheek and I lifted my hand to touch the spot. I glanced around and noticed Karro lightly touching his cheek as well. He caught my eyes and said, "She said she loves me. I heard her in my head. Then she kissed my cheek."

"Yeah, Grandma Lilith is always watching over you."

He blanched. "I hope not *always*."

"I said watching *over* you, not watching you. That would be weird and creepy and trust me, nothing she wants to see. I know, I asked. Connor and I have gotten a little freaky-deaky ourselves."

"Do tell," he said.

"There was this time in Lucifer's office—"

"Lucifer? As in *the* Lucifer?" Shafira asked.

"He's a great guy. Connor works for him and they're best buds. Luc is hotter than any guy you've ever seen—guaranteed."

Karro bit his bottom lip. "Ooh—do tell."

Laughing, I went on. "I adore him. He gives Connor crap all the time and anyone who gives Connor crap is okay by me."

"Connor, as in your protector mate, Connor?" Karro asked.

I nodded. "I love him. He's good to me. The sex is off the charts, but he can be a bit... *ornery* with people." When Karro looked a little taken aback, I went on. "Don't worry. He's a puppy underneath all that sexy hellhound. Anyway, giving Connor crap is one of the great joys in my life."

"What do you need of us?" Adalaide asked, interloping on our little bit of fun.

I let out a breath. Time to work. "Okay, first... I need help rescuing my mate. I escaped capture, but he wasn't as lucky. They have him in a black salt cell and I'm worried I won't get back to him in time.

There might've been a collective gasp from the other witches when I said 'black salt.' Apparently, they all knew its effects on hellhounds.

"And you need more numbers to rescue him?" she asked next.

"No. I need to find him again. I don't know where he is currently."

I kid not, the woman looked at me like I had horns growing out of my skull. "Can't you home in on his location? He *is* your mate, correct?"

"Oh, he's definitely her mate. I was a second and a half away from being ripped to shreds when I teased about sharing him," Karro so helpfully put in.

"Then what is the problem?"

Now I felt incredibly stupid. "Um... I didn't know I could do that. This whole Lilium magic is fairly new to me. My powers had been bound until I connected with him. So... yeah..." I ran my hand through my hair uncomfortably. I *hated* admitting to not knowing, well, anything—but I especially hated not knowing about my magic or the mated bond. I felt like a poser. Like Lilith had put her faith in the wrong person.

Adalaide approached me, placing her hand to my back. "I didn't mean to embarrass you. I'll help you to home in on his location. What can we do while you're hunting him down?"

"This is so important. I need you to get in touch with a woman named Victoria Rivers. She runs Weik Laboratories in Birmingham, England."

She nodded. "I know the name. The Rivers witches are old blood. Strong witches."

"She knows to expect contact from other witch covens. Once I rescue Connor, we'll have to reconvene. We need to plan our attack or defense. I haven't quite figured out which would be the best course of action."

"I will work with my most trusted sisters here and we'll contact Victoria Rivers immediately. But to home in to your mate's location, close your eyes and concentrate on him. On his face. On his smell. You will be able to connect with him like a call connects with a cell tower."

"It's that easy?"

"Easy and difficult."

I didn't want to hear that. But Connor needed me, so I could do this. I closed my eyes and thought of him. His face. That smell of his—the one that got me all hot and bothered. And… nothing.

Nothing?

"It's not working," I whined.

"Try again. Don't let your mind wander. Don't get distracted. He's your mate. I know your mind wandered."

Oh, man… called out by the coven leader. *Just Connor… Just Connor…* I repeated this over and over in my head. I felt my consciousness zipping around the world in an instant. It felt like the fastest rollercoaster ride I'd ever been on. But finally, after more aggravating minutes, I locked on his location.

Only I could hear him, but when he saw me or felt me—however he picked up my presence—he sighed. "*Simone…*"

"Connor, we're coming. Please hold on."

"Trying…" he said. "Hurts…"

I knew it hurt him. I pulled back enough to take him in and my strong, virile Connor appeared gaunt with dark shadows under his eyes and the palest skin. If I didn't move fast, I'd lose him. I locked in my Lilium or mated pair driving directions into my internal GPS, then said, "Hang on, babe." To my friends, I said, "I have to go—*now.*" To Adalaide, I said, "Once you connect with Victoria Rivers, start spelling your asses off. Offensive spells, defensive spells, counter-spells—anything and everything you can come up with. I'll contact Luc and his demons as soon as I can."

Adalaide's pretty face hardened as she locked her hands in front of her with an air of power. "Are you sure he's trustworthy?" she asked.

"Absolutely. You'll get it once you meet him."

Her eyes grew huge and yeah, I forgot given all the time I'd spent with him, that the idea of meeting Lucifer freaked most people out. But I didn't have time to reassure her. She believed me or she didn't. "Victoria Rivers," I reminded her. She startled but nodded.

Then I took off running toward where we'd entered the town. Hopefully, I remembered where the portal to the catacombs was located. Otherwise, I'd be screwed and Connor—*no, Simone, don't even think it. Connor has to be okay.*

Shafira and Karro caught up to me. He grabbed my arm to stop me. "Where are you going?"

"I have to find the portal to the catacombs that we arrived here through."

"Catacombs?" he asked.

I nodded. "Under Hades."

"Wow. Okay, I don't know about any catacombs, but if you need to get to Hades, I can get us in."

'Us'? That concerned me. It steadily became harder to protect the people in my sphere. Still, I asked, "You can get us into Hades?"

"Okay, when I first arrived out here, it'd been months since I'd gotten any and I'd found myself in this out-of-the-way bar in this two-bit town. This man approached me. He wasn't hideous and I saw what he was packing through the outline of his trousers. So I said, why not? I needed a bit of stress relief. He led me down into the basement of the bar where they kept the alcohol. Then he opened a door and led me down another set of stairs and we ended up in this office. People everywhere looking miserable. And I thought, *It must be hell working here.* But then I saw flames on the walls and I *knew* it *really was* Hell. He took me into this empty office—and let me say, he wasn't the best lover I'd ever had, but the size of his meatstick made up for his lack of skill. He calls me or I call him whenever one of us needs a little stress reliever."

I stared at him with my mouth hanging open.

"What?" he asked. "I'm young and it's not like I'm getting any in a coven of witches."

"So what happens if he's not in the mood?" I asked and Karro gave me the *'are you serious'* eyes. "Okay, so what happens when he realizes that you aren't going through with it?"

Karro's gaze shifted to *'oh, you sweet, summer child'* and I gasped.

"You are not pimping yourself out for us."

"Girl, you need an in and I can buy us that time. Plus, Uncle Karro could use a bit of stress relief, so it's a win-win."

"Will you come back here, then?" Shafira asked him.

"No, I'm coming with you."

"How will you find us?" she asked.

"You said you can manifest, right?" he said to me, but before I got the chance to answer, he went on. "I mean, I know you can. You brought Lilith in to talk to us. So give me like twenty-five minutes and then manifest me to you."

"Twenty-five minutes?" I asked.

"It gives us both time to get into it. But he doesn't last long once he is. So that should work."

Without any other plan available to us, I gave in. "Okay, call him."

In a perfect world, I'd have been able to manifest myself to Connor. But that black salt disrupted my ability to get to him. Now that I thought about it, black salt was probably the reason that mates had this honing thing to begin with. I still had so much to learn and no time to study.

Karro pulled his phone from the pocket of his caftan and pressed a contact. "I could use some sexual healing today, how 'bout you?" he asked into the receiver. The man must've said something intimate because Karro smiled. "Great. Meet you in about ten minutes, lover." Then he hung up. "Right. Other way," he directed us and then he turned to start jogging to the far end of the town, where Adalaide's bungalow sat. Both Shafira and I followed. He led us around the bungalow and we passed through the wards on the other side back into the desert. I cloaked Shafira and me, but I manifested for Karro to be able to see us. About ten minutes of walking and we ended up in this two-bit town exactly as he'd described. There were maybe three broken-down buildings. A grocery/gas station type of store. A mechanic's garage and the bar. Karro led us to the bar and we walked inside.

A rather beefy man whom I could tell right away was a demon leaned against the bar. His tight pants showed exactly what he was working with. Karro smiled. "Hey, lover," he cooed. The demon stood straight.

"No one here yet. Let me take ya over the table."

My Lilium cousin shook his head. "Anyone could walk in. I'd rather go to our regular spot. You know how I like to get loud."

"You know how I like to get rough," he replied.

"Do I ever. Your desk is far sturdier than these old tables. You can ram me rough." Karro approached the demon to run his finger along the man's jawline. The demon's eyes heated and he grabbed Karro's hand, pulling him behind the bar. Shafira and I followed.

The demon hurried us down into the basement. It was dark and old with cobwebs and that dank basement smell. But he opened a second door behind the stairs we'd just come down to reveal a stone stairwell that I recognized very well. An entrance to Hades. We descended the step at a pretty quick pace and once we'd reached the bottom, the demon dragged Karro to an office down the main hallway.

A middle management demon.

"Will he be okay?" Shafira whispered.

"He'll be fine. Come on." I picked a different hallway. The setup was similar to Luc's, so it made sense that I'd find the stairs to the catacombs if we went that way. We walked and walked, getting farther and farther away from the office setting and that was where we found the stairs. *Hallelujah!* Or you know, whatever a Lilium was supposed to shout.

"I don't like the look of that." Shafira pointed to the place we had to go. "It looks danker than the last tunnels."

Getting a big wiff of mildew mixed with rotten eggs, I wrinkled my nose. "You won't like the smell, either."

But I felt Connor. My internal GPS kept me going in the right direction. At the twenty-five-minute mark from when we left Karro, Shafira said, "It's time." I hadn't been keeping track. Good thing she had.

I closed my eyes, manifested keeping Shafira and me invisible while bringing Karro to us. He popped into our bubble. His eyes looked glazed. "Did he give you something?" I asked, horrified.

"Oh, he gave me something, all right," he replied. "You caught me cleaning up. That man upped his game. I think I might be in love."

"Seriously?" Shafira asked.

Karro pursed his lips. "With his penis." He chuckled to

himself still with that glazed, dreamy look in his eyes. "Oh—and I found out who he works for."

News. Good. News helped. "Who?" I asked at the same time as Shafira.

"A man named Belphegor? I never heard of him, but apparently, he's a big deal demon, too."

"You've never heard of Belphegor?" I asked.

He shook his head. "I've heard of Lucifer, Satan, and what's his name"—he snapped his fingers to help him remember—"Beelzebub. After that..." He shrugged.

Now the big question was: What did *I* remember about Belphegor? Oh—it hit me. No wonder Mr. Middle Management had time to play snake in the hole with my cousin. He wasn't in a hurry to get work done. Sloth. Belphegor's sin was sloth. Sweet.

"Okay, I think he's one of the tamer rulers of Hell. I've never met the man, but I don't think he's one of them that Luc has a problem with."

"Who does Luc have a problem with?" Shafira asked.

"Well, Connor said Satan is a nasty piece of work and both he and Luc agree that you *don't* want to mess with Leviathan."

"Leviathan?" Karro asked.

I nodded. "His quadrant is the oceans. All the oceans. But we don't have to worry—we aren't going in the water at all."

"You know what would be nice?" Shafira asked. I shook my head. "If we could get out of this dampness. It's frizzing my hair."

"We have a long way to go." I replied, as I thought that was her way of spurring us on. *I got you, Shafira.* Closing my eyes, I focussed in on Connor.

"Simone?" he asked again.

"It's me, babe. I'm still coming."

"Not until... I get... my hands on you..." He tried to laugh, but it came out so frail that tears wet my eyes.

"Don't worry. I'm in need of a little sexual healing."

"I'm in need of healing, period."
*Dammit.*
"Connor," I said softly.
"Hm?"
"Don't die."

e walk forever—hour after hour in those damp catacombs. I craved the sun of the Western Australian desert. I craved just about any sun about now. My skin felt pasty and my clothing clung to my body. But worst of all, I needed to get to Connor. It started getting harder to home in on his location about two hours ago. That meant our connection was growing weaker. Only one reason for that, and I couldn't get myself to even think the words.

Connor had to be okay. He *had* to be. I wouldn't accept anything less. And with keeping us cloaked while trying to keep my internal GPS locked on my mate and walking swiftly enough to actually get us to South America, my energy stores were spent. Hardcore spent. At least I knew where we were heading.

I started to panic when I couldn't feel him. It was like his signal was there and then it was gone.

"*Connor?*" I sort of shrieked, but I shrieked in my head. "Connor, talk to me."

"Sorry…" His word slurred. I was losing him.

"Swear to God, Connor Baghest, if you die on me, I'll kill you!" My lip began to tremble and that just pissed me off more. I hated feeling fear. I hated feeling sad and I hated crying because of any of those. I was a badass woman—no, I was a badass *Lilium* woman.

It took a bit to get him back but then—*whoa!* I felt him. Like, I really felt him. This tunnel would lead me to my Connor. I stopped to fill in the other two. "We're almost there. He's going to be sick. I have to get him out. You'll need to have my back."

"Are you sure you don't want us to get him out and *you* have *our* backs?" Karro asked. "You're Lilith's granddaughter."

"Yes, and you're her great-whatever-grandson. You've got power. Shafira has power. Don't get unsure on me now. I need you to come out swinging with anything you've got in you."

He looked me dead in the eyes. "I won't let you down."

I believed him. Karro wouldn't let me down. We had this.

"My powers lie mostly with brewing teas to cure sickness or elevate consciousness to talk with the ancestors, things like that," Shafira said.

"What do you need?" I asked.

She stared at me blankly.

"To cure a hellhound who has been housed in black salt? I'm running low on energy, but if you tell me now, I can use what I've got left to manifest the ingredients to you right here."

"What about the black salt?" she asked, and good question.

"We aren't close enough for it to interrupt the manifestation, but you all might have to carry me when I'm done. It'll take what I've got left."

She thought about it. And yeah, it'd have been so helpful if I'd been able to manifest us right to Connor, but I couldn't. My magic wouldn't let me. And I had no idea where in South America they held him prisoner. It was safer for us to travel the catacombs for the time being. Trust me, I'd been berating myself this whole time for not just transporting myself to him.

"Well, I need boiling water, ginger, turmeric, cinnamon, clove, calendula, lemon balm, and honey—do you think he has any infections? Feverfew could help with that, too. This is hard. I just don't know what all his ailments are."

"Throw the book at it. We don't have time to mess around."

"Can't she just manifest the finished tea?" Karro asked.

Shafira looked between me and Karro. "She could try, but I worry about anomalies forming." Anomalies forming? That was a thing? "They are two distinctly different types of magic. She is Lilith's granddaughter, so maybe it is perfectly safe for her to mix them. As far as I know, she is the only one who can manifest objects into existence. For the rest of us, we do not mix spellwork with herbal magic."

"Anomalies? So what are we talking? Not strong enough?"

"That could be an issue. Too strong is also an issue. Too strong may hurt him internally, like overdosing on a medication. It also may add rogue ingredients never meant to be in that potion by accident. You are magically creating a potion out of thin air. Much thrives in the air."

Shit. I never thought of that. I couldn't take the chance. Shafira told me way back when we were still sitting in her living room, that everyone had a destiny, a part to play. I needed to trust that the universe sent Shafira with me for this purpose. This was her part to play.

"Don't let me down," I said to her. "I can't do this without him."

She exhaled a short, sharp breath. "Fine, then I need rose hips, lemongrass, nettle leaves, peppermint, red clover, chrysanthemum flowers, Hawthorn berries, rosebuds—I think that should do it. Are either of you good at spellwork? You could amplify the effects of the tea."

"I'll try," Karro said. "My spells have been improving."

"I'm going to have to drop the cloak for a moment. I'm running out of energy. I can't manifest everything and still keep us hidden."

Both of my traveling companions nodded. I sucked in a deep breath, dropped the cloak, and manifested the crap out of those ingredients. I needed this to work. Connor needed this to work. A pitcher of boiling water appeared out of thin air first, followed by the herbs, then the flowers, and lastly, the honey. She used her hands to measure the dry ingredients and poured in the honey according to what felt right to her. She looked up from her work. "Want to try?" she asked. "You're weak. If it helps you, then I think with Karro's amplification, we can save Connor."

Hell yes, I wanted to try it!

"Hit me, bartender," I said, hoping to bring a little levity to the situation as we were running dangerously low on positivity. We gave the tea a little time to steep. I raised the cloak over us again while we waited. In that time, I manifested a backpack for Shafira to store the leftover herbs and flowers in. She slung it securely on her back. I hoped this worked because the cloak fizzled out. We stood in that walkway completely exposed. I dropped to the floor as my legs no longer felt able to hold my weight. She handed me the pitcher and I took a big, burning hot sip. The power of the herbs tingled as they moved through me, invigorating my body, mind and soul just that quickly. "I feel great. Like, I want the both of you to take a few sips to get yourselves powered up."

Karro smiled as if pleased with himself. "So the amplification spell worked."

"Whatever both of you did, I'm feeling like a brand new person. Please" —I handed off the pitcher to Karro— "drink."

"We need to save it for Connor," Shafira argued.

"There's a whole pitcher. I need you full strength." I pushed the pitcher toward her mouth. "It's go time."

She nodded, taking the pitcher from me and lifted it up to her lips to drink. After she'd had her fill, she handed the tea off to Karro. He drank his share, leaving two-thirds of the brew for Connor.

"Let's do this," I said. I held the pitcher close to my chest protectively and had to keep myself from running to him or risk splashing the lifesaving brew all over my shirt. But I had so much spring in my step and we were so damn close, I swore I could smell him.

And then maybe twenty minutes passed before we found ourselves in front of *the* row of cells. The ones where Kamaris held my mate prisoner. We'd found him. I moved us to the center cell, where my usually strong mate huddled in a corner. His ashen complexion made me worry we'd gotten to him too late. I couldn't see him breathing in the low light. But I still felt him—or did I? Maybe it was my excitement. What if it wasn't him, but my excitement to see him that I felt? No. I shook that thought off, throwing my hand out to manifest the cell door opening. The magic fizzled out. Damn the black salt. It shouldn't stop me. I wasn't a hellhound. But then again, I didn't know all the properties of black salt. Connor tipped his head up just slightly and I sucked in a sharp breath. My Connor, still alive! I started to panic.

"What do I do? The magic won't work."

"I got this," Karro answered. He had this? What could he do that I couldn't? Karro reached up to fondle the headdress with the feather. The feather waved and shimmied while his hand roamed for something. Then, smiling big, he produced a hair pin. My mouth dropped open. Picking a lock wasn't as easy as the movies made it look. Karro sauntered over to the cell and dropped to his knees. He inserted the pin into the lock mechanism and started twisting it. I watched in dumbfounded disbelief as the lock popped.

"You did it," I said.

"Some of my foster moms didn't much like finding out I was getting more action from their husbands than they were. Picking locks became a necessary skill."

"You learned to pick locks because your foster mothers locked you in your room?" Shafira asked.

"I didn't mind being locked in the room, but dick is dick—there isn't much I wouldn't do for dick, even back then."

"You are more than that," Shafira said. Karro stared at her. She repeated herself. "You are more than that."

"Right." My cousin cleared his throat. "Let's do this."

"Ready." I told my friends.

The cell door clanked when I opened it, causing each of us to wince. It was comical the way we all stopped even breathing to listen for activity—footsteps or talking—heading our way. I ran to my mate, falling to my knees in front of him and set the pitcher on the floor to gather him in my arms. "Connor, baby... I'm here."

"Took you... long... enough," he whispered and more damn tears spilled from my eyes. The dark circles and bruising aged his face by thirty years or more. When the longing to kiss him overwhelmed me, I gave in, bending in to press my lips to his. He shivered in my arms. I turned myself to cradle his body against mine.

"We have to get him out," Shafira said. Agreed. Even though I hesitated to let him go, I allowed Shafira and Karro to help me carry him out. The man weighed a ton. It seemed impossible. I'd seen that body naked. My mate was all stream-lined muscle. He had the body of a god. We grunted as we moved him through the cell's threshold, setting him down on the damp stone. Along with Karro's power up fizzing in the tea, one had to believe that we'd get him back stronger than ever. I didn't waste any more time, picking up the pitcher to get him to drink.

"Here," I said, tipping it to his open mouth. "Take in as much as you can."

So weak, he never even asked what was in the brew. A full-strength Connor would've ask if it was poisoned. I held back the tears. Tears later—or never. Never would work. I squared my shoulders, tipping the pitcher even more. As my mate drank, Shafira gasped causing my heart to sink.

"Crap," Karro said.

"What are you doing?" someone shouted.

That would be when the shit hit the fan. The demons descended. Karro, whom I was pretty sure had never *fought* a demon in his life, started popping off defensive spells, bless his heart. The man had power. Why could Karro use spells but mine fizzled?

It hit me, we were connected, right? My magic started unbinding when we'd met. If I was right in my theory, that was some shit. I seriously hated the universe if my magic fizzled because my mate was sick and dying. Oh, the universe had an earful coming from me when this was over.

"Drink," I ordered him. Connor must have read the situation and drank. As he healed, my magic tingled rather than fizzled. I threw out spells left and right, trying as hard as possible to miss my friends in the process. Oh yeah—the bitch was back!

I manifested the black salt to transform into black onyx. Connor stumbled back on his feet. Black onyx boosted strength, protection, and focus, among other things. The power inside me glittered over my skin as it built up like charging a battery and then I shot it into the room. Connor's eyes grew huge—then heated.

Finally, Connor grabbed me. He kissed me, growled, and dropped into his hellhound form. Who let the mother-fucking dog out, indeed. *Yes!*

"Drink what's left," he ordered me in my mind. "You can help us once we get out of here."

I lifted the pitcher to drink but had to stop to help Shafira. She screamed when the demon caught her in the shoulder. No— just *no*. Not Shafira. I gulped down the rest of that brew.

Anger roiled inside me. My power rippled in a golden glow over my skin and I rose off the ground. I shot my hand out and several of the demons disintegrated into ash before our eyes. Then I saw him, Kimaris. He scanned the scene and turned to run like a coward without the upper hand. I closed my hand into a fist, manifesting my magic to destroy him. Kimaris's eyes began to bulge as he clawed at his neck to remove the invisible chokehold I held him in while his feet dangled off the floor. His face deepened to an ugly purple. I squeezed my hand tighter, ready to pop his head like a pimple.

"Simone," Connor shouted, but it sounded far away, and like it came from underwater. I squeezed harder. *"Simone,"* he shouted again and I felt him move. He rammed his hard head into my arm, causing me to let go of the demon. Kamaris dropped to the ground, slumped into a heap on the stone. I snapped my glare to Connor, rubbing my arm. That shit hurt.

He mentally winced. "We can't use him if he's dead."

"He's a demon—he won't die for good."

I raised my hand again, but this time, instead of ramming me a second time, Connor moved back into his human form, yes, buck-ass naked because he'd torn his clothing to change. I'd have to manifest new ones. He moved in front of me, placing both hands on my face. "It's done. Let him alone."

"He hurt you. He tried to take you from me. He needs to be punished."

"I'm okay. You saved me." The man bent in to kiss me and I didn't know how to explain it, but it felt like this huge sense of hatred and dread had lifted from my shoulders. I blinked several times before realizing that my mate stood there showing the goods to everyone in the room.

"What happened?" I asked. Karro and Shafira stared at me, which was a feat, given Connor's state of undress.

"What do you mean?" Connor asked.

"It felt like I was here, but I wasn't here. Like, I don't know… I absorbed the power of the space."

"A power-up," Karro said.

"But this place is evil, so she absorbed the feelings along with the energy?" Shafira asked.

"Seems like it." Connor pulled me tighter against him. "Baby, we have to get you out of here."

Yes. Yes, we did. We needed to get out of here. And that was when we heard the slow whistle and all our eyes turned to Karro, who now openly gawked at my mate. "Jiminy Christmas —who gave you the right to have an ass like that?"

"Don't turn around," I ordered the gorgeous man. Karro

seeing the back of him was bad enough. They didn't need to know the heat my mate packed in the front.

"Not planning on it."

"Please tell me you're into threesomes—oh, better yet, where can I get me a hellhound all to myself?"

Connor laughed. Yes, he *laughed*. I wanted to rip Karro's throat out for suggesting a threesome. I had to get out of this place.

"I thought you were smitten with that demon back at Belphegor's place," Shafira put in.

He sighed. "Crap. You're right. A boy can dream, though."

"Belphegor?" Connor asked at the same time I closed my eyes to manifest him a pair of joggers, a T-shirt, and some nice running shoes. The outfit showed off his assets nicely, but in a comfortable, breathable way that allowed quick movements, and right now, we needed quick movements.

"We made a stop at the Western Australian Coven. That's where I picked up Karro, here." I pointed to my cousin. "He's a Lilium, too. But it's a long story. We have to get out and find a place to hunker down for a rest."

"Where do we go?" Karro asked.

Shafira shrugged. Great, another thing left up to me. Or so I thought, but then Connor surprised me—well, all of us.

"There's an abandoned outpost on Antarctica that the demons were talking about," he said.

"Did you hit your head or something? We don't want to go where there are more demons."

He shot me his '*Simone… shut up*' eyes. Kind of ungrateful for a man who had just been rescued from the brink of death, but I digress. And I shut up. "They stay clear of it because it's haunted. It freaks them out."

"Wait, wait, wait…" Karro said. "There's a place that *demons* won't go because they think it's *haunted* and you want us to *go there*?"

"You got any better ideas?" he asked. And not only did none

of us have any better ideas, we heard more of the enemy clamoring down the corridor. We'd literally run out of time to decide.

"Shit or get off the pot," I murmured, closing my eyes as I wrapped us all, including an immobilized Kimaris, in my manifestation bubble. Haunted, abandoned outpost in Antarctica, here we come. I chanted the location in my head over and over again.

We disappeared right as the first demon to enter the room with us yelled, "What the hell?"

Understatement.

And the next thing I knew, we popped up inside a dark room. It looked like some kind of old station with a very dated sofa, chairs, a couple of tables—one for coffee and one for dining—then as whoever had designed it had designed a very open-concept space, to the back of the room sat a full kitchen. The room might've been dark, but waning daylight streamed in through the windows, giving me enough of a torch-like effect to see what we were dealing with.

That was when I remembered the demon along for the ride. I remembered because he began stirring. The arrangement worked for now, but I'd have to keep diligent by watching him like a hawk to make sure he didn't recover enough to become a problem for us. To get anything done, we needed a different method of keeping him inactive and ineffective for the axis of evil. There were some things even I couldn't do, like creating wards. I had no problem breaking them—well, the ones to confine or keep out witches and demons. I'd yet to encounter a ward geared toward the Lilium. To get demon wards, you needed a demon—strike that, you needed a *powerful* demon to create them for you. I figured the Western Australian Coven had contacted Belphegor or one of his upper management. The problem with asking a demon for a favor came in the form of repayment. I'd absorbed that knowledge back in the witches' archives. That seemed like a million years ago. It made me wonder what the Western Coven might have offered up or agreed to pay to get said wards.

"What are we going to do with him?" Connor asked, pointing to the unconscious Kimaris.

"We need wards," I replied. "We can't plan or try to make contact with anyone if we're constantly trying to keep him out. We need Luc."

"We don't know where he is right now," he countered. No. We definitely didn't. But I could manifest myself to wherever he was. Luc loved me. More than that, he and Connor were best friends. He'd make me the wards and probably without demanding payment.

"Can she manifest to him?" Shafira asked. The woman paid attention.

"I suppose we could go. I'm just worried about this guy," Connor said.

I shook my head. "You're staying here."

He shot a death glare at me. "What are you smoking? You're not going alone. *I* go with you."

The man could be so thick sometimes. Of course, I wanted him to go, but I needed him here. "Connor, babe, I need you here to help keep Kimaris subdued until I get back. Shafira is a powerful witch, but her area of expertise is as a kitchen witch. And Karro is stronger than he realizes, but he's never kept a demon occupied—"

"Oh, I've kept a demon *occupied*," he said, cutting me off.

I shot him my *'really?'* face. "With magic, not sex."

"He might be open to—"

"As far as I know, Kamaris wouldn't be," Connor stated with the authority of a man who knew. And given our connection, he knew exactly what I wanted to ask and went on, "Kimaris has a mate. A woman. He can't get with anyone else."

"Demons have mates?" Shafira asked and Connor nodded.

"All supernatural beings have a mate out there. They just

have to connect. Once you do, that's all she wrote," he said. I smiled. "You're stuck," he finished. I frowned.

"'Stuck'?" I raised an eyebrow at the infuriating man. "You really want to go with that?"

He grabbed my hand, pulling me into his arms, and tried to kiss me. I turned my head and he got my cheek.

"Baby…"

"Don't *baby* me, you jackass," I said, but I let him kiss me for real this time and he whispered something Shafira and Karro didn't need to hear in my ear. I giggled under my breath, letting him off the hook for the time being. "My point still stands. I can manifest myself to Luc. You need to stay here and keep Kimaris under control."

"I'll go with you for backup," Shafira said. "I might not be as strong with shooting off spells as you or Karro, but I can be of use."

"I don't like it," Connor grumbled.

"I never thought you would," I told him, "but this is what we've got to work with, so deal with it or don't, *dear*."

He grumbled again and I knew he was giving in. I wrapped Shafira in a manifestation bubble with me and shot us off to Lilith-knew-where. I just kept repeating: *Take us to Lucifer*. Over and over in my head: *Take us to Lucifer*.

The bubble popped, landing us in a posh living room. I dropped into a cushioned chair covered in black fur. I hoped not real fur. Shafira dropped on a black, leather sofa, one of those massive sectionals. I had no idea where we were, but there was no Lucifer in sight. Well, until the door opened at the end of the room and the gorgeous, blond man walked in. He stopped short at the sight of us, pressing the palms of his hands to his eyes before dropping them and openly gaping.

"Nope. Not seeing things," I said.

"Oh my god, Simone—are you okay? Where's Connor?" He turned his head from side to side, scanning the room.

"He's not here. This is my friend—" I didn't even get her

name out when Luc jerked his head back to face us, like he'd just now noticed her in the room, gaping like an idiot before he pulled himself together.

"Shit," he said, turning on the Luc charm. "I'm Lucifer. You are?"

"Not interested in blond fallen angels," she replied. *Go Shafira.*

"I bet I can change your mind."

I snapped my fingers to gain his attention. "Focus, Luc. She's my friend, not your newest booty call."

Luc bit his bottom lip in such a sexy way that even a mated woman got hot and bothered. And I meant me. I was that woman. "She could be both." He never took his eyes from Shafira. "The ladies love it when I do this—" He gyrated his hips and looking at that, I knew from the depths of my soul that the ladies loved it.

"Luc, this is Shafira. Please, we're here because we need demon wards."

That sobered him right up. "Demon wards? Where are you? Where's Connor?"

"We're hiding out, but we have to find out what Kimaris knows and so we need to box him in."

"*Kimaris?*" he shouted. "Why in all of Hades would you be anywhere close to Kimaris? He works directly for Satan."

"He captured Connor and tried to kill him with black salt. We rescued him, Shafira healed him with a powerful tea, and now Connor and Karro, a Lilium cousin of mine, are keeping him subdued until I get back with wards. Please, we don't have time for this."

Opposite his normally fun, sexy demeanor, Luc's face hardened, turning very serious. "I'll make the wards, but you have to take me with you."

"Where are we?" Shafira asked.

"It's one of my safehouses." He tilted his head, smiling and revealed a dimple at the corner of his mouth, quickly shifting back to the flirty Luc I knew and loved. "Why? Do you like it?"

"It's a little gaudy for my taste," she answered and he scoffed.

"'Gaudy'?" he asked indignantly.

I laughed. "Ouch. I think someone hurt his pride."

He shot me a death glare. "I was going to do it for free for you and my boy Connor. Now, you want wards I get a date"—he pointed to Shafira—"with her."

"You're not dating my friend." I couldn't believe that with everything going on he'd let his pride get in the way of helping us.

"We are in a battle to save the world," Shafira countered. She spoke with confidence, but the twinkle in her eyes had dimmed considerably.

"It won't last forever. And when we win..." He let that trail off.

"Shafira, you don't have to agree to anything. I'm calling his bluff."

"Then I'm out." He turned to leave.

"I'll go out with you," she called to his retreating back. He stopped, turned back to us, and smiled. I never wanted to kick a man in the shins so badly in my life.

Here was the thing about Luc—his smiles could be as lascivious as they were sexy. "Shake on it," he said. Shake on it. Binding. She shook on it, she had to go through with it. This was the payment.

Shafira held her hand out. Luc grabbed it, brought it up to his mouth to kiss the underside of her wrist, and then they shook hands.

"Just so you know, I'd have still done it for free. Simone here knows me too well. I'm so glad you don't."

I saw the moment her stomach dropped.

"But you will," he finished and I took it upon myself to use my electric fingers on the man, pressing them deep into the exposed skin of his neck for maximum contact and maximum effect. He dropped to his knees and I still found that so satisfying to witness.

"Stop—" Shafira shot her hand out in front of her. "You're hurting him." She was seriously too nice. But alas, I pulled my hand away.

He grumbled as he stood, rubbing his neck. "You can't do that, can you?" he asked Shafira.

"No."

"Good. Clearly, Simone here needs a round of slap and tickle with Connor. She's only nice after a round of slap and tickle."

"I'm only nice to Connor," I warned.

"Right," he said, shivering. He got me. "Let's get you those wards."

He started for the door again and as we followed him Shafira said, "I cannot believe you dropped the creator of hell. Who does that?"

I smiled. "*Me*. Being the granddaughter of Lilith has its perks."

Luc led us through the safehouse which was seriously nicer than any house I'd ever lived in, to a room off the back parlor. A lab. On one wall, he had shelves of crystals in clear bins and beakers, vials, microscopes, Bunsen burners—the whole shebang.

"Luc, you're a man of science?" I asked.

"Are you serious?" he asked me, then he turned to Shafira. "Is she serious?"

"She sounds serious," Shafira answered.

"Do you not read? Why do you think I got cast out of heaven?"

"I don't know—something about wanting to be as loved by God as the humans."

He sighed. "We really do need better PR. People always turn

shit around. I wanted the angels to have the same rights as humans. I wanted us to have the right to discover all that science and nature had to offer. I got tired of the blindly following 'because I said so' mentality. *Because I said so* wasn't enough. We weren't exactly unionized, so when I voiced my concerns with management, I ended up down here."

"That's rough… and why you allow demons to have unions. I get it."

"She can be taught," he murmured.

"Hey, now, don't be mean. Your side of things is pretty new to me."

Luc gave a slight shrug as he stepped to the far side of the room to a wall filled with bins that contained crystals and stones. I saw onyx glass in a ceramic bowl and next to it, M&M's open and dumped into another bowl.

"M&M's, Luc? What are you, five?"

"I get hungry when I'm working. Sometimes I want a snack. Sue me."

"I don't think there's anything wrong with a man enjoying some candy," Shafira said, snickering. "It's cute.

"Don't encourage him," I replied. "Can we get on with this?"

He looked at Shafira. "Every party has a pooper."

"Hey—that's *my* line. You can't use it against me."

"I'm Lucifer. I can do anything I want—*and* it's fun to see you fume."

Okay, so he might've had a point. About doing anything he wants. Seeing me fume? Oh, if we had more time, the man would suffer. "Can we focus? Connor and my cousin Karro are with Kimaris right now."

That sobered him right up. Luc picked up several different crystals in the shapes of like those batons that runners used in relay events, but they had sharp points at each end. He carefully considered each one, picking two white stones, a pinkish-colored stone, and a gray stone. He brought them to one of the tables, where he picked up bottles that had what looked like oils in them and wiped the oils from each bottle over each crystal. Lastly, he held each crystal in his hand. Power flowed from the center of Luc's chest down into his hand. His body lit up like a beacon. I gasped. The awe-inspiring sight was something that would stay with me forever. How many people got to see an angel imbue power into a ward in their lifetime?

Shafira took a step closer. Since she did, I did too because I couldn't be showed up by her. He carefully imbued each crystal with his magic. The glow faded as soon as he set the last one down.

"That was amazing," Shafira said through a very heavy breath. Luc looked up at her, smiling. Then he winked and she blushed. Luc had that effect on women.

"These should work," he said. "Kamaris is a powerful guy, so I picked out powerful crystals. The oils help to amplify and set the Luc magic into each one."

"I'm so glad you're on our side," I replied.

"You really are," he teased, or I think he teased. Luc had a big head, so it was a toss-up. "Is there food or anything at this place?"

"I have no idea. It's abandoned."

"Right." He tossed me the wards as he passed me to walk out of the lab. Shafira and I scrambled after him. He grabbed a bag from a pantry and started filling it with food, handing the bag off to Shafira and she set it down by her feet. Then he started filling jugs with water. He set those by her feet, too. Lastly, he left us for a minute and came back with an eight-pack of toilet paper. Luc understood the assignment.

Once the three of us stood close together, I manifested a bubble around us and the food and water, and I magicked us the hell out of there, locking in on my mate-GPS. In a blink, we set down back inside the outpost.

"Thank the gods," Karro said. He looked pretty tired. "My

zaps don't pack as much heat as yours do. He just keeps waking up—oh, *hello*, sexiest man I've ever seen in my life."

Luc snickered. The man certainly had prideful down.

"This is Luc, known better as Lucifer," I said, snickering in anticipation of his coming. My cousin didn't disappoint.

Karro started coughing. "Lucifer—like *the* Lucifer?"

Luc threw out one of those smarmy, used car salesman smiles. "I see you've heard of me." I half expected him to cluck his tongue and shoot a finger pistol at the man.

"Luc, brother, leave him alone," Connor said. Luc turned a *'sit your ass down'* look on my mate. Shaking his head he replied, "Everyone has heard of you." Luc's looks didn't appear to bother Connor one bit.

"You always ruin my fun."

"I'll tell you what, you can have fun antagonizing Kimaris if you get the wards set before he wakes up again."

Luc rolled his eyes at my mate but grabbed a white crystal from my hand, ramming the point into the floorboards. Next he did the same with the pinkish one, followed by the gray crystal, ending with the second white one that was diagonal from the first white one, forming a square.

"That's it?" I asked.

"You'll see. He's stirring now." Luc dropped on the sofa, man-spreading his legs to get comfortable and draping his arms over the back of it. He gestured with his head for Shafira to sit next to him. She walked over to him but put a bit of space between them and she took up as little space as possible. It was actually pretty funny to watch. I got it. She was in the presence of greatness. And *he* knew it.

Karro raised his hands, ready to throw down if necessary. As Kimaris roused, he lunged for Karro but hit the invisible shield, cracking his face—well, his whole body—and throwing him backward onto the floor.

"The fuck?" Kimaris raged, and Luc, looking completely bored, sighed heavily for Kimaris to hear him.

Luc never looked up from picking the imaginary dirt from under his fingernails. "Calm your tits. You're not getting out unless I let you out."

Kimaris snapped his head around to look at Luc and I kind of had to feel bad for the guy. He turned green before our eyes and I got it. One really didn't want the fury of Lucifer coming down on them. *"Lucifer,"* he whispered.

"Kimaris… tut, tut, tut… you've been bad. Everyone in Hades knows that Connor here is my righthand man, and you tried to kill him with black salt?"

"I didn't—" he started, but Luc raised his hand to stop him.

"Don't embarrass yourself. We all know what you did. Now I need to know *why*. What's Satan's endgame? Why is he attacking the witch covens? What's his beef with Connor and his mate?"

"Satan has no beef," he replied and that was so the wrong thing to say. I was used to the loveable Luc. Kimaris's lie released the power of Lucifer.

As he rose from the sofa, I'd swear in a court of law he grew by like a foot or more. He loomed over us. A red glow engulfed his skin and his eyes turned to fire. "Do not lie to me."

This version of Luc, the fallen angel, the creator of Hell, scared me enough that I was on the brink of spilling every secret I'd ever kept to the man. Kimaris cowered like a sniveling rat. "We need the Lilium. Word has it she possesses power to rival even yours." He used his head to gesture to me. "And there are two."

"Why is he starting shit now?" Connor asked, well, demanded.

"It's been in the works for some time. I don't know why. I only know that I'll be handsomely rewarded for my compliance."

"Or…" Luc paused for dramatic effect—the man was such a diva. "You can die and we'll go on with our lives as if you never existed." Kimaris swallowed, looking about a second and a half from getting sick all over the floor. But when Luc raised his arm, Kimaris shot his hands out in front of him.

"*Please, don't—*" he begged.

"Then *tell me* what I *want to know.*" A pissed-off Luc got me a little hot and bothered. Damn, I was a mated woman. He seriously needed to dial back the pheromones or whatever he used on the ladies because if Connor knew the thoughts going through my head right now, he'd go ballistic. "What is Satan up to?"

"It's not Satan. I swear."

Luc, not being a demon, had no trouble reaching through the wards. He lifted Kimaris up by his shirt collar until the usually intimidating man's feet dangled off the floor.

"Who is behind this?" Luc spat, giving Kimaris a shake for good measure.

"I don't know. I received an envelope with instructions—I swear. There's a liaison, a man—Cain—he contacts me. He promised that if I helped, I'd be handsomely rewarded. I was told that it was in my best interest not to tell Satan about this or I'd bring revenge down on his entire quadrant."

"And you accepted?" Connor asked.

"I'm a demon. Who's going to turn down an offer like that? I keep my boss safe and get a big payday? I'm evil, not stupid."

In a weird way, I respected his answer. "Who is this Cain?" I asked. "Where can we find him?"

"I don't know. He seeks me out when he has a job for me."

"What does he look like?" Shafira asked.

"Big, burly man. A real attitude on him. He's a human with the balls of a demon. Dark hair. Dark, angry eyes. A neck like a bull. I don't like him, but I have mad respect for a human who thinks he can go toe to toe with one of us."

"A big, burly man with a thick neck? That's all you've got?" I asked. "That describes like a half a billion people."

"He's tan—more like her..." He pointed to Shafira. "No,

more like you," he said to me. I had a natural tan a few shades lighter than Shafira's skin tone.

"Can I kill him?" I asked Luc. "Let me kill him."

We went through all this trouble to capture him and all we got was 'a big man with tan skin'? I cracked my neck, ready to take him out until Connor snuck behind me, wrapping his arms around my waist.

"Enough," he whispered in my ear.

"He tried to kill you and the only reason I kept him alive was to get answers, which he's not giving. Don't tell me *enough*."

"Simone, baby… We still have to get the grimoire, find Lily Joy, and meet up with Sim and Maddi to join the jewel with the hilt of the dagger."

"Not to mention stopping demons from wiping out more covens," Karro unhelpfully put in.

"Yeah, and your point is?" I asked sarcastically.

"We might still be able to use him down the road. He's not going anywhere with the wards in place."

"Have you figured out why demons think this place is haunted?"

Kimaris's eyes went huge.

"You aren't afraid?" Connor asked. "A big, tough demon like you?" And he might have snickered. Oh, Connor Baghest was an evil man when he wanted to be. Was it wrong to be so turned on by that?

"I feel like we should split up to not draw attention to ourselves," I said. "But I worry about Shafira and Karro alone. They're powerful, but demons can be tricky sons of bitches and I don't want them getting hurt in a surprise attack or something."

"I can't cloak them like you, but I can keep them safe." Luc really didn't deserve the bad press he got all the time. I loved the crap out of Luc—in a sisterly way, but, like, not a Cersei and Jamie Lannister sisterly way—although Luc was hot. But no… just no.

"So where will you head, then?" I asked.

He shrugged. "Since we don't have to worry about this guy" —he thumbed over to Kimaris—"I'll take Shafira and Karro with me. We'll see if we're able to hunt down the identity of Beetle."

"Right. Then Connor and I will head back to our place to retrieve the grimoire. Hopefully, we'll be able to contact my brother and Madigan again and find out about Lily Joy. This whole thing got old, like, last week."

"Lily Joy is smart. She's powerful. I'm sure she's fine." Luc was probably right. I certainly couldn't let myself entertain any other ideas at the moment. I cared for her. Once upon a time, I'd thought that going from being completely alone to having this ever-expanding family was so cool, but now they were people I cared about who could be injured or killed if I didn't stop this crap. Another thing to worry about. I'd probably end up with the digestive tract of an eighty-five-year-old by the time this ended.

"You're not going to leave me here?" Kimaris asked.

Okay, so he made this part of the job fun again. "Ready?" I asked Luc. "I'll take you, Shafira, and Karro back to the safehouse and you all can figure out where to go from there. Connor and I will head home."

"Since it's unlikely we'll be able to meet back up for a while, anyone have a phone?" Karro asked.

"I do. Back at the safehouse," Luc answered. "And yes, I have both Connor's and Simone's numbers."

"Check in as often as you can, but we'll set a time for… what?"

"3:00 P.M. Eastern Standard Time tomorrow?"

I turned to Connor. "How'd you decide on that?"

"Shit tends to happen in the morning or at night. It's the calm before the storm. You don't like it, pick something else."

"No. I'm good." I looked to the rest of the group. "You all good with that?"

We got head bobs and "Yeah"s. With nothing for it, I grabbed Luc's and Shafira's hands, as they were the closest to me. Shafira grabbed Karro's hand and I manifested us back to Luc's safehouse.

This was it. I dropped their hands and hugged Luc. "Keep them safe," I said into his ear. "You won't be dead forever. They will."

"With my life," he replied.

Then I moved to Shafira. "Don't let Luc's fallen angel status or good looks intimidate you. You're a powerful witch and I'm proud to call you an ally—but I'm more proud to call you my friend."

She sucked in a sharp breath. "I am not crying. Badass witches do not cry." Shafira wiped at her eyes when I released her to turn to Karro.

"Stay safe, okay? I want you coming over to the house for cookouts. You can even bring your demon lover boy."

Karro's face turned the cutest shade of pink. I thought that maybe it wasn't just the man's penis that Karro loved. I hugged him fiercely. "You have family now," I whispered.

"Right," Karro said, pushing me back. "Don't you dare get yourself killed."

"We won't. Connor will be there to protect me. I'll be there to protect Connor." My time was up. I had to get back to the man, and so with one final wave, I manifested myself back to my mate.

Connor stood near the wards, taunting Kimaris. He turned the moment he sensed me and I rushed him. "I'm usually badass," I mumbled through sniffles.

"They'll be fine."

"I know. It's not them. I just want sex and we don't have time."

He chuckled. "Right, baby. It's just the sex. Remind me, when was the last time horny made you cry?"

"Shut it," I warned with my face pressed against his chest. "Or I'll take the demon with me and leave your ass here."

"That's a great idea," Kimaris said.

"Okay, I'm better," I snapped.

"Not horny now?" my jerkface of a mate teased.

"You are so lucky that I can't tease you about climbing Luc like a stripper pole thanks to this bond."

Connor's grip on my waist tightened. I pushed up on my toes kissing the underside of his jaw and then manifested us home.

*What the hell happened here?*

# CHAPTER
## Twenty-Five

"*My house*," I cried in complete and utter shock. It'd been turned upside-down. Everything I'd worked so hard for lay in tatters on the ground. Stuffing pulled from furniture, glass shattered, tables upturned. My beautiful television smashed to pieces.

Suddenly, my head started to spin and I fell backward ass-first onto the edge of the sofa. I felt sick. Violated.

"It's just stuff," I mumbled, trying to rein in my emotions. "It's just stuff…"

Connor dropped down next to me, pulling me onto his lap. "You've got magic and I've got money. We'll get it all back somehow. I promise."

I nodded, squaring my shoulders. "It was a shock, is all."

"You don't have to be strong around me, sweetheart."

Call it the mania of the moment, but when he spoke softly and sweet to me like that, I lost it in that I shifted on his lap to straddle him and proceeded to kiss the crap out of him. I kissed him with possessive tenderness as if we had all the time in the world. His arms held me tightly against him while he dug his fingers into my blouse and my jeans right above my butt.

He gave me the strength to keep going. He did that.

Just as abruptly, I pushed back from him. "Right," I said while collecting myself. He snickered at my change in attitude.

"Time to find the grimoire," he replied.

I stood from his lap and walked over to the vent in the floor to see if Mr. Pooches might've hidden it there. "You're just a good kisser." I felt the need to defend my actions.

"Sure."

"I'm a strong, independent woman."

"Absolutely."

"Are you mocking me?"

"Never."

"Good, because I can be formidable even with you, Connor Baghest."

"Noted." He winked. I balled my fist, willing myself not to punch him square in his sexy, solidly muscled... What was I talking about?

We started in the living room. Okay, so the first floor vent probably wouldn't have been the best place for Mr. Pooches to hide the world's most important grimoire. Connor and I tore apart the house even more than what the demons had done, just with less destruction.

I plopped down on the kitchen floor, utterly defeated.

"Are you sure he hid it here?"

"It was here. There wouldn't have been anywhere else for him to hide it. Otherwise, I'd have no freaking clue where to look."

Connor grumbled. I felt like grumbling too, but as he did it so much better, I left it to him. My kitchen table had been upturned, as were the chairs. Every cupboard opened. Every pot, pan dish, or utensil lay scattered or shattered on the floor surrounding us. They'd even upturned Mr. Pooches's litter box. Poo and litter all over the small corner. I looked at it. Then I looked at it again. Poo? His litter box had an automatic scoop that moved the kitty waste into a compartment that held a plastic container underneath the litter box so he had a clean box for every use and I didn't have to discard the plastic more than every couple of weeks. If you didn't know about the bin, you'd never find it. It'd taken me an hour to access the thing and I'd had the damn directions. The bin wasn't open. But there was poo.

"I know where it is!" I shouted, totally startling Connor, which always brought me joy.

I crawled over to the litter box, flipped it right-side up, and pressed in on the back to release the compartment holding the bin. And there—*my grimoire*! Mr. Pooches earned all the tuna and sardines his heart desired for thinking of this.

"It's tiny," Connor said, looming over me and the litter box.

"What did you expect?"

He shrugged. "I don't know. It's Lilith's grimoire. I thought it'd be huge."

"She left it with an infant."

"Still... you'd think Lilith, of all people, would know more magic than this." He picked it up from the bin. It fit in his hand. I pushed up from the floor to snatch it back, flipping it open. The inscription with my name appeared on the first page. As I turned each page, I read over names that'd never been there before. Names of Lilith's descendants. They had to be, because I found Simeon, Lily Joy, and Karro in the book. A list of powers opened up to me too and I had to believe that these were powers I could tap into now that my magic was unbound. I saw the Taser fingers, the manifestation, the astral-projection, talking with spirits, and so much more. Lilith gave detailed explanations on how to master each power and corresponding spells to utilize them.

"Connor, you have no idea what's in here."

"I take it by your reaction that none of that was in there before."

"No. None of it—*look*." I shoved the list of names in his face. "Other Lilium. And here..." I turned the pages to show him the powers.

"Are you shitting me? All of those are yours?"

"I assume so. Maybe some are for Sim. Maybe some are for

my cousins—" My next words got cut off by a loud knock coming from the front door. I looked to Connor. "No one should know we're here," I whispered.

"Hide, babe. I'll answer. Something feels off." Goosebumps rose up his arms, which happened just before he shifted. I held the grimoire close to my chest, kissed Connor, and slunk off silently to the back bedroom.

"Let me hear everything that's going on." I manifested and I heard Connor answer the door.

"Can I help you?" Connor asked.

"Is the homeowner home?" the person outside the house answered in a grumbly voice I'd heard before. Detective Shift. *Shit.*

"No. She ran to the store for garbage bags. Clearly, someone ransacked the place. Can I ask what this is regarding…" Connor paused and the detective must've pulled his badge because he finished, "Detective *Shift.*"

"The neighbors reported something going on at this residence."

"But not when someone broke in and leveled the entire place? That makes sense. And since when does the police department send a detective to look into a possible B and E?"

"I was the closest," he countered.

"Right. Well, she'll be back when she's back."

"What are you doing here?" he asked.

"I live here. She's the homeowner, but I moved in a couple of weeks ago. We're getting married."

"And you don't want to file a report?"

"I asked her. She—wait, why'd you ask for the homeowner?"

"Excuse me?"

"Why did you ask for the homeowner? Why wouldn't you have assumed *I* was the homeowner?"

*Ooh… good question. Come on, Detective Shift. Let's see you get out of this one.*

"You tell the bitch that we want the grimoire."

Connor growled. Literally growled.

"She gives it up willingly," Shift continued, "Beetle will spare her life. He said he'll make her his number-one concubine. She fights us, the rest of the demon population gets to play with her."

*Play* with me? I burst from the bedroom in full charge, ready to take that asshole out, but the moment I reached the front door, a literal hole opened up beneath Detective Shift, sucking him down. A portal. The man showed up at my house threatening me and then used a goddamned portal to escape when it had gotten too real for him. And that ticked me off more. He'd chosen his side. He needed to stand up and fight for it. Clearly, Beetle hadn't vetted his minion too well. Next time Beetle might want to check with resume sites like LinkedIn or Monster.

And because of my ADD 'ooo—shiny' brain, I giggled, thinking about searching up minion positions on Monster. Connor shot me the death glare of all death glares.

"You were supposed to stay hidden," he raged.

"Whoa... down boy."

He dragged his hand through his hair so roughly that I thought I spied a bald spot after he'd finished. Maybe it was just my imagination, but it still looked painful. "Simone... Swear to god... How am I supposed to keep you safe if you keep charging head-first into danger?"

"Right. Let's pretend for a second that I'm *not* the grand-daughter of Lilith and *haven't* come into magic that no one on the planet has seen before—oh, right, we *can't*. Because *I am* the freaking granddaughter of Lilith, which is exactly why they're after me. I can't hide from them. I'm in this. I *am* this... this... whatever this turns out to be. I'm connected and you know it."

"But you're my mate—"

"Yeah. And I love that thing you do"—I twirled my finger in the air to remind him of the thing in question—"but I told you before, we're partners in this or it's not happening. I'm not about to play damsel in distress to bolster your ego."

"It's not my ego." He sighed. His rage deflated for the time.

"Good. Now that we've got that settled, you've seen that detective before," I said. Connor narrowed his eyes at me. "That first day we met. You tried to kidnap me."

"You know damn well I wasn't kidnapping you."

I shot him my *'really?'* eyes and waited.

"Fine. I kidnapped you but not in a creepy, *want to wear your hair as a wig* kind of way. You were doing something stupid that could've gotten you hurt or killed, per usual. I had to make sure that didn't happen."

"Aw… such sweet words," I said sarcastically. "Keep talking like that and you might get lucky." I tilted my head, smiling at him as I finished, muttering, "Or I'll get lucky when I cut you while you sleep." under my breath.

He reached out to grab my hand, tugging me against his solid, yet—I'd never tell him this but comforting—body and he just held me. Connor and I would get through this. The universe put us together for some reason. I still sort of thought it was a clerical error, but I the universe *was* the universe for a reason. I held him back.

"What do you know about him?" my mate asked into my hair.

"Not much. I first heard about Detective Shift from Jeffery's mother. He'd come to visit her about Jeffery's case, but it never sat well with me because no Detective Shift had ever come to talk to me and I wondered why. My Spidey-sense told me something was off about it. But then so much happened, I never thought anything more about it until years later when I went to the police station to pick up Jeffery's effects and I literally ran into the man."

"Then what?"

"He was incredibly rude. Again, I sloughed it off because I wasn't exactly looking forward to retrieving Jeffery's things. But then, Detective Shift was the one who responded to the kidnapping call. And I thought I recognized his voice in the cemetery when Beetle's men attacked."

"He's human. Why is a human working with demons?"

"I don't know. He has to be expecting some kind of major payout, right?"

"When will humans learn? Demon deals never turn out like you expect them to."

"Luc would keep his word."

He pressed a kiss to the top of my head. "Luc's not a demon. His demons never strike deals. It's not a job requirement. Plus, that whole pride thing—he'd never let one go back on a deal."

Terror struck me as I realized that I'd set the grimoire down to storm out here and I tore myself from Connor's arms to run back into the back bedroom. The grimoire sat on the hardwood floor exactly where I'd dropped it and I sighed all the relief.

Only seconds behind me, Connor entered the room in full-on hellhound mode. His red eyes glowed. "What happened?" he asked in my head.

"I dropped the grimoire to tackle Shift. While we were standing in the living room, it hit me that I'd left one of the two most important books in the world unattended. Stupid, I know," I said before he could, then I turned to walk over to the pile of Connor's clothing that had once been neatly folded in the drawers broken on the floor. I picked up a clean pair of boxer briefs, walking them back over to him as he shifted back to his man form.

He took the underwear from me without any negative comments for once, sliding them up over his powerful thighs. I paced the room, opening the grimoire again to the first pages where the names of all my cousins were written. I concentrated on the names, manifesting them to copy themselves onto paper that went directly into Karro's hands, making sure to add a note explaining why the papers appeared in his hands. I wanted to send them to Lily Joy too, but I had no idea where she was at.

Was she okay? Astral projection. It ended up being the only way I could think of to contact her and not risk her safety even more.

I turned my attention from the book to the destroyed room then back to the book. "What are we going to do?" I asked.

Being charged with saving the world sucked. Totally and completely. And being completely in my head, I missed Connor move until he reached me, grasping my arms in each hand, he walked me backward until my legs hit the bed and I fell onto the skewed mattress.

"Connor, there's no sheet on the bed. The mattress is half on the floor."

He shrugged. "You take care of the sheets. I got the mattress."

Rather than get up and look for the sheets, I cheated, manifesting the fitted one under me. Connor used his brute strength to swivel the mattress back into place.

"We're going to sleep in our own bed tonight," he said.

"But the world—"

"Won't end tonight. They don't have the grimoire."

"But what about Shift and the demons? I don't have wards. We need Luc for that."

"I work around demons every night. They'll think we've fled because of Shift's visit. No one will expect us to stay. I promise. You need to rest. Tomorrow, we'll tackle the world."

Well, I had to admit that sounded pretty perfect about now. Sleeping in my own bed. I missed this bed. I missed this house, even in its current upturned state. At least that was something I could control.

The food that had been pulled from the refrigerator and freezer for no reason except to vandalize my home more had started rotting and smelled pretty bad. If bugs and rodents hadn't found their way inside yet, they soon would.

I concentrated on the mess. I concentrated on the smell. I manifested them gone completely, leaving behind a squeaky clean kitchen. For good measure, I focused hard on any insects or rodents that might've been hiding in my home and manifested them gone too.

And to think, everyone could've had magic if Adam hadn't been such a major tool.

Connor kissed my cheek. "I'm hitting the shower while I have the chance."

"What do you want to eat? I'm starved."

"There's nothing in the house and you're not going out."

"Whoa, whoa, whoa… despite you *trying* to tell me what to do, let's play the 'all the ways Simone's not stupid' game."

"Simone, I know—"

I held my finger up, signaling him to zip it. "One," I started. "There are demons trying to kill me. Two: According to you, the demons will think we've hightailed it out of town, so going out would give our position away. Three: I have magic. I can manifest us a freaking meal. Four: I don't feel like leaving this bed until absolutely necessary. And let's face it, that tops my list of important things right now."

"You done?"

"Be a good dog and shower. If you're clean, I'll let you sleep in the bed and I might even give you belly scratches before you go to sleep."

He charged me. I might've known exactly what I was doing. I giggled as he trapped me between the bed and his body. "Flea shampoo's on the shower rack." And that was where all teasing stopped, unless you counted Connor teasing my lady bits. I went from zero to naked from the waist down in .057 seconds. His mouth found me and—*whoa! Thank you universe.*

Every touch of his hand, every nip from his teeth brought me closer to my personal heaven. I squirmed beneath him, needing to touch him but whenever I reached a hand out to run through his hair or grab hold of his shoulder, he'd stop, leaving me in carnal agony.

I gripped the sheets instead, widening my legs to give him more access to me.

Everyone… should… have a Connor… I closed my eyes, letting the sensation from his mouth take me over. My heart pounded and my breaths left me in tiny spurts. Nothing in the world felt as good as Connor's mouth—or other parts—on me.

In the middle of finding greatness, my grandmother popped into my head.

"You can't be here," I shouted.

She laughed. *Laughed.* "Simone, do you remember how many children I had? This is nothing."

"It's not nothing to me. And what he's doing won't make children."

My millennials-dead, spirit-guide grandmother laughed even harder at me. I found myself stuck between trying to enjoy every new thing my mate did to me and not letting Lilith know exactly how skilled he was—if you get my drift. Finally, it got too uncomfortable.

"Is there a reason you're here?" I asked. Not harshly, but Connor's tongue made a special kind of magic, the kind that no one else on the planet made. Not even me.

"The vent in the room past the kitchen. There is dried blood from where the intruder scraped themselves while looking for the grimoire. You need to take it to Victoria Rivers."

"Blood to Victoria," I said. "Got it."

"What?" Connor asked.

Lilith left me just as fast as she'd shown up.

If the choice was left to me—and let's face it, all choices in this relationship were mine—I wanted to spend a normal night in bed with my mate recharging my battery, but Lilith showing up meant more than her giving guidance. How selfish of me to sleep soundly in a soft bed when so many of our witch sisters had already lost their lives, and I still didn't know Lily Joy's whereabouts. Was she safe? Was she alive?

"Connor, we need to get the vent from the den and get it to Victoria Rivers."

"That's incredibly random." He started running kisses over

my bared skin and it… felt… great. "You sure I can't convince you to wait until tomorrow?" Yes. Yes, he absolutely could—no, he couldn't. We needed to dress. We had to move.

I reluctantly shook my head. "My grandmother popped in while you were… well, you were *entertaining* me."

He choked out a cough. "Lilith showed while I was going down on you."

I shrugged. "Not the best timing."

To be honest, I thought he'd blow a gasket, but instead, he rolled his eyes to the ceiling and sort of laugh-sighed. "Let's get dressed."

Disappointment. I'd been hoping he'd use his hands and mouth to protest my plan. I frowned, pulling my bra cups back into place under the T-shirt. At least I got to wear my favorite pair of Converse.

With Connor to my back, I walked into the den, over to the back floor vent.

"Fuck," Connor said understandably, because of the blood pooled in a small corner of the vent cover and a disgusting piece of fingernail nestled in the congealed blood. We were staring at the blood and fingernail of our intruder. This person violated my life by destroying my home and was so cocky, he neglected to be bothered to clean up after himself. It hurt. It hurt a lot. I took a moment to let myself feel that hurt and then shut it down.

Time to get to work. Closing my eyes, I manifested a gallon-sized Ziploc bag big enough to hold the vent cover, and I was careful to only touch the sans-blood side, dropping it inside the baggie and zipping it closed.

"Oh, we need—"

"Got it right here, babe." We'd entered the 'reading each other's minds' portion of this mated bond because he absolutely held the grimoire in his hands.

"We didn't even get to eat yet," I grumbled.

"If you ate more protein instead of junk, you wouldn't be so hangry right now."

"Shut it, Baghest. For your information, I planned to manifest a big, juicy double cheeseburger and fries. Cheeseburgers have plenty of protein. And I'm not hangry, more hirritated."

His fingers curled into the shirt at my waist as he pressed a kiss to my hair and I manifested us to Weik Laboratories. We landed in the alley between the two looming block buildings again, but this time instead of shadows, we were cloaked in darkness.

"What time is it?" Connor asked.

I pulled my phone from my pocket to look at the screen. 2:00 A.M. "Early."

"No one will be in. We could've slept in our bed."

"Lilith made it pretty clear we needed to get this stuff here."

"She's dead. Time doesn't mean the same to her."

"I'm sure dear Granny still understands the concept of time for those of us in the meatsuits."

"'Meatsuits,' Simone? Where do you come up with this stuff?"

"You *wish* you had my incredible sense of sass." I loved playing around like this with Connor, but given the time crunch, I grabbed his hand, pulling him along with me out onto the sidewalk. I supposed I could've manifested us inside the building, disabling any security measures, but as it turned out, I didn't need to. As we walked, I spied light coming from the back of the alley next to Weik Laboratories. It happened like a blink, there and gone—or, like a door opening and closing.

"This way," I said to Connor. A cooling breeze rippled over my skin. It hardly felt like the world was on the brink of ruin on nights like this with Connor and breezes.

These were the images I needed to hold on to in the coming days. My future life with the sexy hellhound deserved to be lived. I planned to live it.

With quiet steps, I led us down the darkened alley and to the second partial alley that ran behind the Weik building.

We held back, peeking around the corner to check out the lay of the land. Two women and a man stood under a cloud of smoke sucking down cigarettes like it was an Olympic sport. Given the way witches were being hunted, I couldn't blame them.

I'd never smoked a day in my life, but if I smoked, I'd have been doing the exact same thing.

When they finished, the man knocked on the door—three quick raps and two slow. Then the door popped open.

They walked back inside. With lightning quickness, Connor jutted forward to stick his foot between the jamb and the door to keep it from clicking shut on us.

He nodded at me, knowing exactly what I was thinking, and I cloaked us before we walked in.

People—witches—milled about in the hallway. I figured if Victoria Rivers was here, she'd be in her office.

"Hold on," I whispered to my mate, but a woman whipped her head up. *Whoopsie.* I needed to be more careful. The second Connor's hand touched my shoulder, I manifested us to the top floor.

A woman and child, both in pajamas, walked from the restroom to one of the offices on the floor before Victoria's. Air mattresses and sleeping bags took up the floor space. The desk had been pushed back against the far wall. It appeared they'd turned Weik Laboratories into a Holiday Inn.

We continued on past this band of offices to where the space opened up and Victoria's secretary's desk sat empty. Connor and I moved around the desk and I dropped the cloak before knocking on her door. After a few moments, the door opened. A sleep-disheveled Victoria's eyes went wide.

"Nice jammies," I said, smiling and pointing to the dancing kitties on her sleep pants. She blanched before gaining composure.

"Simone. Connor. What are you doing here?"

Connor handed me the bag with the vent grate. I handed it off to her. As she slowly took it, I explained. "Lilith came to me. She said we needed to get this blood analyzed. It's important."

"Uh, yes… Give me a moment." She walked over to her desk, sliding on a pair of slippers and dropping a robe around her shoulders before joining us at the door.

We followed her to the elevator. She pressed the button to the basement laboratory. Victoria led us into one of the rooms, now empty, where she handed me the Ziploc to suit up. I handed her back the bag. She set it on a metal table before pulling the grate from the bag and placing it on the shiny surface. Victoria walked over to a shelf, grabbing a swab from a cylindrical glass jar with a fitted aluminum lid. She wet the tip of the swab from a squeeze bottle marked 'Distilled Water.'

Victoria rubbed the dampened cotton over the dried blood. She did this three more times with three more swabs. Then, snipping off the reddened tips, she added those tips to a smaller tube containing a clear liquid. She added drops of two others before stoppering it, giving the liquid time to turn red, then used a dropper to suck up the red liquid that she squeezed into yet another smaller tube, and another, and another.

Each of the smaller tubes got the testing treatment. I'd never considered that Victoria would know how to test the DNA. When we met her before, she'd seemed so *company president. Go, Victoria.* Sisters doing it for themselves and all that.

"Now we wait," she said. "Have you eaten? Are you tired?"

As my stomach grumbled from hearing the word 'eaten,' I shook my head.

"We've been busy," Connor replied for the both of us.

"Since we've been hosting witches from covens all over the world, I've kept the kitchen open. Staff has been taking all shifts. If you go up to the cafeteria, you can get food. I'll set you up with an office for a few hours of rest."

"Thank you." I reached my hand over to Connor. As he took it, I added, "Food is great. Rest depends on what you find with the testing."

The woman turned a look of '*girl, please,*' on me. "You might be Lilium, but you still need rest. Tired minds make mistakes."

I should've thought of that.

"Fine. We'll eat and rest for just a bit."

The idea of resting or sleeping irritated me. I agreed because Victoria made a great point, but it wasted time we didn't have to waste.

Connor and I took the elevator up to the cafeteria level. Several people sat at tables eating and talking. Most of them stopped to take in my mate. He still had that effect on me. Why should they be any different? So what if covens were being attacked and people were dying—a foin man was a *foin* man.

After scanning the room, my sights landed on just the thing to lighten the mood. "Pasta!" I semi-shouted, starting for the pasta bar set up on the far side of the room.

"I thought you wanted a cheeseburger."

"Well, now I want pasta. Don't judge me on my lifestyle choices."

This pasta bar held every kind imaginable, I swear. They even offered a high-protein chick pea option that put Connor into the throes of foodie passion.

I opted for loaded mac and cheese and creamy chicken alfredo, then I finally got my baked ziti, this one with mini meatballs.

He laughed at the delicious disaster on my plate. "That's gonna put you in a food coma."

"Only for the untrained. I'm a professional." And I plucked a meatball from my plate, popping it into my mouth.

We ate in comfortable silence until I started dozing off and Connor decided that we needed to rest for a bit. He cleared our plates while I waited at the table. A pretty woman maybe in her mid-thirties walked through the door. She stopped to scan the room and when her eyes landed on me, she smiled, making her way over.

"Hi. I'm Layne," she said by way of introducing herself,

uncomfortably tucking strands of her light-brown hair behind her ear when Connor joined us. I was totally aware of that feeling, internally listing all of your visible flaws and hoping that someone as gorgeous as him wouldn't call you on them, or even bother to notice them in the first place. He never would. He saved his attitude for me alone.

"Hi," I replied. "I'm Simone and this is Connor."

She dipped her head to each of us. "I'm Victoria's secretary. I have a room set up for you upstairs, if you want to follow me."

Talk about timing.

Connor linked our fingers together and we held hands as we followed her to the elevator. She hit the button for the top floor. Then Layne, the secretary, led us to a conference room where the tables and chairs had been removed, and a queen-sized air mattress with pillows and sleeping bags sat on the Berber carpeting in the middle of the floor.

"This okay?" she asked.

"It's great," Connor replied. "Thanks."

"Victoria will be in touch when the test results are in."

"That'll work," I said, yawning.

"Well, that's my cue…" she said, turning to leave us. As she shut the door, I kicked off my shoes.

Seriously, my eyes fell shut as soon as my head hit the pillow. The next thing I knew, my consciousness roused to the feeling of someone shaking me. My eyes cracked open. "Need sleepy," I whined.

"The two hours you got is what you're gonna get. Up. Let's go."

I narrowed my eyes on him. "I know twenty ways to kill a man without lifting a finger."

He laughed at me, tugging me up. I stretched then slipped my Converse back on. Rather than hit the elevators again, Connor turned us in the direction of Victoria's office. He gave one knock and opened the door.

"I'm sorry I had to wake you," Victoria said. "I wanted to let you sleep a bit longer, but this seemed very important."

That caught my attention. "Important?" I asked.

"Please, have a seat." She flipped her monitor around for us to see the screen. "This is you." She pointed to the line that represented me, the one she'd shown me before. "Now, this"—she pointed to a second line—"is the results from the blood on the vent."

*What in the...?* I leaned in, trying to reconcile what I was looking at with some shred of reality.

"What exactly are we looking at?" Connor asked.

"He's above me," I replied. "Not below."

Victoria nodded. "That's exactly right."

"What does that mean?"

She pointed out more lines. "This line here means that he—and yes, the DNA is male—he and Simone are related, but only through one line. In my opinion, you're looking at the DNA of your half-uncle."

"The fuck," Connor spat, but I had a different reaction.

"Cain."

"What?" Victoria asked.

"Cain," I repeated. "Cain was my mother's younger half-brother through Adam and his second wife, Eve. Hell, I suppose he could be Abel, but if history is at all accurate, Abel was a decent guy who was killed by his brother. Were there any others?"

Victoria shrugged her shoulders, shaking her head. "I'm a witch. We didn't spend much time in church."

Connor outright laughed. "I'm a hellhound.We hung out with Luc and his demons."

"Well you know I was brought up in foster homes. I'm surprised I know as much as I do."

"So, just to be clear, given our collective lack of biblical knowledge, we're thinking Cain is in our time?" Connor asked.

"If it's him, he's definitely out of time, like you, Simone,"

Victoria said. "But he holds no magic. We checked for markers and there was nothing. He's completely human. Not one drop of super."

"I feel it in my gut, we're dealing with Cain, and neither Adam nor Eve held magic. That was why Adam wanted my mom to get with his son, to get the magic back in his family. But Lilith brought me forward. Only she'd have the power to do that and she'd never have. *Never.*"

"Lilith and demons," Connor replied. Victoria gasped and I whipped my head towards him fast enough to cause whiplash.

"Demons can do that?"

"The kings can. And angels."

"Like Lucifer?" Victoria asked.

"Not Luc," I said sharply. "He's good people. The man is on our side. He'd never stoop so low."

"He wouldn't, but Satan might," Connor said. Freaking wrath.

Why did every road lead back to Satan?

"I guess it's time to pay him a visit."

# CHAPTER Twenty-Six

We thanked Victoria for her help and really, the fastest way for us to get to Satan was through manifestation, but Connor insisted that we get to the closest portal so we didn't drop in somewhere that might get us killed before we could react.

His plan made more sense.

I closed my eyes, manifesting us to the closest portal in Satan's quadrant, which, you know, given we were in England, wasn't that far. The math mathed, right? Given the extended history of warfare in the country alone, not to mention Europe as a whole—no one but Satan could've controlled this quadrant.

Our feet touched ground at the far end of an archeological dig not currently in progress next to a large stone that concealed the both of us. The holes of the dig had been covered up by large plastic tarps, probably blue. The sun just started to peek above the horizon line, causing half of the tarps to fall into shadow and the others—well, it blinded me to look at them. Sunrises here were beautiful. I took a minute to enjoy the sight, a reminder of what we were fighting for. Not that Satan could control the sunrise, but our ability to enjoy them.

It hit me right then that my shop had been closed for an extended period of time. Customers had no idea that I was fighting to save them and were probably plenty pissed that they couldn't get their herbs and stones. Despite our circumstances here, I felt the need to shoot off a text to my employees telling them I'd been called away on an emergency and forgotten to contact them. If they wanted overtime, open the shop every day until I got back.

"You're texting now?" Connor asked accusingly.

"My girls. My store. It's been closed and I needed to—" I stopped trying to defend myself, letting my shoulders fall instead. I thought he'd make some sort of crack at my expense, but instead, he pulled me into his arms, placing a kiss to the top of my head. God, I loved when he did that. I felt safe. I felt loved. I felt... *happy*. In a time where I should've felt anything but, Connor made me happy.

He held me a few beats before saying, "We'll get you back to your store."

Connor got it. He got me. Now, I'd never tell him, but right here, right now, I decided the universe had gotten it pretty right pairing us together. Whatever deal Lilith made to make this happen, I owed her big time, too.

"Right," I said, pushing back from my mate but not letting him go completely. "Let's go bust some heads."

"I was thinking capturing Satan and forcing him to talk might be the better strategy here."

"Semantics."

As he laughed at me, I dropped a cloak around us. Connor pushed on the large stone and it made no noise as it scraped across the ground to reveal the entrance. We moved as a seamless unit down into the portal. Since I'd asked for one that would bring us to Satan's headquarters, the stone stairwell led us into Hades.

I'd snuck through this office space twice before and still

disliked it just as much. Sad. Beige. Fluorescent lighting. Shivers always accompanied thinking of the poor demons who suffered this place day in and day out while Luc had people laughing and lounging in the big common room. Luc's half-walls of fire gave an exciting flair. Nothing exciting happened here. Or at least no good excitement. Satan seemed the type to tear apart an unsuspecting demon just for shits and giggles.

We stopped in the middle of the hallway until Connor got his bearings. "Not the usual way I get here." Made sense. He turned us to the right and there—the office of the Goodfella came into view.

I cracked my knuckles, getting ready to manifest us inside the office when the door opened and a man in a tie, button-down, and suit pants stepped half out of the room. He stopped and turned back to whoever was in the office. It wasn't Satan. No one would dare speak to Satan in that tone—not if they wanted to live.

The man walked out without shutting the door, his whole body tight. He was not happy. Connor and I moved into the office where a woman had her ear pressed against the receiver of a beige, corded desk phone straight out of the 1970s. A closed door came into view behind her desk and I knew in an instant *that* was Satan's office. She had her mousy, brown hair pulled back in an extra-tight bun and she wore a blouse and a herringbone pencil skirt. She clicked her blood-red nails on the desk as she appeared to be waiting for someone to answer.

Finally, she spoke. "Please tell Mammon that Satan isn't in. He's been called away on important business."

Important business? You mean like hitting covens and killing hundreds of witches? I looked at Connor. He nodded once and clicked the door shut as I dropped the cloak. She gasped as anyone would then narrowed her eyes at my mate. She tilted her head, pulling her eyebrows together.

"Connor Baghest? Is Lucifer here?"

"No," he growled.

The woman hung up the phone, taking a step back to put more distance between them. "Wh-What's going on?"

"Where is Satan?" Connor demanded.

"He's been called away."

"To where?" he barked and she straight up jumped.

"What's his game?" I asked and she finally turned to look at me, startling as if she'd just now noticed my presence.

She cocked her head giving major haughty vibes, hand propped on her hip. "What are you?" she asked.

Really? She had a very pissed-off, menacing Connor baring teeth at her, looking a minute from going full-on death hound on her ass and that was what she chose to ask?

"You don't talk to her. You address me. Where is Satan? You've got two seconds." Connor's eyes started to glow red and *oh, man*—shit was definitely about to hit the fan.

Her face went completely ashen, zombie gray. "He got called away," she replied. "Things have been happening—things he hasn't approved." She finished fast. Well, this was a new development.

"What things?" Connor roared. "Where is he?"

The woman threw up her hand as if that would stop my mate from ripping her throat out. "He's taking a meeting… at a place called Monnie's. I don't know it. I can try to find out where it's located."

"No need." He turned to me. "Simone." I used my Lilium magic to make sure she couldn't move or speak for at least an hour. We didn't need her warning Satan. Then I took Connor's hand, cloaked us again, and manifested us the hell out of there.

We landed by the big, green dumpster behind Monnie's Bar.

"I don't understand," I whispered to Connor. "I thought Luc was with us."

"There's no way he's involved."

"But this is *his* territory."

"I'm aware of that."

"*Shit*—we left Shafira and Karro with him."

"They'll be fine. He's not involved."

"Connor, you know I think the world of him, but this is a bit too sus. Who'd dare hold a meeting in Lucifer Morningstar's quadrant without his approval?"

"I don't know, but I'm about to find out." Connor started stripping off his clothes. I bent to pick them up as he dropped into his hound form. The giant dog still took my breath away. I draped a cloak around us and we snuck into Monnie's through the back door. We entered the kitchen area, which appeared cleaner than I'd expected it to be. Somehow, given it's role as *the* hangout for all the bad men in Luc's territory, I'd expected dirty dishes piled up in the sink with food rotting on the plates and flies buzzing around. But no, it looked like a clean, up-to-date bar kitchen. Who knew?

*Focus, Simone.* We walked through the kitchen to emerge behind the bar. A hallway sat across from the bar. Signs pointed out the restrooms. Instinctively, I felt like that was where we needed to be. With Connor at my side, we headed in that direction. The door at the end of the short hallway opened up and ooh—that man gave me the willies. That man being Satan himself, looking every bit as menacing as the last time I'd seen him. The scar that ran along his face appeared thicker, deeper now. As if all his stress manifested through that ugly feature.

"See that it doesn't," Satan said to someone and clearly, we'd missed a large portion of the conversation. The door opened wider and Connor snarled and barked, gnashing his teeth. Both Satan and the other man turned to see where the sound was coming from.

Connor charged and it took everything to keep up with him. The man was fast in his hound form. In the melee, I didn't notice Satan slip away, but he did because when we reached the office, Satan was gone.

Our timing—*perfect.* I dropped the cloak and Connor changed back to a man. "*Damien,*" he snapped and he lunged, capturing the guy I assumed to be Damian as he tried to escape.

When would these guys learn? Connor was not a man you pissed off or played with—well, unless your name was Simone Lamia. How I enjoyed the perks of being me.

A third man, the other man still left in the room, whom I assumed to be the owner of Monnie's, sat behind a desk. His eyes darted back and forth between us. I used my magic to ensure neither bad dude could leave, before handing Connor back his clothes.

"What in all of Hades were you doing meeting with Satan?" my mate asked as he dressed, and I really thought it behooved the man to answer. Unfortunately for this Damien, he thought with his bravado rather than his head.

"The world is changing," he replied, sneering in a way that was just asking to get his head torn from his nasty demon body, and Damien reminded me of a reptile when he spoke. Like the equivalent of a human gecko. I disliked the man on sight.

"Not today," I said and the man glared at me.

"You think you know—you've got no clue, girlie. Either of you. No amount of bitches—*oops!* I mean, *witches* are gonna keep us from turning the Earth into a literal devil's playground. Watch your back, girlie. They're *all* coming for you."

Connor moved so quickly at his threat, I didn't have time to react. He used his bare hands to rip the demon in two. Blood and guts spurted and spilled all over us and the desk before it all disintegrated into ash. I didn't even have the chance to vomit, it went that fast. So I conjured up a breeze to brush it away.

Then Connor turned to the man still stuck to his seat. The man's eyes went huge. "I have nothing to do with this." The man sniveled. "When the leader of Hell calls a meeting, you don't argue."

"He's *not* the leader," Connor snarled. And I got it but this wasn't helping.

"Why did they call the meeting here?" I asked.

He turned his head to me. "Because of Lucifer. It's his quadrant."

My stomach dropped and I felt all kinds of nauseous. "We have to get to Shafira and Karro," I said.

"We need the amulet," Connor returned.

He was right. I could drop Luc with my Taser fingers, but to end this, we needed to unite Lilith's blade.

"You'll forget all about this meeting the moment we leave," I said to the man, manifesting that into reality. He neither nodded nor shook his head—more he sat in his chair staring at us like he'd missed our entire exchange. I grabbed on to Connor and popped us out of Monnie's.

We touched down in the field next to Lily Joy's cottage, the place I'd last seen my dear cousin. The house looked empty. I ran for the front door, using magic to push it open. "Lily Joy," I shouted. "Lily Joy, it's Simone and Connor. We're back."

Nothing. No one. Abandoned.

"Where could she have gone?" My heart hurt. "I feel like we take one step forward and fifty-seven steps back."

"She's okay. I know she is. Lily Joy is a powerful Lilium. But we don't know where she is or what we'd be landing in if you manifested us to her. We want her unhurt, but the world *needs* you alive, babe. We can't risk it."

"Don't be logical with me, Baghest. I'm not in the mood." I made the sorry attempt to lighten the atmosphere. It didn't work.

"Let's go upstairs and get your backpack."

"What if it's not here?"

"I highly doubt demons searched the place after we left. Their mission was to kill us. We got away. They were scrambling."

That gave a little comfort, given how things kept going from bad to worse and I had no idea what came after worse. I didn't want to know. What I wanted and what I got always seemed to fall at the far ends of the spectrum from each other. Pulling up my big-girl panties, I marched upstairs to the bedroom Connor and I had shared while staying here.

I immediately saw my backpack squished between the bed and the bedside table, where I'd stuffed it before all literal hell had broken loose and I sighed all the sighs. Every single one. The universe allowed us to take a big step forward. *Thank you, universe!*

Connor made it into the room right behind me, but I'd already bent down to retrieve the pack. I could be quick too, when I needed to be. With Connor next to me, I crawled onto the bed, leaning back against the pillow to open the pack, reaching inside to find the amulet. I pulled the ruby-red gem out, holding it protectively in my hand—not that I thought Connor would try to take it, we just had no idea when some janky demon might appear out of the floorboards and snatch it after catching us unawares.

At this point, we couldn't discount any scenario, no matter how ridiculous it sounded.

"It's hard to imagine that little thing will kill demons as powerful as the leaders of Hell."

"Hades might be a nicer place to work, then," I replied.

He shrugged. "I guess depending on who you work for. I know there's a high rate of job satisfaction in Asmodeus's quadrant—and I've always enjoyed working for Luc."

We both fell silent. Luc. How could he have been involved? It didn't make sense. The man had far too much pride in the Hell he'd built.

"What do we do now?" I asked.

"He's not involved. He's not. He's being set up. You know Luc has the most territory. It's a perk of creating the realm for yourself."

"You have to be prepared if he is involved—"

"He's *not*," Connor snapped.

I wrapped an arm around his waist, leaning my head on his bicep. "I have to get ahold of Sim. We need to meet. We need to join the hilt of Lilith's dagger and the amulet to activate it. Then we need to end this."

The grimoire poked painfully into the skin of my back in this seated position. I reached behind me to pull it from the waistband of my jeans, dropping it on my lap.

"So much trouble for this thing," I said, casually flipping it open. And it appeared Lilith answered me in the form of an entry not there before. "'Once the witches be slain, the world shall crumble in pain.'"

"I think your grandmother heard you."

"I'm sure she did." Then I looked to the ceiling as if she hovered above me—ridiculous, I know. "I didn't say I was quitting. I just said it's a lot of trouble for a little book."

More words appeared on the page. My grandmother, it seemed, had a flair for the dramatic. "'With your family you will overcome, without them, evil will overrun,'" I read to Connor. Then I looked up to the ceiling again. "I got it the first time. Your little rhymes don't make me like it any better."

"Simone," Connor replied in his gentle voice. Yes, his *gentle* voice.

"What? I don't like being pressured. I know I have the entire fate of the world in my hands. She could've killed Adam years ago and been done with the man. Instead, she drops this on me and I'm supposed to be happy about it? I'm tired, Connor. I'm tired and people die when I make mistakes. I feel old—like I've aged five hundred years in the last week." I slapped the book shut, swiping it from my lap to land on the bed next to me.

"We're not going anywhere right now. You need to rest."

"Connor, that's not—"

"I know what you meant. But you still need to rest and this way, you can try to contact Sim."

My shoulders slumped. "Okay."

"Babe?"

"Yeah?"

"I'm here. You can't carry it all—give some to me. My shoulders are strong. Let me do some heavy lifting for you."

Stupid, hot tears leaked from my eyes. "You are so getting

laid when this is done. Spectacularly. Spectacularly laid, Connor Baghest."

He leaned in to kiss me, snatching the grimoire from the bed as his lips pressed to mine. He dropped the book into the backpack without missing a beat. After pulling back, he helped me lie back onto the bed. Connor still kept one arm looped through the backpack straps as he held me.

With his warmth to my back and his arms protecting me, I let myself succumb to the sleep weighing my eyes closed. I started to dream of Connor and me back home packing to go on a beach vacation. I had no idea if Luc would allow Connor to take a vacation, but we deserved one and I could be pretty convincing when I needed to be. But as we packed the last bag into my Jeep, I felt myself lifting up from the ground and I realized that the astral projection just started separating me from my body without me even trying.

The door appeared, floating in front of me. It opened the moment I approached and I glided through. Wherever they were, it appeared to be night. The entire room cloaked in blackness.

"Sim?" I whispered, which yes, I know—ridiculous. Madigan wouldn't hear me if I spoke in regular tones. I couldn't help it, though. Whispering seemed somehow more respectful. Whatever. Moving on.

His eyes opened and he sighed, pushing up from his body to join me hovering over the bed. "Hey, sis. Are you okay?"

"I'm ready for this to be over."

"Before you showed, I was dreaming about Madi and me packing for a beach vacation. How great would that be?"

I startled. "Packing for a beach vacation?"

"Yeah…" He drew the word out. "You don't like the beach?"

"I—yeah, I love the beach—it's just, I was having the same dream. Packing up my car for Connor and me to take a beach vacation."

"That's odd. We're fraternal, so we can't really chalk it up to being a twin thing."

"No. Maybe it's a reward for a job well done?"

"I'm down with that."

"Where are you now?"

"Back in Michigan. Northern part of the mitten. I grew up about three hours south of here. I had a foster dad who wanted all the kids to learn how to hunt. He'd bring us here. Seemed safe."

"You grew up in Michigan, too?"

"*Too*? You mean Lilith placed us that close to each other and we never met. Damn. I can't believe my sister was so close yet we both had to grow up alone." He shook his head. I got that.

Damn was right. Okay, I'd have to unpack all that later—like once the world was safe. Right now, work.

"Listen, I've got the amulet and the grimoire. There's so much going on, but here's the condensed version. Someone, probably the demon responsible for this whole thing—we think it's Satan—brought Cain, Adam's son, forward in time. Why? I don't know yet. But new pages have been appearing in the grimoire and we need to meet up. I need you to head for the witches' archives so we can join the dagger and try to end this."

"That's the condensed version?"

"I know. The safest place for us to meet is the Knap of Howar. That's where the archives are located."

"Knap of Howar? Sounds old."

"And crumbling. There's a little entry connecting two larger crumbling rooms. It's hidden from people walking up because of how it's situated. I need you to say: *Cuir isteach mar chara*. Can you remember that?"

"*Cuir isteach mar chara*? Yeah, I can remember that. A keen memory is one of my abilities. What does it mean?"

"Basically, 'open up and let me in.' I don't know the exact translation. But a stairwell will open up out of nowhere and that will take you down to the archives. Madigan needs to be holding you, your hand, or shirt. The door will close behind you. The room will give you whatever you need if you're hungry or tired. But don't let anyone hear the password."

"What about Lily Joy?"

"I'm trying to locate her and I hope to Lilith that she's safe, but you and Madigan are part of this in a way that not even Lily Joy is. So please, be careful and get to the Knap of Howar."

"I'll get us there."

"Can you do two days? I don't think we can wait much longer." I manifested him money, exactly as I had the first time we'd met. "There's a private side to MBS Airport in Saginaw."

"I know MBS."

If anything, that made life a little bit easier. "Get to hangar nineteen. Inside, there'll be a plane and a pilot waiting to fly you to Scotland."

"How do you know there's a hangar nineteen?"

"I don't. But there is now. I've thought about trying to manifest you and Madigan here, but I've never done it remotely before and my powers—I don't know if I'm strong enough. I scramble a hangar, oh well. I scramble you and Madigan..." Not a thought worth thinking.

"I have to get home first. I need the hilt."

"And the book. Please don't forget the book."

"I won't."

"Repeat the directions for me, then."

"Hangar nineteen. MBS. Private plane. Scotland. Knap of Howar. *Cuir isteach mar chara.*"

"Right. Okay, be safe, brother. I'll see you in two days."

"Two days," he replied as I started to drift back through the door.

The door clicked shut and then disappeared. I drifted down into my body, very aware of my surroundings. Connor watched me with concern. "You find Sim?" he asked.

"I did. We're meeting at the witches' archives in two days." I sighed. "I should manifest myself to them and bring them here instead of making them get there by themselves."

"Simone, babe, he's got power and you have to let him do his part. You can't keep taking everything onto yourself. He'll get them there. Let him get them there."

"But I know I can get it done."

"Not if you make yourself sick and right now, we don't have a witch to heal you."

Why in times like this did he have to make sense? "I manifested him money to help."

"I trust my sister. I trust your brother. You're not alone."

"Connor?"

"Yeah, babe?"

"I have to find Lily Joy. I'm going back under. You have to be prepared to bring me back if necessary."

His whole body went rigid. "You think she's in trouble?"

"I don't know. But I have to find her. I have to help her. You heard Lilith. The family has to be in on saving the world. She's family."

"Do what you have to do. I'm awake."

I leaned in to press a kiss to his furrowed lips. "We're going to the beach when this is done. You, me, Sim, and Madigan. A long beach vacation. I will end Luc if he tries to stop you."

Connor rolled on top of me to press a longer, lingering kiss back. Then with my eyes still closed, I started concentrating on finding Lily Joy. It took me manifesting the astral projection this time rather than it happening naturally. I floated through the door, but instead of finding my cousin, my spirit zipped through the sky at breakneck speed, finally plunging me down into the water of probably the Pacific Ocean. Instinctively, I gulped a large breath before my head went under, which was dumb because I didn't need to breathe. My body lay in a comfy bed back in England next to Connor. Still, I held my breath until my chest burned and I let it out. The bubbles from my exiting air must have hit a sensor because a door opened. It opened without any water rushing inside. A forcefield?

My spirit passed through and the door slid shut again. I continued down into Hades. This had to be Leviathan's quadrant. Lily Joy slept on the ground leaning against the largest tank I'd ever seen in my life, containing a giant squid that would've made Captain Nemo pee his pants. As I watched this monster sleep, I thought maybe *Twenty Thousand Leagues Under the Sea* might've been more of a biography than a fantasy novel.

As I floated down toward Lily Joy, the squid's eye popped open and it made this horrendous sound. Who knew squids even made sounds? It began to glow a bright red and the energy in the room turned hostile.

Lily Joy's eyes popped open, and she gasped. "Simone?" she asked, rubbing at her eyes.

"Are you hurt? Are you trapped? What can I do?"

"You're floating," she said.

"My body is with Connor. How are you?"

"I'm fine. Leviathan offered me sanctuary."

"Leviathan? He's… He's…"

"A really nice guy. Did you know it's all an act? He's an introvert who prefers to spend his time with his pets. Apparently, he's surly to everyone else to keep them away and keep them from trying to take his territory."

I didn't know how to feel about this. Both Luc and Connor had said I didn't want to deal with Lev. "Are you sure we're talking about the same Leviathan?"

She nodded. "He's willing to help us. His pets are at our disposal should we need them. He just doesn't like confrontation himself. He wishes he was a go-getter like Luc, always willing to help to make himself look better with the ladies—Lev's words, not mine."

"You're on a nickname basis with one of the kings of the underworld?"

"Two if you count Luc. But I can tell you that Lev hates the idea of Hell taking over. He says they have a good thing now and wants no part of it."

So we had Leviathan on our side? This war just kept getting weirder and weirder.

"I need you to get to the Orkney Islands. Knap of Howar. It's important. Can Lev help you get to the Orkney Islands?"

"It's islands. I'm sure he can."

"Great." That was a load off. "Sim and Madigan are meeting us in two days. If I had my body, I'd manifest you there right now, but given my current state, I don't think it's possible."

"No biggie. I'll be there as soon as I can—oh, don't tell anyone else about Lev. It would upset him. He likes his privacy."

"My lips are sealed." I could've cried from relief.

"Do you know what happened to Daniel?"

"Daniel would be?"

"The hellhound who helped me escape. We got separated after he helped me find a place to rest. He showed up the day the demons attacked. He was very intense and spoke very little—he generally acted like every breath I took upset him, but he helped me, so I want him to be okay."

"No. Sorry. I have no idea, but I'll ask Connor to keep his ear to the ground. I have to go now. I'm starting to wake up."

"See you soon, then." She smiled up at me as I bent my energy in to hug her. I fizzled in and out a bit when we touched. Ask me if I cared. Hugging Lily Joy meant everything in this moment. Sooner than I wanted, I let her go, zipping back to Connor the exact way I'd gotten here, but in reverse.

My spirit reentered my body and my eyes popped open. Connor had been shaking me. "What's wrong?" I asked.

"Another coven was hit, but Victoria had already gotten the witches out."

"How do you know?"

"You got a text from Agatha."

"Agatha? Where is she?"

"I don't know."

"She's my friend. She helped us. We have to make sure she's okay."

"Not arguing with you, babe," he replied, handing me my phone. "Do what you've got to do."

We'd come a long way from him trying to control every move I made. Better for him.

I popped off a text to Agatha.

And I waited...

It felt like forever before Agatha texted back. Agonizing minutes passed where I wondered if my friend was safe or not. At least Victoria had gotten the witches out before they'd hit the latest coven.

ME: Where are you?

HER: …

HER: …

HER: Been hiding. Large demon presence. It's bad, Simone. Been in hiding.

ME: Can you get to MBS?

HER: Don't know… People going crazy… It's like *The Purge* out there.

My mouth literally dropped open. "Connor, are you reading this?"

"Fuck! We need to stick to the plan, get to the archives."

I text back to Agatha: Going to try something I haven't before. Bringing you to me.

"Won't that drain you?" Connor asked.

"Do I have a choice? Agatha can help me. Then I can get us up to the Orkneys."

ME: Where are you, exactly?

HER: Farmstead outside of Reese.

ME: Get ready.

I closed my eyes to concentrate without distraction on Agatha at her farmstead outside Reese. I'd manifested us to different locations a hundred times by now, but this would be the first time I manifested someone to me. It took different energy. It took more energy to make sure I got the right person, no hangers-on. Just Agatha. And yes, I'd been too scared to try this exact thing on Sim and Madigan, but if this worked, then that would open so much up for us. *Please, Universe, let this work.*

Taking two long breaths in and out to clear my head, I focused on bringing my friend to me. Sweat dripped down my brow. Connor cleared his throat, momentarily breaking my concentration. I had no choice but to shake it off, hoping that I brought all of Agatha to me.

*"Holy…"* I heard Connor mumble and I opened my eyes to see a very intact Agatha standing in front of us.

"You did it," she said, and yeah, you could call *astonished* an understatement.

I smiled so big and stupid, letting out the longest sigh of relief, and laughing from getting to release all that pent-up tension. Then I hugged my friend.

"You're here," I said into her ear.

"I must admit, I was worried about getting here in one piece. I should've never doubted you. Your abilities are beyond anything I've ever seen."

"There's so much to fill you in on, but we have to get to the witches' archives. It's the safest place for us right now."

She blinked. "Excuse me? The witches' archives? You want to bring me there?"

I nodded. "It's so cool. It'll totally blow your mind."

"Simone's powers lie more with magic and manifestation than healing arts. Bringing you here took a lot out of her,"

Connor said and I realized I'd sagged against him, letting his body weight prop me up. "Can you brew her something? Lily Joy's cupboards are full. You'll find what you need here."

"'Lily Joy'?" Agatha asked.

"My cousin. I'll explain everything. You'll meet her soon."

Connor slid my backpack off his arm, slipping it up my arms. Then he scooped me up to carry me downstairs to the living room, where he set me on the sofa. He walked Agatha into the kitchen to show her the pantry and Lily Joy's stash of every herb imaginable.

Seeing as she and Connor, who acted as her assistant, stayed in the kitchen, I hefted myself up, using all the spares to walk my butt into the kitchen too, plopping down in the closest chair surrounding the table. My body felt so heavy—like the Earth's gravitational pull quadrupled around me alone.

"Babe, you're too weak," Connor scolded.

"I don't like being left out. You know this."

"She really doesn't," he replied to Agatha, who laughed at me.

"Do you have strength to talk? Can you fill me in?" she asked.

"Girl... do I have the tea to spill."

Agatha stopped abruptly in the midst of scooping a measured tablespoon of some herb, holding it hovering above the jar. "You're a Lilium, aren't you?"

"She's not just any Lilium," Connor answered for me.

"What does that mean?"

"It means I'm out of time. Lilith is my grandmother—like my mother's mother, not distant in any way."

The tablespoon clanked against the counter, herbs scattering across the countertop. She collected herself quickly, cleaning up the mess and measuring out another spoonful. "It has to be exact measurements and we can't risk something else, a particle from the countertop, getting in the brew."

Made sense to me. From what I'd heard, changing an herb ratio even that minusculely could alter the desired result. I didn't need to end up as a mermaid because Lily Joy had a rogue fish scale on her counter or something. And that was in no way demeaning Lily Joy's housekeeping skills. I saw no fish scales, for the record.

"I've been finding my cousins—other Lilium—and witches. When Lilith left Adam, she took the magic of the garden with her. Outside the garden, small pockets of magic began to form. I don't know if Lilith inadvertently did this being outside the garden, or if the universe gifted others because of Lilith's caring, but I do know that Lilium are directly related to Lilith, whereas witches come from those who'd been granted less powerful magic. But it all stems from Lilith leaving the garden."

"What does that have to do with covens being attacked?" she asked.

"I don't know yet. I know that somehow, Adam sent his son Cain through time. I've had a few run-ins with him. He's *unpleasant*. We think Satan might be behind it, but we're not sure why."

She threw her hand to her chest. "Satan? As in *Satan* Satan?"

"Unfortunately," Connor added.

Agatha appeared to collect herself and began brewing my healing tea. "It makes no sense. Why kill witches?" She handed me off a large mug of steaming liquid. I drank the herby concoction sweetened with honey. And this was why witches rarely had to see the doctor. I felt the healing begin immediately. I could see Big Pharma going after wi—hey, did Satan invest in Big Pharma? Could that be why? He certainly could control a lot of people that way. But still, bringing Cain forward didn't fit into that equation.

"Okay, I'm feeling better. We need to get to the archives." I held my hands out to Connor and Agatha. I must've been getting stronger because it took much less time for me to recover this time. Then I tried to stand, swaying infinitesimally, but still enough for quick-eyes Connor to see me struggle.

"Simone needs another cup," he ordered Agatha. "Don't argue," he said to me.

I put my hands up. "Not arguing."

Agatha quickly brewed me another large mug and I chugged it down without coming up for breath. I for sure knew I could get us there now. And with a witch by my side, it didn't matter how much energy drained from my body, she could fix me up with one of her teas. Agatha was exactly what I'd been missing since parting ways with Shafira.

Right after closing my eyes, I pushed the thought of the three of us at the Knapp of Howar and as I opened them again, the crumbling stones greeted me. I felt rather proud of myself for accomplishing this every time, without fail, and turned my eyes to Connor. He flashed me a smoldering smile that screamed pride and... *other* things. If only.

When I turned to Agatha to ask if she was ready to go in, nothing short of awe shone on every bit of her face. I'd forgotten that she'd never been here before. "Ready?" I asked. Slowly, she nodded, her eyes roaming over every pebble, and reached her hand out to touch the remains of the Neolithic structure.

I spoke the words to open the archives and gestured for her to enter first. Smiling, she sighed and tentatively stepped inside the stairwell. Connor went next and then I ended the parade, making sure to lock the door behind me.

The archives came to life when we reached the bottom. Agatha gasped as the purple flames ignited in the hearth, crackling softly. Pots and kettles appeared along with plates and cups, as well as flatware. She ran her finger reverently along the table closest to her. I recognized that feeling of awe, the same one I'd had the first time Connor and I found ourselves here.

A comfortable, cushioned chair pulled out by itself for Agatha to sit in. She looked at me, I nodded once to tell her it was okay, and she sat. "What now?" she asked.

"It looks like the archives are preparing to feed us. So we'll eat and wait."

"I have to say, knowing about the archives and being here are on opposite ends of the believability spectrum. I'll need a minute to adjust."

"I get it. But you're a powerful witch. The archives will show you things that it won't show the less capable magic holders. So if there are things you think will help, just ask the room. It will provide what you need."

Slowly, she shook her head, then said, "I need information on Cain, Adam's son." Three different ancient texts pushed forward from the back shelves. Agatha walked over, plucking up the tomes, cradling them reverently in her arms as she walked back to the cushioned chair. "I'm going to start reading. I think we need to know about Cain. There's a reason Satan brought him here."

"You okay?" Connor asked.

"I hate waiting."

He snickered. "Take the reprieve. You'll be dreaming about it soon enough."

Too true. "Sit with me?" I asked. It hardly took any convincing. A cushy, two-person loveseat appeared against the wall opposite the hearth and we walked over, Connor holding my hand. He dropped on the loveseat first, pulling me down to rest half on him.

"I feel like I should be doing something, but I'm not sure what that is right now."

"Simone, baby—swear to Hades," Connor said in his irritated, *'Simone is being a pain in my ass again'* way that I've grown to love. "you have to take the downtime when it comes your way. Company'll start showing soon enough."

"I feel like I need to be active," I replied on a yawn and felt my eyes droop. Now? I couldn't help feel like Lilith had something to do with this. What did she have in store for me now? Because I didn't sleep. I floated above my body, watching as

Connor bent in to kiss the top of my head. The door appeared again, opening, allowing me to move through it. On the other side, I found Luc, Shafira, and Karro. A beautiful bronze-skinned man in a linen suit sat at a table—more like lounged, half-slumped with his arm over the back of the chair. As I took him in, I noticed his stunningly deep-brown eyes and hair so brown, it could almost pass as black, feathered back from his face. New guy had that cocky-hot vibe going on. That popular jock guy who knew all the girls were hot for him—yeah, that. In truth, it made him less attractive. But the more I took him in, I realized he wasn't a man. He was a demon. A powerful one. I felt his power radiating off him in waves—and I found it interesting that Luc stood between him and Shafira.

Karro practically drooled. Who was this guy?

"So you're with us?" Luc asked. With *us*? Which us? The 'take over the world' us or the 'save the world' us? What were you trying to pull? If you picked the first option and had the mind to bring my friends down with you, Lilith as my witness, I'd cut off your balls.

"Listen, I don't know what's going on out there, but I'm a lover, not a fighter. When people die or are forced into servitude, I can't partake in my favorite pastime. You know me, Luc. I'm a total grump when I don't get my fill."

"I'll help you get your fill," Karro offered and the man turned a twinkling smile at my cousin. He eyed him and blew a kiss. I swore Karro started drifting over to the man until Shafira quickly reached out to grab his wrist, yanking him back by her.

"Aren't you in love?" she asked him.

"Am now," he replied dreamily.

The gorgeous man chuckled. "Love." He sighed as if bored. "The bane of my existence."

"I'm not in love," Shafira said, but Luc held tight.

"Can you tone it down?" Luc asked the man and I watched the glow around him dim significantly. It hit me. A demon with his power. Love the bane of his existence. Asmodeus. It had to be. *Oh, wow.* Asmodeus. That man was everything I'd ever heard about him. From the top of his head, down down to the bottom of those cool, suede leather loafers he wore without socks, he oozed sexuality.

Given how I watched him play with my friends' emotions without a second thought, I couldn't have been happier to turn my nose up at his supreme hotness. The demon of Lust didn't hold a candle to my hellhound.

"I'll talk to Bel," Asmodeus said. "You know he's not a part of this. We'll hunt down Mon. There's no way this crap would be good for business. He can't be involved. I'll contact you as soon as I know anything."

"Thanks, man." Luc held his hand out. Asmodeus gripped it, pulling Luc in close, giving him a hug and back pat.

"You know, I've been wanting to try you out forever. If you want to thank me..." He let his words trail off. I bit back my laughter.

"Sorry, man," said Luc. "I keep clear of workplace entanglements."

That was a diplomatic answer.

Asmodeus shrugged. "If you ever change your mind, we can bring in your chick there." He gestured with his chin to Shafira. Her cheeks pinked. I'd like to note, Luc didn't deny *anything.* Interesting. "You know I'm down for anything."

Luc shot him a regal, angelic glare, the one that committed him to nothing. "Just let me know about Bel and Mon."

Asmodeus nodded, blew a kiss to the room, and blinked out.

"I can't believe they've been using your quadrant to hold these meetings," Karro said.

Luc's normal smile dropped into a frown. "I've been so busy helping Simone and Connor that I had no idea." Anger rolled off the man in waves.

"It's not their fault," Shafira countered, defending us.

"Of course not. Connor's my boy and Simone is cool. She's a friend and a powerful ally. I'm glad to have her on the team. I've worked hard to create a space where humans can feel safe to be themselves and give them knowledge of how the world works. The last thing I need is a demon on a power trip trying to hack away at my baby."

"'Baby'?" Karro asked.

"The world," Luc replied. "The world—this world—full of math and science, an inquisitive zest for learning, is what got me kicked out of heaven. I stand by the choices I've made and won't let anyone ruin it."

Luc wouldn't let anyone ruin it. I wanted to kiss him but thought better of it. For one, a kiss without him knowing I was here might give the man a heart attack. Secondly, Connor would blow a gasket if he found out and we all knew that Luc would *absolutely* kiss and tell.

So checking that impulse, I manifested them to see me. Shafira gasped. Karro shouted, "What the fuck?!"

Luc simply smiled at me. "I thought I felt a presence here. Did you hear what you needed to hear?"

"Hey—the evidence against you was pretty damning. You can't blame me for not announcing my appearance here today. But it's good to know we still have you."

Luc waggled his eyebrows. "Oh, Simone… you can have me."

"Shut it," I warned and he laughed at me. "I need these two now."

"Anything I can help with?"

"I have to bring them to the witches' archives. But the archives won't let you in."

"If you've got them, then I have to bust some heads in my quadrant. We'll meet up when I'm done."

Then he popped out. Gone.

"I've never manifested people while in this spirit form before, but I've done money, so I'm fairly confident I can get you there safely." Lies—all lies. I had no idea if I could get them to the archives safely.

Karro blanched. "Was it a lot of money?"

"Not necessarily." I felt so stupid admitting that. But if I could manifest them to the archives now, then I could bring Sim and Madigan there, too, if necessary. *And this boys and girls, is how I use my cousin and my friend as guinea pigs to make sure I don't kill my brother and sister-in-law.* Horrible person—party of one, your table's ready. But with Luc gone, what choice did I have?

"I trust you, Simone," Shafira said. "I'm ready to join you."

"Karro?" I asked and he nodded.

"Grandma trusts you—I do too."

"Grab on to Shafira." Closing my eyes, I shot off a quick prayer to my grandmother. *Lilith, help me make this happen.* The pair held hands as I began chanting, "Bring Karro and Shafira to the witches archives." Over and over, I kept the chant going until the floating door opened up sucking me back through.

My consciousness hit my body right as Agatha said, "Someone's here." She placed her book on the table to jog up the steps, walking back down moments later with Shafira and my cousin in tow. "They said you brought them here?"

*Thank you, Lilith!*

"I did." I started to get up, but both Karro and Shafira walked over to hug me, so I kept my butt planted next to Connor, who acted as the most comfortable body pillow ever invented. I reached up to hug them back.

"Connor, good to see you," Shafira said.

"*Very good,*" Karro said.

It appeared my mate resolved himself to the fact that when you married, you got more than a wife, you got her family too because he simply shook his head. For my part, I found myself able to check the *rip-his-head-off-for-flirting-with-my-mate* impulses, so wins all around.

"Luc left to go crack heads," I told him, taking in his strong profile and feeling grateful that I was surrounded by or made contact with the people I cared about most. "It looks like someone informed him of what we saw at Monnie's."

"Asmodeus showed. He's pissed, too," Karro put in. "He said this crap is bad for business."

"Asmodeus is with us?" Connor asked. "Brilliant. He's a good ally to have."

"He's taking meetings with Bel and Mon," Shafira said. "Though he didn't elaborate, I feel as if he meant Belphegor and Mammon." And we had Leviathan.

"We're already pretty sure Belphegor is on our side," I put in. "Remember Australia?"

"Right. But I think it'll be good to get confirmation."

She wasn't wrong. Four of the seven leaders of Hell on our side were far from bad odds. If they gave confirmation, we could work on an alternate plan where demons got involved. Lilium, witches, and demons. Earth might not fall, after all.

From that point on, A never-ending stream of witches and new Lilium started to show. Things got a bit crazy for a while. When Lily Joy arrived I felt a huge sense of relief. After surviving losing someone I cared about once already, I couldn't go through that again.

The door to the archives opened, tearing me from my somber thoughts while allowing more witches to enter. The room didn't look big enough to accommodate us all but somehow did. It expanded as we needed it to. Victoria Rivers understood the assignment and had done her job. Witches kept showing. We needed all of them we could get.

When I sensed the next new Lilium arrive, I started feeling even more confident about this war. Witches held power, but Lilium held *power*.

"Hello?" the voice called out in a distinctly Southern accent as they descended the stairs.

I smiled so big at the bottom waiting to greet her. "Hi. I'm Simone. Welcome to the witches' archives." I slowly waved my hand out like a gameshow model presenting a new car.

A woman appeared from the staircase. Big, bleach-blonde hair pulled back in a ponytail, but she had almost a pompadour poof in front. I immediately thought: Texas. Then I dropped my eyes to her Cowboys T-shirt, confirming my suspicions.

"Simone? Simone Lamia?" she asked.

"The one and only," I replied, standing a little taller. Proud of what we'd been able to accomplish so far. Yes, we still had a monumental challenge ahead of us so I'd be a fool to get too confident, but we deserved to take a moment to pat ourselves on the back for getting this far.

"A Victoria Rivers contacted me. She said I had family—and I ain't never had family, but she sounded serious. Next thing I know, I'm on a plane to Scotland. Victoria Rivers said you're my family. What's going on? Do you know how dangerous it is out there? Mine was the last flight out. They shut down the whole airport for security reasons. People are going crazy."

Yet another ancestor of Lilith who'd grown up alone. Why? Why didn't we deserve to have the love of a family in our formative years? What happened to make this our reality? Grandma and I needed to talk. It seemed she'd left out some information.

"What's your name?" I asked.

"Alexis Smith."

"It's good to meet you, Alexis. Do you know what you are?"

Her head jerked. "What I am? Not you, too. I didn't fly across—"

"So you've heard that a time or ten. I wasn't insulting you. I was asking a legitimate question."

"Do you know… you know, what I am?"

Smiling, I nodded. "You're a Lilium. Like me. Like Lily Joy." I pointed to Lily Joy conversing with one of the witches. "Like Karro." I pointed him out, along with the two others he talked with. More were on the way. I felt it. I felt our connection.

"Lilium?" she asked. "What exactly is a Lilium?"

"A direct descendent of Lilith," I replied. Alexis's head jerked again. I loved this part. "Go join Karro. He volunteered to fill in all our new cousins who arrived. The two he's talking to showed up maybe ten and thirty minutes ago, respectively."

She let a tentative smile replace her shocked expression and slowly made her way over to Karro, who threw his arms out with a welcoming, "Girlie… let Uncle Karro take care of you." He enveloped her in a hug. She melted against him and I felt okay to get back to my business.

Connor sidled up behind me, wrapping his arms around my waist as he rested his chin on my shoulder. "How're you doing?" he asked.

I sighed. "I'm okay. Relieved Luc is working with us and not against us."

"One of us said that would never happen. Can you remember who that was?"

"You have to admit it looked bad for a while."

"So what's next?"

"I like that subtle change of topic. Smooth, Baghest."

He pressed a kiss to my neck. "I have my moments."

"I'm waiting for more witches and Lilium to show and then I'll address the room. Since I'm winging this, I have no idea if it'll work or not."

"Winging it, my ass. I hear the thoughts spinning in your head. You have a plan."

"A tentative one, I guess. I studied business and finance at community college, not battle strategies and the art of war."

"Babe, Lilith put you in charge for a reason. I like Sim, but he's following your orders like the rest of us. Lilith put *you* in charge."

"What if she made a mistake?"

"Don't start second-guessing yourself now. My Simone is a strong, badass woman who knows she's the shit and will kick any ass that gets in her way. Including mine."

I chuckled. "I have other plans for your ass."

"When we're done with this, I'm keeping you naked for at least a week. I don't care if your grandmother shows. She'll get an eyeful because I won't stop for anything."

"It's a date." I meant it. I wanted that more than he knew. Me and Connor bumping uglies like couples should on their honeymoon. We'd earned a honeymoon. And when we came back, we'd throw the biggest reception anyone had ever seen. For me and Connor, for Sim and Madigan, and for anyone else who had a reason to celebrate. A smile crept over my face as I closed my eyes, picturing our life post-possible apocalypse—*no*. It was our job, it was *my* job to make sure this never reached apocalyptic proportions.

The hearth glowed purple from the flames as it expanded to allow more pots to appear and bubble over the fire. More loaves of bread magically widened the bread oven. Ramakins of butter materialized onto the tabletops along with condiments. The archives knew where our witches visited from. I saw diced raw onions, cilantro, fresh lime, and a few salsas on the table by the witches from Mexico. Then over by Shafira, who'd tracked down her sister and nieces—they'd be staying at one of Luc's safehouses during the fight—the table produced sumac, dried limes, and a sauce that looked like a thick, spiced yogurt sauce, among other things.

I let the room of mostly women eat and settle in a bit before dropping the heavy on them. The door at the top of the stairs cracked against the wall. That unmistakable sound reverberated down to us, catching all our attention. Then throngs of witches and Lilium flooded into the archives, which just kept expanding to hold them. The door clicked shut again and a disheveled, very injured Victoria Rivers stumbled into view. Connor and I rushed to her.

"Weik was hit..." She stopped to catch her breath. "I don't know... how they found us..."

Weik was hit? How? She'd had wards up all over the building to keep the undesirables out.

"Lily Joy, Shafira," I shouted, but the women were already moving through the throngs of bodies to get to us. They, along with other witches, jumped in to assess the situation like a group of EMTs.

At this point, the smartest option for me was to step back out of the way and let them help. They knew how to heal. My natural inclination to manifest her better felt like it would hurt us all in the long run. I saw visions of me trying to use manifestation to heal people rather than focusing on the fight and becoming overwhelmed because everyone just expected me to take care of it. And I knew in an instant, even though I held that power, that I couldn't.

Every witch or Lilium in this room had their part to play—a destiny to fulfill. I couldn't go against the universe and deny them their destinies, as scary as it might be. I didn't want to lose any of them, and they surely didn't want to die, either. But who was I to play God?

"You can't save them all, babe. I hear your thoughts. They know the danger witches face out there. You'll tell them the risks. Some may opt out of fighting, but my guess, they're here because they have people they love. People who need protection."

Most of the witches and Lilium were either helping take care of the wounded, or pressed in close to those witches, waiting to help if necessary.

"How is she?" I asked, concerned about Victoria's condition.

"Her injuries are bad, but she's stable," said a witch, a middle-aged woman who wore a shag-style haircut that flattered her face and made her icy-blue eyes the focus of her face. With her golden-blonde locks, she reminded me of the acting icon Farrah Fawcett. I didn't know most of these witches, and truthfully, I lacked the headspace to bother with getting to know them, so for the time being, I'd think of her as Farrah.

As for Victoria, that wasn't the best news—not as bad as it could've been, but I liked her. I wanted her to be okay. And truthfully, we needed her.

Given we were running out of time, I decided to address the witches and Lilium present and just fill in any new ones who showed up. I clapped my hands to get them to look at me. "I need your attention. Witches, I need you to break into groups. Raise your hand if you're a kitchen witch."

A bunch of hands shot up into the air.

"Great, you all congregate over by the woman in the blue boho blouse," I ordered. The woman in the blue boho blouse waved her hand and the kitchen witches started moving over to her. "Crystals?" I asked. More hands shot up. A woman with bright-pink hair caught my eye. "Crystal witches head to the woman with the bright-pink hair." And yes, I had to make that distinction, because we had witches with a rainbow assortment of hair colors. The crystal witches moved to stand by her. "The rest of you do spellwork?"

I got a bunch of nods and mumbles of "Yeah" or "Yup" or "Yes."

"You guys stand next to the goth practitioner," I directed next. The goth waved their hand to get the others to see them, though I found a goth look to be rather hard to miss. Lastly, I addressed the Lilium. "Lilium, now that you all know what you are, if you're not already by Karro, then I need you up there."

Most of the Lilium already stood in a huddle close to Karro. It'd been a shock for most of them to finally find out what we were. A few already knew, but for most of us, it was a big shock to the system. Most supers knew the legend of the Lilium, but no one had ever met a Lilium. So then to find out you *were* a Lilium —yeah, mind blown.

"Okay," I called out. "You all know that this is literal life and death out there. I need the kitchen witches to start brewing up anything and everything for healing, for forgetting—anything that will aid us in the fight. Crystal witches, start using oils to anoint the crystals. We'll make them into necklaces for everyone to wear for protection. Spellcasters, we need offensive and defensive spells that will stop humans without killing them if possible, maybe knock them out for a while, but do what you need to do to the demons. Lilium, do your thing, whatever that may be. You need to be able to use your magic, both offensively and defensively, as easy as Harry Potter flicked his wand and shouted, '*Expelliarmus.*' I got a lot of snickers from that, but they all got to work in their groups.

Karro's group looked to him for input and he totally took to this new leadership role like he'd been born to do it. But then again, maybe he had been. What did I know?

I stayed next to Connor. He kissed the side of my temple. "How're you feeling about all this?"

"I'm good at manifesting. I think I'll be okay, but I don't know if Sim has the hilt and his book yet. We need him here to join the dagger and those plants from the garden were given to him for a reason. I have to talk to him so I can manifest them here."

"Babe, I know you want them here, but I think you need to give them the chance to do what they've got to do."

"You want me to leave them out there with *The Purge*?"

"No."

"So then I have to."

"He was bound for most of his life just like you. My gut tells me he needs this time to find out what he's capable of."

"But I need to know if he has the things yet."

"Then talk to him—don't just bring them here, not yet."

We were running out of time but as I kept finding new achievements to unlock, I had to assume Connor's point held merit. A *lot* of merit. Of course, I'd never tell him that. We didn't need him thinking I'd ever let him win an argument.

He looked around the room and then said, "We need a private room, something quiet."

The archives answered right away, with a door shimmering purple into appearance at the far end of the room. We started weaving our way around the throngs of bodies to get to it. The door opened for us without even a push or twist of the handle.

When we stepped inside, the smaller room held drinks on low-lying tables set next to these huge, beanbag-style chairs. I dropped on a lavender one, sinking into the cushiony softness.

Connor dropped onto the second black one. Assigned seating. The room had a reason for this—I just didn't know that reason yet.

"Okay, let me see my brother, Simeon, and his mate, Madigan," I said, manifesting the hell out of this. The air between our seats swirled and then a picture showed, like watching television without the TV.

It was dark there. I manifested letting them talk to Connor and me, and to hear our responses. I hoped this worked. "Sim," I whispered, in case he wasn't safe. Simeon twisted his head from side to side, probably to see where my voice came from. "Sim, straight ahead. Up."

He tipped his head up, looking straight ahead. "Simone? Where are you?"

"The witches' archives. We need you here. You, Madigan, your book and hilt."

"We're trying to get home. It's crazy out there."

"Okay, where are you?"

"Right now, we're in Bay City. We broke into the State Theater. I have to get to Corunna. That's where I live. It's where my things are."

"Hold on to Madigan. I'm going to try to manifest you home. Once you get there, get your things."

"You can do that?"

"I can now. New abilities keep popping up."

"Same here. Each new thing that pops up, I'm like, where have you been all my life?"

"He's amazing," Madigan said.

My brother leaned in to kiss her cheek. "Thanks, babe."

"If you're anything like Simone, you can do whatever you set your mind to," Connor replied.

Simeon chuckled. "I hope that's true because I wish I had the kind of power she does."

"You have great powers, Sim," Madigan countered.

"Guys—*focus.*" I snapped my fingers to get their attention. "I'm manifesting now."

I watched Simeon wrap his arms around Madigan's waist and then I closed my eyes. "Get Simeon and Madigan to Simeon's home in Corunna," I began chanting over and over. *Please let this work.* We needed this to work. The manifestation pummeled my insides. Maybe because I'd done it too many times today. But moving people from their location, and not physically being in the room with them, to a different location kind of sucked. My body bruised from the inside out. I couldn't stop. I just kept chanting over and over, no matter how much it hurt. How hard I breathed because the magic knocked the wind out of me.

The pair disappeared from view, the TV went black, and they appeared in front of a cute, well-landscaped house. The door had been kicked in. Someone knew about his book. I hoped it remained where he'd left it. Madigan pushed in front of my brother and I saw the look on his face when she did that. No way was he comfortable with his woman going in first, even if she could shift at the drop of a hat and had been mated to him for this exact purpose.

"Back bedroom," he whispered. She nodded once and started for the hallway. The woman knew exactly where to go, which meant she'd gotten to spend a little time there before they'd gone on the run. I mean… good for her. And my brother.

Exactly as they'd done with mine, demons—or Cain—had trashed his place. Sim and Madigan walked into what must've been the master bedroom. The mattress lay half on the frame and half on the floor. Everything he'd ever owned was smashed or strewn over the carpeting. He walked over to the bed, popping up the bed platform. It had a false bottom. Connor and I watched him pick up the small botanical book and the hilt from inside the nook the false bottom created. He ran to the closet and pulled junk from the floor, throwing it over his shoulder to get to what he needed: a leather satchel with a crossbody strap. He shoved the book and hilt into the satchel, zipped the top, and secured the over-flap with the buckles.

Then he held his hand out to Madigan, who grabbed hold. "Ready," he said to me.

I cleared my throat, closed my eyes, and started chanting. Like with Agatha, it took more effort to get them to me. Instead of an instantaneous movement, they zipped through the air at lightning speed. I started sweating and my mouth went dry. Pain throbbed in my head like someone continuously beat me with a sledgehammer, but I couldn't let myself lose focus. The room started to spin and I felt a second and a half from passing out.

Why was this so much more difficult than bringing Shafira and Karro to us? I heard an answer to my question in Lilith's voice: "Angel magic." Angel magic boosted my magic? Good to know. I pushed her voice out of my head to keep myself on task.

"Baby," Connor said, falling down by my side. He pressed his hand to my forehead. "Clammy. You've got to stop."

I dared not speak, pushing his hand away. I couldn't let go of my focus. Out of the corner of my eye, I saw the glass next to my beanbag chair start to glow. Connor noticed it too. That had to be why the room had given us different-colored chairs. He lifted it to my mouth and I drank the sparkling liquid down. The pain eased right away. My body temp started to regulate itself again. The sweats stopped.

The room knew exactly what I needed. When I tried to manifest them into this room, the energy of the archives zapped me. Apparently, they had to enter the same way everyone else did. I moved my destination to the Knapp of Howar. Two people really put a strain on my magic. I kept drinking the witchy beverage and when I reached the bottom of the glass, it refilled to allow me to keep drinking, which I did until I saw them land outside the crumbling monolith.

My brother and Madigan were here. I dropped the glass, spilling the rest of the drink, pushing up out of the chair to run. The door opened for us, letting me speed up rather than slow down to get to my brother. The hilt and amulet were so close to being joined.

Excited, I ran up the stairs and outside. I could've cried from happiness. But before I reached Sim, a demon lunged at me. A freaking demon? What? How'd demons know we were here? I had just enough sense to lock the archive doors behind me before taking a shot to my middle, knocking me to the ground.

I screamed, partly from pain, but given the adrenaline surging through my veins, mostly from anger. It took major gall for a demon to surprise attack me when I was about to hug my brother. I shot my hand out to grab for the demon when more started appearing. There was me, Sim, and Madigan, who dropped into her hound form.

And holy hell—Sim controlled plants. I watched as grass shot up around a demon's foot, winding and twisting to keep him anchored to the spot. Madigan lunged and ripped his throat out. Black demon blood sprayed us. Vomiting would have to wait until we took care of these creeps.

Somewhere along the way, Connor had joined us, and he fought alongside his sister. As I cast out my hand to fire off some spell or other at a charging demon, I looked up for a split second to see a man standing off in the distance. Beetle. But Beetle wasn't Satan. This was the man I'd talked to at Monnie's what seemed like a lifetime ago. Same stature. Same style suit. Hair slicked back. Without thinking, I took off in a dead run. He wouldn't get away from me. Not this time.

I became vaguely aware of Connor at my side, and as we ran, I manifested to bring Beetle down. I wanted that man trapped. But somehow, he deflected my shots. That shouldn't have been possible. Rather than take more time, I reached over to touch Connor's head and manifested us to him. We popped into the place where he'd been just a second before, but that coward was gone.

"No!" I shouted. This was our shot and I'd blown it. I dropped to the ground crying angry tears. How did Lilith expect me to save the world when I couldn't catch the man trying to ruin it? I had one damn job—to defeat Beetle, and I let him get away.

Connor dropped his arms around me, holding on as tightly as he dared while I sobbed. "He wanted to see what you've got, babe. No doubt he's reformulating his plan."

"Because I screwed up."

"How? You did exactly what you needed to do."

"Then why did he get away?"

"Because he knew he was coming here. You didn't."

Well, it was an answer—maybe not a good one or one I liked, but it answered some questions.

"You ruined your clothes again," I said dryly, waving my hand in the air to manifest him simple jeans, a T-shirt, and Converse. I didn't have it in me to be more creative. As we made our way back to Sim and Madigan, we stepped in puddles of demon. Lucky us, we'd gotten there right before the bloody debris turned to ash, blowing away on the wind. I manifested joggers and a T-shirt for Madigan. They flitted to the ground next to my brother, who stood between us and Madi, blocking her naked form. He nodded his thanks in passing. Connor kept his head turned away, no doubt not wanting to see his sister *au naturel*.

When we reached the door, I unlocked it, letting us inside the archives. Madigan was the last to enter, pulling the door shut again, and I locked it.

"That's a badass power you've got, brother," I said to Sim.

He smiled. He looked like me when he smiled. "It's been getting stronger." Simeon flicked his hand in the air and the sound of thunder rumbling overhead filled the stone stairwell with us.

My eyes bugged. "You can control the weather?"

"At least we'll always have good beach days," he replied, shrugging. Shrugging, my ass. That was huge. He could control weather and plants. Somehow, we needed to use this to our advantage because Beetle had skipped out before seeing Sim's biggest power-up.

"Achievement unlocked," Connor teased.

"I'm thinking of planning a BBQ in January," Madigan said while smirking. "Mom will trip."

Connor threw his head back, laughing.

# CHAPTER
## Twenty-Eight

We let Sim and Madigan get settled and have something to eat before getting down to the heavy. "Can I see the book?" I asked my brother.

He gave a quick nod, unclasping the buckles from the satchel he wore. After unzipping the top, he reached inside, pulling the small, leather-bound book out and setting it on the table. I stood to retrieve my backpack. When I rejoined them at the table, I had the grimoire in hand.

"May I?" Sim asked.

"Please."

Ever-so-gently, he picked it up like he thought it was fragile, then opened the book. His eyes grew as he read the names of all our cousins, and reverently ran his finger down the page. When he flipped to the next, new pages had been added. They gave detailed diagrams of spells from Grandma Lilith.

Spells for our cousins to try. Ideas for me to manifest.

"Open your book," I said and Sim opened it. I manifested a pot with dirt. "Touch the plant and touch the dirt." He did as asked and I told the dried, pressed plant to grow in the pot. A strong stalk shot up out of the pot with vines winding around it like a slithering snake. Beautifully vibrant, blood-red flowers, the likes of which I'd never seen before, blossomed in front of our eyes. Spiky thorns protruded from the stalk.

"What is it?" Madigan asked.

Words appeared over the dried plant in the book: The Death Bloom.

"Death Bloom?" I asked.

My brother read on. "It looks like if the thorns scratch the skin, it poisons the person. Lesions will bubble up over their body and the pain is so intense, it drops the person where they stand."

"Will it kill them?" I asked.

"In larger doses. But we could use this to quell the uprising of humans out there."

Exactly my thought.

"The flower can be used to brew an anti-poison." He turned the page. And with each page he turned, I started seeing a pattern. I absently pulled the amulet from my backpack and for the first time noticed the gem was porous.

"Connor, wasn't this smooth before?"

His head jerked as he took in the bauble in my hand. "As a baby's butt," he replied.

"Extract the poison," I told my brother. "Make it as potent as possible." I started manifesting pots for more plants. Sim touched each new leaf, stem, or root and the dirt in the pot to create the plants. Each had a description above the name. As I read them, I understood why she'd chosen those particular plants from the garden. Our witches could use these plants to make the most powerful destructive and healing brews.

"What are you thinking?" Sim asked.

"I'm thinking that we make a brew from all of the poisonous plants and soak this gem in the poison before joining it to the hilt. This is what's going to kill Beetle. This is what made Lilith's dagger so lethal. It's why no one could touch it—because the gem held the poison."

"What good is a dagger without a blade?" Madigan asked.

"Let's try this and see what happens."

Well, there we had the start of a plan at least. As my brother tended to the plants from the Garden of Eden, I walked around the archives to let the witches and Lilium know that we had stronger plants to work with.

Seeing all these people from different walks of life working together for the sake of humanity did my heart good. We spent far too much time at each other's throats because of this bullshit thing or that bullshit thing. Politics and narrowed points of view had separated us—all of us—for too many years. But now we'd come to a precipice. We stood together or we fell apart. Us against them. Them being demons of the underworld, which probably hadn't been on *anyone*'s bingo card this year. I digress.

But here was the problem: I hated feeling useless and right now, I felt useless. Yes, I walked from group to group checking on witch and Lilium progress and fetching anything they might've needed, but all I could do was manifest. Since the moment my powers opened up to me, I'd been practicing and perfecting my manifesting game. So now there was nothing for me to do. I walked—no, strike that—I paced the room growing more and more agitated until Connor snagged my hand, dragging me to the special private room the archives had created for us.

He tossed me down on the purple beanbag chair. "What are you doing?" I asked, irritated.

"What are *you* doing?" he repeated in a dumb voice. "What does it look like I'm doing? I'm calming my mate the best way I know how." It hardly seemed like the time or place for this, but when his hands found the button of my jeans, I sort of lost all rational thought. He stripped my lower half but kept his pants on, unzipping and unbuttoning his fly and tugging his jeans down around his ass. Connor's lips found my neck and his fingers, my center. Oh, dear god! As he sucked the skin into his mouth, I squirmed beneath him and his strong hold.

My eyes closed and I stretched my neck to give him more

room to roam. "Connor, please," I begged. He moved his fingers from my center to rub himself against me there. "Connor, *please*," I cried this time. He tore his mouth from my neck to press a heavy kiss to my lips. I'd like to think he just couldn't resist kissing me, but I felt like he'd done it more to shut me up. Ask me if I cared. In this moment, he had my permission to press his whole hand over my mouth if it meant keeping the ecstatic shivers coming.

Everything but the feel of neurons firing fled my brain as my body took over, reaching to get what it wanted by rocking and rubbing against Connor. He growled low, tearing his mouth from mine, pressing his forehead to mine, and draped each of my legs over his thighs. He plundered the spoils of this battle. A meeting of hearts and bodies and minds. We took off, lips and tongues and teeth. Touching everywhere we could touch. Moving with each other in a way that no other lover could give him or me. Mated sex reached heights that no other sex reached. For the rest of my life, I got this. I got Connor, a partner who read my mood and went out of his way to calm me. As our momentum built, the pulse of culmination reached the breaking point and I lost all sense of space and time. My damn mate drove in one last time and I lost it all over him.

While he came down, he pressed his forehead to mine again, sighing in that heavily contented way he had. I loved that sigh. It meant I gave him exactly what he'd given me. I felt humbled and powerful all at once.

Connor rolled us to drop his butt into the cushioned seat, pulling me onto his lap. Both our chests heaved while we struggled to find reality again. "I can die happy now," I said, teasing him, but that was *not* how he took it.

His whole body went rigid. "Don't ever say that again."

"Connor—"

"I'm serious, Simone. Don't say that shit again. You're not dying now or anytime soon. I will not lose you. Do you hear me?"

Talk about an open mouth, insert foot moment. I tipped up my head to kiss the hinge of his jaw. "Sorry, babe. I won't joke like that again," I said, getting the words out over the hard lump in my throat. Joking about death with Connor came easy given our expert level banter. But with facing our impending doom, I needed to make better word choices. "I forget how intense the bond can be sometimes. I'll get used to it."

"Babe, even if we lost all our magic, including the mated bond, I couldn't survive losing you. I'm in it."

I threw my arms around him, pressing my face against his chest, holding on with everything in me.

*Okay, enough of that.* I shook my head, letting my arms drop from around him. "So we're done with vulnerable Simone, then?" he asked.

"I have a reputation as a supreme badass to protect," I said to his ensuing snicker. "Plus, I wanted to discuss something with you."

"Shoot," he replied.

"Adalaide said that Mr. Pooches is my familiar."

Given how he nodded, I figured he'd come to that conclusion as well. "Does Sim have one? He got a hellhound for a mate, so it seems likely he'd have gotten a familiar, too."

"Note to self, Baghest, do not bring up my brother when I'm leaning on you with my junk hanging out."

He barked out a laugh. "Baby, what you got ain't junk and it's not just hanging out. *My* junk is hanging out. I could take you again in any position."

"Why do you have to be so *you* and ruin something beautiful?"

"That sounds like a you problem. Nothing's ruined on my end. Well, except that pu—"

I slapped my hand over his mouth. "If you know what's good for you, you won't finish that sentence."

Removing my hand, he kissed the palm. "I know what's good for you and you love it when I finish."

"I think we need to clean up. If I stay in here any longer, the world is gonna burn."

Connor laughed even harder. "I'm not complaining."

Oh, lord… I manifested a basin, water, and soap to clean myself up. Yes, it was difficult to do something so common in front of him, but he took pity on me and stepped up next to me to clean himself off rather than keep watching me, and he achieved his goal of settling me.

When we left the room, several sets of eyes found us, crinkling with humor. Okay, so they knew we'd been getting down and dirty in the other room. The fate of the world fell on my shoulders. It was a stressful position to hold. And yeah—it all sounded like excuses to me too. I just had to be okay with people knowing we'd knocked boots at what amounted to a highly inappropriate time. Privacy and leadership didn't really mesh together.

I wandered over to Simeon and while my brother worked, I asked him, "Do you have a familiar?"

He shook his head slowly. "Had one. Ruby. She died right before Madi and I went underground. We hadn't… become official yet," he said, smirking at the memory. "Madi'd been checking something out, so we weren't together. Ruby threw herself in the path of a demon blade that I'd never seen coming. She sacrificed herself to save me. Stupid thing is, I never knew what she was until she died. I thought she was just a raven that I'd fed and talked to while she ate. Stupid, right?"

"No. I had no idea about Mr. Pooches until a few days ago. But I haven't seen him in a while and now I'm really worried about him."

"I'm sure he'll show up again."

"He curled up on my lap every night after Jeffery's death. He took care of me until I could take care of myself."

"Pooches will show up," Connor said, startling me. I didn't realize he'd been listening.

If I'd known he was there, I wouldn't have mentioned Jeffery.

I turned sorry eyes on him. "I was just explaining why Mr. Pooches—"

"It's okay."

My head jerked back. "What?"

"He ever get what we had in there?" Connor pointed back to the room.

Uh… I narrowed my eyes on him not understanding. "Did he ever get sex?"

"No babe. We got deep in there. We had *connection*."

Oh, right. I got it. Jeffery and I had great sex over the years, no doubt. But no. "No," I replied honestly. The universe gave me Connor and now it appeared that the jealousy portion of our newly mated bond hopped a bus to some other couple's relationship. Connor draped his arms around me and I couldn't help but notice the smug, *'and that's how it's done'* look he shot to my brother.

"Don't you love it when they're docile," Simeon said and without even lifting my head, I let go of Connor's waist, rearing my arm back to punch Sim in the gut. Hard.

"You know what's good for you, Baghest, you won't answer that," I taunted Connor, but I taunted him sweetly.

"I ever hear that again, Lamia, you'll beg for a quick death." At first, I thought Madigan was talking to me and come on—Sim deserved it. But I realized she'd been talking to my brother when she said, "As useful as it is to me, I will rip your dick from your body, cram it down your throat, and laugh while you choke slowly to death on the impressive meat stick."

*Ew.* I didn't need to know that my brother had an 'impressive meat stick,' but good for Madigan. You know, girl camaraderie and all that.

Speaking of meat sticks, though, I decided that my brother and his mate should get one more time to bump uglies before the world completely turned on its head. "Sim, how's it going?"

He pointed to the pot simmering over the fire at the hearth. "I'm just waiting for the brew to reduce enough."

"There's a special room in back. I think you and Madigan should check it out while we have a little downtime." I pointed my thumb behind me.

Simeon raised his eyebrow. "Sister, I like the way you think." He grabbed Madigan's hand, leading her to the back of the archives.

"I know why you did that," Connor said low.

"We don't know what's going to happen. I want them to have what we had."

Connor held me tighter. "No one will ever have what we had, babe." I started to sigh, thinking how romantic the big, dummy hellhound could be until he opened his sexy yap again. "Because there's not a man alive who's as good a lover as me."

"I'm sure you need to think that." I patted his stomach before walking over to the sofa where I plopped down very awkwardly and unladylike, folding my feet under me. Connor's phone rang from his pocket. He fished it free, answering. "Luc, what's up?" He paused and then said, "Babe, manifest to hear the call. I don't want the rest of the room hearing, but Luc says you need to and we can't go in the private room now."

Did that bother me? Nope. I regretted nothing. They deserved the slap and tickle. I nodded, closed my eyes, and thought, *Let me hear Luc over the phone. Let Luc hear me.*

"She's here now, isn't she?" Luc asked. "I feel her."

"Dude." Connor growled. "You don't *feel* my mate." Okay, so maybe the jealousy only took a day trip. Rome wasn't built in a day and all that.

Luc laughed.

"She's here," I said, though I said it in my head. Because I'd joined his pack, if you will, I didn't have to manifest for Connor to hear me. He already could. "But she prefers to be addressed as 'Her Excellence, the Exalted Simone' from now on."

Both men started laughing.

"Right. We ready?" Luc asked.

"I've been ready," Connor answered.

"Her Excellence the Exalted Simone?" Luc waited for me to answer.

"I'm ready."

"Great. So after I looked into shit going on at Monnie's, I took a meeting with Mike."

"Mike?" I asked.

"Mike—*Michael*. We're still close."

"As in Archangel Michael?"

"You know where I used to live."

"Right," I replied sheepishly. "Sometimes I forget. You're so… so… *regular*."

"Sweetheart, I'm anything but regular."

"Then maybe you need more fiber in your diet. I meant you don't sound regal."

He laughed. "Neither are they. I promise."

Okay, that made me chuckle and I noticed eyes of witches turning to the crazy woman laughing at nothing—and to be clear, *I* was the crazy woman.

"Focus," Connor snapped. "What did Mike say?"

"He said they're out."

"Surprise, surprise," Connor muttered.

"He has a point this time. They can't get involved."

"*Why?*" I asked, hanging on his words. I found myself totally invested.

"We know a demon is leading this charge, but he's charging against the Earth plane, not Heaven. If Heaven gets involved, it's the same as declaring war."

"Declaring war?" I asked.

"Armageddon," Connor replied.

Ooh—yeah, the last thing we needed was *actual, real life* Armageddon, not the esque version that I'd been planning for.

"I'm heading to the union hall, been spreading the word that the hounds need to congregate. Let me know where and when we need to meet."

"I'll let you know," Connor answered him.

As they hung up, I felt a presence approaching the stones outside. Really? A presence? I sighed until I felt with everything in me that the presence was my beloved Mr. Pooches. Finally.

"Pooches," I cried, springing up from the sofa. I ran up the steps, throwing open the door. Mr. Pooches limped. His tail bent at an unnatural angle. My poor kitty was battered and beaten down. I bent to pick him up and he winced.

Cradling him in my arms, I moved us back inside to safety. "What happened?" I asked.

"I barely got out with my life," Mr. Pooches said.

"We'll get you fixed up." I gently ran my hand down over his back. He closed his eyes, leaving me wondering if it was out of relief or pain. A tear ran down my cheek. I hadn't realized how much Mr. Pooches meant to me until now. Would Connor, a death hound, be okay living with a cat familiar? Could hounds and cats get along? Well, they'd just have to because I clearly couldn't get rid of Connor. He was my family, but then again, so was Mr. Pooches. "You'll be okay," I whispered. "I'll take care of you."

Mr. Pooches snuggled his head down into my arms. Whatever I'd done to have been given him, I once again thanked the universe. I'd spent my early life being alone. Now I had more people/demons/fallen angels to care about than I knew what to do with. Oh, and a mate that I'd die to protect. My family had grown exponentially at a really bad moment in time and I felt the weight of that realization settle in my heart for the long haul.

Shafira met me at the bottom of the stairs. She gasped. "*Mr. Pooches*." Pooches lifted his head, smiling at her as best he could through his pain. "Let me." She reached out and I bent to kiss my familiar on the head before handing him over.

Connor found me again, nuzzling my ear with his nose and his warm breath tickled. "He'll be okay. I trust Shafira."

"I do too."

After a couple of minutes, Shafira called us over to where she had an IV running into Pooches' front paw. She had his tail bandaged. He looked pitiful. Smaller than he'd ever looked. "He needs to speak to you," she said.

"Mr. Pooches?" I asked, in reality asking him what he needed to tell me without saying the words.

"The possessions have begun," he said low.

"'Possessions'? As in demon possessions?" Shafira asked, throwing her hand to her mouth. Yeah, I felt that too.

"I know where the demons are amassing. They've been called back…" He took a sharp breath. "To receive orders. This is an organized attack. I fear they plan to attack at once."

"Attack at once. Fuck," Connor muttered. "So we have to go on the offensive. We have to hit them before they split up. They won't expect us."

"My thoughts exactly," Mr. Pooches agreed.

An offensive attack. We had to plan for every problematic scenario that could arise because this was a dangerous undertaking. Very dangerous. How did we plan for every counterattack? We hardly had time to pee, let alone plan our mobilization. And how did I get all our witches there without the demons knowing?

Lilith help me.

"Lily Joy, Karro," I called to my family. "Oh—Agatha, I need you too." As my brother and Madigan were still occupied in the other room, I'd have to fill them in later. The witches and Lilium joined me, standing next to Connor and Shafira. "Mr. Pooches knows where the demons have been mobilizing."

Everyone turned their attention to the injured familiar. He had a hard time lifting his head, turning it to look at us. "Outside Göbekli Tepe," Pooches said.

"'Göbekli Tepe'?" Karro asked and the cat nodded the best he could.

"I know of it," Shafira said.

"Me too," I replied. "I watched a NatGeo program about it. It's one of the oldest settlements in the world."

"Türkiye," Lily Joy said softly. "Demons are amassing in Türkiye. I wonder why."

"That whole region is considered the cradle of civilization," I offered as a possible reason. I supposed it was as good as any other reason. For all we knew, demons had a love of ancient stone architecture. Okay, so that idea gave me a chuckle. Architecture-loving demons—if only.

The door to the back room opened. My brother and Madigan exited. He held her close and tight as they made their way over to our group. "What are we talking about?" he asked.

"Türkiye," Lily Joy said and he shot her a curious expression.

"What about it?" Madigan asked.

"Demons are organizing there." Connor did the honors filling her in. She gasped as one would.

"Demons are organizing?"

"Is the potion ready?" I asked Simeon.

"Give me a sec." He walked over to the pot using a rag that magically appeared to lift the handle off the hook, walking the pot back over to us. It bubbled thickly. A deep, reddish-purple color. The brew smelled cloyingly sweet, causing me to gag.

"Connor, my backpack?"

My mate walked over to the table where I'd left the backpack sitting. When he returned with it, handing it over to me, I reached inside to pull out the amulet.

"Ready?" I asked. The group nodded or gave confirmations of "Yeah" or "Yup" and I tossed the amulet into the pot. The bobble plopped, causing a large splatter to hit the sides of the cauldron. It bubbled and hissed, steaming up from the surface. "How long do we leave it in for?" I asked and Sim shrugged.

"Let's give it at least ten minutes to steep," he replied.

"Okay, so we need cloaking wards. A lot of them." I looked to Lily Joy, who already knew how to make wards. "We'll need Luc to zap them with his angel mojo." And that got me thinking, "How did you make the wards before?"

"A recipe I found on the counter in my cottage. I left them there overnight and the next morning a jar of this glowing, swirly goo sat next to them. I rubbed them down with the goo and let it dry. Oh, and I'm on it." She turned to walk over to one of the tables, where a group of witches made room for her. My cousin started giving directions and the witches got down to work. Glowing, swirling goo? That had Lilith written all over it.

"I'll help," Shafira said.

"Take the grimoire." Opening the pack again, I fished around for the grimoire, pulling it out, handing it off to Shafira. "Lilith has good spells in here."

Shafira took the book, reverently holding it in her arms as she turned, jogging over to the table with Lily Joy.

"Once the wards are finished, we'll have to start moving witches to Göbekli Tepe. I thought about manifesting us all there at once, but—"

"No." Connor cut me off. "You're powerful, but that's too much, even for you. We need you strong and healthy."

"Calm your tits. I was just going to say I thought that was too much for me to do."

He growled. "Good. Then we're on the same page."

"So now that we all know I wasn't going to risk it, I think we need to move the witches and launch our attack from there. We'll hit them first, when they least expect it."

"It's the best strategy," Madigan said. "They won't see us coming."

"That'll still strain your energy," Connor protested.

"Do you have a better way of moving this many witches to a camp without them getting caught?"

"We could try the tunnels."

"With this many witches?" I countered.

"Brother, I know you don't like it," Madigan said, "but she can manifest for a reason. She's powerful. She can do this."

"Sim, you and Madi will go with the first group. I'll send Lily Joy, Shafira, and Karro along, too. We'll need Madi in hellhound form for protection while the wards are set in place. Then I want you to form a perimeter of poisonous plants just inside the wards, leaving openings for the witches to get out. That way, if some stupid demon does venture too close, they'll regret it."

"Got it."

"We need Luc's number to call him in."

"I have it," Shafira said, and when we all turned slowly to

stare at her she finished, "he gave it to me because of our agreement. I can use Karro's phone."

"That'll work. Connor and I will help the witches, unless I can get him to stay at the camp and help protect everyone with Madigan."

Connor shot me a *'woman done lost her mind'* look. I knew he wouldn't leave me again, but it was worth a try.

"What about joining the hilt and amulet?" Simeon asked.

"I'm formulating a plan for that."

I had to wait for Connor and Madigan to break off into their own little group—I heard something about battle strategies—and I pulled my brother aside. "I have an idea, but my big lug of a mate would throw the hissy fit to rival all hissy fits and I don't think your mate would be too comfortable with it, either."

"Lay it on me," he replied and I did.

He started to fidget, as if uncomfortable.

I told him, "If you can think of anything else, I'm open. But I'm trying to end this with as little loss of life as possible."

"I know. But I just got you in my life. I'm not ready to lose you. And Connor—"

"Would eventually understand. But let's not dwell on that part right now because we only have to consider it if the rest doesn't work."

"Jesus," he whispered.

"I know."

Sim pulled me into a tight hug. I sighed one of those heavy, *'I hate this'* sighs that said so much of what I was feeling without having to say the words. Yeah, we'd officially reached *that* point in our quest. The point where Frodo had to come to terms with the prospect of *not* coming down from Mount Doom in Mordor. Note: The part of Frodo Baggins to be played by Simone Lamia.

It took a while, but Lily Joy came to me when the wards were finished. "Grandma Lilith knew her stuff," she said and yeah. They didn't call her 'the mother of all witches' for nothing.

"We ready?" I asked, and when she nodded, I called to the room, "First group of witches and Lilium. It's time."

My cousin and I were joined by Shafira, Agatha, Karro, Sim, and Madigan, along with several witches and Lilium, including Alexis Smith. She might've grown up without family like the rest of us, but she'd embraced her power and I was glad to have her on the team.

"It'll work best if everyone hangs on to each other in some way," I said. "I'm going to manifest us downwind as close to the demon camp as possible without being detected."

Everyone started grabbing hands, arms, shirts—whatever they felt comfortable with—and I closed my eyes. Right as I thought *downwind from the demon camp at Göbekli Tepe*, I felt Connor pressing himself to my back, wrapping his arms around my waist.

"I've got your back," he whispered. Always. He always had my back.

*Downwind from the demon camp at Göbekli Tepe.*
*Downwind from the demon camp at Göbekli Tepe.*
*Downwind from the demon camp at Göbekli Tepe.*

I repeated it over and over, feeling Connor and me disappear from the archives. The weight of the others pulled down on me as if I were transporting a bin of large stones, but it made me glad for the feeling, knowing that I'd successfully brought them with us.

Moments later, we set down behind a rocky outcropping of hills. I cloaked Lily Joy, Shafira, and Karro as they went up the hills to place the wards. The others placed the wards on flatter ground where we'd directed them to. Sim went to work springing poisonous plants to life out of literal dirt. Connor and Madigan remained on guard during the whole process. The wards they cooked up kept the camp undetectable from the demons and humans alike—well, once Luc gave them an angel powerup. We couldn't take any chances.

"Okay," I said to the crowd. "Shafira, call Luc. The rest of you, take this time to focus and get your spells in order. I'll be back with the next group as soon as I can get them together. Be careful. Keep vigilant." With that done, I reached for Connor and manifested us back to the archives. They still wouldn't let me manifest directly inside. We had to use the door like everyone else.

Inside, I gathered up the next group, this one larger than the first. This group was mostly made up of our healers and they carried salves, elixirs, bandages, you name it—something I'd neglected to account for when determining the weight of transporting them.

Still, pulling up my big-girl panties once again, I gave myself a small pep talk and then started manifesting. *Our camp downwind from Göbekli Tepe.*

*Our camp downwind from Göbekli Tepe.*
*Our camp downwind from Göbekli Tepe.*
*Our camp downwind from Göbekli Tepe.*
*Our camp downwind from Göbekli Tepe.*

It took everything I had in me to move a group this size and weighted down, but we needed this to work and so I fought through the pain to deposit them where they needed to be. On our third trip to the camp, Shafira grabbed my arm before we could leave.

"Luc was here but he could not stay. He is 'working his angles' whatever that means. He wishes Connor to call him when he needs him again."

Connor turned to me, "Working his angle?"

"He's *your* friend. I have no idea."

As a fallen angel, Luc could do whatever he wanted. We still had witches to move. Trip after trip, dozens of them, Connor and I moved the witches and Lilium to the camp. By the end, my head throbbed and I needed to recharge. Lily Joy and Agatha met me with a yummy rum tea cake and a mug of healing brew.

I welcomed their offerings, hardly taking time to chew. I mean, it was *cake*. One didn't get a booty like mine by hating cake.

Scouts volunteered to go out undercover, counting the growing numbers of demons and reporting back—a dangerous but necessary job. We needed the demons all present and totally unaware they were about to die. Hearing about the numbers of humans camped along with the demons hurt my heart, but I had to remind myself that not all humans were good and wanted the best for the world, but also, that most of them were forced to be there by possession or enslavement.

Connor's phone rang with Luc on the other end. He asked Connor to put it on speaker so I could hear too. "You good?" he asked.

"So far," I answered.

"Right. So I got tired of waiting for Connor to call. You need to know what I've been up to."

"What have you been up to?" I asked.

"I've been creating wards, gathering up all the hellhounds and rounding up more witches."

"*Wow.*"

"Wow is an understatement, but I need your help—you and Connor. I need to know your exact coordinates to set up our camps in the right spots. We're surrounding the demons from all sides."

"Two camps of witches?" Connor asked.

"Not even close. I popped back to Antarctica and guess who'd been eaten?"

I swallowed hard. "Kimaris was eaten? By what?"

"Remember that monster who scared the demons? It's real. Ancient. They call him 'Átahsaia.' He was created by a few of our disgruntled upstairs neighbors who didn't much care for the creation of Hell or the offices of Hades. As I was busy setting up shop, he flew under my radar. When the continents broke apart, he ended up down in Antarctica because they'd neglected to give him anything useful like flight. For a bunch of Kevins and

Karens who were always up in everyone else's business, they certainly weren't that smart."

"So how did you get away?" I asked.

He chuckled. "Not a demon, sweetheart. He's actually a decent guy, but he's ravenous after all these years of fasting."

Átahsaia. A demon eater. We had a demon eater on our team. I left Connor to the coordinates, then he and I manifested to meet Luc. Maybe I was biased, but hellhounds were a good-looking bunch. Several men took their lives in their hands by turning their swagger my way. Everyone of them knew the Baghests were hellhound royalty—well, practically. They didn't actually have a monarchy, but if they did—all hail the Baghests. Still, Baghests or not, it appeared that hellhounds thought highly of themselves. I laughed and laughed at their antics and Connor's reaction to them. I kept them cloaked while the wards got put in place. We'd left Sim back at our camp. I thought it best not to risk tangling up a bunch of unruly hounds in poisonous vines as that sort of screamed *disaster waiting to happen.*

"Witches next," Luc said. "They're coming up through a portal." Connor shot me one of his smug, *'what did I say?'* looks, to which I responded with a *'don't go there'* of my own. He shook his head, snickering. And on that note, we gave our 'goodbyes' and 'be safes' to the hellhounds, then I manifested Luc, Connor, and me to the area of the portal. This one was trickier because we had to place wards inside the tunnel to keep demons from entering the camp that way, along with placing them around the perimeter.

More witches than I'd realized existed started funneling up through the portal into the basecamp we'd set up. But it was when regular non-magic humans started following them up that I just about lost it. Men and women with no abilities aside from courage and love for their children and grandchildren, who were willing to put their lives on the line to make a safe future for their loved ones.

"Connor," I cried in his ear. "They can't be here."

He held me tight to my spot. "They volunteered."

"But they'll be slaughtered. I can get them safe."

"Everyone has a stake in this fight. They understand the risks and are willing to fight for what they believe in."

I gasped as I remembered the protection stones—plus, you know, my brother. Along with Sim's plant protection duty, our crystal witches had spent hours creating necklaces with protection stones. "We need to head back to camp. The witches—they made things that could help them."

After letting Luc in on my plan, I manifested Connor and me back to our camp. Right away, I started gathering up necklaces and we even had some weapons—poisoned maces and even spray bottles full of the poisoned brew my brother and the witches had created. I didn't have enough for everyone, but at least it was something.

We manifested back to the second witch camp, where Sim got to work on the poisonous barrier. I started distributing necklaces and Connor, the weapons. "If you don't have a weapon," I called to the group, "then hang back to help the injured. We'll need people who are quick on their feet. Triage is as important as the fighting."

They seemed to be okay with this plan. No one looked forward to dying, and I'd told the truth.

"Okay," Luc said, turning to Connor and me. "We have to move Átahsaia to his location. You ready for that?"

Ready or not, we needed a ravenous demon-eating monster on our side. "Ready," I agreed. Before taking off, I manifested my brother back to our camp. As his protector, Madigan would go crazy not knowing if he were sick or injured. Plus, for my plan to work, I needed him close to me when shit started to hit the metaphorical fan.

Luc and Connor each grabbed one of my arms and I manifested us to the outpost on Antarctica.

The ground shook beneath us as a sinkhole the size of a herd of elephants opened up in the ground about a hundred yards away. This massive, gnarled hand with fingernails so long and thick, they appeared more like tree roots, grabbed a hold of the edge of the sinkhole. The loudest grunt echoed up. The sound almost knocked me to the ground. This giant mountain pushed up from the hole. A bent knee and thigh thudded on the ground, allowing the rest of the monster to reveal his form. He had a long, gray beard that almost reached the ice under his gigantic feet and gray hair that he kept pulled back in a knot that must've reached his calves when undone.

He had these bulging, brown eyes. But even though he never once blinked, I felt no fear. As unsettling as his appearance was, his eyes exuded kindness. I expected him to lumber, slow and clunky, but he moved with speed and grace.

"Hello," I said. "I'm Simone Lamia."

He smiled, showing me a mouthful of yellowed teeth. "I am Átahsaia," he said, introducing himself.

"It's a pleasure to meet you," I replied. "This"—I pointed to Connor—"is my mate, Connor Baghest."

"You wish for my help." It wasn't a question. "Lucifer told me of the demon uprising."

"Yeah, they've gotten a bit unruly and since you haven't eaten in a while, we thought you might like a snack."

The laugh he let loose reverberated across the frozen land, causing cracks in the ice. "I will eat my way through your demon problem."

I'd never moved a giant before and the prospect of it made moving all those witches laughably easy. One long, cleansing breath in, then slowly letting it out, I looked up at him. "I have to touch you to move you. Is that okay?"

He nodded. Connor and Luc joined me. After sending a quick prayer to Lilith and the universe, I manifested us to a spot behind the Göbekli Tepe archeological site, which lay opposite the hellhound camp. I swayed.

"More cake," Connor ordered. "As soon as we get back."

I nodded because the way my head spun, I felt like vomiting. Moving a giant—not fun.

"Warm," Átahsaia said of the surroundings.

"It is." I loved that in his long life, he got to experience the sun and warmth again. Now to get down to work.

When I say it took everything in me to keep the big guy cloaked, I was *not* exaggerating, but with no one else able to keep him hidden while Luc put the wards down, the job fell on me. I wanted to kiss Luc with tongues when he put the last ward in place. Then I was free to drop the cloak, which—record time on that one. I had enough left in the stores to manifest him a giant watch to wear around his neck. I set the alarm.

"When the alarm goes off, that's when you come out eating. Not any sooner, okay?"

"'Alarm'?"

"It'll sound like this high-pitched rapid beeping. You press the button on the side to turn the beeping off and then it's time to feast. But we can't let the demons know you're here until that moment."

"I will not fail you," he replied.

"Okay, well, we have to get back to our camp." I hugged his leg as much as I could and finished with, "Good luck—or um— *Bon Appétit*." How else did one say good bye to a demon-eating giant? I snagged the hems of Connor's and Luc's shirts, manifesting us back to our camp.

Yet again, my mate forced me to sit while he grabbed me tea and cake. Yet again, I woofed them down. Keeping a giant incognito robbed me of so much energy, I ate five rum cakes each as big as my hand, and drank an entire pot of the tea. I took breaks between each round of cakes and cups because that was a lot of food for me, but I had to be at full strength for this battle and my body told me in no uncertain terms that I was *not*.

In a moment of downtime, Connor dropped down next to me

on the ground. He placed my hand on his lap, intertwining our fingers. "Feel ready?" he asked.

"I will as soon as I've had enough tea and cakes."

"Not what I mean."

I sighed. I knew what he meant. "Can anyone truly feel ready for something like this? But it seems a little too late to catch a bus to Hollywood and try to fulfill my secret dream of becoming a famous actress. So I might as well do this."

"You wanted to be an actress?"

"No. Just trying to—"

"I know what you're trying to do, babe. No one will get to you. On my life, no one will get to you."

On his life. We'd hardly had time to be a couple, yet here we were '*on my life*'ing. It sucked. We were mated. What kind of life would I have without him around, being all grumpy and bossy? I leaned in to press a kiss to his lips. I wanted him to know everything in my heart at this moment. He wrapped an arm around my back, tucking me in closer to his body. We sat that way for a little bit. Not speaking, just being together, right up until Lily Joy approached us.

"I'm sorry to interrupt, but it's almost time."

Almost time. Right. I stood first, pulling Connor to his feet. I supposed they needed me to say something. Luc had gone back to the other witch camp. Where was Bill Pullman and his *Independence Day* presidential speech when you needed him? Five hundred years from now, that would still ring true as one of the most iconic inspirational speeches in movie history. But right now, all these people had was me.

"Everybody," I called out and the groups of witches and Lilium stopped talking, turning to face me. I looked as many people as possible in the eyes. They deserved to see my sincerity. "When the alarm goes off, we will launch an offensive the likes of which the world has never seen. All of us magic holders. You were given your power for this reason. *This* reason." I paused for effect. "We will fight a threat greater than humanity has ever seen. A demon uprising has never been recorded in all of human history. Today, we must put aside our differences and cling to what bonds us. Life. Love. Future." I paused again to swallow and just breathe. "We stand together or we fall apart."

At that moment, the alarm beeped.

War.

# CHAPTER Thirty

Both Connor and Madigan dropped into their hound forms. Come hell or high water, this was it. *"For Sparta!"* I shouted, because *300*. It seemed relevant to the situation. I ran for the opening we'd kept clear from poisonous vines exiting the camp with Connor at my side. I saw my brother and Madigan run through a different opening out of the corner of my eye.

All around me, witches, Lilium, humans, and hellhounds ran into battle. Átahsaia moved with graceful quickness. The whole of the world magic holders—we had to be at least a million strong—rushed into battle, taking the demons completely off guard. We descended into their camp just outside Göbekli Tepe in an attack they never saw coming.

Demons scrambled to organize and retaliate, but they came out swinging with everything in their arsenal. Blades, bombs.

I heard a scream and turned in horror to see Adalaide, the leader of the Western Australian Coven, fall. "No!" I screamed and brought down a half dozen demons at once. Átahsaia double-fisted two demons. Ripping the head off the first, he sucked the insides out, dropping the lifeless body to the ground to disintegrate into ash as it hit the dirt. He tore the head from the second demon consuming his insides and dropping him almost on top of the first.

Hellhounds ripped into demons, shredding them.

But this was far from a slaughter. Demons fought with a fury that rivaled the deadliest wars in human history. When a winged devil launched into the sky, I shouted to our fighters below it as the beast dropped black powder onto them. It burned through the flesh of everyone it touched. So many of them dropped, writhing in pain. My brother shot his hand up to the sky, causing dark-gray clouds to form, and he let loose a torrent of rain to wash away the demon poison. But he wasn't done. He shot lightning from those clouds, disintegrating that winged devil.

Holy hell, my brother had power.

The other demons got that too and turned their attack on him. Madigan jumped in front of him in time to save him from the dagger that would've taken his life. She dropped. He screamed. I screamed, manifesting every destructive painful way to die my brain could come up with in the moment, directing my hits to the ones who'd hurt my sister-in-law.

Humans rushed to Madigan, lifting her. My brother, in a state, tried to fight them off, but they knew their job and they would try to save Madigan. Given what I'd just thrown out, the demons turned their attack on me. Three hellhounds surrounded my brother to give him protection and I watched as Lily Joy and Karro ran to his side. My family fought hard. I had to fight just as hard.

Demons kept pouring out of their camp. We had to be outnumbered ten to one at least. I found it hard to accurately math in times of crisis. Connor stayed at my side. A gaping, jagged cut on his shoulder that badly needed stitches oozed blood. I took my attention from the fight for just a moment, enough time to seal his cut, and got knocked on my ass. Connor lunged, ripping the demon's throat from their body. It turned to ash. My tailbone smarted where I'd hit the ground hard.

While the chaos ensued around me, I felt him, and whipped

my head around to find Beetle. He'd shown. I'd known he would—it was only a matter of time. But I had him in my sights and wouldn't let him live. Not this time. I took off in a dead run, parting the sea of demons like a modern-day Moses.

"What are you doing?" Connor barked at me in my head.

"Beetle," I yelled back, not letting up. Beetle was going down. Lily Joy, Karro, my brother, and Shafira must've seen me take off —I mean, I'd parted demons, that was probably hard to miss— and they ran alongside me. Simeon caught up to Connor and me. He needed to be here for my plan to work.

Luc held off the legions of demons while we raced to take out the man himself. When we'd just about reached him, Beetle raised his arms, and bringing them down fast, captured Connor, Sim, and me in this transparent cube-like cell along with him. Neither Lily Joy, Shafira, nor Karro was able to penetrate the invisible barrier muffling all the outside sounds.

"Beelzebub?" Connor said, shocked. "You're Beetle?" He stood there completely naked, so I manifested him clothing because I felt like it put my mate at sort of a disadvantage. But manifesting was all I could do, as I found myself unable to even move a pinkie. Somehow, Beelzebub managed to immobilize us with this cage.

"Ah… Lucifer's little pet," he said, sneering at Connor. "So nice of you to join us."

"What are you doing this for? You control the second-largest quadrant behind Luc."

"Oh, you dumb dog—why have the second largest when you can have it all? Humans have everything, yet they still fight each other for more. Lucifer lost control of them years ago."

"Luc never wanted control. He wanted to give them choices."

"Now, they'll have one master."

"Why'd you kill Jeffery?" I asked, non-sequitur, I know, but I needed to know the point of it.

"Because of you. I thought you'd have hunted down his

murderer two years ago when the police failed to bring his assailant to justice."

"I know why they failed to capture his assailant. You had one in your pocket."

"So you figured it out."

"Why Cain?" I asked. "He's not a magic holder."

"I'll let him explain." Beelzebub waved his hand and a portal opened, floating above the ground, large enough for a man to walk through. Cain.

He sauntered over to me all cocky and I wanted to punch him in the gut so badly, but I needed to hear what he had to say, and I'd accidentally knocked into him once before. That man was solid muscle. I didn't need to break my wrist at this crucial point in the war.

"Simone Lamia. It took me a long time to hunt you down. Bitch kept a low profile, but I found you."

"Why?"

"That magic belongs to me. The magic of the garden should've been mine. It should've been passed down to my children. We'd have been the most powerful family in the world. But your whore mother refused to give me sons."

*Gross.* "That's incest, you perv."

"Now the power goes to me."

"It doesn't. Whatever he promised you, he was lying. Even if I die right now, my power goes into the ether. You won't get a drop. Magic gets passed to the offspring of magic holders. You've been unremarkably ordinary your whole life."

He shot his hand out, slapping it hard across my cheek open palmed, hard enough to bust my lip. I bit the inside of my cheek, causing my mouth to fill up with blood. I spat the blood onto his shoe.

"Make you feel like a man? Slapping a woman. Just like your dad. You want to blame someone for not having magic, blame him. The magic of the garden never belonged to him. It belonged to my grandmother. Had he been kind, she'd have shared it. But not him, not Adam. Oh, no—he abused Lilith and his children until she had no choice but to leave the garden."

"I will end you, bitch."

He meant it. Cain wrapped his meaty fingers around my throat and began to squeeze. I couldn't move. My body wanted to drop me to my knees, but I had no choice other than to stand there while he squeezed the life out of me. "Beelzebub," he screamed. "I've done what you asked. Give me my magic!"

Beelzebub shot his hand out.

Connor screamed, "*No!*"

Sim shouted, "*No!*"

I'd have shouted or screamed my own *no* if I'd been able to. And before my eyes, Beelzebub's strike hit Cain square in the back. The large man dropped to *his* knees. He turned his stunned, dying eyes on Beetle and I swear I saw a betrayed '*why?*' right before he slumped to the ground.

Gasping for breath, I took in large lungfuls of air that burned my throat and lungs. "What just happened?" Sim asked.

"Ah… Simeon. Brother to Simone. That was quite the show you put on out there." Beelzebub pointed outside the cube. "I didn't see it coming. Rarely does anyone get one over on me." Then his voice turned serious. "It won't happen again."

"You always planned for him to die," I said, assessing the situation.

"Well done, Simone. Yes, he always had to die."

"I get why he wanted to come forward in time, but why did you bring him?"

"So greedy and power-hungry, he actually thought I'd give him your magic. How would that have benefitted me? *I* get to control the humans. Not Cain. But to answer your question, your grandmother is why. I put out feelers all over the world to track you and your brother down, but the witch had bound your magic. I couldn't find you. I *needed* to find you for any of this to work. So, since he'd already killed off his own brother, I knew Cain would be more than willing to come forward in time—see,

I needed his blood to track you down. You share DNA, as Adam's child and grandchildren. We isolated DNA in Cain and I have people in my employ who were able to use that to magically locate your brother."

"You went after Sim first," I muttered.

"When I found out he had no idea you even existed—well, let's just say my staff learned to never disappoint me like that again. So we had to expand the search. You took longer, as you'd been bound tighter than your brother. And now, here we are."

"But you're Beelzebub. None of this explains why you went after us in the first place."

"Magic," Connor said softly.

"Oh, good boy. You got that."

Connor growled at the Prince of Hell.

"That garden held all the magic of the universe. Hell holds the magic of one fallen angel. Powerful, but not nearly as powerful as what you and your brother have flowing through your veins. I need to resurrect the garden and I need your blood to do it. Sorry you have to die, but it's for the best. You'll never use it to its full potential." Beelzebub walked over to me like he didn't have a care in the world, then he turned first to Connor and then to Sim. "Now, you get to watch as I drain the life from Simone first."

"Why me?" I asked, trying to distract him or give me time to get Simeon's attention.

"You haven't figured it out? You're a woman. All women hold tiny bits of magic. Why do you think men sought to subjugate them? Men were never meant to be the dominant force on the planet. They were destined to be the soldiers who protected the ruling queens. And as women were busy creating life and knowledge, some men grew resentful and then, my dear Simone —they struck, spinning the world off its intended axis. Given your power, you have to die first. I can't have you trying to kill me while I'm killing your mate or your brother. As I will have your power inside me, they'll be no trouble to me."

Now we'd all seen movies where the bad guy spilled his nefarious plan right before getting defeated by the hero. Up until this moment, I'd thought that was a product of subpar storytelling, yet here we were.

"Smart," I said. "You played the long game and got one over on all of us."

"Really, Simone?" Connor snapped at me.

"What?" I asked. "I got to give credit where credit is due. That was a smart plan. Think about how much patience it took to get here. Lilith knows I'd never be able to hold out that long."

"I appreciate the compliment from a queen such as you are," Beelzebub said, "but I have a world to dominate, so I'm afraid it's time for you to die."

As he walked up to me with a demonic pep to his step and as he raised his hand, I shot a glance to Simeon. He dipped his eyes to his pocket and I manifested the hilt of Lilith's blade from his pocket into my hand. I manifested the amulet into my other. Lilith appeared inside the cage.

"You will die for your sins against my family," she warned Beelzebub. He turned his head to her and with her magic, she unbound me. I joined the amulet to the hilt and a glowing, ethereal blade shot up from the hilt. Beelzebub turned his attention back to me in time to see me thrust Lilith's blade into his heart and twist. The blackest demon blood spurted from the wound as he dropped to the ground. He screeched and writhed and squealed in agony while I stood over his dying body.

"The magic will never be yours," I spat.

Then, as the last bit of life left him, the bindings on Connor and Simeon dropped. The cage disappeared and I saw the destruction from the battle outside. It enraged me. I looked to my grandmother, who hovered above the ash pile that used to be Beelzebub and she nodded once. I threw my hands into the air, invoking the power of the universe. I had no idea I had this power until this very moment. The universe downloaded into my system, filling me with more and more of its magic. The power levitated me off the ground. Vaguely I became aware of my brother harnessing the clouds as the sky grayed. Bright, white-hot light shot out from every surface of my body targeting the demons, who fell in piles of ash—no warning. They died where they fought.

The last thing I noticed were the bodies of fallen witches, Lilium, hounds, and humans. I shrieked so loudly, it shot my light out for miles and miles. Mile-high flames charred the world around us. Átahsaia dropped his massive body to the dirt and sighed a breath that came out like a large gust of wind. He leaned his chin on his fist as if upset that his meal had so abruptly ended.

"Simone," Connor hollered my name. I lifted my hand setting the hills ablaze. The current of power rolled through me. I *was* the power. "Simone—*stop!*" He lunged for me but was thrown back by the electromagnetic field radiating off me. He hit the ground hard. I blinked. Then I dropped.

And my world went black.

I woke up with a splitting headache and as I got my bearings, realized I was in my bed back home. Mr. Pooches lay snuggled up on the pillow next to my head.

Something nagged at the back of my brain, but I couldn't figure out what that something was. I felt gross, like I hadn't showered in a hundred years. When I tried to sit up, my body felt sluggish, like after you slept way too long.

"Ready for some yum-yums, Mr. Pooches?" I asked and I'd swear that he nodded at me as he pushed up from the pillow and stretched his kitty stretch. "Let me shower first," I said. He meowed. "I'll be quick."

Well, like it or not, I needed a shower, but more than that, I had to pee like a racehorse. I knew there was more to that saying, but hell if I ever remembered it. Mr. Pooches mewed his displeasure, but I ignored him and his attitude to pull clean undies and a bra from the top dresser drawer. I took a peek outside, pulling back my curtain to see what the weather was like. The trees had turned. Vibrant red, orange, and yellow leaves on the sugar maple in my front yard greeted me rather than the lush greenery. Boy, that had happened overnight. The sun shined brightly, though, so I pulled out a pair of leggings that I'd had printed with Mr. Pooches's face on them from the second drawer from the bottom, and one of my soft, oversized T-shirts. Today felt like a comfy kind of day.

Mr. Pooches didn't follow me into the bathroom. I supposed he was still in a snit. Whatever. I peed, then got the shower going. My muscles were sore, probably from sleeping hard, and I noticed yellowish-blue bruises—big ones—on my arms and legs and even my torso. They looked the color of fading bruises. What the hell had happened while I slept?

After washing my hair and gingerly giving my body a scrub down, I dried off, dressed, wrapped a towel around my hair, and left the bathroom to take pity on Mr. Pooches. He mewed a kinder mew at me this time.

But when we passed the den, I saw a bunch of dudes and a few women watching the Red Wings play on a big, big screen that I didn't own.

"What the hell?" I shouted and all the eyes in the den turned on me. They smiled, as if happy to see me. "Get out! I'm calling the cops."

A couple of heads jerked like they couldn't believe I'd threatened to call the cops. I turned, running to my bedroom, and slammed the door, locking it. Then as someone pounded on my door, trying to pop the lock, and shouting, "Babe? Open the door," I frantically searched for my phone, which, as it turned out, wasn't in my room.

"Leave. I won't call the cops if you just leave." What did I do? The intruder popped the lock, pushing open the door. I grabbed up the lamp from the bedside table closest to me to use as a weapon if necessary.

"Baby, put the lamp down."

"Get out. I swear you don't want to mess with me." Then in a flash I felt the magic tingling under my skin and realized that we must've been at the full moon of the lunar cycle. I didn't need a stinking lamp. I had Taser fingers. He didn't know what he was in for. The man kept walking forward and I kept backing up until I hit the far wall and he easily pried the lamp from my hand. I let him to distract him. Like a one-two punch. He took the lamp from one hand while I pressed my other to his neck, expecting to see blue magic zap the shit out of this guy.

Instead, I got, "Not this again."

Excuse me? Not this again? I pressed harder.

"Simone, baby. You know that doesn't work on me."

Simone. He knew my name. He was very handsome. So handsome that I started to get turned on by his closeness. How inappropriate. The man probably had a mind to violate me and I was turned on?

A second man with golden-blond hair and other worldly beauty stood in the doorway chuckling. "Dude, she doesn't remember you," he said.

"*She* doesn't know *any* of you," I said, getting irritated. "Get out of my house."

"*Our* house, babe."

"Am I being pranked? This is a prank, right? I live alone."

"No. You don't." He gently grabbed my hand, still pressing against his neck to lead me into the closet. If I'd chosen a dress or a blouse, I'd have seen the men's clothing hanging in there.

My mind felt like it was reaching for something it couldn't grab on to. He turned me around to see that the otherworldly blond man had been joined by more men and women. "The blond guy is Luc. He's a friend and my boss. The guy who looks like you is your brother, Simeon. The woman next to him is his mate, my sister, Madigan. On the other side of Luc is your cousin Lily Joy. Shafira is the woman behind her. Next to Shafira is your other cousin Karro."

"'Karro'?" I asked. "That's a fantastic name."

He snickered. "You liked it the first time you heard it, too."

First time? What was I missing?

"Who are you?" I asked the sexy man still holding my hand.

"Baby, I'm Connor, your mate. Fuck me, you don't know how glad I am to see you awake."

"My… *mate*?" I asked hesitantly and he nodded. "I don't have a mate," I whispered.

"You do. Me."

"But I don't remember you."

He walked me to the door, closing it in the faces of all those who continued to stand in the doorway, and backed me up against it. "I want to jog your memory."

"Jog my memory?"

He leaned *way* into my space, fingers gently holding my face. "May I?" he asked and I thought, *What the hell?* At worst, I had a sexy man kiss me. At best, I found out this sexy man was indeed my mate.

"Connor, you say?" I asked on a hitched breath because as he nodded, he slowly ran the tip of his nose up and down my jawline. My heart rate sped up as he breathed in deeply then brushed his lips over mine. *Wow…* As he deepened the kiss, my every muscle in my body felt ready to seize up and liquify at the same time.

A plethora of memories flooded my head starting from the first time we'd met and I laughed. "Oh… *Connor*."

———

THANK YOU FOR READING! I hope you enjoyed meeting Simone and Connor and all their friends. If you haven't read my first Rom-Com series yet, let me introduce you to SKYDIVING, SKINNY-DIPPING & OTHER WAYS to ENJOY YOUR FAKE BOYFRIEND, you can read it here.

CLICK HERE TO READ SKYDIVING… >>

Don't miss sweet fur-babies. Read the HOLIDAY BITES SERIES starting with BABY, IT'S COLD OUTSIDE

I appreciate your help in spreading the word, including telling a friend not only about my rom-coms, but about my romantic suspense, too. The Brimstone Lords. The Bedlam Horde. Reviews help readers find books! Please leave a review on your favorite book site. A review on Amazon helps the most.

If you want to see what happens to Simone and Connor after the story ends, click to join my newsletter and get your Witch-ish Bonus Scene.

You also might be interested in The Consolation Bride. It's the first book in the Unexpectedly Married series.

### First Chapter

*The Consolation Bride*

"AND SO IT BEGINS." I leaned over to whisper to Gabby, my sister's best friend, as my mother, Mrs. Evelyn von Dutton—yes, of the Grosse Pointe Shores Von Duttons—clinked her crystal champagne flute three times to get everyone's attention. Her delicate, bird-like physique was accentuated by the golden cream silk dress that she wore tonight to upstage the bride in her stunning green. My mother and her magical superpower, her ability not to age. Flawless porcelain skin kept tight and elastic. Thick hair pulled up in a twist. We got the "are you three sisters?" question all the time.

It was a well-known secret that mother took trips to "rejuvenating spas" every couple of months and came back having shaved years off her appearance. Funny how the spa was located next to one of the country's most renowned plastic surgeons. She used to be a deep brunette just like my sister and me, but after each of those refresher visits, she returned with hair a little bit blonder than before. Evelyn considered aging a congenital disease that we Von Dutton women inherited from her and were expected to fight to the very end.

My father stood to her left and slightly behind her with his hands resting on her hips in his stance of solidarity. He looked as handsome as ever in his silk Armani suit. He felt no need to cover the slight graying at his temples because for a man, especially a man of wealth and power such as my father, gray looked distinguished.

"Thank you all for joining us today to celebrate the engagement of our beautiful daughter Gretchen and her perfect match, Mr. Stanton McCain. Gretchen and Stanton have been in love for as long as any of us can remember. We are so pleased to finally be uniting our families." My mother had a way of making every word out of her mouth sound pretentious. Like Mrs. Howell from *Gilligan's Island*. I held an affinity for vintage things such as vintage television shows thanks to my defacto-grandparents Alessandra and Rochester our married housekeeper and grounds chief who'd taken me and my sister under their wings years ago—without my parents' knowledge—and given us, or at least me, a relatively normal childhood when our parents were simply too busy to parent.

Everyone clapped. Of course they did. My eyes slid over to where the happy couple stood, Stanton's arm wrapped around my sister's waist, both of them wearing huge smiles. Beautiful Stanton, tall and broad-shouldered, with a face like a movie star. He wore his deep chestnut hair styled business cut but his most defining feature had to be his storm-cloud gray eyes. I sighed, momentarily forgetting myself. My sister in her emerald green silk looked just like our mother, but still wearing her naturally deep brunette hair twisted up in a ridiculously expensive updo. I tended to do my own hair. It was fun for me to play with styles and I'd gotten good at it over the years. Only a professional could touch my sister's locks. But maybe that was why *she* got Stanton.

Our fathers had done business together for years. Our

mothers sat on boards for charities together and lunched regularly.

Stanton and Gretchen: the perfect couple. *Not.*

It wasn't sour grapes. I was happy for them if this was what they wanted, but I'd just never understood it. Ant and I—Ant, the name I'd called Stanton since probably the first day we'd been introduced as kids. "Stanton" had seemed too stuffy. Ant, he and I always had more in common. He loved going down to Comerica Park to watch the Tigers play. I loved going to Comerica Park to watch the Tigers play. Gretchen only went to PGA tournaments and tennis matches. Ant and I both loved the travel channel and cooking. Two things that my sister would have nothing to do with. Forget about eating a drippy burger, Gretchen never ate anything without a knife and fork unless it was an hors d'oeuvre like caviar.

Seriously, only two years separated my sister and me. So it wasn't like he'd be robbing the cradle. But for Ant, it had always been Gretchen. Maybe because of that more refined, highbrow nature or maybe because her boobs were about a half a cup larger than mine. It could've been her chiseled cheekbones or her deep, ocean-blue eyes. My cheeks had a bit more roundness to the apples and my eyes… Somehow, I'd ended up with a muddy brown.

The worst part for me had to be that my sister simply wasn't nice. The world revolved around Gretchen. If by chance, you found yourself in the position where you outshined her in some capacity, big or small, her congratulations came in the form of an obvious backhanded compliment.

Matthews, our butler, because yes, our family had a butler, approached my mother. "Ms. Von Dutton, lunch is ready to be served." He came to work for the family a couple of years ago after our first butler, Randall, retired. He was nice but kept to himself or the other staff, never engaging much in conversation with me. Tonight he wore his navy blue jacket with the family crest embroidered over the breast pocket. Again, *yes*, the family had a crest. My mother had the staff dress in uniforms at all times while out among the family and guests. Why? Just–why? But he learned the hard way, from what I'd been told after the fact because I'd still been away at school, that he learned the hard way to always defer to my mother in the presence of large groups. Parties were her artistic medium. Gretchen was the apple that didn't fall far from the tree.

"If everyone would please make their way to the dining room. Lunch will be served," Mother said.

Let me just say, the Von Duttons didn't do anything on a budget. There were so many options from seared swordfish to grilled eggplant, two kinds of pasta, one Italian white truffle, and one with lemon and walnuts. Soup courses. Salad courses and more dessert options than a small island nation could consume in a year.

Gabby, Gretchen's best friend, dropped into the seat next to me. She looked beautiful in black. She came from a well-respected Mexican-American family out of Texas. They didn't come close to the wealth and prestige of the McCains or Von Duttons, but they had enough means to allow her to continue to be friends with my sister. "Have you tried the swordfish?" she asked. "It's heavenly."

I shrugged. "It's not my thing." My mother had us eating off personally monogrammed china she'd purchased specifically for this lunch—white porcelain with real gold edging and letters. Talk about OTT. "But I can't wait to see how they top this at the wedding."

At least we didn't have to deal with a bridezilla. My family had the wealth to buy anything and everything Gretchen's heart desired. With that kind of cake tossed around, people didn't tell her *no*.

As we ate, more glasses clanked and the speeches started. Gabby's face fell and *she* sighed.

"What's wrong?" I asked.

"Oh, nothing."

"It's not *nothing*, Gabs. You don't sigh like that unless something's bothering you."

"Once she's married, she won't have much time for me. Your mother already has her life planned out. The charities she's to join. All the dinner parties she's to host."

"You're her best friend. She'll always make time for you."

"No. Your mother has already set up play dates with your sister and other married socialites."

I popped out a laugh loud enough to catch the eye of Ant. I shrunk down in my seat and mouthed, "Sorry." But come on, *play dates*?

"What? I'm serious. She had lunch with Christina Rivers the other day. I've known Christina Rivers as long as Gretch has, but I wasn't invited."

"That doesn't mean—"

"Sylvie Sheridan was."

"My sister can't stand Sylvie Sheridan." Secretly, I couldn't stand Sylvie Sheridan either. If there was ever anyone on the planet to out-pretentious my sister, Sylvie Sheridan took that trophy.

"*Exactly*," she practically shouted with exasperation. "The only things those women have in common are wealth and husbands. I have a little wealth, but not a husband and that makes me a lesser class."

"Well, it's not much of a consolation, but you still have me."

She squeezed my arm. "The sister I never had."

Here's the thing. I really hoped Gabby was wrong about my mother, but as the lunch wore on, it became blatantly obvious that only the married couples got my sister's and Ant's attention for more than a few exchanges of "Thank you for coming" before my mother swooped in, shuffling them off to another table. Crappy, right?

Well, as it turned out, what they lacked in manners, my parents totally made up for with copious amounts of Dom Pérignon, of which both Gabby and I indulged until, for my part,

I couldn't feel my feet and walking seemed more of a concept than a tangible state of being.

Gabby leaned in conspiratorially. "She's making a big—*huge* mistake." Either her words slurred or my hearing slurred. Fingers crossed on her slurring because I never met anyone drunk enough to have slurred hearing. "She doesn't want to marry him. He's a good guy, but they have nothing in common."

"That's what I'm saying," I slurred back, slapping the table hard, then I hiccuped because *hello*—classy. "You know she'll never make him happy the way he deserves." And I punctuated my point by waggling my finger in the air because nothing says '*I'm right*' like a finger waggle.

Ant looked so beautiful as he and my sister moved from table to table talking with their guests. In my opinion, nobody in the history of the world came close to everything that was Ant. As I scanned the room, I noticed a room full of tawny-haired men, but none of them had the richness of tobacco with the highlights and lowlights that I'd give almost anything to run my fingers through. The tiny flips and waves that never seemed to be tamable enough for my sister's taste. He caught my eye again for the briefest second. Every time he looked at me, it felt like looking into a thunderstorm.

Ah, well… Look at me waxing poetic.

It took them long enough, but they finally made their way over to Gabby and me gliding into the two empty chairs at our table to take a necessary reprieve from being the perfect couple entertaining their guests. Why did every thought in my head make me feel like a terrible person? I should be happy for Ant, finally getting what he'd always wanted.

"What are you doing?" my sister snapped at me low so only those of us at the table could hear.

I looked at her, dumbfounded. "Celebrating your engagement? Just like everybody else."

"Everybody else doesn't look a second and a half away from falling off their chair."

"Oh, no… I'd need to be *way* more drunk to fall off a chair."

Ant snickered and my sister shot him a "don't encourage her" glare that he completely ignored because we'd always been friends and I'd been making him laugh most of his life. Strangely, Gabby just sat there silently glaring at both Ant and my sister. She was really upset by this marriage. I understood. The four of us hung out all the time. The three of us—me, my sister, and Ant—growing up. Gretch met Gabby in college. Ant and Gretch applied and got into the same college, Brown University, the one I'd applied and gotten into two years later. Sure, my other friends or Ant's other friends would join us, but at the core were the four of us. Not that I particularly liked hanging with my sister all the time, but given the incomes of my friends in high school, my parents didn't trust my friendship decision-making skills. And now? We'd hit the end of an era. I doubted it would be too long before my sister pushed out those anticipated 2.5 kids, widening the gulch between us. That angered me even more. I wasn't ready to lose Ant to his responsibilities. I needed more time. *Gabby* needed more time–see? I wasn't being selfish. Altruism at its finest.

I cleared my throat and with a newfound sense of drunken stupidity or clarity, the jury was still out on which, I said, "I don't think you should do it."

"Do what?" Ant asked.

"Get married, *duh*. You're twenty-five. Why rush?"

"This is where it was always leading," he answered paradoxically. Why paradoxically? Because his lips tipped up in the corners indulgently as if speaking to a kid sister, but his eyes–if I had to give the look in his eyes a label, I'd call it resigned. "So why not now?" he finished.

*Because I'm not ready,* I wanted to scream yet I held my tongue saying nothing. Go restraint!

By his reaction, I didn't appear to have ticked him off, even though I internally kicked myself for blurting that out. My sister, however… Her face darkened to this beet shade of anger.

"Pen," she hissed, "just go." But Gabby placed her hand on my sister's arm, causing Gretchen to close her eyes and compose herself. "You don't have to go, but for God's sake, sober up."

She stood up to leave. Ant stayed seated a moment longer before joining her. "I'm done," I said to Gabby, pushing up from my chair. I'd be lying if I denied that my gaze lingered on Ant as he and my sister laughed at something some other guest had said.

Today totally sucked.

The Consolation Bride

I've been lucky enough to survive in this author game for many years now, and I've thanked a whole lot of people over those years, too. Well, I hope you know—yes, *you*! The one reading this note—that I want to thank you too.

You're here. You've read the book. You give me a reason to keep on writing. So thank you, from the bottom of my heart.

Years ago when I started down this author road, I did it because I had stories to tell, but also, as a single mom, I needed to be home for my sons. That decision helped us remain close now that they're adults. I'm grateful every day of my life to not just call them sons, but friends.

Love and light to all of you!

# About the Author

A former preschool teacher, chef, and lastly, a stay-at-home mom, Sarah Zolton Arthur has worn many hats in her life, until graduating with a Bachelor's Degree in English/Creative Writing and finally finding the hat that fits: writing romantic comedies.

Above all else, she lives by these rules. Call them Sarah's life edicts: In Sarah's world, all books have kissing and end in some form of HEA, because all romance heroes deserve love.